'In Fine Est Pincipium' In the End is the Beginning

The End of an Eon

ESSENCE OF THE STORM

S. M. SAVOY

Published by
Ace Lyon Books
July 2020

Ace
Lyon

First Edition
Cover Design by S. M. Savoy
Essence of the Storm S. M. Savoy
Paperback ISBN 978-1-947122-37-6
eBook ISBN 978-1-947122-31-4

Books by S. M. Savoy

VALOR SERIES

Valor
A Warrior's Fury
A Sun Priest's Magic
Beyond Valor
A Rogue's Passion

RETURN OF THE FAE SERIES

Return of the Fae
Enter the Frey
Danu's Children

Contents

ESSENCE OF THE STORM

The First Sign

Friday, 4: 30 in the Afternoon 1/5

Anne peered from her kitchen window over the back fields to admire the first fat snowflakes of the year. Her gaze landed on evenly spaced maples, naked now without their covering of leaves, lining the lane between the lower cow pasture and the small peach orchard she and her husband had planted eight years ago.

Her grandfather had planted those maples. His foresight let her family enjoy the sugaring season; four weeks of collecting sap and boiling it down with the cheerful assistance of friends and family.

Every weekend during sugaring season, the Sugar Shack would be crammed with volunteers who enjoyed the opportunity to sit and visit while the evaporator that reduced gallons of sap to sweet maple syrup heated the air with fragrant steam.

The children would tromp through the snow, getting cold and wet, and return for homemade mulled cider made from their apples, and fresh waffles, which were Ben's specialty.

Her husband didn't cook often, that was Anne's thing, but he always supplied as many waffles as you could eat topped with fresh syrup and Anne's homemade preserves or butter, or ice cream made with fresh milk in the churns they brought out just for the occasion.

Reminded, Anne called down the basement stairs for her daughter. "Jill, can you stop by the Sugar Shack before you go out today, please?"

Boomer ran up the stairs, and Anne bent to ruffle the dog's silky black ears.

"You're getting fat," she said, but she offered him a doggy treat from the jar on the counter anyway. Merlin, her small dog, pawed at her knees. She scooped him up, handfeeding him a treat as she crooned, "Who's mommy's little magic man?"

Jill snorted, and Anne glanced at the basement door as her daughter entered.

"Disgusting," Jill said with laughter in her voice. "You spoil Merlin rotten." She wiped her hands on a white rag already speckled with various colored paint stains and tucked it absently into a back pocket of her jeans.

Anne made a mental note to remove the rag before doing the wash, although Jill was getting better about keeping her painting contained to canvas and not clothing.

Reminded of her daughter's imminent departure back to Brown, where she minored in art, Anne grew sad. The house seemed quiet and deserted without her daughter's cheerful presence and soon it would become even emptier when Doug married and moved into the house he and his fiancée planned to build on the lower road.

"Look who's talking." Anne said with forced good cheer as she gestured at Boomer who greeted Jill with a happy bark and a hopeful glance at the treat jar.

Trained well, Jill threw him a treat.

Boomer snatched it from the air and crunched with slobbering joy.

"Tell Dad the sledding party is officially on. Bring him the churns; they're on the bottom shelf in the basement, and stop at the root cellar for, say, five pumpkins."

Jill grinned, her gray eyes sparkling. She loved fresh-roasted pumpkin seeds, and Anne promised herself to make them more often.

She tugged her daughter's ponytail. "Remind him to drag the sleds out too."

Jill's smile widened, and Anne wondered how much longer sledding parties would thrill her daughter. Her son still enjoyed them, but not with the same excitement he'd had when young.

Anne's smile brightened as she contemplated her son's upcoming wedding. Maybe she'd have grandchildren soon to sled with and cook for.

"Is Johanna coming?" Jill asked, and Anne laughed.

"I was just thinking of her. Her entire family is coming. Dad has promised them another batch of the Rhode Island Reds that hatched last week, and he was even going to build a fire on the point. Maybe you could hook Thunder and Lightning to the sled and give some sleigh rides?"

Jill nodded eagerly. "I'll call Stacy and see if she wants to bring Margo today before the roads get bad. Her mom was thinking of getting another horse she could train to pull a –"

Jill stopped speaking abruptly and grabbed for the counter. Anne swayed and reached for her. The air vibrated as a noise she felt more than heard built to painful pressure in her ears.

Earthquake, Anne thought, shocked, and tried to step forward, but the air felt solid, and she couldn't make her feet move. The noise that wasn't noise, built. Air vibrated along her skin so hard she expected the windows to blow out any second if not the Earth itself to shatter. Jill staggered in slow motion as if the air held her in place too. Her hands rose slowly to block her face as she fell into Anne.

Anne clutched her and bent over her daughter's head. She knew they should run outside but she couldn't push through the pressure of the air. As suddenly as it had begun, the pressure and sound ceased as if it had never been, leaving Anne disoriented but everything else exactly as it had been.

"What the heck was that?" Jill asked as she straightened, lifting shaking hands to her head.

Merlin cowered on the floor and the sharp scent of urine laced the air.

Anne rummaged beneath the sink for the paper towels as she said, "Earthquake, I think. Check the news. I've never felt one before. That was terrifying. How does anyone live in California?"

Adrenaline made her hands shake and a cold sweat still beaded her brow. She never wanted to feel anything like that again. Her uneasiness grew, and she was tempted to rush outside and wait for an aftershock but nothing at all had happened.

Nothing I can see anyway, she thought nervously as she swabbed up the urine and petted both dogs.

Merlin still trembled and cowered against her legs now. Boomer gave her his goofy dog grin. Whatever had happened hadn't affected him at all, which surprised Anne when storms terrified him and didn't bother Merlin one whit.

Jill reached for the laptop open on the counter, her troubled gaze flicking from the screen to the dogs. "Is it over? Merlin's still freaked out."

"I'm still freaked out," Anne said as she rose to brace her hands on the kitchen island to peer out the bigger windows in the adjoining dining room.

Snow still fell, and smoke rose from the chimney of the Sugar Shack. The cows were clumped together by the side gate but that was typical in winter. They rarely wandered the fields in cold weather. The corner of the barn she could see from where she stood looked normal, but it didn't feel normal. The air still felt weighted and laced with dread.

She'd expected to see dark clouds and tumbled trees or buildings, maybe cracks in the earth or rock falls from the ledge to the west, but the snow still fell in light flakes and settled to the exposed branches, leaving them laced in white. *The trees hadn't even trembled enough to dislodge the snow.*

Anne shivered and rubbed her arms. "Anything on the news?"

"No, nothing."

Anne reached for the phone on the counter and called her husband. Jill left the laptop on the weather channel and headed into the living room. The television came on as Ben answered.

Anne glanced around at her kitchen. Something had changed. She couldn't put a finger on it, but her simple white appliances looked different to her. The day felt darker, the air oppressive. *Something was coming,* she thought. *Something big, something huge, something bad.* A shiver traveled her.

Ben sharply saying her name brought her attention back to the phone she held.

"Did you feel that earthquake just now?" she asked.

"Earthquake? No," he said, sounding surprised and somewhat relieved. Her long silence must've worried him. The phone grew muffled as he called, "Hey, Sam, did you just feel an earthquake?"

Talking too muffled to make out filled the line a moment before Ben said, "Wayne and Sam both say they didn't feel a thing. You sure there was a quake?"

"Both Jill and I felt it," she said, "But there's nothing about it on the weather app. I'll check the news; maybe there'll be something about it there."

"Call me if you hear anything. I better run out and make sure the water heaters weren't dislodged."

"Check for cracks in the ice on the pond too. I'd hate for someone to fall in while skating tomorrow."

"Sure thing. Love you," he said and hung up.

She slowly replaced the phone and then hugged herself hard, almost afraid to look out the windows again.

"Nothing is on the news either," Jill said. She stood by the door, her troubled gaze scanning the windows, and Anne gave her a quick hug.

"That was bizarre," Jill said, then shrugged and shook herself. "I'll go help Dad, then I'm going to run to the mall with Donna and Stacy."

"Be careful," Anne said, giving her a wan smile. She wanted to forbid her to go but overreacting would just annoy her— or scare her. So, she smiled and waved from the front window when her daughter drove away before hurrying back to her kitchen.

Consumed by nervous energy, she defrosted all the hamburger from the last cow they'd butchered and made enough chili and meatballs to feed an army.

On her second trip to the basement freezer, she paused to eye the rows of shelving holding her canned goods. Ben had just put in a new shelf she'd intended to fill with maple butter for sale at their farm market. Cases of empty canning jars and packaging waited to be filled. She ran back upstairs to order more taps for the trees. Ben had wanted to run a new line, and she'd talked him out of it, but a new line would mean fifty more gallons of maple syrup— and she suddenly wanted those packages filled.

Proof of Premonition

Saturday Morning 1/6

The next day, Anne stood at the stove making herself eggs. She knew no one else would want anything. They never did for breakfast.

Ben grabbed the coffee she had waiting for him and gave her a quick kiss.

"Doug!" he called up the stairs. "You up? I'm going to need help moving that bale and then we need to make sure the chicken barn is swept out upstairs and the mouse traps are reset. I'm expecting that feed delivery, and we have to be ready before everyone gets here for the sledding party."

"I'm up," Doug groaned, and they both heard his feet hit the floor with a loud thump as he got out of bed.

They grinned at each other.

"That's our early bird," Anne said with a smile, and Ben laughed.

"Yeah, now you go wake our night owl. I want her help sweeping up today."

"Oh no," Anne said, shaking her head. "You're on your own

there, pal. I know better than to wake a sleeping tiger. I'll send her out when she gets up. Take Boomer with you; he needs the exercise," she added, petting the black speckled dog on his soft head. "For a cattle dog, he enjoys being inside way too much."

"What about your mutt," Ben teased. "He's always in the house."

"My dog is a pedigree, a very rare breed," she said in a fake British accent, "and can't be expected to go out with the working dogs."

"Your dog is a ba—"

"Stop!" she said, leaning over to pick up the small black and white dog in question. She covered his ears with her hands. "My dog is fabulous. You're just jealous 'cause he loves me best. Don't you, little man?" she crooned to the small dog. Merlin obligingly licked her nose. She placed Merlin back on the floor and kissed her husband. "I'll be over to the shack at noon with the chili, and I'll get Jill out before then, I promise."

"*I* love you best." He gave her another kiss, then yelled for Boomer and headed out.

Doug thumped down the stairs into the kitchen. "Where's Dad?"

"You just missed him. He and Boomer headed out to the barn. Want any eggs?"

"No, just coffee." He hit the brew button on the coffee machine and opened the cabinet to get a plastic top for his Styrofoam cup. "How many of these do we have left?" he asked, holding out the lid.

"About a thousand."

She laughed when he grimaced. She'd bought the wrong kind. He rolled his eyes.

"What," she said defensively. "They were cheaper by the case at the Restaurant Supply Store, a lot cheaper."

"Our basement looks like a mini warehouse," he said with a

small laugh. "You need to stop going there."

"I told Johanna I'd take her next week," Anne said with a fond smile.

She liked Johanna quite a bit and approved of her son's choice. Johanna's mother, Carmen Martinez, raised goats she milked to make soaps and lotions and bred pedigree sheep she had hand sheared. The hand-dyed wool clothing she made sold for a fortune in a New York boutique. She wasn't what Anne would consider a farmer, their animals were kept in pens inside a designer barn and hired hands took care of the day-to-day work, but she was comfortable around livestock and had taught her children to be as well.

The Martinez's had recently added chickens and a few fruit trees, gifts from Doug, and Doug had helped them make a small root cellar to store the fruit in.

"Johanna wants to go to Restaurant Supply?" he asked in surprise. "What for?"

"I told her what good deals you can get, and she was interested."

"*Uh huh*," he said dubiously and grabbed his coffee.

"Was Jill up yet?" Anne asked.

"Yeah. I heard her moving around. You two we're making enough noise down here; how could anyone sleep?"

"She'd sleep all day if we let her."

"Well don't let her," he said. "I don't want to sweep that barn alone." He grabbed his brown barn coat from a hook by the door and headed out.

"Make sure your dad wears his coat; it's freezing out there today!" she hollered after him.

He lifted his hand to signify he'd heard and keep going. She closed the door behind him.

"Jill!" she yelled up the stairs, "you want any eggs?"

To her surprise Jill yelled back she'd like an egg sandwich.

"One runny egg sandwich coming up," Anne said and went to crack the eggs.

"Mom!" Jill yelled, and her feet clattered against the wooden stairs. "Did you hear this?"

Anne paused in her cooking to peer out the window over the sink, once again expecting to see a storm cloud brewing or scarred earth. Snow-covered fields met her searching gaze. The day remained sunny and bright, but unease overtook her.

Jill ran into the kitchen. Her hair was still wet and uncombed from her shower. Her feet were bare, peaking from beneath artistically ripped jeans, and she was pulling on a yellow sweatshirt over her pale face. Only her wide eyes were visible, and she looked scared.

"What?" gasped Anne. "Are you okay?" She reached for her daughter.

"I'm fine." Jill held out her cell phone for Anne to see. "But you have to see this."

Message icons littered the screen. Anne held the phone closer to read the top one.

'Omg did u c the news!!! all flights canceled some kind of attack!!!'

She quickly scrolled to the next one. *'Jill did u c about the planes?? wasn't Greg taking a plane to Florida? Call me!!!!'*

And the next; *'Call me I can't believe this.'*

Sweat beaded Anne's brow. "What's going on?"

"I don't know. I got like all these messages saying someone shot down all the planes and all flights are canceled. Everyone is freaking out."

"This must be a hoax." *Please let it be a hoax,* Anne thought while she rushed to the living room to turn on the television.

It was on every channel. Twenty-eight planes were missing so far. All flights over the Atlantic were canceled. Not terrorists, a storm. NASA was showing pictures from space of what they were calling the storm of the century. Swirly white clouds covered the entire ocean and half of Greenland.

"Our earthquake!" they said simultaneously.

"Holy cow; look at that," Anne said nervously.

Storm warnings ran along the bottom of the screen. Every station showed experts of one kind or another talking about global warming and solar flares.

"Call your father," Anne said sharply as she flipped through the channels.

I knew it, she thought, *I could feel it coming. This is going to be bad.* "I'm going to the store," she said as she ran into the kitchen. "Tell your dad to come home. He needs to see this." She grabbed her old blue barn jacket hanging by the door, then changed her mind and ran into the small home office off of the kitchen. She logged on quickly and went to their bank site and moved ten thousand dollars into their ATM account—everything they had in savings. She flicked a glance to the safe where she kept about eight thousand in cash, then opened her top drawer to remove the business checkbook from the desk.

Guilt made her hesitate. She should clear major purchases with her mother and husband first, but she didn't want to take the time to explain or risk being turned down.

Decision made, she yelled out, "Jill, get in here!"

Jill still spoke on the phone, talking excitedly. "I called Dad. He's on his way home."

"Good," Anne said absently. She grabbed Jill's arm and pulled her over to the desk. "I want you to make some calls for me while I'm out. If they give you a hard time, have your father call them." She shook Jill's arm a little trying to impart the urgency she felt.

"Okay." Jill pulled her arm back and rubbed it absently. "Who am I calling?"

"First, call the oil company. Tell them it's urgent, that you have a plant shipment and need the tanks in all three greenhouses filled completely and ask them to fill up the tow motor's extra tanks. Get all four filled. Tell them to stop here and fill both ours and Grandma's tank." She reached over and pulled a page from the rolodex. "Then call this gas company and tell them to come fill our barn tanks, we need it for the tractors. Make something up if you have too but get them here as soon as you can. Have them fill the bakery and the winery tanks as well," she continued urgently.

Her daughter was starting to look scared.

"What's going on, Mom?" she asked in a small voice.

"Just getting prepared." Anne reached out again and grasped her by the shoulders. "Jill, without gas we can't farm. This storm will likely disrupt the oil deliveries. If we can't get fuel, our crops won't get planted and our animals will starve. We could survive without one baking or wine season but the animals...We'll lose everything. We need to get the gas now before the prices rise."

Jill made a sharp sound of distress, and Anne hugged her a moment, smoothing her wet brown hair. "We need to hold it together. This is bad. But we can do it, okay?"

"Okay," Jill said in a soft, scared voice "Then what do I do?"

The kitchen door slammed. "We're in the office!" Anne yelled. "But go see the news first!" Doug and Ben headed to the living room, talking softly. "Okay," she continued to Jill, "call the vet and make emergency appointments for Monday."

"For what?"

"I want every animal on this place to get rabies boosters, Lyme vaccines, vitamin shots, and anything else you can think of. Get as much penicillin as you can from her."

"What for?" Jill asked in confusion.

"If this storm is as bad as I think it will be, we might not have power for months. We need it just in case the chickens or cows get sick from the storm; bacterial pneumonia is a real possibility in these conditions."

Jill nodded in agreement.

What else, Anne asked herself. Her sense of urgency mounted as she considered the oncoming storm. "Dad can go to the feed store today and get a truckload of feed for the goats. I'll order a truckload for the cows and horses," she said absently as she began jotting down a quick list. "You take grandma's car and follow him. Get at least five big bags of dog food and cat food. Buy all the tarps they have. I'll call our food supplier for the bakery when I get home and see what I can get delivered. Oh, and if they have water and gas jugs, buy them all."

"All?" Jill rose an eyebrow.

"Well, all you can fit in the car," Anne amended.

Her daughter looked nonplussed at this but said nothing.

"Holy cow!" Ben exclaimed in the living room.

Jill turned to go, but Anne grabbed her by the arm again.

"Calls first," she said firmly and pushed her down into the seat she'd vacated. She leaned over and kissed her forehead. "Be careful," she said and ran to Ben.

Ben turned to her, his eyes stunned.

"It's bad," she said.

"A storm," he said airily, trying to placate her, but she knew he was worried by the way his eyes squinched. "A big one, but nothing we haven't done before."

"Not like this," she said firmly, shaking her head. "No one ever saw a storm like this."

Doug was still glued to the TV.

"It could still blow out," Ben said hopefully.

"It won't." Anne knew it wouldn't blow out; she felt it coming like pressure in the air. Pressure that weighed more every second.

"It's going really slow," Doug said, and they both turned to look at the television.

"What?" Ben strode to the center of the living room

Doug pointed at the big picture of the storm that was being shown live on their local news channel. "See that in the corner there? That's a real-time clock. NASA is measuring its progress. It isn't really moving just growing bigger, gaining about a mile diameter an hour.

"A mile per hour? Ben said in a surprised voice. "Are you sure?"

Doug shrugged. "The reporters are. Look at that graph! The electric fields are off the charts! All contact is lost for people in the storm, and approaching it is impossible, so they know it's bad. NASA has pictures miles out of what looks like severe lightning and they're tracking wind gusts at over two hundred miles an hour."

They all stared at the satellite pictures behind the reporter. The commentator described the severe conditions in an exited tone.

The man was thrilled, Anne thought bitterly as she contemplated what winds of that magnitude would do to their trees.

Bright lights flickered in the storm clouds that the commentator said where fires cause by static discharge.

"There's too much electrical interference for them to know for certain. He's just guessing," Doug said and grabbed the remote to switch to the weather channel. "That announcer just said it will be at least two weeks before it hits our coast at that rate, and it's bound to peter-out before then."

"I hope so," Ben said and placed an arm around his son's shoulders.

"It won't stop," Anne said with certainty. "It's going to be bad. We need to be ready. I'm going to the grocery store right now. In fact, I want you and Jill to go to the feed store and stock up. Doug can wait here for the chicken feed delivery."

"Sure, Mom, no problem. I'll get it ready. I'm gonna go call Johanna and see what she heard." He walked out of the room, grabbing for the cell phone strapped to his belt.

"Overreacting a little there, don't you think?" Ben asked with a smile.

"Not reacting enough," she said and shivered, hugging him tightly.

He kissed the top of her head. "Hey, we'll get through it. It's just a big storm, and it probably won't even hit our shore.

She said nothing just hugged him tighter.

Hunkering Down

Sunday Noon 1/14

"Last reports say the storm will hit our coast in four days." Doug said as he stabbed the reload key a few times as if that would make the internet connection work. He pushed his laptop away with an annoyed huff. "They don't know anything though. It could still blow out, but it's acting so oddly."

He turned on the television, catching the news mid-broadcast. Radios hadn't worked in days. There was too much electrical interference and only the one television channel came in now. All the rest of them had gone off air to harden their equipment.

A female reporter Anne had never seen before said. "I'm Sonja Arnault, and I'll be keeping you informed up to the last minute."

Ben and Doug complained about the regular reporter being replaced so abruptly a week ago, a complaint they'd voiced daily as the channels shut down and new reporters replaced the old ones, while Anne shivered as she contemplated the newest maps.

After swirling in place for a week and growing to enormous proportions, two days ago the storm had formed a wedge shape, aimed itself at the northeastern seaboard, and begun to move. The wedge had flattened out when the storm began moving and now formed a mile-deep jagged line that would hit the east coast along the entire length. Theories abounded for its odd behavior, but no one really knew what was causing it. All anyone could say with certainty was that it knocked out all electronics on contact, even the hardened ones. The experts had taken to calling it a sustained solar flare. Thirty-foot ocean swells had blossomed to fifty-foot ones. The surf was too dangerous for boats to get close enough to take readings. And the only thing they could do was build homemade faraday cages and bury any electronics they could.

Doug glared at the computer screen as Sonja spoke.

"—arrested for market manipulation if he can be found."

Doug slapped the laptop closed and said, "Why would he need to manipulate the market? He's already one of the richest men in the world."

Ben said, "Who knows why people do the crazy things they do. I bet he made millions from that footage though."

Doug said, "That's just stupid. He spent millions, maybe even billions burying that city like he did."

Jill said, "He must be crazy like they said."

On the screen Sonja said, "It's clear he's suffering from delusions and psychosis." The picture behind her changed to show the footage Doug had been examining on his laptop and he stood to lean into the screen.

Sonja said, "Common sense tells us that the pictures are computer generated but if you look closely you can see the debris pattern is not only inconsistent to the supposed destruction but identical. The footage was clearly made in a hurry."

"It looks real to me," Doug said.

Ben rolled his eyes.

Anne shook her head. She'd seen the footage before. It had gotten over a billion views and would have gotten more if the web hadn't gone down days ago. Doug had saved the footage to his laptop and watched it over and over and it was beginning to worry Anne. She wasn't certain if he believed the conspiracies or if he just wanted to ride out the storm somewhere else too. Guilt assailed her but she couldn't make herself leave the farm.

Ben said, "You couldn't join them even if you wanted too. He's keeping his whereabouts secret, although, I suppose, you could join one of the countless groups who are mimicking him."

Doug snorted.

"We'll be fine here," Anne said, grimacing ruefully, feeling a hypocrite when she wanted to ride out the storm in her root cellar as well.

On screen Sonja smiled and shook her head as the images behind her changed from the picture of the boat being disintegrated by purple gas to a view of a night sky and a round glowing disk. Yellow light shone from the disk over a stretch of rough waves and the waves grew ten times higher with visible roughness from photo manipulation. The lightning that followed was clearly fake as well and Anne laughed although the footage made her uneasy.

Sonja said, "This footage is clearly fabricated as well and yet rumors of alien interference abound." Her smile widened as the picture changed again to show an enormous sea creature thrashing the waves as lightning flowed from its eyes and the tips of its tentacles. "Now this one looks real, but I assure you, there are no ravening sea creatures approaching."

More videos taken from the web followed. The newscasters all laughed and commented on the footage, pointing out the mistakes in the videos and complimenting the cinematography on the realistic looking ones.

Ben and Doug laughed and commented too but Jill looked uneasy and Anne took her hand.

Sonja finally said, "Spreading rumors, while amusing, does have drawbacks. Looting has been reported, a serious incident that killed thirty-seven and was perpetrated by a militant group who believe the radio silence to be purposeful. The death toll is rising, and we expect to hear of further casualties caused by the storm although hopefully not by looters. Please, stay calm and stay indoors. I assure you, the radios should be back on the air within days. This is the latest live footage."

The screen behind her played storm footage of a US Coast Guard vessel floundering in high waves. Lightning flickered in the distance and rain and spray limited visibility, but the sea was obviously rough and the lightning intense.

Anne wished they could get news from the Carolinas where the storm would hit first, but all cell lines had been down for three days now while the phone companies attempted to harden their lines according to the new regulations. Even land lines were spotty.

Lawsuits and counter suits were already being filed by service providers and their customers for the lapses in coverage, and Anne dreaded the resultant rise in prices that were sure to follow.

Prices of everything had risen drastically, and shelves had emptied. Anne had spent every dime they had, and had borrowed heavily, to stock up. She'd gotten good prices because she'd acted so quickly.

Their basement bulged at the seams, and she'd filled the storerooms at work and the walk-in cooler they used in the fall to store the apples. Guilt flushed her cheeks as she glanced at Ben. He had no idea how much she'd spent.

The pressure of the approaching storm weighed so heavily on her now she barely slept, waking nightly from night terrors. She knew Ben was worried about her compulsive shopping and fear, and he'd humored her as best he could, but no one except Jill seemed to sense the impending doom like she did.

Most treated the approaching storm as an enforced holiday. Restaurants and hotels advertised for storm parties and storm watchers had flocked to the east coast to see the storm hit land.

Hotels had sold out and people had even started renting floor space in their homes for exorbitant sums.

The television warned repeatedly for everyone not to rely on restaurants or hotels to provide and to ensure they had supplies of food and water for at least a week while roads were cleared and the electricity was restored. But Anne thought it would more likely take months to clear the storm damage.

A banner ran along the bottom of the screen beside a time clock ticking down. "This channel will be off the air in twelve hours and forty-six minutes," Sonja said, "Reports have come in from Newfoundland and parts of Quebec where the storm has already touched the ground." Behind the reporter, a rain-swept landscape lit with bright streaks of lightning played.

"Jeez," Doug said.

Jill squeezed Anne's hand. Anne bit her lip, eyeing the dark purple sky on the screen with trepidation. Light rain fell in slanting sheets, melting the snow on a bluff overlooking the sea. Small whitecaps foamed, and the grass and trees swayed lightly. It was clear the winds weren't too bad except for the occasional hard gust but the lighting was brighter and more frequent then she'd ever seen. Metal rods attached to enormous white buoys stuck from the waves. Streak after streak hit the buoys and even from a distance the force of the impacts was clear.

Sonya gestured, facing the camera, not turning to view the scene. "As you can see, reports of the severity of the storm haven't been exaggerated, but the lightning rods are doing their jobs. Remain indoors away from windows. The storm will pass over your location within an hour, but experts warn there could be residual storms and less frequent lightning for the next twenty-four hours."

The camera switched to a male reporter. "All airports on the east coast will be closed by eight p.m. tonight. Flights still remain open. Take advantage of the low fares and go on that California vacation you've always dreamed of. For those of you toughing it out, and by our lasts reports most will be, the curfew will be enforced at ten p.m. along the entire east coast, starting tonight. Anyone caught out after ten o'clock can expect to be fined and perhaps detained for the duration of this emergency. The exception is emergency personnel, but please respect these safety procedures. All lights will be out, including traffic lights. All stores, gas stations, restaurants and public buildings will be closed. Hospitals will remain open, and emergency medical teams are standing by, but they too will be affected. Be prepared to help yourselves before the storm passes out of range."

The picture behind the reporter changed to a close-up of a car engine compartment. "Unplug all electrical appliances. Remove the battery from your car and store it away from your home or deep in a cellar." As the reporter spoke, a man removed the battery from the car with exaggeratedly slow movements, pointing at bolts and holding up tools while directions ran along the bottom of the screen. "The electrical panel inside the car should be wrapped in plastic as we've shown here and then tin foil. Homemade Faraday cages work best nested, which means two layers at least. Use copper, tin, or steel. We recommend wrapping all cell phones and computer equipment, and then storing them inside your dishwasher, which is insulated and sealed. Do not remove them until the storm has passed completely. The lightning will pass within one hour, but the electromagnetic energy will remain invisible to the naked eyes for up to eight hours; four proceeding the storm and four after."

The camera switched back to Sonja. "Television, phones, and internet will remain offline for an estimated thirty-six hours on the east coast. Because the storm appears to be traveling in a straight line, and has shown no sign of stopping or slowing, expect to remain out of touch until the storm passes and the western states get back on the grid."

The camera refocused on the man. "While power and phone companies are doing their best to shield their hardware some losses are to be expected. Normal operations might take as much as six months to resume."

The picture behind the reporters changed to another storm shot, and both reporters glanced over their shoulders. The screen focused in on the storm, and a new man spoke in a voice over.

"I'm here in Cape Freels North Newfoundland, reporting live." The man who spoke wore a bright yellow rain suit and carried a bulky radio encased in thick plastic in one hand and clutched his hat to his head with the other. The camera panned, revealing sleeting rain and brilliant white lightning in the distance.

"My equipment is shielded but untested. We'll have to retreat when the storm gets within range of us." He jumped and spun as a bolt of lightning hit an exposed rod behind him. "As you can see, the rods work." He laughed nervously and wiped his brow.

"Don't put yourself in danger, Ron," the woman reporter said.

"We've been experiencing small lightning strikes for the last hour and still have two hours until the storm passes over us," Ron said. "The rain has been steadily increasing, but the wind gusts are holding steady. None have been over sixty miles per hour. Wind damage should be low, but the possibility of fire exists. We saw some smoke in the north earlier, but it disappeared within thirty minutes. I think the rain itself put out the fire. We've been monitoring the emergency channel, but no fires have been reported."

The camera switched to a cut scene with the male reporter. "I want to remind all you good people, the emergency channel is just for emergencies. A power outage is not considered an emergency. Neither is storm damage that doesn't affect the safety of our citizens."

Another bolt of lightning slammed into the rod behind Ron, and the screen flickered.

"My crew has informed me we need to move further away." The screen flickered again, and the reporter cut in and out. The two reporters in the studio held their hands to their ears and tried to ask questions while the earlier storm footage played in a loop behind them. Sonja finally shook her head and smiled. "We seem to have lost Ron. I'm sure he's getting us some good pictures we can see after the storm passes. Please remain safely indoors. Cameras will be recording and while you won't see it live, it'll be safer to wait out the storm in enclosed basements."

She turned, and the camera panned with her to a man in a fireman uniform who walked onto the set.

"Blah, blah, blah," Doug said and put his feet on the living room couch. "We've heard this so many times already. How many times will they tell us what to do if your house catches on fire?"

Jill shrugged and released Anne's hand to sit beside her brother. "You know half of these idiot storm watchers won't listen."

"And that's why we aren't going out until the storm passes," Anne said firmly. "Let them watch, but we aren't risking our lives to help those struck by lightning because they couldn't follow simple directions. We'll watch it approach, but when we start seeing lightning, we'll come back to the house and watch from the basement."

"The bunker, you mean," Doug said and snickered.

"And you'll be glad of it when the storm arrives," Anne said.

"We'll be perfectly safe." Ben kissed Anne's brow. "If the house catches fire, we'll run to the root cellar, but Doug and I put in so many lightning rods, we'll be fine."

Doug grimaced at his calloused palms. "I'm just glad most of our equipment is so old it doesn't have electronics. It was a bitch getting to the new tractors electronic panel."

"All the batteries are out?" Anne asked.

"Yep. Some of the neighbors asked to store theirs in the old root cellar too. Even if lightning does hit them and they blow, it won't do a damn thing except blow a bigger hole in the ground. It's too marshy to burn there."

"And you filled the water tanks?"

Ben tweaked Anne's ponytail. "And the sap holders and the evaporator and all troughs. We can go for three days without pumping water at the barns, and we have the hand pumps and hoses if we lose the generators, but we've put them in Faraday cages too."

"We'll lose the greenhouses though?" Jill asked.

"Maybe." Ben shrugged uncomfortably and put an arm around Anne's shoulders. "We did put in lightning rods, but the buildings are metal. We got the oil tanks buried and disconnected, but you saw the pictures." He jutted his chin at the television screen still displaying the same loop of footage while the reporters repeated their advice and warnings.

Anne's eye caught on the clock ticking down and she shuddered.

Ben shook his head at Anne and muted the television. "Stop worrying. The storm could blow out anytime and all this would be unnecessary. Its criminal they didn't pre-shielded though. I see some major lawsuits looming. Moving the patients because the power companies didn't shield their computers… well, I'm certain those families will sue over the deaths."

"I backed up all our computers and triple wrapped the hard drive." Doug rose and stretched. "Cloud storage will be decimated. You mark my words. Our info will be safe inside the root cellar."

"Will the web be down a long time, you think?" Jill asked as she fiddled with her phone.

Anne hid her grin behind her hand. The lack of internet and phone service seriously annoyed her children, but she found it relaxing.

Doug said, "Some service providers will be gone for good if

the storm continues like this, but it could stop anytime. I bet some of the towers are already gone, damaged beyond repair when they started their emergency shielding. It's so stupid they didn't have them shielded already."

"It wasn't like they knew this would happen," Ben said.

Doug said, "Sure they did. EMP is a known weapon. Granted this is a natural event, but still…"

"Let's not argue about it," Anne said. "Take the photo albums to the root cellar too, Doug, and go ask Grandma if she has anything she wants to save there. But make sure you leave room for everyone to squeeze inside."

"What about Lighting and Thunder?" Jill asked, darting a worried glance from Ben to Doug.

"The horses will be fine in the barn," Ben assured her.

"What if it catches fire?"

"I'm sorry, honey, but we don't have any other options. They would be scared to death if we left them outside. We got the tranquilizers from the vet, but it's just a mild sedative, not enough to make them sleep."

Anne said, "And, before you ask, no, you can't wait with them. The animals will be afraid and dangerous to be near. We'll tie them tightly and wrap their feet good so if they kick at their stalls they won't hurt themselves, but that's all we can do. We can't risk our lives for them, even if the barn does catch fire."

Tears filled Jill's eyes, but she nodded.

Ben hugged her. "It'll be fine, honey. We've put in lightning rods, and it'll be raining hard by the time the lightning is on us. The house is higher than the barn. After seeing that"— he gestured at the television— "I almost think we should just go to the root cellar and not even try to stay here."

"I agree," Anne said, trying to keep her tone even and not I told you so. She'd wanted that since the moment she'd heard of the storm.

Doug frowned and gestured to the fire extinguishers lined up beside the door. "But if we're here, we could try to put out a fire. We have extinguishers."

"Which are metal. I'm torn," Ben said and pointed at the television. "Look at that. I don't want to run through it to reach the root cellar, and I don't want to be holding anything metal while exposed to it. We have insurance. I'd rather lose the house, then you."

Experts spoke endlessly on the television about hardening the electronics while others claimed it wasn't necessary, and still others warned the government wouldn't be able to recover, and Anne was reminded of the Y2K scare.

A different newscaster came on and warned again that calling to report trees down or power outages would be considered inappropriate for one week and the fines would be hefty. Only life and death emergencies were to be reported. Scrolling banners at the bottom of the screen warned of the fines that would be levied for inappropriate use of the emergency channels. A list of numbers to call was followed by another list of organizations who'd accept volunteer help and what types of help they were looking for.

Ben and Doug had signed up with the local fire department to help with road clearing. Anne planned to open the bakery and supply food and drinks to the volunteers. She and Jill had spent the last two days rolling plastic silverware in napkins and preparing pots of stews and soups. They'd filled the coolers that normally held the fresh pies. The ovens were ready to go even though they generally only used the bakery in the fall.

She was as ready as she could be and still felt in her soul she should be doing more, that it wouldn't be enough.

With begging, bribes, and threats, Anne had talked most of her family into riding it out at her house. She couldn't explain even to herself her deep unease.

She returned to the kitchen and began making cookies.

27

Essence of the Storm

"This is surreal," Ben said. He scooped a dollop of raw dough from her bowl and ate it. "Come see the president's speech. You've made enough already." He took the bowl from Anne and placed it on the counter.

She wiped her hands and followed. "I need to make something, to do something."

Ben nodded and kissed her cheek. "I love how caring you are, but we're prepared." His glance flicked to Jill who stood before the television and stared with a terrified expression. Ben's slight nod conveyed more than an hour-long lecture. She was scaring their daughter.

Anne pasted a fake smile on her face and sat, trying to project relaxation, not the terror she felt. She'd closed the curtains, but Ben opened them to peer out at the storm.

"Look at that lightning," he said and shook his head as a rolling peal of thunder rumbled down the river valley, followed immediately by brilliant flashes of light.

The meteorologist on the screen warned again of severe lightning and heavy rains as the storm passed over. The storm was already affecting television reception. The picture flickered, and lines scrolled through it with every crash of lightning from outside the house. Rain drummed against the roof. It had washed the snow away days ago and still fell in thick sheets. The storm still crawled at the same leisurely eight miles an hour but was now a ten-mile thick mass that reached from pole-to-pole and was proceeded and followed by tropical storms. No one could explain the storm's odd behavior. It neither veered nor altered but flowed relentlessly west, growing bigger daily.

Ben and Doug had spent the last week driving lightning rods across the crest of the hill behind the house. Anne knew it wouldn't be enough. Nothing would be enough. This storm was as inevitable as time.

She shivered and clutched her sweater tighter. Ben gave her a worried glance but turned back to the television as the president began his address.

Marshal Law had been declared in their town yesterday. It had taken Anne over an hour to get through the roadblocks set around the city limits as barricades went up and soldiers set up small camps to help prevent looting. The president warned that interfering with the soldiers and looting would be taken very seriously, then went on to reassure them that the government was prepared and emergency personnel and supplies would be forthcoming for those in need.

He smiled into the camera, saying, "Stay home with your families. You know we've encouraged the families of our brave soldiers to join them at the bases on the coasts where storm shelters have been prepared, but please, unless you have adequate shelter waiting, remain in your homes. The streets will be unsafe and clogging them will slow our relief efforts."

The picture panned to the base behind the president where trucks loaded with supplies passed in the background. Men and women in Army uniforms bustled about, heading into the underground shelters that had been erected over the last week, *a massive effort that had cost them billions*, Anne mused, and wondered when the press would begin accusing the president of overspending. He'd sanctioned the funding needed to build or reinforce already existing shelters to house the nations national treasures, using an emergency decree that was already being debated by congress.

"As you can see, we're taking every precaution with our national treasures. The contents of the Jeffersonian that have been deemed at risk from an EMP are being moved as we speak. But it isn't things that make our nation great, but people. Take every precaution to safeguard our real national treasures, yourselves. The storm should pass overhead relatively quickly but the electrical surges will be dangerous for some time both preceding and proceeding it, so, please, remain inside and away from windows."

Nothing he said reassured Anne in the least, and she tuned him out as he again went over the procedure for hardening personal electronics.

"We'll see," she said gloomily.

"Don't worry so much, Mom," her son said cheerfully. "We'll be fine. We're so prepared we could go a year with no electricity."

She shuddered again. "I can feel it coming; can't you?"

"I can," said Jill who sat beside Anne and opened her drawing book. The page before her remained blank. Jill had also begun to suffer from insomnia and nightmares. Anne hoped she herself wasn't the cause, that her fear hadn't transmitted to her sensitive daughter.

"You guys are worry warts." Doug grinned and ruffled his sister's hair.

"Don't worry so much, sweetheart," Ben said as he sat beside her and took her hand. "It'll be fine. We're all prepared. Hell, we're over prepared. Everyone is coming over. It'll be fine, you'll see," he repeated when she bit back a sob. "We'll have a storm party. Even if we lose power, and they close the roads for a week, everyone will stay here until they open again."

She nodded unhappily against his shoulder. "Don't worry," he said again, rubbing her back.

She leaned back to look him in the eye. "You told them to bring their pets, right? They might be stuck here a while. I wouldn't want them to worry about them alone at home for a few days."

"Yes," he said exasperatedly. "Pat said they'd bring their dog and cat. Dave and Kate said they'd bring the new kitten." He laughed and rubbed his hands together. "They also said they'd both bring their bows. They're hoping we get stuck here a few days at least so they can show off their mad skills. When Pat heard that, he said he'd bring his too. So, we're going to have a shooting contest while waiting for the storm to pass. Doug already rigged a firing lane in the lower hay barn."

"Oh, that reminds me, Dad. My new scope came in. Wanna help me put it on before then?" Doug asked.

"Sure. We can't do anything else in this soup." Ben stood. "Let's head to the workshop and put it on now." He leaned over and kissed Anne on the forehead. "It'll be fine," he said softly and headed to the door. "Come on, Boomer!" he yelled, "let's go the barn." The dog rose excitedly, wagging his tail at the word barn.

"Your dog is getting fat!" Anne called after him. She scooped Merlin from the floor at her feet and cuddled him, giving Ben an insincere smile. She knew she was worrying her husband with her rising fear and panicked spending, but she couldn't make herself stop.

"I know," he laughed.

"Too much beer," Doug said and grinned, bending to pet the dog. "I'll meet you there. Gotta grab my bow," and he headed up the stairs.

Jill and Anne stared at each other; their expressions grim.

"They don't get it," Jill said. "I feel—" she broke off and shrugged. "I was going to say the impending storm, but I just feel an impending." She made a wide-armed gesture, and Anne nodded.

She felt it too. A weight hovered, growing closer every moment and when it arrived it would crash over them and obliterate everything.

"No, they don't feel it," Anne said softly.

"They can't feel it," said Jill.

"No" –Anne shivered harder—" they can't," she whispered, and they both turned to stare out the big picture window that looked east over the snow-covered fields— toward the storm they could both feel coming.

The Storm Draws Closer
Wednesday Afternoon 1/17

Anne glanced at Merlin when he jumped to his feet and both turned to the doorway. The small dog perked his ears and wagged his tail but didn't bark.

The back door opened, letting in a gust of cold, rain-laden air and the smell of wet wool. Boomer bounded into the room followed by Ben who yelled," Out, dog!" He snapped his fingers and pointed to the door.

Boomer gave Anne a beseeching glance but obediently turned and plodded back into the rain.

"How bad is it?" Anne asked, dreading the answer.

"Doug and I got all the machinery out of the lower barns, but that hay is a total loss. We won't have any to sell if we want to feed our own herd until spring. The river is over the banks already. I ran into Roger and he told me they've opened all the flood gates on the dam to ease the pressure. We can expect it to reach record highs."

"The shop?"

"Should be okay even if the dam gives way completely."

Anne's eyes widened, and she stood. "Will it?"

"The engineers say it's safe—"

"What's Doug say?"

Ben grinned at her, and she smiled back. They were both so proud of their engineer son.

Ben said, "He thinks it will hold unless too much debris is knocked loose, but even then, he thinks it wouldn't be enough for a total collapse, but if I lived on the River Road I'd ride it out somewhere higher just in case. I'm a bit worried about the cars parked in the lower lot."

Anne peered worriedly at him. "They signed releases, and we can hardly be blamed for flood damage. Can we?"

"No. The releases will hold, but..." Ben shook his head and pursed his lips. "I just hate that trying to help might hurt instead. It just seemed like a good idea to get the cars off the street, and all the experts say most cars should come through it fine or with little damage if they're parked on dirt."

Anne snorted and stood to give her husband a quick kiss. They both knew the experts had no idea what would happen. A sustained electric magnetic pulse of this sort had never been seen or posited before.

She helped him tug off his drenched coat as she said, "Fools keep coming despite the warnings. They're camping in their cars like idiots."

Ben crossed his leg to rub his foot. "Doug checked, and no one is trying to hide out in any of the cars parked in our lots. It's a bitch working around them though. I'm glad the lightning seems to have stopped. Maybe we can catch up on debris removal now. This is the storm of the century, and you can't really blame people for being interested, especially as it's impossible to film it."

"Film what?" Jill asked as she entered the kitchen. She placed her laptop on the counter and bent to pet Merlin.

"The storm. And I thought you packed up your electronics

already," Ben said in a disapproving tone.

"I did. This is an old one. Doug told me he'd dig a hole out on the point. We plan to use this with his old cell phone to record the storm. We'll plop them into one of the cooler bags and bury them. He's rigging a voltage meter, so we should be able to disconnect before we're surged." She grinned and shrugged, straightening to tap the laptop. "It's no great loss if we lose it, but if we get some good footage, it should be worth a lot of money."

Ben laughed and tweaked her ponytail. "Well then, I hope the storm doesn't blow out before it reaches us."

"It won't blow out," Anne said, and rubbed her shoulders. She tried to smile naturally, but knew Ben saw the lie on her face. She let her smile die.

Ben sighed and smiled crookedly when she winced. She turned away and began neatening the files she'd spread over the kitchen table. "Did you check the silo's and granary?"

"Triple checked it. And we got the plastic rolled off on one of the greenhouses and tied down as tight as we can make it. We'll get the others tomorrow if we get the chance but it's a bitch of a job in this weather. I'd rather just replace it after the storm passes.

"You say that now, and I bought the liners, but you know what a pain it is to roll it out."

"It's no easier to roll up. And being on those metal bars is nerve wracking."

Anne immediately felt guilty. "You're right. Let them blow off. We can fix them later. It isn't worth getting killed or hurt. It won't ruin us to keep the greenhouses closed for a year either." She flicked a glance to the kitchen window but saw no sign of lightning. Thunderstorms had rumbled through the valley for a week now, but the rain had been a warm deluge today with no sign of thunder or lightning. But she couldn't blame Ben for being nervous. They'd had some spectacular displays.

"We won't have to close them. We might have to cut back and

just open one or two but that's probably a good idea anyway. People will still be recovering from the storm damage and won't have money for frivolous things. We should put in more vegetables and maybe some extra grain for us. We're bound to lose some grain to water damage. I'm more worried about erosion than the buildings being damaged. We have insurance and can rebuild but crop loss will be a big hit. Hopefully, the ground doesn't thaw enough to erode too much. I hope this warm front passes. I'd rather have snow," he finished.

"It would be feet," Jill said.

"Yeah, but snow insulates. It's easier to keep snow out of the storage buildings than water, and running water does more damage than piles of snow."

"It's more fun too," Jill said as she lifted the curtain over the sink to peer out.

Anne followed her glance but could only see their reflection in the rain-splattered glass.

Merlin stood and wagged his tail, and Anne knew Doug was coming. He let in another burst of rain and a swirl of cool air when he entered.

"Grandma's basement is FUBAR," he said as he stripped off his gloves and shook his hood off. "It's flooding faster than the pumps can keep up. I moved the Christmas decorations, but all the packaging will need to be cleaned. I told you that you were getting too much."

Anne frowned and sat back at the table.

He said, "Most of the glass bottles will probably break. Those cardboard boxes they're in will just disintegrate when we go to move them."

"Then you'll just have to be careful!" Anne narrowed her eyes at Ben when he snickered.

He made a warding off gesture and lifted his other foot to rub it. Anne was happy to note his socks appeared dry. She'd bought everyone new rain gear knowing Ben would go out in the old set despite the way the way rain funneled into his boots.

She frowned at him; he'd been working too hard if his feet were tired. Doug reached into the cookie jar on the counter beside the door and grabbed a handful of cookies.

Anne nodded to Jill who heaved a heavy sigh but went to pour her brother a glass of milk.

Anne said, "This storm is going to screw up everything. You mark my words, the prices are going to go through the roof, and we can't wait for them to settle back down. We need those jars for sugaring season."

Jill and Doug exchanged amused glances.

Ben said, "You're too young to remember, but your mom is right. The last time we had a big storm and lost power it took two weeks to get it back. Now, when you add in that all the electronics have to be either hardened or they'll be ruined, I predict it will be months before things are back to normal."

"You think they'll cancel school for the rest of the year?" Jill asked as she handed her brother the glass.

Ben said, "I'm sure the schools will remain closed until they restore power. And it will take a lot of work to get everything cleaned up. They were predicating high winds with the possibility of tornados."

Doug sipped the milk, then said, "You know some idiots will leave their cars in the road. I saw Mr. Brooks yesterday. He was driving his new Lincoln and stopped to tell me I was crazy for putting Mom's Nissan into storage. I warned him the electronics on his car would be fried, and he called me gullible. Said I was buying right into the propaganda like they wanted. He hasn't prepared at all."

Ben said, "I'm sure there are lots like Henry, which is why we bought extra chains and winches. Those dead hulks will have to be towed away. The old Ford is purring like a kitten. We'll be out and clearing debris the minute the storm passes."

"Speaking of that," Anne said. "I spoke with Lydia from the church, and they plan on running a soup kitchen to feed those without power to cook for themselves, and she asked if you'd be willing to pick up donations? She thinks, and I agree, that they'll get lots of donations when the power goes off tonight and everyone realizes they'll lose their frozen foods."

"I can do it, Mom," Jill said.

Ben gave her an approving glance. "Jill can handle that. I want to clear out the root cellar by the barn in case we need a tornado shelter for the neighbors. I wish they'd give us another day of power, but I know they need time to harden the plant. But call Lydia back while the phones still work and tell her to ask for blankets and cots. I think freezing will be a bigger problem than going hungry. Once the power goes out, so does the heat in most homes. Henry for one will be looking for a warm bed."

"Well, he ain't staying here," Doug said and grabbed the coat he'd just shrugged off. "I'll call Janice and see if she can help Jill while Will and I move his grandmother."

"She's still there?" Anne asked in alarm.

"The crazy old lady won't leave her furniture behind. I told her everyone's already put their cars into storage and packed up their electronics, but she won't hear it. I'm meeting him there in a few minutes to start moving her out."

"Where will she go?" Jill asked.

"His mom's. It should be safe there. The entire dam would have to fall down before they flood."

"Tell them to come here," Anne said.

"I'll tell them, but you know they won't."

Ben shook his head and stood to stomp his foot back into the boot he'd just taken off. "I appreciate he wants to get right to work on replacing his electronics, but he should just come with us in the truck."

"*Ha*, he's afraid you'll put him to work in the barns," Jill said, and Doug laughed.

Ben rolled his eyes. "Keep being a smart ass and you'll be the one I put to work." He paused at the doorway and said, "Rich called. Molly has a fever and he's staying home. He doesn't want Ricky to get sick too."

"Ben...."

"What do you want me to do? Kidnap them? We'll see them when she's feeling better. Keep dinner warm, we won't be long!" he called over his shoulder as he followed Doug out into the storm.

Anne hurried to the living room to watch them go. They took Doug's new truck. The old red Ford was already loaded with chainsaws tools and fuel and parked in the lower level of the barn. She made a mental note to add food and blankets when she put the first-aid kit in tomorrow.

She stood at the window long after the truck disappeared into the night. Few lights glimmered on the road and none lit the streets. Most people had already done their best to harden their car's electronic systems as best they could. Garages were charging exorbitant fees to remove the sensitive electronic systems and store the newer cars. Every underground parking lot in the state was full and the trains had been running non-stop.

She frowned as she considered the lights sparkling like jewels on the hill across the river. People were flooding the state, wanting to see the storm for themselves while others were packing up and heading west. Ben would go if she asked him, but she couldn't bring herself to leave the farm. In fact, she thought he didn't ask for her sake. Guilt made her head throb, and she rested her forehead against the cool glass.

"We're prepared," Anne whispered, trying to convince herself, but Jill heard and said, "At least we still have power."

Anne nodded. The generator Ben had installed ten years ago would keep the lights on in their home.

"I hope the phone lines don't go down."

"They will," Anne said and picked up the cordless phone to call Rich and beg him to come.

"Mary is having a party—"

"Don't be ridiculous!" Anne took a deep breath and tried to talk in a calmer tone, but the idea of Jill being away filled her with dread. "You could get stuck there for a week or more, and we need you here."

Jill sighed hard but smiled. "I know. Sorry. It's just all my friends are going."

"Invite them here instead. We have more than enough supplies for a week. How is Mary even planning on heating her apartment? Don't you kids have any sense? As soon as this warm front passes, that rain will be snow. Without power, her apartment will be freezing."

"You worry too much, Mom," Jill said without conviction. She hugged herself and rubbed her shoulders. "I'll call and invite her again. It's going to be bad, isn't it?"

"Very bad," Anne whispered.

Storm Party

Thursday Noon 1/18

Long strands of Jill's hair flicked into Anne's face. She absently brushed them away, and Jill mumbled an apology. The fear in her daughter's voice tore her attention from the approaching storm.

"How are they not terrified?" Jill whispered as a shriek of laughter rent the air.

Anne wondered that too and had no answer. Stormy skies, distant rumbles of thunder and flickers of lightning had ceased to hold anyone's attention except Jill's and Anne's. The firepit and coolers full of food and drinks set up under the pavilion at the top of the hill drew everyone.

Johanna and Doug were talking and laughing with a group of their neighbors. Johanna's family had called to say they'd come help in the kitchen once the storm had passed and they'd assessed the damage on their farm.

Anne's mother had left a lantern on in her kitchen window and another in the upstairs window of the front bedroom where she likely watched from. Ben's mother had elected to watch from there too, neither woman wanted to wait in the rain.

Anne's house remained dark and deserted except for a lantern hanging from the front porch, and she couldn't see her sister-in-law's house because of the contours of the land. But Angie stood with her husband and stepson, holding her grandson's hand beside the fire. She looked for Ben's brother Dean and didn't see him. Her niece Julie would be with Jill if she were here, so Anne assumed Dean and his family hadn't arrived yet.

Anne's best friend, Kate, held up a glass of wine in a would you like one gesture, and Anne shook her head, turning away to face the approaching storm again.

It embarrassed her that she was being such a poor hostess when she'd insisted everyone come, but she couldn't drag her attention away from the approaching storm.

Anne's offer of the bakery as a staging area for the cleanup crews had been inducement for her friends and family to weather the storm with them. The River Road that bordered the lower fields of the farm passed through the center of town and connected to a highway. The volunteers would be able to start clearing the roadway as soon as the storm had passed, and, hopefully, get that major travel artery clear for emergency vehicles.

Anne considered the distant flashes of lightning and frowned pensively. The reporters had warned of the danger of fire and lightning strikes and spoken endlessly of the first-aid measures to take for burns and shocks, but Anne wasn't certain her medical skills would be up to it. The sight of blood unnerved her, *and it's clear I don't handle pressure well*, she thought bitterly as she eyed her in-laws laughing with the Russo's. No one else seemed nearly as worried as her. Except Jill, she mused and turned to inspect her daughter again.

Jill's eyes were closed, and an intense expression lined her face. They'd come out to the pavilion atop the promontory that overlooked the river valley, the hill everyone called the point because of the views it offered. They'd closed the business for the duration of the storm, not allowing anyone to use the walking trails or picnic areas, so only her invited guests were present beneath the wooden building.

The pavilion was open on three sides with an enormous fireplace making up the fourth. A bathroom was built into the back side of the fireplace and kept warm with a kerosene heater. Picnic tables and benches, unused now, were tucked beneath the maple trees that lined the wider walking trail leading to the winery.

The point was a popular picnic spot year-round. On cool nights, they usually had a bonfire burning in the fire pit adjacent to the pavilion but now just a small fire burned in the fireplace. Doug had hung tarps on the south and west sides of the pavilion in the hopes of keeping some of the rain off while they watched the storm approached, but it was pouring so hard Anne suspected everyone was soaked already despite staying mostly under the pavilion.

Her cheap raincoat was doing a good job of keeping her dry although she'd managed to tear her thin plastic pants and her left leg was slowly getting soaked through the small hole. She'd bought a case of the one-size-fits-all rain gear the first day and would've bought more but they'd sold out within the week.

Rain snuck into the edges of her hood, trickling down her neck and splattering her face, but she thought it was easing off.

From this vantage, she could see for miles both up and down the river valley, and the visibility was growing as the rain lightened. The slowing rain sounded almost musical as it pattered against the nearest grapevines, a delicate species they mulched and wrapped in plastic to winter over. Grape vines lined the hillside before her and behind her until the hill flattened out, turning into fields they'd plant in vegetables come springtime but now were covered with winter rye. No houses lined this side of the road for a quarter of a mile or so, but houses lined the opposite side, each one set on a double lot.

The hillside overlooking the river valley was also covered in grapes with tree-lined pathways that lead through the arbors and to the winery. Only the black slate roof of the winery was visible from where they stood. The bakery, shop, and greenhouses where hidden by the curve of the hill.

Ben had driven lightning rods along the eastern perimeter of the hill, and Doug had attached an alarm. At the first strike, they'd know to pack up and head inside.

Reassured that her family was safe, she turned her attention to the storm. She could feel it growing. The weight of it pressed on her, an impending she didn't have words for.

✲ ✲ ✲

"I'm glad you made me get those extra fire extinguishers," Ben said.

Anne hadn't noticed him arrive and wondered how long he'd been standing beside her, scanning the horizon with his binoculars.

Wayne handed him a beer, taking the binoculars from Ben. "I'll admit, I thought Anne might be overreacting, but she sure was right. Look at the lightning! I'm worried now about my house."

Anne looked too and was surprised to see how bright and frequent the lightning had gotten. Time had run away from her while she pondered the approaching storm.

Ben said, "Let the fire die out." He handed Wayne one of the lanterns she'd bought. "Nope, you use this one," Ben said as Wayne's son, Cole, reached for a lantern. He handed him one of the smaller crank-operated lanterns she'd bought in bulk for the younger kids.

A lone car chugging up the steep hill opposite them drew Anne's eyes to the houses on the hillside. Unlit windows gave them a vacant air, and she shuddered, glad she could see the approach, not have it creep up on her, but at the same time she wanted to be closer, to touch the purple wall.

Ben said, "A fire in your neighborhood would be hard to contain. It's safer to wait it out here."

"I wish I'd put in a hand pump though."

Ben laughed. "That's from having a three-hundred-year-old farm, not foresight."

"Five more minutes!" Pat called after his girls.

"*Aww*," Emily complained.

"You're watching from the house with Mrs. Carmichael," Pat said in a no-nonsense voice, squelching the protests before they got started.

"She has cookies and snacks waiting," Ben added.

"They should all go inside," Anne said absently.

The approaching storm enthralled her in a way she didn't have words for. It seemed to call to her, and she understood the reluctance the kids had to leave, although it was already clear it wasn't safe to remain. The entire horizon glowed an eerie red and flickered with bright lights, which Anne assumed was lightning. Wind speed picked up and dark clouds she thought were smoke scudded across the distant treetops. A tall hill across from the river blocked the view east. The hill lowered and flattened as it went west, leaving distant rolling hills visible. Normally, you could see taillights and house lights flicker through the trees but with the electricity off, the hillside appeared deserted except for the smoke from a few of the chimneys. She hoped most of them had generators so they wouldn't freeze when the warm front passed with the storm. The dark purple cloud to the east captured her attention, pulling her thoughts from the houses on the hill.

The cloud seemed to glow and stretched across the horizon as far as she could see. The wall of purple roiled but seemed constrained, having an even height and edge, not wispy like clouds but dense and roiling.

The men chattering by her ear were distracting and Anne

wished they'd go somewhere else to talk and then felt bad again for being such a poor hostess. She'd come out before everyone, meaning to get the chairs and food set out, but the storm had utterly distracted her, and she'd left the set up to Ben. She hadn't even made sure he'd set out the food and snacks as she'd intended and couldn't bring herself to do it now.

She turned to see what the children were up too. They giggled and leaned over Doug who was doing something she couldn't make out at the fire pit. The rain had lightened farther but sharp gusts of wind picked it up and sent it at odd angles, splattering her face with what felt like handfuls of water. She closed her eyes and tried to understand the sensations she felt when she contemplated the storm.

"Just a few more minutes!" Sue called, but Anne didn't turn to look this time.

The lack of rain felt ominous, like being in the eye of a hurricane, she thought as the rain faded to nothing. A steady wind picked up and grew until she could hear the branches creak on trees six-hundred yards away. *Or maybe it just seems loud without the noise of cars*, she thought as she turned to scan the road that bordered the lower riverbank. Water had risen and escaped the confines of the riverbed, partially covering the roads on both sides of the river. The road had been closed for almost two days now although she'd seen some use it despite the warnings and barricades.

The air felt weighted as if it muffled sound. Pouring rain had been such a continuous background noise for days now that the lack felt jarring. But the sky was the scariest part. Deep purple clouds, lit by flickering light, swirled over the hills to the east. The purple mass filled the horizon as far as she could see. A neon green glow lined the treetops with streaks of lighter green, bilious yellow, streaks of red, and white, leading up into the roiling purple clouds. A million pinpricks of light shone among the distant trees and she would have found them beautiful if it weren't so odd. She'd never seen anything like it.

"That must be some lightning storm," Ben said as he put an arm around her.

Anne said nothing. Terror and a feeling she didn't have a name for kept her mute. Every second the unnamed feeling grew and pressed upon her, leaving her breathless and weak.

The men and women gathered on the hill continued to talk and laugh, acting as if they couldn't see the enormous storm bearing down on them. Anne wanted to shriek at them to shut up so she could concentrate. She thought if she just tried hard enough, she'd reach and important understanding. The epiphany was tantalizing close and the distractions were maddening.

"Can't you see that?" Jill yelled, startling her.

Anne jerked and glanced at her daughter. Jill stood beside her so pale and drawn Anne thought she might faint. Apparently, Ben did too. Instead of rebuking her for being rude, he took Jill's arm, then put an arm around her. "See what, honey?"

"What, Princess?" Kate called.

"That!" Jill said and pointed. "How does that cloud not terrify you? What the hell are those lights?"

"The cloud?" Ben asked, frowning at the sky. "You mean the lightning? I think the glow is a fire. It's nothing to worry about. Everything is so saturated a fire won't burn long. We're ready to put out any fires the lightning starts in the buildings."

"No, that!" Jill said, making a frustrated gesture. "The lights. What the hell is it?"

"Maybe it's lightning too," Anne said doubtfully.

"I wish we were closer," Jill murmured and stepped forward.

Ben pulled her back.

"I wonder what it feels like? I bet it feels amazing."

Anne glanced at her, alarmed at her tone although she wanted to touch it too.

"Have you been sneaking beer with Julie?" Ben asked suspiciously.

Jill didn't answer. She lifted her hands as if she could grasp the cloud from here.

"No, she's been with me. Don't you want to touch it too?" Anne reached as well. Every second the cloud grew more enticing.

"What the hell are you talking about? What lights? The lightning? That red glow is freaking me out though. It must be a huge fire if that rain didn't quench it."

Anne didn't reply, she was caught by the sheer power of the approaching cloud. She took Jill's hand.

"Fairy lights," she tried to say reassuringly. There were so many she didn't see how it could be lightning and hoped it was some sort of optical illusion or a harmless manifestation like Saint Elmo's fire. It didn't appear to be burning the trees. The lights just flickered, growing and fading in a pattern she could almost make out.

Jill nodded and withdrew her hand to gather her hair into a ponytail.

"Fairy lights?" Ben asked, and his scowl deepened. "It's regular lightning. Maybe you need glasses. Or do you mean the way the storm clouds are lit?"

"Not the clouds the lights on the trees. Don't you see the lights there?" It shocked her that he couldn't see it although she shouldn't be surprised. It explained his nonchalance. But how do I see it? A sick feeling rose in her stomach and her hands began to shake.

Ben lifted a hand to feel her brow. "I think it's time to head inside," he said.

"Not yet." Anne shook off his hand and took a step away. She closed her eyes and tried to decide if she could feel the storm like Jill could. But it didn't feel like static although she felt that too. The small hairs on her arms were standing upright beneath her plastic raincoat and thermal underwear she wore underneath her winter clothes. She could smell the ozone in the air under the odors of rain, wet earth, and fresh popcorn. She turned to peer over her shoulder at the fire pit. She'd been so lost in her musings she hadn't heard Doug making the popcorn. To her surprise, the kids had already gone in. Just the adults remained.

Jill gasped and moaned, falling to her hands and knees.

"What," Ben asked and leaned to her as Anne did.

"No!" Jill yelled and pushed his hands away. "I almost know!"

The words rocked Anne. She almost knew too. She closed her eyes and sought knowing.

What's Happening?

Thursday Noon 1/18

Ben pulled his daughter to her feet, and she thrashed wildly, hitting and scratching at him in a complete panic to get away. It shocked him so badly he dropped her.

"Jillian?" Kate called, then, "Princess, you're scaring me!"

"Jill!" Doug yelled, then, "look out!"

Ben turned to look. A purple glass ball fell at his feet. Surprised, he bent to see it as Pat's wife, Sue, screamed.

"Jill!" Doug yelled again, and Ben left the ball and Sue to look at his daughter. She lay motionless on the ground, her eyes wide and staring at nothing. Before he could reach forward the three inches to touch her, another purple sphere landed at his feet. Doug yelled a wordless shout of fear, and Sue screamed again. A cascade of sharp tinkling cracks, as if it hailed ice, muffled the sounds of his friends exclaiming in fear. Ben fell to his knees to feel Jill's pulse amid a flurry of purple spheres that fell like rain, expecting one to hit him in the head and knock him out any moment.

"Get her inside!" he said as Doug loomed over him. He glanced at Anne, surprised she'd remained motionless through the commotion. She held one hand before her face, staring at the rings on her hands as if they were the most fascinating thing she'd ever seen. A purple ball the size of his truck barreled toward them. It rolled through the air against the wind, but before he had time to react, it veered sharply and fell to the lower field.

"What is that?" Doug yelled.

Kate crouched beside Jill, feeling for her pulse and glaring over her shoulder at Anne.

Without warning, rain began to fall in thick sheets accompanied by sharp cracks of thunder. More purple spheres appeared and careened past him, and Anne laughed. She held out both arms and laughed again, the sound sending goosebumps down his spine. Her hair rose, despite the rain, and waved about her head, each strand lit with blue sparks of static electricity

Ben said, "Get Jill inside. I'll get your mom."

"No," Jill moaned when Doug yanked her up.

Johanna hoovered uncertainly. "Jill, Anne? What can I do?" she asked.

Ben spared a glance for his gathered friends who stared up at the sky in horrified fascination. A roiling mass of purple filled the skyline now. It flickered and blazed in shades of purple and gray lit with bright skeins of light as if the sky itself burned. Purple spheres the size of cars floated from it, racing across the sky to land in the field below them. A thin purple haze trailed to Anne, growing thicker by the moment. He couldn't see the streamers for very far, they condensed too quickly into the purple balls that continued to fall at Anne's feet, but he was certain the haze was part of the thicker clouds. An enormous mass was gathering and pulling away from the approaching clouds. It was moving unnaturally fast and headed straight toward them. And within the roiling mass, a million small lights flickered

"Fairy lights," he whispered. He wanted to stare too but was afraid his daughter was having a seizure.

"Get her inside!" Ben yelled and ducked as another large sphere whipped past his head.

Kate reached for Jill, and Doug bent to lift her, grunting with effort. He pulled Jill over his shoulder and staggered to his feet. She made no resistance but began to scream as if in agony.

"Dad?" Doug asked in panic.

"Jilly," Kate said breathlessly.

Ben shoved Doug away. "Go! We can't help her here."

Doug hesitated, his face white and strained, his gaze flicking from his mother to Johanna and then to the roiling clouds.

Kate pulled his arm.

"Go!" Ben yelled and turned to Anne as Doug reached a hand to Johanna.

Ben grabbed his wife's arm, and she shrieked a sound he'd never heard her make before.

"Dad!" Doug called, and Ben peered over his shoulder to wave his son on. "Go!" he yelled at Johanna who'd started back to him.

She bit her lip and hesitated before turning and running after Doug.

"All of you, get inside!" Ben yelled as he struggled with Anne

"Is that aliens?"

"What the hell is that?"

"Oh my God!"

"It must be electricity."

The comments and exclamations tumbled over themselves so fast and in such frightened tones Ben couldn't decipher who was speaking. He had no attention to spare anyone. Anne fought him, scratching at his hands and straining hard to get away. He slapped her cheek, harder than he'd intended, and she opened her eyes.

"Ben?"

For one second, he was sure she saw him. Her eyes were wide, terrified, and confused. But she slumped without saying more and her eyes closed. He thought she'd passed out, but she spoke a moment later without opening her eyes. "Go! I need to stay. I need to! Go!" she shrieked and tried to crawl away from him.

"What's going on," Wayne asked as he ran up to squat beside Anne.

Kate stared at Anne in shock, exchanging worried glances with Ben as his friends gathered around.

Ben shook his head, his eyes on his wife who crouched, clutching the grass to balance herself with her head tipped and eyes squeezed closed as if she were listening hard.

"Oh, dear god! Look!" Sue cried out in a terrified shout, and Ben turned.

Sue staggered forward, falling to her knees. Mud splashed and coated her face, but she didn't wipe it. She held both hands up, shading her eyes from the sluicing rain and stared with wide eyes and an open mouth. Pat reached to pull her up and froze, his own eyes wide and suddenly terrified, locked on the hillside before them. Kate began screaming and Dave grabbed her in a hug. Ben rose slowly to his feet. Like Sue, he used his hands to shade his eyes, thinking what he saw was a trick of the rain.

"Dear God," Wayne whispered and held the binoculars out to Ben.

Ben took the glasses in his trembling hands and focused on the hill across from them. Green phosphorescent fire coated the trees. It didn't appear to be harming them. The trees glowed so brightly he could see with perfect clarity despite the storm wrought darkness. A red mist bubbled along the ground and coated the trees, dissipating into a bilious yellow glow that fed the green, but the bark and boughs remained mostly intact. Not so the house the green phosphorescence touched. The green turned red and the red mist thickened into a dense cloud that rolled and billowed and grew so fast the eye couldn't track it. It obscured the house until the green cloud engulfed it and dissipated the red into wisps and streamers that faded to yellow that were swallowed by the green. And where the house had stood was a pile of rubble. It had taken mere seconds.

He lowered the binoculars to scan the hillside, and Wayne took them from him. Ben looked to where he knew houses had been and spotted nothing except more of the green glow that writhed like flames over small piles of rubble. The glow advanced in a straight line while above it the purple fire burned the sky.

He figured they had maybe ten minutes before that fire passed over them.

"There are people," Wayne said in a strangled voice.

Ben grabbed the binoculars and swung them back to the destroyed house. A naked man held a naked child. The lightning revealed his anguished expression as he turned to the house. Ben lost sight of them as the man ran with the child behind the pile of rubble.

"Pat, get to the house and get them out!" Wayne called.

Ben grabbed Wayne's arm. "Take them to the root cellar and barricade yourselves in. Make it as airtight as you can. There should be enough air from the ventilation shaft in the back. If this is like radiation, it won't be able to travel around the corner of an underground pipe, so make that door tight!"

Wayne slapped his shoulder, gave Anne a grim look, and ran off calling for Dave to follow.

Anne and the Storm

Thursday Noon 1/18

The storm had answered Anne's call. It raced to her without appearing to move at all, but she felt its potential growing closer. It burned along her skin. The magnificence of it staggered her, and she braced herself against its power.

Giddy excitement made her sway. It wasn't a storm at all but a wall of information as if every thought in the world was condensed before her. Each flicker was a new piece of knowledge and she wanted to explore them all.

She could sense Jill beside her, reaching out to the information, accessing it somehow but her excitement made it too hard to focus. She wanted to know everything, but she knew she'd only have a few brief moments to access the information while the storm passed overhead and that thought brought tears to her eyes. To lose the knowledge after these small enticing glimpses would be like becoming mute, going both blind and deaf. She wanted to keep it with her.

Her ring cut into her palm she was clenching her hands so tightly and the diamond on her finger caught her eye. And suddenly she saw it, every microscopic spec, and she understood why diamond was so hard, why it shone, what it had been and what it could be. She knew the essence of it, and she laughed as she held up her hands.

I can encase it in diamond, she thought, and a purple sphere fell at her feet.

Vaguely, she heard people scream, but she couldn't pull herself away from the enticing knowledge to see who screamed or what they screamed about.

Time ceased to have meaning, and she no longer knew herself; she was the storm. Possibilities crashed upon her, and she strained for understanding, trying to form a question, the question, knowing the storm held all the answers if she could just ask it the right thing. And she wanted the knowledge, craved it, needed it.

"Anne, stop!" Ben shook her shoulder. "Stop!"

She glanced at him as he brushed his hands over the static jumping across his arms.

Anne didn't want to stop. She closed her eyes again and reached.

"Please!" Ben shrieked.

She opened her eyes and lowered hands she hadn't realized she'd risen.

He sounded terrified. "Look!"

She followed his pointing finger. It took her a second to see what had horrified him. The purple cloud was destroying every house it passed over. She staggered and fell back to her knees. Ruins covered the hillside where houses had stood moments before.

She was too far to see the panicked people, but she knew they would be panicked. Clouds of roiling red mist grew and spread, changing to green and being swallowed by the advancing purple wall. The red haze grew and mixed with the green and it appeared as if the purple cloud burned, an effect the lightning enhanced.

A distant corner of her mind wondered if it were burning, if the storm would sweep everything before it in a wave of fire, but she couldn't muster the attention for the thought to scare her. The cloud brought her knowledge without her will as if a billion men were shouting what they knew.

She could see the life fading from the people across the hill and without thought or planning she grasped at the fading life forces and somehow meshed them together. The moment she did it, she knew it was a mistake. The separate life forces weren't meant to be shaped and they screamed in fear and pain. It was a perversion of a life, a wrongness she didn't have words for. Horror made bile rise in her throat and she yanked the muddled mass she'd made apart.

The life faded to deadness and she was afraid to try again. She was afraid to even contemplate the lives she could still sense. Seeing the pain and fear was horrifying and she wasn't sure she'd be able to resist trying to help. She gritted her teeth and turned her attention back to the storm.

She could no longer consider it a cloud. It was too dense, to solid, to everything. The potential of it caught her again and it took her a few minutes to respond to Ben who called her in increasingly panicked tones.

"We have to get to the root cellar before the lightning reaches us," he yelled to be heard over the now howling wind. Anne hadn't even noticed the weather, too caught by the purple wall of knowledge. She glanced back at her mother's house. Distance and heavy rain hide the identities of the people who ran hunched over and clutching bags to the west where the root cellar was.

The horror of the imminent destruction of her home could barely penetrate the glory of the cloud. It pulled her so strongly she had no room left to be afraid.

"You go," she said.

"Anne…"

"Go!" she shrieked. "I have to stay. I have to know. I have to—"

The look on Ben's face seared her soul, but she didn't have words to explain her need. Ben took a step back and hesitated. He reached out as if he would drag her, then dropped his hand. She was glad he had, hating the thought of fighting him, but she'd fight to remain. It must've been clear in her expression because he took another step back. Rain came down so hard now it was difficult to see his face. Anne wanted to comfort him, but the purple wall called her.

"I need it," she said and turned away.

"Please, Anne, I love you. You'll die. Look at that lightning."

As if to emphasize his words, lightning arced over their heads and slammed into a lightning rod. The hair on Anne's arms rose, and wet strands of hair that had escaped her ponytail lifted. She cringed from the next strike but couldn't make herself go.

"I need it," she sobbed and rose her hands again, wishing she could explore the purple wall in peace, but she'd explore it in any way she could. Pressure built in her ears and along her skin, reminding her of the moment weeks ago when she'd felt the wall be born.

The leading edge of the storm touched her land and the land shrieked. The sound and shock of the pain that accompanied it drove her to the ground. She landed gracelessly in the mud. Pain like she'd never felt before lanced her body. Her land screamed again, and she felt it in her soul.

"Mine," she snarled and shoved Ben away. He'd pulled her up, and she hadn't noticed caught by the earth's agony.

Ben cried out and jerked away as a rippling series of lightning strikes lit the bank of the river below them.

"Mine!" Anne screamed and grabbed the purple wall. She

forced it up and over them. It could have the entire world, but this land is mine. The effort left her weak and gasping but she forced the wall of purple to her will.

Trust is Hard

Thursday Noon 1/18

Ben glanced at his wife and jumped a step away. She'd risen to her tiptoes and her hands were still lifted. All the hair on her head still floated as if she were covered in static. But it was her expression that shocked him. Her lips were lifted in a soundless snarl and she glared up at the sky. The rain cut off as if someone had turned a spicket and the sky grew darker.

"This is mine!" Anne shrieked, startling him. "You can't have it!"

He took a hesitant step forward, not sure what to do.

"Mine!" she yelled again, and the sky darkened so fast that for a moment he thought he'd gone blind, but the lanterns still burned behind him, and Helen's house lights twinkled in the distance. He heard a quad start up and a truck engine and hoped they thought to use the tractor to make an earthen barricade.

"Anne, we have to go!"

She made no reply.

"Anne, please, when it reaches us, we'll die! Who knows what breathing it will do! We need to get underground!"

A motor approached, and headlights lit the dark hill.

"Dad," Doug called, speaking as he drove up. "Wayne said the buildings are crumbling, that the storm is destroying the houses! What the hell is happening?" He pulled to a stop beside Ben and leaned from the cab of the two-seater MULE he was driving.

"Help me get your mother. How's Jill?"

"Crying and comatose by turns," Doug said grimly as he reached for Anne's arm.

"No," Anne said calmly and clearly. Lines of strain bracketed her mouth and she'd lowered her hands and clenched them into fists. Her posture said she was willing to fight, but her attention wasn't on them. Her open eyes looked right past him and into the sky.

Ben grabbed Doug's reaching hand.

"Trust me," Anne gasped out as if the effort to say them was beyond painful, and Ben wasn't certain who she spoke to.

"Dad?"

"I don't know." He crouched to peer into his wife's face. His boot nudged a purple sphere, and he eyed it thoughtfully. None of the spheres that littered the hillside had hit anyone. Despite heading directly toward them, they'd all turned and veered off.

"Is she controlling them?" Doug asked as he kicked the sphere away from Ben's foot. "Is it aliens?"

"I have no idea. She's doing something though."

Whatever she was doing was hard work. The strain on her face was apparent, and she was breathing so hard and fast Ben worried she'd have a stroke.

"Ten more minutes," Doug said.

Ben spared him a grim smile. "You timed the approach?"

"A rough estimate. It looked to be moving forward at a steady rate. If I had to guess, I'd say the same rate the reports warned of. But that isn't an electrical storm. Or not just an electrical storm."

Doug turned in a slow circle, his eyes scanning the black dome of sky overhead. "It's a barrier of some kind. No wind, no light, no rain…"

"No air?" Ben asked grimly.

"It's a big dome with trees beneath it. Air shouldn't be a problem for a good long while."

Another motor and headlights passed on the road behind them, and they both turned to look.

"I told Wayne to come back for the guns," Doug said as he watched the taillights disappear around the curve.

"We should go let the cows out…"

Doug shrugged and glanced at his watch. "No time." He cleared his throat and wiped his face on his sleeve. Ben laid a hand on his shoulder, then hugged him tightly.

Anne moaned and sank to the ground, her head hanging and the panting escalating.

"I'm trying," she gasped, and again Ben didn't know if she spoke to him or herself or the cloud.

He hesitated, not knowing what to do. Time ticked by while he dithered, and Doug's timer came and went, and still Anne struggled.

"We have to do something," Doug said in a tortured voice.

Ben bit his lip. Whatever was happening might be killing her, but he wasn't sure taking her away was smart either— and she'd asked him to trust her.

He reached out and pulled Doug away. "No. I've never forced your mother to do a thing in my life, and I'm not starting now. Whatever she's doing, she wants to do it—

"She's dying!"

"Maybe, but it's her choice."

He yanked Doug back, gripping his arm tightly. "I think she might be saving us too. If you stop her, will that fire descend and burn us all?"

"We can't let her die!"

Tears thickened Ben's voice, and he said gruffly," She'd rather die fighting. You didn't see…

"I saw," Doug said grimly and shook loose Ben's grasp. Ben tensed, but Doug merely crouched. Being careful not to touch Anne, he leaned closer.

Doug said, "The storm is destroying shit just like in that video. The one they claimed was a hoax."

He clamped his lips together and they were both silent except for the sounds of Anne's panting breaths.

It was hard to judge time, but Ben thought a good fifteen more minutes had passed before Doug said, "She's in pain, Dad."

Ben turned away and rubbed his face hard, then lifted his head to the sky but he couldn't see more than a few feet. The headlights of the MULE lit only a small area, leaving impenetrable blackness around them. He'd never been outside in darkness of this sort. Even on stormy nights, when the moon was small and the nights cold, his eyes would adjust and reveal at least the outlines. He shivered as he considered maybe the blackness was total and world-wide. Maybe the stars themselves had gone out and they'd never see sunlight again.

"Is this the end of the world?" Doug whispered.

"No, it's everything," Anne gasped out, then fell face down.

Light resumed along with the sound of rain although none touched them.

Thunder like Ben had never imagined crashed continuously while brilliant streaks of lightning flashed above them and slammed into the hillside across from them. The sound was so deafening and light so bright it amazed him that he hadn't heard it through whatever it was that had covered them.

Static flickered along his exposed skin, little tingles of electricity that grew by the second. He could feel the strike about to hit them. The purple fire was descending, but the green phosphorescence had passed over them and lit the hills to the west.

Doug whimpered as he reached to Anne. Ben grabbed her by the waist and the two of them lifted her while she moaned, trying to talk but not managing more than a mangled gurgle.

Ben flicked a glance to the sky as he staggered to the MULE with his wife's limp form.

"No," Anne groaned and the fire above them halted its downward motion.

"Is she doing that, Dad?"

Ben had no idea.

She'd fallen completely limp. He wasn't even sure she was still alive.

"Dad!" Doug screamed and dropped Anne's legs to race around the MULE. Ben dropped her in the small truck bed in the back of the mule, wincing as the tools beneath her clattered, and jumped into the passenger side, his terrified gaze on the lowering sky. Green phosphorescent fire had sprung up and rippled above them, casting an eerie green light over the fields. He half knelt on the seat to stare east.

"Go east, Doug! Look! It's clear! Go the other way!"

Doug glanced over his shoulder and swore. He swerved hard and they raced across the field. Ben stared upward into the writhing green flames. The purple clouds had stopped descending again and appeared to be moving west. The green fire was so low now he could see a thin smoky-black barrier between them and the fire in the sky. The green fire appeared to grow brighter, and he realized it was the barrier melting away that was improving visibility. He hoped that barrier was thick enough to keep the green fire away from them.

They reached the lower field and the path that cut across the hill and through the vineyard. Doug halted at the intersection and leaned out to stare up at the sky. "What way?"

"It looked like it was clear over Myer's farm. Cut through the back way and we can probably get a good view from the hill over the barns."

Doug nodded and gunned the engine. Ben braced himself with both hands, kneeling on the seat now to stare back the way they'd come. The tone of the light changed to a more normal nighttime glow. Trees blocked the view of the sky overhead, but he could see the lightning flaring and hear the thunder. It still crashed in an almost continuous peel and seemed to be farther west now. He was tempted to tell Doug to turn around again. They were likely to be struck by lightning on the hill. It might be better to follow the edge of the sky fire.

As if reading his mind, Doug slowed. "Maybe we should head for the winery. The cellar there should be safe from the storm.

"Yeah, I was just thinking that, but damn, I hate not knowing what that fire is doing."

Doug drove without speaking, going slower now on the narrow, curving path. He turned off at the intersection and slowed even more. They'd put in multiple pathways, most too narrow for a car, and kept them clear for the hikers and walkers who visited the winery. For a small fee they even allowed horses and bicycles. It was a popular place for the local horse set to visit year-round, but the trails were steep in areas, mostly the ones above the winery itself, and all were dirt and very slippery now.

The rain resumed, at first in fitful dribbles, and then a torrent that made it hard to see. The MULE splashed through deep puddles, sending cascades of muddy water over their legs and feet through the open doors.

Doug swore again as they slid sideways, and he slowed even more, clutching the steering wheel with both hands, leaning forward with his eyes narrowed, trying to see through the sleeting rain.

"Is Mom okay?"

"She hasn't moved," Ben said. He was tempted to ask him to

stop so he could check her pulse but the lightning that continued to strike the hill behind their head dissuaded him. The lightning rods they'd hammered into the top of the hill seemed to be doing their jobs but there were so many strikes one was bound to head for the metal canopy of the MULE. *It wouldn't do anyone any good to be hit,* he told himself firmly and turned to sit on the seat.

"Jesus," Doug said when they broke through the trees.

"Keep your eyes on the road," Ben snapped but he couldn't blame his son for staring. The winery sat on the hillside beneath the point and overlooked the river. It wasn't quite as good a view as the top of the hill, but it afforded a great view of the destruction that had followed the dam's collapse.

"The purple fire must have washed over it," Ben said.

"Will," Doug said grimly.

"High enough I think."

"Jesus, his parents…"

"We can worry about that when we're safe."

"The road is gone—"

Ben nodded. The force of the water had uprooted trees and left a wide path of devastation behind. He imagined it must've been a loud and terrifying sight, but they'd seen and heard nothing beneath the black dome. Reminded, he leaned out to stare up at the sky. Normal storm clouds floated overhead but he could see the glow of the purple and green fire further west.

"We're out from under," he said. "Jesus, I hope it passed the root cellar."

"I wish we had a radio."

You couldn't use it anyway. It would attract the lightning."

"They didn't lie about that at least."

Ben's lips tightened. He'd been thinking the same. The fury of the storm, the effects, all must've been known. The video he'd seen online that the reporters had called a hoax had been true and they must have known it.

"We can worry about that later too," he said as Doug pulled up to the back of the winery.

He jumped out and grabbed for Anne.

She didn't make a sound and lay limply in his arms. Doug reached past him to feel for her pulse.

"Get the door," Ben said and shifted his grip, laying Anne over his shoulder.

"Want me—"

"I got her. She barely weighs more than a sack of grain."

"Fuck!" Doug yelled as a bolt of lightning hit the metal roof of the MULE. He laughed nervously as he ran to the back door and fumbled with the padlock.

"Hurry up!" Ben said as another bolt slammed into the MULE with a crash that seemed to shake the earth. Every piece of hair on his body stood up straight. A piece of something whizzed past his face, and he could smell the chemically oily odor of burning rubber. He practically pushed Doug down he crowded so close to get inside the door.

Doug flipped the light switch, then swore when he remembered there was no power.

"I left my flashlight in the MULE."

"Leave it," Ben said and shouldered past him. He led the way through the dark room by memory, and Doug reached past him to open the cellar door.

The noise of the storm lessened with the closing of the door, and he eased carefully down the stairs. The room was pitch black. He couldn't see the steps or his hand in front of his face. The concussion of the thunder sounded like cannon fire and shook the floor beneath his feet.

"I'm going for the fire extinguisher," Doug said.

"Grab the first aid kit under the counter but stay away from the windows. And don't you fucking dare go outside for that flashlight!"

Doug huffed a small surprised laugh. "Yes, sir."

Ben smiled, imagining his son was saluting as was his habit when he gave him the sarcastic title although he usually said sir respectfully. His smile faded as he reached the bottom step and placed his wife on the floor.

"Anne," he said, patting her cold cheek. He felt for the pulse in her wrist, relieved to find one, and then chaffed her cold hands in his. She was soaked beneath the rain slicker, and the skin of her stomach was just as cold as the skin of her hands.

He stripped off her wet clothing, and then removed his outerwear. His thermals were still dry, so he removed them too and dressed Anne in them before putting his damp jeans back on. He gathered the wet clothing and piled it to the left of the door, except for his raincoat, which he shook out and put back on before picking Anne up and sitting to the right of the doorway with his back to the wall.

"I wish we'd bought you better rain gear," he mumbled as he settled her in his lap, putting his raincoat over both of them. She'd bought he and the kids the best rain gear she could find and had bought herself cheap ones, and he'd said nothing. He'd thought her preparations had taken on obsessive dimensions, but she'd sensed it coming.

A wave of guilt brought tears to his eyes. Anne never bought on impulse, but she'd been shopping like a lunatic, and he'd never considered how frightened she must've been to do so. The only thing he could remember her buying without planning was Merlin, despite Ben's objections on the cost. She'd seen him and fallen in love and it had been mutual. Merlin was just as devoted to her. Ben spent a second hoping the dogs were okay.

He was pondering his wife's' improbable actions when Doug returned.

"How is she," Doug asked as he clambered down the wooden stairs. He halted at the bottom, a thin beam of light lingering on

Anne's head. Ben was about to yell when he realized it was light from a cell phone.

"Unconscious but alive," he said as reassuringly as he could. "I'm trying to warm her up."

Doug squatted next to him and offered him the first-aid kit he carried. "I left the extinguisher outside the door, but the strikes were slowing already."

"I figure it will last a few days at least but slower like it was with the storm's approach," Ben said as he took the kit and examined the contents. He'd thought the lightning of four days ago spectacular until he'd seen this.

"Here, let me," Doug said and took the kit back. He began pulling out gauze and tape as he said, "There's nothing in it that will help her, but your cheek is bleeding." As he spoke, he opened a tube of antibiotic ointment and smeared it on Ben's cheek.

Ben didn't even remember getting scratched.

"There's food in the vending machines upstairs if you're hungry."

"I'm good. I wish I knew if the others—"

"Yeah, me too. What do you think that was?"

"Some sort of acid rain maybe, but I can't figure out why it didn't destroy the trees just the buildings."

"The manufactured stuff. Did you see the road was all eaten away on the hill across from us? It looked like the telephone poles had been dipped in acid. I think that red gas or whatever it was just ate the wood away when it boiled off the impurities."

"I didn't notice the road, but that seems like what it did to that house."

"If you're okay here, I'm going to go upstairs and see if I can see anything."

"Stay away from the windows."

Doug kissed Anne's cheek and then Ben's. "I will," he said gruffly.

He halted as he stood, and the light played over the aisle.

"What's all that?" he asked, but Ben was wondering the same thing.

Doug stepped forward and peered around the stacked barrels of wine.

"Holy shit, this aisle is full too!" He walked the wider path and disappeared from sight, only the muted glow of his light betraying his path around the room.

Three wide aisles bisected the room leading to a ramp that lead outside that they used to bring in the barrels of wine and cider they stored here. There was another bigger storage cellar beneath the shop, but this one was open to the public and the barrels were stored on fancy wooden shelves with name tags and decorative taps for when they held tastings. Doug's light had revealed the center aisle was full of boxes. It looked like Anne had emptied the accounts and bought the packaging and supplies for the entire year.

He frowned as he considered she'd done it without consulting him or her mother.

"Why?" he whispered as he kissed her cold forehead. He slipped a hand beneath her shirt to see if she was getting any warmer. To his relief, the skin of her stomach felt warmer to him now. He kissed her again and snuggled her closer. They'd have to talk about her sudden penchant for hoarding, although he supposed it didn't matter now.

He wasn't naive enough to think the world was going to be the same, not after the lies were revealed and the deaths and damage counted. *Doug's fucking cell phone worked.* The ramifications of that were just sinking in. A sob clawed its way from his throat, and he breathed hard a minute, knowing if he started crying, he'd continue, and his family needed him to be strong. Despite his efforts, tears trickled down his cheeks and he was soon bawling like a baby. It took him minutes to regain control, and he was still taking hitching breaths when Doug returned.

"It looks like she bought all the supplies we usually get and then some. Every aisle is full. How did she know?"

"She didn't," Ben said and had to clear his throat.

"Are you okay?" Doug asked and squatted to place a hand on Ben's shoulder.

"No. Doug—" He cleared his throat and tried again. "Doug, that purple fire will pass over your Uncle Rich's any minute. God, I wish he'd come…"

Doug sat back on his heels and rubbed his face.

"They'll all die."

"Yes."

"Even if the fire doesn't kill them, they'll die."

Ben nodded.

"Jesus!" Doug jumped to his feet and began to pace. "Jesus," he said again this time angrily. He kicked the wooden shelf and then leaned his head against it, letting the phone fall to the floor.

"Doug," Ben said, heartsick to hear his son cry but unable to comfort him.

Tears welled again in Ben's eyes. The entire world would be crying. Who was to say if the fire would die out? It might travel the world, destroying everything, leaving naked shocked survivors who would die of exposure or the effects of the gases they inhaled.

Doug cried for a few more minutes before he straightened and wiped his face. He sat beside Ben, resting his hand on his mother's shoulder.

"Even if the fire dies out soon, it still killed millions. New York, Boston… Would they have time to get out, to get underground?"

"Maybe some. When the storm breaks, we'll get the radios out."

Doug nodded, then leaned forward suddenly to glare at his phone.

"I forgot Jill and I planned to record it…" He frowned as he trailed off and examined the phone. "It works fine. Those fuckers!" He threw the phone across the room, swearing as he leapt to his feet and stomped after it. He snatched it up and dropped it in Anne's lap.

"It works. There was no electric magnetic pulse, or it'd be FUBAR. All that work… Jesus Christ, we could've been building shelters! Those fuckers!" he continued to swear and rant, growing angrier by the second.

Ben wanted to be angry too, but he was too worried. Worry had formed a knot in his stomach and made his head throb. He closed his eyes and leaned his head against the wall, letting his son rage and trying not to picture his family beneath the purple fire.

Waiting Out the Storm

Thursday Dusk 1/18

Ben lifted his head, surprised he'd dozed off.

"I think we can go," Doug said.

"How long was I sleeping?" Ben reached to check Anne's pulse.

"About forty minutes. It's still raining but the thunder and lightning are back to normal. The MULE burned; we'll have to hike back."

"We can't take your mother out in the storm." Ben lifted his raincoat off Anne as he said, "You wait with her. I'll go check on—"

"I'll be faster, Dad."

"But I need to see Jill. Please, just wait with your mother. If someone doesn't come by morning, leave her here and go check on them."

"Morning," Doug said dubiously.

"If I don't come back, it means I'm dead and it's too dangerous to go out. Wait until morning before trying. Your mother needs you."

"Johanna—"

"Is either dead already or waiting in the root cellar. I'm sorry, son, I really am, but there's no sense in both of us going and getting killed, and I can't send you out in this. I can't!" he repeated emphatically when Doug opened his mouth to protest. "Wait here, and I'll take care of our family."

Doug nodded, ducking his head and rubbing his face with both hands. Ben placed Anne gently on the floor, stooping to kiss her lips and feel her pulse a moment before straightening to stretch. His head throbbed hard with the change of position. He had the worst stress headache of his life. Each heartbeat seemed to echo in his skull.

Doug offered him the phone, but he gestured him away.

"You keep it. It's better if I have no metal on me. Check the boxes and see if you can find anything we could use."

Doug nodded grimly.

Ben hugged him quickly and headed up the stairs. Rain drummed against the tile roof and the occasional flash of lightning reflected off the metal tanks, lighting the dense gloom of the winery. The building seemed to have come through unscathed. He debated a moment, then headed for the front door. They'd removed the expensive electronic keypad and replaced it with a padlock. He'd be unable to open the doors from the inside, but the front room was used for sales and sported floor-to-ceiling windows that looked over the grapes that lined the hillside and afforded a great view down the valley. The tables and chairs had been stacked along the bar to leave the floor clear for the outdoor furniture to be stacked until they opened again in the spring. The big empty room echoed as he crossed it. A flicker of lightning revealed handprints on the glass, *Doug must have peered out the same window*, Ben mused as he placed his hands where his son had and pressed his nose to the glass.

Essence of the Storm

The rain still fell in thick sheets and night had fallen. The western horizon glowed that eerie green, and he turned away, not wanting to see. Darkness obscured the view before him with only the intermittent flashes of lightning to light it. His forlorn hope that his recollections of the devastation were only a nightmare died as another flash revealed the destruction the water had wrought. He turned his eyes away from the destroyed homes on the hill opposite and stared hard at the roads that glistened oddly as if slicked with oil. Trees and downed telephone poles made viewing the roads difficult, and he gave up on trying to figure out what had happened to them. The damage was worse than he'd imagined possible. He turned from the window and headed to the back door.

The rain that slapped him in the face was colder than he remembered it being. Icy rivulets snaked beneath his collar and chilled him as he powerwalked along the lower trail. He'd been tempted to cut straight up the hill but wanted to see if the bakery and greenhouses still stood. If they stood, there was a chance the wider paved road that cut down the hill from the barns would be intact, and he might be able to take the truck down it. There was no way he could go the usual way, following the road as it wound along the edge of the farm then joined the River Road and turning up their private road that lead to the lower parking lots so he didn't have to stop and open the gates, one of which always got stuck and he'd been meaning to fix for ages but had somehow never gotten around to it. But sticking gates were the least of his worries now. Carrying Anne through the rain to the upper parking lot would be much faster than carrying her all the way to the root cellar. If the cellar was still intact.

"Don't waste your breath, old man," he said, when his breath hitched on a sob. He clamped his lips together and picked up his pace until he was jogging. The roof of the bakery came into view, and he slowed to catch his breath and left the path, cutting diagonally up the hill, climbing over the trellised grapes, not caring when he bent the wires and broke the vines. He reached the path again in minutes and paused to glance back. The metal bars of the greenhouse were visible in the dim lit. Brighter flashes of lightning revealed the tattered plastic coverings.

At least they're still there, he thought, allowing himself to feel hope that the root cellar would be untouched as well. As fast as his legs would take him, he climbed the steep hill, huffing and puffing with the unaccustomed exertion. He'd thought himself in great shape for his age; he was able to lift bales and bags of grain with no problems, but he wasn't used to running up hills. His pace slowed until he was walking and clutching his side, but he pressed on.

Lights in the distance caught his eye as he crested the hill, and he lifted both hands to shade his face from the pouring rain. The electric lanterns they'd left on in Helen's and his house still twinkled in the windows. The sight invigorated him, and he picked up his pace again on the flatter ground. *The purple fire in the sky had passed from view or maybe went out,* he thought hopefully. He could see the darker shape of the barns to his left and took the fork in the road that led to it. A tiny glimmer of light swayed, the corner of the barn cutting it off.

"Who's there?" he called.

"Me!" Wayne yelled back, and the light grew brighter, revealing a dark shape.

"Jill? My family?"

"Safe inside! Where've you been? I ran up to the point as soon as the storm passed over us. Jesus, did you see that sky? And that blackness?" Wayne clasped his shoulder with a trembling hand. "How's Anne? Where's Doug?"

"Doug is with Anne. Jill?"

"Still out, but she thrashed about a few times. I think she's coming out of it." Wayne gave him a quick hug. "Pat went with his brother Kate and Edward to check the houses. We figured it was safe to go back now, and it'll be warmer there." He glanced over his shoulder and lowered his voice. "They don't know, not really. I saw it though. It's all gone. We need to get out there. If there are survivors, they're going to need help."

"Go get Doug at the winery, and we'll take Anne and Jill home. I need to see Jill, and then we'll go. And, Wayne" – he gripped Wayne's shoulder hard— "Grab one rifle and five pistols."

Wayne nodded grimly and ran for the front of the barn. Ben continued along the back, heading for the root cellar that Anne's great, great, great, great, grandfather had dug by hand. They used it now to store apples and pumpkins. Anne had been after him to build another for squash and onions, and he'd been putting her off for years with no intention of actually building one, but now he vowed to do it the first chance he got.

He had to knock on the thick wooden door, it hadn't budged when he pulled the handle.

"One second," Sue said, her voice muffled by the thick wood.

Ben waited while listening to muffled exclamations and soft clinks and clanks. The lightning that flickered overhead made him nervous, but the rods still appeared to be drawing it.

The door finally opened, and Sue greeted him with a quick hug. She stepped back to let him enter as everyone tried to greet him or ask questions at once.

"Let the man breath," Sue said, and everyone quieted.

Three lanterns hanging from hooks in the low ceiling cast wavering light across their strained faces. He was happy to see the kids all appeared to be sleeping on blankets spread across the top of planks that lay over the bins in the back. *Someone had been thinking on their feet*, Ben thought approvingly as he eyed the thick roll of plastic that they used to cover the greenhouses had been spread out to cover the walls. The plastic was nailed to the wooden beams that formed the deep bins that lined the walls, and two-by-fours had been used to lift it to the ceiling, leaving the aisle completely cocooned.

A very crowded aisle, Ben noted as his sister held up a hand to wave to him. She sat in her husband's lap holding her sleeping grandson. His niece and brother sat beside them. Ben had to turn away from his brother's face. Dean knew. Julie still had hope though, it shone from her eyes as she stared at Ben as if she expected her mother, Andrea, to follow him in, and Ben didn't know which was worse. Only the sleeping children looked comfortable. Everyone else looked scared to death *but at least they were safe.*

Ben said a prayer of thanks as he reached for his mother who sobbed quietly, muffling the sound with her hands pressed to her face. Sue pressed hard against the wall to make room for him to pass her and reach his mother.

"Wayne told us to stay inside. Is the storm passing?" Sue asked.

Ben hugged his mother as he said, "A bit. It's still raining but the worst seems to be over. "How's Jill?"

Jill lay right inside the doorway, the widest part of the aisle, with a light directly over her. Her head rested on Wayne's wife, Marie's, knees, and Abby and Johanna hovered, standing behind them, being there was no room to sit. Ben hoped they'd taken turns and that Abby and Johanna hadn't been standing the entire time.

His gaze flicked to Abby's husband Dan who nodded acknowledgement. *Dan had aged ten years in the hours since the storm arrived,* Ben thought as he nodded in reply. His grim expression and tight-lipped pale face told Ben that Dan knew the storm had devasted the coast.

Johanna gestured to her feet. "Sick. Where's Doug?"

"He's fine and at the winery with Anne," Ben said as he gave her a quick hug before kneeling beside his daughter. Her pulse beat steadily against his fingertips. She was warm to the touch but not feverishly warm. Her skin didn't have the same pallor Anne's did, he was happy to note, and she moaned softly when he patted her cheek.

"It's best to let her lay still," Marie said. She reached down and felt Jill's pulse, turning to Abby. "Nice and steady."

Abby said, "Check her pupils again before we take her out. I'm worried moving her will be bad for her, but she needs somewhere warmer."

"The houses are"— he'd been going to say fine but cut himself off. The houses were destroyed; it was only his that were fine. The thought left him feeling sick with guilty nerves. "My house is still standing, and the winery came through with no damage. Wayne went to pick up Anne. He'll stop here for Jill, but the rest of you can walk. We need to get on the road as soon as we can to help the survivors."

"How bad is it?" Dan asked.

"Bad. The dam went. The River Road is unusable. All the roads will be blocked with debris." He took a deep breath and gathered his thoughts. They needed to know but he dreaded the telling. "That red gas stuff seems to have disintegrate anything man-made it touched. The telephone poles and road across from us look like swiss cheese. I think we can expect the same kind of damage on our side."

Helen furrowed her brow and pursed her lips. "But you said the winery is fine."

"It is. Look, I don't know what happened, but somehow the storm passed completely over us."

"We saw the lights go out. It scared me to death," Helen said.

"Well, whatever turned off the lights also blocked the fire in the sky from reaching us. I don't really know what damage that fire caused, but we saw what it did on the hillside across the river. There will be people out there who need help. And the flood damage… well, we need to get going or the elements will kill them if that gas didn't."

A truck approached in the distance, and Ben turned to the door.

"But that means they're all dead," Helen said in rising horror.

Ben stepped outside as she began to cry. The headlights of the truck cut a broad swath through the darkness as Wayne pulled to a stop.

"Johanna is fine," Ben said.

Doug stuck his head out the passenger window and said, "Mom's still out. Wayne says Jill is too."

"Yeah, take her with you to the house. Get her and Mom settled while I talk with everyone. We need to get going if we're going to make any kind of difference."

"Those goddamned bastards," Doug muttered as he rolled up the window.

Ben returned to get Jill and was greeted by crying and grim faces.

"That can't be true," Helen said through her sobs. Johanna leaned down to pat her shoulder. Tears trickled down her pale cheeks, but she was crying quietly.

Ben didn't answer. Marie rose as he did, supporting Jill between them. Her voice shook as she asked, "Are you sure?"

"Yes." Not knowing how to soften that blow, he shouldered Jill in a fireman's carry and headed to the truck.

Anne was wedged between Wayne and Doug on the bench seat. He placed his daughter in Doug's lap and reached to feel his wife's cheek. Doug held his sister against his chest and said nothing as the cold rain soaked him.

Ben stepped back and closed the door, watching the taillights until the curve of the land took them from view. He straightened his shoulders and went back to ask for volunteers.

No Time

Thursday Evening 1/18

The adults gathered inside the main door of the barn. Lantern light revealed their tearstained faces were pinched and pale, but all wore determined expressions.

"There will be dead, you should stay," Ben said to Kate.

I'm going. I can run a chainsaw."

Ben nodded and glanced at her husband. Dave appeared dazed, not angry like his wife. He picked up the pistol and loaded it with quiet competence. The two exited the barn, and Ben turned to Sue.

But before he could ask, she said, "I'll look after everyone. And see to getting the soup ready." She used two fingers to rub her right eyebrow. The familiar gesture almost made Ben smile. Sue was one of the smartest people he knew, and whenever she was deep in thought, she rubbed her eyebrow just like her father.

Ben's burgeoning smile died. Her father would be dead by now as would everyone else who'd resided in that apartment complex. Six stories of concrete that would've collapsed like the storage unit across from them had. He'd used the binoculars again and seen more than he wished too. He'd hoped it had just been the homes with vinyl siding, but the concrete buildings had also fallen. He prayed it had been quick, that they hadn't seen the destruction coming and their fate approach, that they hadn't run into the storm and been gassed, their clothing scoured from their bodies and been left to die a slow agonizing death from gas inhalation or the cold rain.

"Bring them home—" Sue's voice hitched, and she began to cry, waving her hand in a go gesture as she rubbed her face with her free hand.

"I'll get the kids home," she said through her tears.

"I'm so sorry, Sue. So damned sorry." He kept his gaze from Edward who looked as if he might be sick any moment. His wife had stayed home with a headache, and Edward hadn't said a word since stepping from the root cellar.

"It's not your fault. Go. I'm fine." She waved him away again.

The lie was apparent, but he left her to cry in peace.

"Where's Doug?" he asked when he reached the truck.

Wayne frowned. "Saying goodbye to Johanna. She's in the root cellar with the kids in case one wakes. I don't like leaving them defenseless like this."

Pat yanked the strap he was tightening, talking without looking up. "Sue will be with them, and she has a pistol."

Ben said, "As does my family. They'll be fine. The house alarm will still work."

"Fuckers," Wayne mumbled, then pounded his hand on the steering wheel. "Goddamned mother fuckers! My truck's in fucking storage! What the hell for? They had to know! They had to!"

Pat shrugged and pressed his lips together. "We have two trucks, and it's a fucking miracle that we do. I don't know how Anne did it— What she did, but..."

Wayne gave Pat a dubious glance. "Anne? What could she

have done? No, it must've been a fluke, like the eye or something. We got lucky. Or unlucky. Jesus, this can't be happening. I keep expecting to wake up or look out the damned window and see the houses. The goddamned houses…"

"Maybe we're overreacting," Pat said encouragingly, but his eyes remained bleak and he flicked a guilty glance at Edward. Ben thought he didn't really believe they were.

Doug hailed him, and he turned. Johanna waved but ducked back into the root cellar.

"The kids are up. She's taking them to the house. They think this is great," Doug finished bitterly.

"Let them have a night. The truth— whatever it is— can wait."

Pat snorted and stomped through the mud to yank on the strap that went around the hood and under the truck. He tugged the ratchet back, but it was already as tight as he could make it.

Another strap went through the windows and over the cab roof. Doug leaned down and ran his hands over the tape that covered the edge of his wellingtons.

"Dry?" Ben asked and rose an eyebrow in a you better not lie to me look.

Doug huffed a half laugh and nodded. "I'm fine. Let's go. Every minute we spend…."

"It won't help anyone if you kill yourself getting to them either," Ben said.

Doug climbed onto the roof of the truck without answering and began connecting the safety line to his belt. Pat slapped the side of the truck and climbed into the back where Kate Dave and Edward huddled under a tarp. Pat remained standing, holding the strap with one hand. Ben handed him the battery powered LED lantern they'd taped to a hoe, and then reached into the back to withdraw the massive flashlight Anne had insisted they buy and stored in their microwave to protect it from the electrical storm. *Maybe the dome blocked the pulse from us too,* he tried to tell himself as he gave the flashlight to Doug after testing the strap himself. But he couldn't banish the images of Sonja Arnault's face as she told them to stay indoors while the fake footage played behind her.

Ben got in on the driver's side and rolled down his window a few inches. Rain immediately dampened the seat back, but he left it open.

"He has a radio," Wayne said.

"Yeah, but if he's falling, will he use it?"

Wayne shrugged and used his flashlight to examine the map he held. Ben drove slowly from the barnyard.

"You can speed up," Doug said over the radio. "The strap is secure, and I have a good grip."

"Slow and steady wins the race," Ben said. "Keep a sharp eye out for downed trees and debris in the road." Thunder rumbled softly, and lightning lit the sky in brief flashes. Ben worried for Doug on the outside of the truck, but the thunderstorm seemed to be heading away at a rapid pace.

"Roger that," Doug said, and the flashlight beam swung from right to left, lighting a much broader stretch than the headlights but the motion was dizzying.

Ben narrowed his eyes and leaned forward, trying to keep his gaze in the center of the road and resist looking to either side.

"Tree," Doug said, and Pat jumped from the back before Ben had brought the truck to a stop. Doug slid off the roof, and Ben rolled the window farther down to peer out.

"Just a small limb," Pat said on the radio. "We got this."

The truck shook slightly, and Ben realized Edward had climbed out as he climbed back in.

"Nice catch," Wayne said.

"I should've rigged a quick release," Doug complained.

"I got this. I don't even need the chainsaw. One minute," Pat said.

Ben rolled the window up and leaned forward, trying to see

through the rain. Pat's lantern bobbed and weaved but didn't cast enough light to show his surroundings much. He was headed back though, and Ben leaned back, stretching his tense shoulders as much as he could in the cab.

Doug halted them again less than a minute later, but Ben had been expecting it. The lights revealed massive storm damage, trees toppled, burnt, and blown apart.

"Lightning damage," Wayne said in an awed voice, and pointed to a swath of fire-darkened trees. "Lucky the rain was so hard or it would've burned the entire forest. And, Jesus, look at the road!"

The road before Ben ended abruptly in a glistening rubble track. He opened his window and leaned out. The damage appeared to begin abruptly and curved away to the left and right until darkness hid the view, but he'd seen enough to realize whatever had protected them from the purple fire in the sky had also protected from the storm itself. He'd been so consumed with the purple fire that he hadn't realized the extent of the damage the lightning and wind were doing. It appeared as if mini tornados had touched down and uprooted trees, flinging them amongst their brethren where they hung entangled together while others lay on their sides or leaned precariously.

Everyone exited the truck to examine the damage. Ben squatted to run his hand over the pitted surface of the road while Pat and Wayne discussed the best way to clear the fallen trees.

"What is it, Dad?" Doug asked as he poked the remains of the road with a shovel he'd taken from the back of the truck.

"Oil, rock… whatever the hell is left when you boil asphalt down to its base structure." Ben wiped off his oil slicked hands on his pants and gingerly stepped forward, pushing down before committing his full weight to it.

"Think it will hold the truck?" Wayne asked.

"There's lots of give, and it's slippery as hell," Pat warned as he stamped across the slick surface. He waved at the remains of a telephone pole, saying, "It could fall any second. We should've brought hard hats.

Ben turned to the pitted driveway. A tree had landed and burned, blocking the drive, but the remains of the house looked untouched by fire. He took out his flashlight and cautiously approached. Doug followed with his bigger light and the shovel. Neither man spoke as they clambered over fallen tree limbs to reach the wreckage.

"Is anyone here?" Doug yelled. "Do you need help?"

"If they were inside…" Ben trailed off and shook his head. *The Andrews had been a nice family.*

"The girls," Doug said, sounding sick. He glared at the remains of the house and tried to pry what Ben thought had been a window header loose from the rubble. The wood disintegrated into thick splinters and the house settled further with a crashing groan of sound. Ben jumped back, pulling Doug with him.

He cupped his hands around his mouth and shouted as loudly as he could, "If you can hear us, holler back!"

The rain beat down, deadening his shouts. Behind him, the horn blew, three long blasts. Wayne joined them and shook his head. "It's no use. If they don't answer, we can't take time looking. Not when there could be people we could save out there."

"They were so small," Doug said and began to cry.

Ben put an arm around his son's shoulder and led him back to the truck. He tried not picture the two little blond girls who'd loved to come feed the cows with their mother and chattered happily while trying to shovel manure with him. To think of them trapped inside that house hurt his soul. But Wayne was right. As much as he wanted to tear the house apart searching, he knew it was pointless. They had no time to search when there were likely others they could help in the freezing rain.

A chainsaw whirred to life, and Wayne left them to grab a saw from the back of the truck.

"We should check the other houses," Doug said in a choked voice.

Another chainsaw joined the first. Ben glanced down the dark, devastated street and his heart constricted. He didn't want to see his dead neighbors.

A wavering light approached as Kate returned. Fresh tears had reddened her eyes, but she spoke firmly. "I'm going to run back for the dogs. Dave says it will take about thirty more minutes to clear this section. He thinks we should get the tractor too."

Ben rubbed his forehead, angry with himself for not thinking of it but his wits felt dull, the shock he supposed. "Go to Kevin Carrillo's and see if we can take his backhoe. I know he didn't put it into storage or take it apart. They might not even realize… Jesus, we'll have to tell them."

Fresh lines etched Kate's face as she glanced back at their road. "I'll stop and talk with them."

"I'll come with you," Doug said and held out the flashlight to Ben. "No one should go out in this alone, and I'll bring the smaller quad and extra gas cans. Should I change out the forks for the plow?"

"No. Leave it. We can use the forks to lift." Ben gazed up at the sky and frowned. The rain was thickening to sleet. They'd need to come back for a plow if it began to snow.

Kate followed his gaze and said," I'll grab a snow shovel too."

"Don't wait for us," Doug called back as he began to jog back down the road. "We'll catch up!"

S. M. Savoy

The Search for Survivors

Thursday Evening 1/18

Ben straightened and turned off the chainsaw when he heard the rumble of Doug's dirt bike.

Dean followed on the quad. The deeper rumble of a bulldozer told Ben Kevin would be on his way.

"Kate's grabbing supplies and bringing my truck," Doug said as he brought the bike to a stop, his voice muffled by his helmet. "I'm going to head down Dover and see if I can reach Will's."

"Not alone," Ben said.

Dean stopped the quad and got off, reaching for the chainsaw Ben carried. His bleak expression hardened as he examined the storm damage.

Dean said, "Take the quad. There's a small chainsaw and rope on the back under the tarp. Sue put some supplies in there. The radios get crap reception, so send Doug back if you find survivors. Marcus is heading out on his mountain bike to search the housing development up on Oak. Sue is organizing search parties to go out on foot. The sooner we reach them...."

Ben gave his brother a hard hug. They both knew Andrea would be unreachable without bridges to cross the rivers. Ben couldn't imagine the pain of knowing your wife was dying alone in the cold. It hurt his soul to think of Andrea alone and suffering and she was only his sister-in-law.

"Julie?"

"Is watching the kids who thankfully have no idea. She'll keep an eye on Jill and Anne."

"I'm so sorry," Ben said.

Dean slashed his hand through the air and turned away. He stomped through the mud and yanked on a limb Ben had just cut loose.

"Leave him, Dad," Doug whispered. Gram is just sick about this. I can't believe this is happening."

Ben gestured to the pack on Doug's back. "What's in the bag?"

Two tarps, a Duraflame, half a case of those cheap rain ponchos Mom bought, and bandages. Uncle Dean worked out a route to clear. We're supposed to be setting up small aid stations where people can get warm while they wait for the truck to come through and pick them up."

"Well, we better get going then."

Doug reached into his pocket and pulled out a pink whistle on a purple cord that he handed over.

Ben grimaced and put the cord around his neck.

"She'll be oaky," Doug said encouragingly.

Ben smiled ruefully. The whistles were from Anne's Girl Scout Supplies.

"Let's go," he said gruffly and started the quad.

Doug slapped down the face shield on his helmet and drove slowly over the downed tree limbs. Ben followed on the quad. Limbs cracked and settled deeper into the muck, and Ben hoped none would puncture a tire. He breathed a sigh of relief when they reached the turnoff onto lower Dover. The houses here were closer together without the thicker trees that had lined the upper street. The rubble of the street itself was slick with rain and an oily substance, but Doug appeared to have no problems traversing it. The quad slid, and Ben tried to stay in the yards instead of the road to spare the tires.

Doug slowed and came to a stop. He got off his bike and squatted, pulling branches back. Ben stopped beside him and turned off the quad to crouch by his son.

"Lightning," he said grimly as he eyed the blackened foot protruding from the foliage. He gingerly reached to feel for a pulse and wasn't surprised there wasn't one.

Doug ripped off his helmet and vomited, then lifted his face to the rain.

"Jesus, Dad."

Ben gripped his shoulder a moment, releasing him when Doug put his helmet back on. They'd gone only another few feet when he stopped again.

This time it was a man and a young girl laying in the street. A charred meat smell lingered beneath the rain, making Ben gag as he examined the corpses. Severe burns marred the girl's body. The man's hand had burned to the bone but the rest of him appeared untouched by fire but was covered with a red rash.

Ben examined the ground, frowning thoughtfully.

"Looks like he was hit by the lightning and it lit the road on fire and caught the girl."

A dog barked and both Ben and Doug turned to look. Rain made visibility low, but the distant flashes of lightning revealed a dog running down the adjoining street. It barked again, a sharp spate of sound.

"Here boy!" Ben called, and the dog stopped and glanced over its shoulder.

Ben straightened but hesitated. The dog was going away from Will's house, but it acted as if it was waiting on a person. *It was likely a corpse*, Ben mused as he debated following, and Will was like a son to him. He'd watched him grow from a boy to man alongside his own son and wanted to know his fate as much as Doug did.

"Follow it," Doug said, shrugging from his pack. He handed it over and remounted his bike. "Meet me there." Doug shook the pack at him when he still hesitated. "Take it!"

Ben took it.

"I'll be fine," Doug said in a softer voice.

Ben watched his son drive away and slogged back to his quad, the cold rain mingling with his tears. The thought of his son alone in this storm, among the dead and sure to be desperate, made him feel sick.

He followed the dog. The dog ran back down the road, and Ben lost sight of it behind a fallen tree. When he caught up, the dog waited with its tail wagging and tongue lolling and a doggy grin. It was having fun running in the rain.

Ben stopped the quad to call it again.

It barked and wagged and darted away. Ben hesitated again but knew if he didn't follow the not knowing would haunt him. A minute later he was glad he had. He could smell smoke. Tumbled debris had formed a crude cave, and someone had made a fire inside the rough shelter. The dog was heading right for it.

"Hello!" he called as he turned off the quad and stooped to examine the carefully laid out corpses someone had covered with pine boughs.

"Move," a woman said as another said, "Marge, don't be silly."

Load crying and sobbing obscured what they said next.

The dog barked in obvious excitement when he heard the woman.

"Move!" the first woman said again in an angrier voice "We're in here!" she called out.

"You can't go out there," another woman said, sounding

scandalized at the idea.

"Get out of the way, or I'll make you move!"

"You're naked," the other woman protested.

"Don't be an idiot!" the first woman snapped as her head emerged from the shelter. Her hair looked frayed and rough as though it'd been singed.

Ben hunkered and offered his pack.

"There's rain ponchos inside."

She ignored the offered bag and continued to crawl out. Once out, she snatched it and squatted to thrust it into the shelter. A red rash covered her shoulders with a bright line of red crossing her back. When she turned again, he saw the rash covered her breasts and thighs too with another dark red line at her waist.

The woman inside were talking and crying but Ben couldn't make out more than arguing complaints.

"Thank God," the woman said and hugged him.

Ben awkwardly patted her back, trying to avoid the rashy parts.

"I have a tarp. We can set up a shelter—"

"Our men have gone to look for help." She turned to stare at the quad while absently patting the dog. "How do you have a vehicle?"

"It's a long story. How many are you?" Ben began removing the tarp from the back of the quad.

"Thirteen here now," she said and shivered, crossing her arms over her breasts to hug herself. She glared up into the sky and hollered, "Shut up!" over her shoulder.

The complainer quieted, and she shook her head hard, sending wet strands of hair over her cheeks.

Another woman emerged from the shelter, this one wearing one of the rain ponchos. It wasn't quite transparent, but the thin yellow plastic molded to the woman's body with the force of the rain. Her hair had almost completely burned away. The red rash was brightest on her legs and ankles, fading to nothing at her knees but he couldn't see the rest of her.

"Can you set this up if I go for the men?" Ben asked.

"Yes…"

Ben handed her the tarp. "The Carmichael farm is still standing. And we have more search crews out. They're clearing Hillside now. If you can walk that far—"

"We can." She shaded her eyes with both hands, peering up into the sky.

"The lightning has tapered off here," Ben said encouragingly. "I hate to send you out in this but it's just a ten-minute walk to the trucks."

Two more women had joined them while Ben spoke. One of the new arrivals handed the woman Ben spoke with a poncho and then held out her hand, saying, "Here, Trish, it helps a bit with the cold. Claire Egan," she said to Ben. "My husband went to search Popular Drive with Trish's son's. We have some kids…"

Ben shook her hand, surprised to find it warm. "Ben Windsor. I can take them back on the quad."

Clair pursed her lips and glanced back at the shelter. "Kathy and the baby will need a ride or better clothing." She gathered the poncho tightly about her and peered down at her feet. "Thanks for this. God, I can't believe this— I thought we were all dead." She shook her head hard. "Trish and I will set up a shelter. Virginia, you go with the first group and send back the ponchos with Mr. Windsor."

"We can't give them back," a woman said from inside the shelter.

Clair rolled her eyes. "Marge, you can stay inside and freeze to death. You can do whatever the fuck you want, but if you come with us, you're giving the fucking poncho back when we reach the trucks. No one cares about your fat ass."

"There'll be clothing there," Ben said.

"You should've brought it with you," Marge said as she

crawled from the shelter.

"I can't bring much on the quad." He eyed the red rash that speckled her cheeks, deepening to an angry red on her neck.

"Perv," she snapped and pulled the poncho tighter, which made her large breasts more visible through the thin plastic.

Ben held up his hands and made a warding off gesture. "I was looking at your rash. It seems to be so randomly placed."

"It's from the clothes," Trish said as she gazed down at her legs. "Polyester, nylon, all those sorts really boiled hard. Cotton and wool weren't too bad."

"He shouldn't be looking," Marge snapped.

Trish said, "Don't be a ninny."

Clair squatted to yell into the shelter. "Wait inside, sweetheart. It won't be long now, I promise."

Ben turned his back on Marge's glare. "Ask for a road flare when you get to the truck and send it back with whoever returns with supplies. Warn the kids I'm going to shoot my pistol."

Clair squatted again as Ben took out the radio.

He clicked the button and said, "Can anyone hear me?"

"I hear you," Wayne said.

Ben mentally smacked himself for not knowing the names of the small streets. It was going to be a logistics nightmare to organize search parties with no road signs or way of knowing where the roads had been. "I'm on Elm, almost at the intersection of the next street over with thirteen survivors. I'm sending some back—"

"Thank God," Wayne said, and Ben took a moment to compose himself. He'd choked up just saying the word survivor. Finding no one alive so close to his home had made him think everyone had been killed.

"There's sixteen men out here somewhere too," Trish said as she opened the tarp and awkwardly wrapped it about the women who'd emerged from the shelter.

Ben said into the radio, "There's sixteen more out looking for help, and I'm going to fire my pistol. Can you send Dave or Kate with more supplies? We've got some children here."

"Thank God, Ben," Wayne said again. "Yes. And tell them food and warm clothes will be waiting."

"Will do," Ben said through a throat thick with unshed tears.

"Get going," Claire said and shooed the women away.

They stood in a clump huddled beneath the tarp whispering together.

"Take Buddy with you," Trish said to Ben. "He might be able to lead you to my sons." Trish bent to hug the dog. "Go find Marty," she said and pushed the dog away.

The dog followed her as she began jogging away. The other women stopped whispering and ran after Trish, letting the tarp fall to the ground.

"Go to Marty," Ben heard her say again, but she didn't try to push the dog away.

Claire squatted again and called, "Sharon, can you manage the fire?"

"Yes," a woman, Ben assumed was Sharon said.

"He's going to fire a gun to gather the men. If any return, tell them to wait or go to Hillside. We'll send back supplies."

"Mommy!" a little girl wailed.

"Where are you going?" Sharon asked.

"To look for my husband. Sweetheart, I'm going to go get Daddy and come back for you. I promise you'll be dry soon."

Claire pushed her sodden hair from her forehead and stood.

"You must be freezing. You should go to the trucks. I'll look for him," Ben said.

"He'll be freezing too."

"And killing yourself won't help him a bit. Go get some clothes and proper rain gear, and then help us search."

She frowned but nodded and wiped her face on her arm. Ben

realized she was crying and wanted to hug her but didn't want her to take it wrong. He was fully dressed, and she was practically naked. Marge's words were holding him back.

"My daughter's clothes will fit you. Tell Helen I said you can borrow Jill's rain gear. But take a few minutes to rest and warm up."

"We don't have a few minutes. The cold will kill them."

"Let's pray this warm front lasts a bit longer."

She wrung the water from her hair as she said, "Let's pray the damned rain stops."

"Can the kids hold out until the supplies arrive? Or should I take them now on the quad?

"It's too cold out here. I hadn't realized how warm the shelter was. We're burning the rock from the road but it's smoky as hell."

"Wait inside then. Forget the tarp."

She shook her head and lifted a leg to rub her foot. "The Carmichael farm is what, a mile, mile and a half away? I can make it there and back in thirty minutes."

"Without shoes? Don't be silly. Wait with your daughter and get a ride in the truck." Ben lifted his gun and fired it. "I'll go look. How long ago did the men leave?"

"Thirty minutes or so. I can catch up to Trish," Clair said as she began to jog away.

Ben squatted to yell into the shelter, "I'm going to fire the gun again and then go, but someone will be here soon with supplies!"

"Thank you!" Sharon called back, having to yell to be heard over the crying children. The little girl calling for her mommy was breaking Ben's heart.

He fired his pistol and started the quad, wondering if Doug had heard the gun shots.

He drove away, heading for town as the men had. He drove as fast as he dared while trying to figure out how fast a naked shoeless man could run through a storm. *How far would they go looking for help? Would they stop and come back if they reached the town and saw it was destroyed too? How long could a naked man live in this rain?* The questions swam in his head.

They needed more people out searching. They needed more supplies. He tried to tell himself they were lucky to have the supplies they had but the sound of the little girl crying seemed to follow him.

How many children had died already? And might they be alive if they'd known to get out of the houses? Could they have buried supplies or made shelters? Anger warmed him sufficiently that he didn't really feel the cold rain on his face.

He slowed, intending to fire his gun again when he heard shouts.

He withdrew his whistle from his raincoat and blew three sharp blasts as he peered through the rain in a slow circle.

"Hey!" A man yelled as he ran up, clutching his side and breathing hard. He glanced over his shoulder then leaned forward, bracing his hands on his knees.

"More are coming," he gasped out.

"Are you from Clair and Trish's group?" Ben asked.

"Thank God you found them. We were beginning to think this happened all over."

"It did. How many are with you?"

"Three. We split up into four groups." The man straightened and approached.

"Can you get to Hillside or back to your shelter? We have help coming.

"Yes."

"I'm sorry I have no supplies. I left it all with the women. Where were the men headed?"

"Albert took his group over to West Main. Bigs headed to the Carmichael Farm. And Sam Holloway was going to check Forest. The library there has a fallout shelter."

Ben took out his radio. "Okay, I'll call it in. Wayne, do you copy?" He tried twice more before shaking his head and putting the radio back into his shirt pocket. "No reception. The radios are complete crap, but I'll go look. Tell them I'm planning on doing a loop from West to Forest.

He drove away before the man could answer.

Reaching Will

Thursday Night 1/18

Cloud cover obscured the stars and left the night midnight dark although it was just a little after seven. A twinkle of light in the distance eased Ben's tense shoulders.

A tent had been set up in a cleared spot among the fallen trees at the intersection of Hillside and Dover. Two of the smaller crank lanterns hung from broken limbs, swaying gently in the breeze.

Another lantern hung beneath the tarp set up in the roadway. Men and women scurried about, and it eased Ben's heart to see so many strange faces.

The little girl he carried continued to shriek. The two small boys behind him hadn't said a word. He'd driven as fast as he could, but he was certain they were freezing in the wet clothing they wore.

A man exited the tent and rushed toward the quad.

Ben handed the crying toddler to her father.

"Thank you," the man gasped out, clutching the crying child to his chest. He wore a wet sweatshirt of Doug's and a bleach-stained beach towel. The child also wore a sweatshirt of Doug's and it covered her completely, but it dripped water from the strength of her father's embrace.

"Get her inside," Ben said as he turned the quad.

"God bless you!" the man called after him.

Ben parked the quad half under the tarp that sheltered a small fire. Claire nodded acknowledgement but didn't stop flicking through a notebook she held. Men and women Ben didn't know were hanging wet clothes from tree limbs jammed into the ground.

"Has anyone heard from Doug?"

"That's the last from our group," Claire said and flipped the notebook closed. She stuffed it into a plastic Ziploc bag she pulled from the pocket of Jill's raincoat she wore as she asked, "Doug?"

"My son. Has he come back on the dirt bike?"

"Not that I've heard."

Ben's unease turned to fear. Sue hadn't heard from him either. He was kicking himself for not sending the radio with him.

Clair said, "Marcus DuBois located another group by the park. We're moving further north now and plan to put up another shelter by the high school."

"Great. Is there extra gas here?"

"No. It'll be in the truck. Which should be back in fifteen minutes or so. Once we get Sara settled, my husband and I will return here to do another run through the streets, but I think we'd have found any survivors by now with all the noise we've been making.

"I think so too. I hate to leave injured to their fate, but it might be better to spend your energy running through the housing complex by the high school."

Ben started the quad again and was relieved when it started right up. They'd been using it hard, but the old engine was chugging along. He made a mental note to ask Wayne to send out some two-stroke for the quad. "Tell whoever comes with the truck that I'm heading to Will's house, and if anyone hears from Doug, I want a call."

"Yes, sir." Claire saluted, the gesture respectful yet friendly, and so like Doug's habitual response it brought tears to his eyes.

He drove back into the night, searching the skies, but he hadn't seen a flicker of phosphorescent green or red. The purple storm clouds seemed to have passed completely and the thunder and lightning had faded into the distance. Rain still fell in thick sheets, and the wind gusted hard, jarring loose the occasional tree limb or pile of rubble.

Visibility was crap and the road slippery. *Doug could've had an accident in his hurry to reach Will.* That thought haunted Ben as he drove with reckless speed down the center of the street, slipping and sliding and bouncing across fallen tree limbs. His headlights shone on corpses who'd fallen in the streets and yards, but most people appeared to have died inside their homes— or were hidden by the darkness. He shivered and hunched lower, hugging the right side of the road as close as he dared, not wanting to miss the turnoff in the dark. Water gushed down the street in muddy rivulets and gathered in treacherously deep puddles, making swales of the edges of the road.

The lack of homes as landmarks made the familiar neighborhood strange. He felt as if he drove on another planet. The world had become a strange place, and he wondered what other surprises were in store for them. *Had the storm been a natural phenomenon or a man-made one? Or had aliens invaded?* His thoughts circled and collided. He couldn't concentrate on any for more than seconds. His soul cried out for Doug and pity for his brother grew. It must be killing him to not know where to start looking for Andrea. She was miles away across a river, unreachably far now, but the not knowing if she lived or had died already… Picturing Andrea's fate made Ben cry, and he swore as branches hidden by his tears lashed him in the face.

"Pay attention!" he screamed into the night, baring his teeth in a fierce grimace. He kept his teeth clenched and kept glaring, afraid he'd start crying again if he relaxed.

A flicker of light in the distance caught his eye and he headed directly toward it, cutting across the yards and driving around the smaller piles of debris. The road Will lived on was just one up from the River Road in a poor section of town. The houses were small and set close together and separated by cheap fencing, the remains of which disintegrated under his tires.

He could hear the whine of a chainsaw ahead, and he slowed to wipe his face, so relieved he had to stop completely and grab some leaves to blow his nose.

Doug was fine if he was using the chainsaw, he told himself and continued forward, cursing when he had to backtrack to get around a row of uprooted trees.

"Dad!" Doug called, and the saw cut off. "I was getting worried!"

"Yeah! Did you find them?"

The light dipped and bobbed, but Ben had to keep his eyes on the ground before him. What he'd thought a puddle was fast running water that he realized with horror was part of the river. He stopped the quad again to withdraw a flashlight from his pocket and shine it around him.

"The water's rising fast," Doug said. He stomped through the muddy water, gesturing back the way he'd come. "I can hear Murphy barking inside the garage. I'm almost out of gas though."

"Are they—"

"I haven't heard anyone, but they could be alive in there. His garage was built half into that bank."

Ben turned off the quad and reached for the tools tied onto the back. He handed Doug the tarp and rope and took the small chainsaw and the three-gallon container of gas for himself. He shook the container and grimaced. It was less than half full.

Doug gave him a quick one-armed hug and lead the way back. Ben's frown grew as they approached the shattered remains of Will's garage. The trees he'd driven around had flattened the building before the storm had hit. The dispersal pattern of the debris made that clear.

"Look at those scorch marks. It must have been hit again after the storm."

Doug's light followed Ben's as he examined the mess of downed trees.

"That's why I think they could be in there, Dad. Murphy would've been with them. If the trees knocked it down, and then he saw the storm damage maybe they hid under it but then the lightning knocked down the last ones and they're stuck."

"Maybe," Ben said doubtfully, but he yanked the cord on his chainsaw.

Doug wiped his face on his wet sleeve and set down the tools to yank on a limb Ben cut loose. A shower of debris and smaller broken limbs rained around him.

Ben climbed carefully over the smaller limbs to the thicker trunk and began a new cut. He thought it was futile, Doug had already cleared a huge mound of wood in the hour he'd been here and hadn't heard them calling, but Doug needed to see for himself.

Ben cut while Doug hauled.

"Use the rope on this one and watch your legs," Ben said as he turned off the chainsaw. Murphy immediately began to bark.

"We're coming dog!" Ben yelled.

"Hang in there!" Doug hollered and grunted with effort as he yanked the knot tight. Ben wedged a thick piece of cut limb under the tree and pushed while Doug pulled.

"Watch yourself!" Ben hollered as the trunk rolled loose

Murphy continued to bark, and it didn't sound like they were getting any closer to him.

Doug scrambled over the trunk they'd just moved, and half lay across it to shine his light into the space revealed.

"Mud but no fire damage."

Ben pulled Doug back and lowered himself into the hole.

"Be careful, Dad."

Ben poked gingerly at the mud wall before him. Dirt crumbled and fell into the water at his feet. "This water is frigid and rising. How much farther back did the garage go?"

"About fifteen feet or so into the slope at a slight angle. Remember how he used to complain about the oil spilling when he changed it? It looks like the trees wedged themselves into the walls as they were dissolving. Can you see any of that white powdery stuff concrete turns into?"

"I can't see shit. We need a shovel."

"I could go back for one."

"Do we have time? Jesus, this entire thing could collapse any second." He didn't know what was holding it up now. If Murphy weren't barking his head off, he'd have assumed the entire interior had already collapsed.

The dog sounded hoarse now and desperate.

"Hand me that stick I used and see if you can find some more around the same size."

He took the limb Doug handed him and jammed it into the earth as hard as he could. "Get me a rock or something to pound this in!"

While he waited for Doug, he cautiously scrapped at the dirt, releasing small dribbles and some larger chunks to fall at his feet.

"Here— and take the rope." Doug handed down a rock from the wall in the front yard and the rope.

"Tie the other end to the quad. If it starts to fall in, pull me out.

"I should do it."

Ben didn't bother answer. He formed a crude harness with the rope and stepped into it. He'd smother before he could be pulled free— *if* he could be pulled free. He was going to die for a damned dog, but he knew if he didn't do it Doug would, and the thought of his son trapped in this pit kept him cautiously pulling the mud away with his bare hands.

Doug lowered a handful of limbs, and Ben braced them in the mud at head height. The dog sounded louder now, and the earth was crumbling away on its own. It wasn't packed tightly at all but held together with pine limbs and chunks of the silty, rock-like substance the concrete had turned into.

"I think Murphy is trying to dig free," Ben said and grasped the next limb Doug handed him in both hands. "Here goes," he warned and began to gouge at the earth.

Murphy broke through before he did. The dog whined as it struggled through the small hole it had made.

Ben tugged it free and petted him a moment before squatting to peer through the hole.

Will's car was a heap of metallic dust. The back of the garage had sunken in but the center to the left of the car was a large pocket of open space. About six inches of water covered the ground.

"They're in here," he said and halted the flashlight beam on the naked feet protruding from the pine needles. One set of feet twitched, and he heard a muffled groan.

He used both hands to make the small hole bigger.

"Hand me Murphy," Doug said.

Ben stopped digging and turned to the dog. It had laid in the water and was licking its bloody paws.

"Good boy," Ben said as he gathered the dog into his arms. Murphy licked his cheek and whimpered. Ben lifted him to Doug who grabbed him by the scruff and yanked him out,

"Good Boy, Murph."

"Hand me the small chainsaw. They're under some trees."

"Alive?"

"I don't think so," Ben lied, praying that the soft moans weren't carrying far. Doug would never leave them. He'd kill himself to get to them.

"Jesus…" Doug's voice broke.

Ben said, "I'm going to go see. Don't come down here. If it falls in, go for help." Ben steeled himself to leave them behind if they couldn't be safely extracted.

"Maybe you shouldn't," Doug said.

Ben was tempted to climb out, but those wiggling toes pulled him in. He wouldn't be able to live with himself if he left now.

It took him another five minutes of digging to make the hole big enough he could crawl through it. Five minutes of worrying that the entire thing would crash down on his head any second.

He crawled through the hole he'd made and onto a bed of broken pine limbs. From this close he could see the red rash covered their feet and legs beneath the mud.

"Ben," Janice said weakly when he grabbed her foot.

"Hold on, honey. I'm coming," Ben said.

"Will, wake up! He got hit in the head and has been drifting in and out," she said to him and then in a cajoling voice, "Please, Will, you have to wake up. Don't leave me alone like this, please!"

"Just relax and save your strength. I'll get you both out." He knelt in the water to peer up at the interwound branches that were keeping the roof from falling in. Dirt and water trickled down with his every movement.

"My arm is broken," Janice said. "I can't turn myself over or crawl out."

"I'm afraid if I cut you lose, the entire roof will cave in. I'll have to pull you out."

"Maybe we should wait for the firetrucks."

"They can't get here. You'll freeze first."

"I'm freezing now."

"I know, honey." Ben removed his raincoat as he spoke. "I'm going to pass you—"

"Dad?"

Ben turned to glare at the hole. "Janice is alive but a bit stuck! Stay out there, and I'll pass her to you!"

"Oh, thank god. How's Will?"

"Haven't checked him yet."

"Doug?" Janice called.

"I'm here!" Doug said. "Hang in there, and we'll get you out."

"Get out of the hole!" Ben yelled as he wrapped his coat around the limb to push it to Janice.

"Janice, try to grab my coat and wrap it around you as best as you can. These limbs will scratch you when I pull you free. Keep your free hand over your eyes."

"Ben," she said in a quavering voice.

"I know, honey, but scratches will heal. I'll go nice and slow. Tell me when you're ready."

"We shouldn't have climbed under here. God, what were we thinking?" She began to cry, the crying escalating as she struggled with his coat. Her movement dislodged bigger chunks from the ceiling, and Ben stared upward with worried eyes until she told him she was ready.

"Take a deep breath, honey."

He grabbed her ankles, and she moaned. *The red rash must be painful to touch,* Ben thought and winced when he considered her entire body was likely covered with it. He pulled her slowly forward, and she shrieked.

"Dad?"

"Stay there!" Ben bellowed.

"Sorry," Janice gasped. "It hurts so bad. I can't do this."

"You have to, honey. Scream if you need to, but don't tell me to stop unless a stick is actually stabbing into you. I'm sorry but this is the only way."

"Ben, I can't," she said through sobs.

Ben released her feet and felt for the pulse in Will's foot, shocked to actually find one. He couldn't see through the brush well enough to tell if any limbs entangled him or not.

"I'll move Will first."

She continued to cry.

Ben pulled Will out, wincing at the sharp snap of breaking branches but none really impeded him. The ceiling was another matter. The branches above them shook and settled with a sharp crack of sound.

Will's entire body and the left side of his head was covered with the red rash. A purple knot on his temple was the only color in his face. He dragged him to the hole.

"Doug!"

I'm here. What can I do?"

"I'm going to put the rope under Will's arms. Pull him out nice and easy. When you get him free, find me something to tie her arm with."

"How bad is he?"

"Unconscious with a knot the size of an egg on his head. Worry about his injuries later. Let's get them out of here." While Ben spoke, he was busy removing his harness and refashioning it to put on Will. He passed the rope to Doug and grunted with effort to slid him through the hole.

Large chunks of debris-laden dirt broke away and splashed into the water, leaving the once small hole a large crater that water poured through. The limbs he'd used to brace the dirt had fallen and the dirt on the sides had slid down with only the pressure of the downed tree's branches to hold it back. The limbs they'd been laying in were almost covered with water now.

"Honey, the ceiling is going to go any second. Brace yourself as best you can."

He didn't wait for her answer just began tugging her loose. He gritted his teeth and kept pulling while she screamed shrilly for him to stop.

"Dad, Take this!" Doug crawled partway into the crevice to

thrust his ripped-up shirt to him.

"Get out of here!" Ben snarled as he snatched the garment.

A chunk of roof fell in, landing on the remains of the car. Puffs of metallic dust billowed into the air and sharp cracks warned more limbs had broken.

Janice lay shivering and crying in the water, half sitting to cradle her broken arm. Blood dribbled from her cheek and a long gash in her arm.

Ignoring her protests and screams, he bound her arm as tightly as he could across her chest and grabbed her by the waist to drag her backward.

Doug reached past him to grab her under the arms, and she shrieked as he lifted her from the hole. Ben scrambled up the slick slope and flopped to the ground, adrenaline leaving him feeling weak and sick.

Doug spoke reassuringly to Janice, but the words buzzed in Ben's head.

"You okay?" Doug asked, and a flashlight beam shone directly into his eyes.

Ben waved him away with an irritable, "Yes," and pushed himself to his feet.

Janice huddled against Doug's feet, crying. He'd wrapped her in Ben's coat and spread his over Will.

"Get the coat on her and zippered up. She can ride with you. We'll have to tie Will to me. Make sure his feet are clear of the ground."

As he spoke, he was putting Doug's raincoat on Will while Murphy whimpered and tried to lick him.

"Hand me the dog. He can ride in front."

Doug snorted a small laugh, ruffling Murphy's ears when he released him. Ben tucked him as tightly as he could against his chest.

Murphy let out an excited bark and wriggled.

"Make sure his feet are clear," Ben said again as he lifted his arms for Doug to wrap the rope around them. "Stay still, mutt, or your walking," he grumbled while Doug tighten the tarp over them by tucking the edges under the rope.

"Go. We'll catch up." Doug slapped his shoulder and stepped back.

Ben eased on the accelerator, driving slowly through the foot-high water and over the downed trees. Once on the road, he gave it more juice and crossed the road at an angle to reach the grass. Water running down the hill forced him back, splashing against his tires and into his face with the force of its passage. He drove on the muddy grass over the downed trees and remains of the fences until the road leveled off.

"This has to be hell on the tires," he said at the loud crunching sound he made as he drove faster on the flatter road.

The lantern marking the tent seemed shockingly bright in the darkness, and he sighed with relief to be back as helpful hands unwound the rope from around him.

"Trish," he said in surprise when he realized who was helping him.

"This is my post until morning," she said, flashing him a rueful grimace. "Let's get him inside and into a sleeping bag."

"You're here alone?"

"I volunteered. How many did you find?"

"Just the two, and Murphy here."

"You know him?"

"Yes. He's family."

"And lucky to have you." She held the tent flap open and gestured him inside, turning to peer over her shoulder at the approaching dirt bike. "Make them as comfortable as you can. I have orders to run back to order transport if needed, and he sure needs it."

"Doug will go. It'll be quicker. Janice is injured too. One of the worst rashes I've seen yet and a broken arm. Maybe worse."

While he spoke, Trish was busy removing the raincoat from Will. She checked his scrapes and pulled open a sleeping bag.

Trish said, "Abby— Mrs. Russo— thinks the rash is just surface abrasions. It isn't spreading or weeping. She thinks it's just bad road rash from the force of the disintegration."

Ben laid Will on the cot, and Trish tucked the sleeping bag around him.

"Well, that's good news."

"Isn't it though?" Trish flexed her arms and shrugged. "No one's seen a zombie yet either."

Ben snorted, and she laughed.

"Hey, I'll take whatever good news I can get. Speaking of which, they've found another big group."

"That's great," he said as Doug pulled to a stop. They exited the tent, and he handed Doug his coat.

Ben said, "Take Janice to Abby. She's probably at Helen's— and send a truck back here for Will. No. Stay on the bike," Ben said to Janice as she tried to get off. "Trish and I will look after Will." He kissed her forehead and waved Doug away. He and Trish watched the dirt bike until the taillights disappeared.

Trish said, "Thank God the storm missed you. You're saving all our lives." She flashed him a smile and gestured him back to the tent. "Come get something to eat and drink while you wait. It's going to be a long night."

Ben pressed his lips together. It was clear Trish had heard nothing about how the storm had missed them and thought it a natural phenomenon. He wondered if she'd be so friendly if she knew his wife was a witch.

The thought shocked him, and he pushed it from his mind, He had bigger things to worry about and maybe Anne had nothing to do with it.

The Dead and the Desperate

Friday Dawn 1/19

A bulldozer rumbled and men shouted directions in the distance. Two chainsaws whined closer but still far enough away Ben thought he might be able to hear cries for help. He brought the quad to a stop and pushed his hood back. Rain immediately soaked his hair and trickled down his neck to make his wet clothes even wetter. He'd been out searching for hours now. A hint of dawn light made the sky a lighter shade of black. He flicked off the headlights and closed his eyes, tipping his head from side-to-side as he tried to hear. He listened hard for a minute before raising a whistle to his lips and blowing, then hollering, "If you can hear the whistle, answer now!"

A dog barked in the distance.

Again, he strained to hear but heard nothing except the distant sound of his friends and family clearing the road. After waiting another minute, he started the quad back up and continued. The neighborhood he drove through had been a nice one with two-family homes on small lots set close together. There weren't many trees to block the roads, and he could generally get around them if he couldn't go over them and seldom needed the small chainsaw he carried.

He drove slowly, both to avoid hitting debris and to scan for lights. The survivors they'd found so far had almost all managed to make fires and crude shelters from the remains of their homes.

A flicker of light caught his eye, and he headed toward it at the fastest pace he could safely manage. He called again when he stopped the quad, but no one answered him. He hoped it was just a fire caused by the storm, but his hopes were dashed when he came upon the tiny campfire beneath a pile of debris and leafy branches. The fire was almost out. The man who'd been feeding it lay dead beside a dead child. The woman had been killed in the storm, the burns on the head and feet were familiar now to Ben. The little boy had burned, *his mother had probably been holding him when she'd been struck,* Ben mused as he closed the father's staring eyes.

He was reminded of the man he'd seen across the river and wondered if he and the child were still alive, or if the father had seen the winery still intact and had tried to cross the river to reach it. He'd have no way of knowing the same devastation waited on this side of the river. Not that Ben thought anyone could cross the raging river and live. Debris hurtled through the storm-tossed froth of the frigid water. That man and boy would die and there was nothing Ben could do about it. He pushed his dark thoughts way and knelt beside the dead man.

"I'm sorry we didn't get here sooner."

He said a quick prayer, the only thing he had to offer them. He couldn't take the time to bury them, not when there could be others who'd survived the storm but might not survive the dropping temperatures much longer. He blew his whistle and called out as he trudged back to the quad.

It took him more effort than he liked to think about to get it started again. All of his muscles felt laden, and he shivered continuously, the wind and rain seeming to cut right through his clothing. The sky began to lighten, turning a dull gray that promised another long day of rain as he drove down the next street. He could no longer hear the chainsaws or bulldozer and wondered if they'd moved on or if he was just too far. He nudged the radio on his shoulder and said, "Ben checking in. A-Okay, nothing to report."

"Copy that, Ben," Wayne said. "We're clearing South Street now. Sue reported, B-Team has reached Popular Drive and already found thirty people."

"Thank God," Ben said with heartfelt sincerity.

"Jill has woken, but Anne's condition is unchanged."

"Is she…"

"Sleeping. Jill woke hysterical. Joyce sedated her, but she says there didn't seem to be any physical damage."

"How bad," Ben asked.

"She was raving, nothing they could really make out, and she kept trying to get outside. Marie was worried she'd make it outside and run off. She should wake again in a few hours. Maybe she'll be calmer by then."

"Maybe," Ben agreed although he doubted it. Even if the storm hadn't done permanent injury to her body, finding out the world as she knew it had ended was sure to be traumatic. "Out," Ben said and started the quad.

"Out," Wayne replied.

Ben made sure the radio was tucked beneath his rain slicker before tightening the hood and driving into the wind. He crisscrossed the streets, stopping to blow his whistle and call. The sun rose fully but the day remained dreary and dark. The morning light also revealed the corpses.

It gave him the willies to think he'd been driving past or over the piles of dead all night. He stopped to examine the first mass of huddled people, hoping some would be alive but all were stiff and cold. The survivors must have gathered together to try to use their body heat or for mutual support. And it had been a fatal mistake. Almost every group he stopped to examine had been killed by lightning, the burns on hands and feet were unmistakable.

"Poor souls." Angry and sickened, he laid them on the cold ground. The rain beat down on their terrified faces. They'd died scared and cold. The waste of it infuriated him, the anger giving him false energy. After the third pile of dead, he quit stopping to examine them, instead calling and waiting and looking for movement. He was stopped before his fourth bunch when a man grabbed his arm. Shocked, he fell off the quad as the man ripped at the pack on his back, swearing savagely.

Ben rolled and slid an arm free.

"Fucker," the man snarled. Fucker!" He kicked at Ben, catching him in the stomach but the kick was without much force. Ben rolled with it, letting the pack fall off his shoulder and got to his feet as the man snatched the pack and ripped it open.

His adversary's skin was blue from cold. He'd wrapped limbs and shrubbery around himself and tied it with vines, but large gaps of skin showed through the leaves and bark, and Ben wondered how much it really kept out the cold.

"Calm down! I can help you," Ben said, holding out both empty hands.

"Fucker! The man snarled again and threw the bag at Ben's head. Ben ducked, batting the bag away as the man lurched forward and swung at his face.

"My fucking wife!" the man yelled and grabbed the shoulder of Ben's raincoat, trying to tear it off.

"Knock it off," Ben said as he punched the man in the stomach and then the face. The man was moaning and growling, not saying anything now as he bent to bite at Ben's arm, trying to grab him as Ben pushed him back.

Ben hit him again, as hard as he could this time, and followed it up with a hard shove from his shoulder. His assailant fell to his ass, and Ben drew the pistol from the holster at his side.

"Stay down! One more fucking move, and I'll blow your head off! Now, where's your wife? I'll call the rescue crew and get you both somewhere warm and dry."

The man on the ground glared up him with such a heartsick expression of fury on his face Ben took another step back. He didn't want to shoot this man or leave him to die.

"Look," he said again, trying to sound reassuring and reasonable, not frustrated and scared. "Get control. We're all in this together. Calm down, and I'll give you my coat, okay?"

The fury melted from the man's expression. He crouched, putting his arms around himself and staring at his bright red feet.

"They're all dead. We're all dead."

"No. Not all of us," Ben said and squatted beside the man. He offered him his hand and pulled him up. "There's a coat and socks in the bag."

The man nodded but stood unmoving. Ben grabbed the bag from the mud and opened it, removing his wife's cheap plastic raincoat and holding it out. Ben realized the man was crying when he didn't take the offered garment.

Ben placed it around the man's shoulders and then flicked the switch on the quad to turn it off. The rain sounded louder and harder, and Ben hoped that was his imagination.

"Sit," he said and rummaged in the bag again for the socks.

The man sat on the quad and rubbed his face, then jumped to his feet, his eyes wide and panicked. "My wife! I heard you and left her! Hurry!" He snatched the pack from Ben and ran.

"Damn it," Ben swore as he started the quad back up and turned. The man was running down the street and darted around a corner before Ben caught up.

"Wait!" he yelled but he knew the man wouldn't. He wouldn't

either if Anne waited alone and freezing. The thought spurred him on, and he drove recklessly across a downed tree to catch up, nudging his radio with his chin, "This is Ben. I have a survivor, over."

No one replied, and he swore softly as he wondered if he'd broken it in the fight, if the battery had died, or if it were just dislodged. The radio he was using was an old toy one of Doug's. It was part of a set meant to mimic police radios, but it had a very short range. The new ones Anne had bought to use during the cleanup were packed away somewhere, and he had no idea where. He was certain she'd remember where they were, but he hadn't paid attention. It had never occurred to him his wife would be incapacitated. Now he was kicking himself. He should've made a master list. He should've left detailed directions on everything. He'd thought he was so prepared, but he'd been arrogant, thinking he could assure his family's safety with lightning rods and root cellars.

Ahead of him, the man was crawling beneath a pile of thick timbers that had once been part of a small barn. *He'd probably thought he'd prepared for the storm too*, Ben thought bitterly. But no one could've predicted the storms effects. *Except the government had to have known,* he thought again for the millionth time. The thought bewildered and angered him. *The shutdowns hadn't been necessary— they'd been a ruse to keep them from communicating.* He told himself they'd done it to prevent panic. *They couldn't have predicted someone like Anne would be able to protect them from the storm.*

"Electrical fields, my ass!" Ben snarled as he ducked to avoid a tree limb.

A tree had fallen and smashed through the roof of a barn. One of the walls remained standing with only light pitting from the red gas. *It must've been really old untreated wood*, Ben thought as he slid to a halt.

"Please be okay," the man was repeating in a hysterical tone.

Ben reached into his raincoat and withdrew his radio.

"Damn it," he muttered as he eyed the new crack in the case. He fiddled with the knobs until he heard static and said, "Mayday— Mayday— Mayday— I'm on West and Third with at least one survivor who needs immediate evac." The radio clicked and whirred, but he couldn't tell if someone had heard and was trying to respond or not.

"It's broken?" the man asked, his gaze darting to the quad.

"Seems to be, but I can get us all out." Ben began to remove his coat. He took a step back as the man stepped forward. "Look, let's get something straight right now. I have supplies, and you need them. Killing me to take the quad won't really help you. You need food and shelter, which I have and will share, but you won't be able to take it from us. We have to give it to you. Do you understand me?"

The man had been nodding along and held up both hands. He smiled a hard smile and said," Yes. Sorry, I don't know what came over me. Thanks. I'm Phil— Philip Auburn, and my wife is Annie."

"Ben Windsor." Ben offered his hand. "My wife is Anne too. She's..." He trailed off and stripped off his jacket, thrusting it angrily at Phil and gestured to the rubble. Rain immediately soaked through his barn coat, making him shiver. "There's a mylar packet in my bag. Try not to tear it. I have matches and a lighter, but if you can stand it, it would be better for me to bring you to the truck than to try to make a fire in this."

"I don't... she's pregnant," Phil said, darting a worried glance over his shoulder.

Ben examined his quad, considering his options.

"The kids used to ride backward. But the weight..."

Phil grimaced.

"Honey?" a woman called in a quavering voice.

"Stay in there! It's warmer!" Phil called back. He turned from Ben to crouch in the small opening and half crawled inside. "Take the coat. He has friends and help is coming. Just hang in there."

"You'll be warm and dry soon!" Ben called. "Can you drive one of these?" he asked in a softer voice.

Phil hesitated, then nodded, and Ben sighed hard. "I can't bring both of you at once. The shocks just won't take it, not over this terrain."

"I can do it," Phil said.

Ben held up his hand, and Phil stopped speaking, snapping his mouth closed and looking grim. Ben didn't like the way Phil eyed him and the quad as if he still debated making a try for it.

"We're going to the Carmichael farm. The barn's still standing, and we have a generator. A truck will be waiting at the intersection of Wilbur and North Cedric."

Phil's expression lightened, and his tense shoulders eased a bit. "I know the place. I went to school with Doug."

"The quad is tricky to drive, especially up hills in this slop. If you stall or flip it…"

Phil's expression made it clear he wished to lie and claim he could handle it, but before he had a chance too, Ben added, "Twenty minutes, ten to get her there and ten more to get back to you. I'll cut up to Elm and across to Wilbur."

"Go," Phil said tightly and dropped to his hands and knees to crawl back into the shelter.

"Go with him, honey. He'll take good care of you, and I'll be right—"

"Come with us," Annie begged. "You'll freeze. No! You take it."

Annie said something Ben couldn't make out. She was crying, and Phil's voice dropped until all Ben heard was a mummer under the rain. He started the quad and called, "We should go!"

"Annie, you have to go!" Phil said, and a moment later a

woman crawled from the shelter.

"I'll be as careful as I can," Ben said. The wind whipped the mylar blanket, and she cried as she tried to hold it around her protruding stomach. Phil had given her Anne's coat too, and she wore both pairs of the wool socks, but her legs were bare and her lips blue with cold. His coat covered Anne's, but she hadn't been able to close either. Scratches and angry looking red welts covered her, and Ben assumed she'd been wearing twig clothing too.

"Sit as far back as you can and hold the rail behind you. If you need me to stop, ask."

She got on behind him, ignoring his advice to hold the rail that edged the supply platform and clutching him tightly around the waist.

Ben began driving as he said, "I've been driving this thing for years. We're perfectly safe. Just close your eyes and don't worry a lick if you feel us slide."

He could feel her shivering and wished he'd had warmer clothing to give her, but he and the quad could only hold so much. "Ten minutes," he said more to reassure himself than her.

He guided the quad through the yards, avoiding the road as much as he could. He'd slid down them easily but the oil that the red gas had released combined with the rain to form a slippery barrier that was hard to get traction on unless he drove over the rougher chunks and he worried he'd blow a tire doing so.

He went as fast as he dared, hoping speed would work in his favor to get them up the steep hill on the smoother but slippery muddy verge. She cried against his back interspersed with small moans he hoped weren't labor pains.

"How do you have this?" she asked.

"It's a long story."

"Phil went out after he made the shelter and the lightening had passed and said all the houses—"

Ben interrupted, not wanting her to get her hopes up that

119

whatever had happened had happened just in this small area. "He's right. Everything is gone, but we have supplies. Hold on tight now." He gunned the motor and crossed the next street on an angle, sliding farther down the street from where he'd started but making it across.

"Will we make it up Wilbur?" she asked.

"I think there was only one fence, maybe two, so we should be okay if we stay in the front yards. The trucks have no problem on the hills really. It's just the quad is old, and the motor is even older. My son and I fixed this up…" He clamped his lips together and forced himself to stop babbling. She wouldn't want to hear how he and Doug had changed the motor out six years ago the summer before Doug had gone away to college. Those days felt like a dream. Summer sunshine and sweating. The picnics Anne had made and brought them while he and his little brother Rich had taught Doug and Ricky how to change out the motor and his nieces had played with Merlin and Boomer, tossing sticks into the pond and daring each other to go in with Jill. His beautiful fearless Jill who swam in the pond daily, not at all afraid of the turtles or icky bottom as Molly used to call it.

His tears felt warm on his cheeks.

He crossed the next street the same way and sighed in relief when he spotted Wilbur.

"I smell smoke," Annie said.

He sniffed deeply but all he smelled was the quad and the mud. "I'll come back and look," Ben promised.

She nodded against his back and relaxed her hold a degree, pointing over his shoulder. "There!"

He followed her finger to see a thick cloud of black smoke at the top of the hill.

He was instantly consumed with worry. He half stood but the steepness and rain defeated him, and he sat and leaned forward, urging the quad up the hill with a mumbled, "Come on, come on," under his breath.

His tense shoulders relaxed when the blue tarp came into sight. A woman he didn't know, wearing Helen's coat and the pink wellingtons Anne had gotten her mother for Christmas, was tending a camp stove beneath the tarp tent. His brother-in-law was burning something in a nearby yard that gave off the thick black smoke. Roger hailed him and spoke into a radio he carried, Ben assumed to tell whoever was on the other end that he'd returned safe and sound and with a survivor.

"You must be freezing," the woman at the smaller fire said to Ben's passenger as he slid to a halt in the grass on the side of what once was the road.

He was freezing. The rain had soaked through his barn coat and saturated the clothing underneath, but he still had to be warmer than the naked woman and he felt renewed guilt for leaving her husband behind.

"You're freezing too," Roger said disapprovingly and waved to a plastic box sitting on a folding table, the only furniture in the tent besides two folding chairs. "Come in and change. Or better yet, go home and take a break."

Ben shook his head, turning the quad as soon as Annie got off. "Can't. I left her husband behind."

"Wait, take this," Annie said and thrust the mylar blanket at him.

"Hold up!" Roger called after him, and Ben stopped to peer over his shoulder.

"Take the mylar. It's better for the rain. We have a real blanket for her."

"Come sit by the fire," the woman said and made a tsking noise. "Your feet are blue from cold. I'm sure that smarts. When's the baby due?" she continued to chatter as Roger grabbed the mylar from her and ran to Ben.

"Thanks," Ben said briskly and wadded the thin metallic fabric to stick it inside his coat. He wished now he'd encouraged Anne to buy more instead of discouraging her. She'd been worried that people would be freezing without power, that they weren't preparing like their neighbor Henry Brooks who'd stubbornly insisted the coming storm was nothing to worry over.

Ben snorted as he slid back down the road, going much faster now, and wondered what ol' Henry thought about his situation now. "Probably doesn't even realize a thing happened," Ben said sourly as he averted his gaze from the burned body of a dead woman lying in the street.

It took him only a few minutes to get back to Phil. Phil must've started to walk as soon as Ben left because he was running toward him as fast as his branch clothing would let him. Ben handed him the mylar blanket as Phil asked, "My wife?"

"Safe with my brother-in-law."

"So, it's just this neighborhood? I'd been worried. I thought it happened everywhere."

"It did."

"But—"

"It's a long story. One I'm not sure I even know. But, for whatever reason, it missed us."

"Maybe—"

"No. We have teams out. Everywhere we've been is the same."

"But you have this quad, and gas?"

"And food and houses. I can't explain it. We were prepared to help with the cleanup. My wife—" Ben had to take a deep breath to clear his throat— "My wife is a worrier. She stocked up, made me fill the tanks, bought us the rain gear, made me put in fifty lightning rods… She was so worried, and I didn't heed her. How could I not have seen?"

"Who could?" Phil asked bitterly. He gestured at the houses, but Ben didn't look, he didn't want to see the dead he knew were there.

"Jesus, so many dead. Have you found many survivors?"

"No. Most seemed to have stayed inside."

Phil made an angry sound. "Annie and I wanted to see it. We were in the car, you know, for the lightning. I wasn't even that worried. Our car was ancient with no electronics. I thought it'd be cool to see. The pictures, the ones they showed on the news, I thought we'd get some great ones with my old camera. I'd packed a chainsaw in case a tree fell and blocked the road, but we didn't plan on going far, just to the winery parking lot."

Ben snorted softly, and Phil shrugged.

"I knew it was closed but figured who would care if we watched from there? It would be a great view and not too far from our house."

"How'd you get past the gate?"

"Bolt cutters. And Annie was pissed. She made me promise I'd replace it. But then the storm came, and we forgot all about it. I never saw anything like it. Annie got hysterical and insisted we go home. I knew we couldn't outrun it. I never saw lightning like that in my life. And the sound of the water… Even without that acid cloud I knew we were doomed. I told Annie to keep her head down and I drove like a madman trying to outpace the cloud in my rearview, but the street was so flooded I stalled it. I was scared to death we'd get blown up by the lightning."

"You should've stayed," Ben said and felt Phil shrug.

"What else could I do but run? The storm caught us and destroyed the car around us. It took everything. We'll probably die anyway."

"The rash?" Ben asked.

"Her back is just shredded. We got out of the car but there was nowhere to run. Everything was falling down. So, we headed to the bushes, and I made us the clothes. Mine had just sort of fallen off but hers boiled. I thought it would kill her."

Phil's voice reveled the pain of that thought.

"Our doctor thinks it's just a reaction from the violence of the disintegration. She doesn't think it's harmful itself. I bet your wife was wearing polyester."

"Maybe. I hope so. Jesus, to survive this and then die of radiation poisoning… or frostbite."

"Sorry, we're almost there," Ben said as reassuringly as he could.

Phil grunted and neither man spoke again until the tarp came into sight. Kevin's pickup was parked beside it now, and men and women Ben didn't know, wearing badly fitting clothing, were unloading supplies from the back.

Pat greeted him with a hard slap on the shoulder. "Who's your friend?"

"Phil Auburn," Phil said as he got off the quad, ignoring Pat's outstretched hand. "My wife?"

"Here!" Annie called, and a woman said, "Stay there!"

Ben followed Phil to find Annie swaddled in blankets in the cab of the truck. He was happy to note color had returned to her cheeks although she still shivered. The woman thrust a cup of something hot to Annie and motioned Phil forward. "Take off the twigs. Good idea that, and get in. She can share her blankets. We're waiting for Mr. Foster to get back. He found a few more and took them supplies."

"I'm taking the quad," Pat said. He glared at Ben as if he'd soaked himself on purpose. "And you know the fucking rules. We keep our gear on! Getting sick won't help anyone."

Ben snorted and gave Annie a pointed glance, making Pat laugh. His laugh sounded odd, shrill and dark, and Ben winced and waved him away.

The woman said, "Sue says you're to take this next lot back and take your mandatory four-hour break." Her voice softened, and she patted Ben's hand. "Thank you. But your friend is right. Killing yourself won't help us. We're setting up these aid stations and lighting the smudge pots. We're doing everything possible."

Ben sighed and rubbed his throbbing head.

"Have some tea and sit a minute." She left Ben to bustle around her camp stove, a stove he recognized from their camping gear. He spared a moment to wonder where the rest of the camping gear was but couldn't muster the concentration or energy to really care. He felt numb and not even cold anymore. To his surprise, he dozed off. Pat's arrival woke him. He'd brought three people in, and Ben hoped he'd slept through it, that Pat wasn't overloading the old engine. Without the quad and the dirt bike, they'd be screwed. The trucks weren't practical for searching. It took too long to clear the debris to make the roads passable. It was quicker to run through the neighborhoods on foot. But quicker didn't mean quick. It would take weeks to check just their town.

"This rain," Pat said and shook himself off, sending water droplets everywhere. "Sue is monitoring the temperature, and it's down two degrees. If this keeps up, it'll be snowing by nightfall."

"Great," Ben said sarcastically and heaved himself to his feet.

The new arrivals clambered into the back of the truck where they huddled miserably on a bed of straw beneath a tarp

"Well, maybe." Pat waved his hand side-to-side. "The snow will insulate better. It'll be colder to be outside but warmer in their shelters, and they'll leave footprints, so they might be easier to find."

"Who will? The dead? You think they'll rise up as zombies?"

Horrified silence met that quip, and Ben was instantly sorry he'd said it.

"Zombies are impossible," he said with as much firmness and sincerity as he could muster. "This isn't a zombie apocalypse."

"We should burn the bodies," someone muttered to loud assent

"We should, but not because they'll turn into zombies. For crying out loud, that's crazy!"

Pat slapped his shoulder, giving him an annoyed glance. "We

can worry about the dead later. Right now, we need to concentrate on the living. Let's make this tent as snug as we can with a supply of wood and food. We can't stay here, but we'll send someone to check it and make sure the smudge stays lit. Barbara, pack up the stove and grab your gear. We're going to the school to set up another station."

"The school? That's so close, why bother?"

"It's a good ten-minute walk. Ten minutes is a long walk without shoes," Pat said.

Barbara bit her lip and nodded. "We don't have anything we could leave them?"

Pat rummaged in the back of the truck as he said, "Like what? Anything we leave behind means someone else can't be using it. Sue is working on supplies, but for right this second, this is the best we can do." He emerged with another tarp, one Ben didn't recognize, and a brown canvas bag that he slung over his shoulder, grunting slightly as if it weighed a lot.

"Send back gas," Pat said as he tied the tarp to the back of the quad beside the small chainsaw and rope already there.

Ben headed to the truck and got in as Pat and Barbara continued to discuss ways to help the survivors.

Toasty warmth enveloped him, and Ben began to shiver as soon as he sat down. He glanced at Phil who sat quietly beside him. Annie's head rested on her husband's shoulder, and her eyes were closed. *She was a pretty woman when she wasn't terrified*, Ben mused as he started the truck. It started right up, and he headed back down the road, being careful to stay in the cleared lane.

Daylight revealed a few disintegrated hulks he assumed had been cars, and he was surprised so many had ignored the advice to stay off the roads.

"Older cars," Phil said quietly when Ben slowed to go around one. "Bet they thought they could get good pictures like we did. Poor souls. Wonder what killed them?"

"If they were inside them…"

Phil nodded, his expression bleak. "We almost stayed in ours. We saw the houses going in the rearview, but scraps were left, and I thought maybe the metal frame would protect us. I'd stopped the car and gotten out to get in the back with Annie when that first green tendril touched."

"Did it burn?"

Phil shook his head. "It didn't give off heat. It just sort of dissolved the metal into smoke. You could see it bubble, breaking up into tiny particles but it happened so fast. I was trying to find a spot to run too. The car and our clothing were gone in seconds. I couldn't decide if the green or red gas cloud was more dangerous but green, you know?" He shot Ben a rueful grimace and continued, "We headed into the green cloud. Couldn't feel it at all but maybe that was because of the shock. We didn't really feel the rain either until we stopped running."

"And now? Any ill effects from breathing it in?"

"Who knows? I feel like shit but is it from the gas or the cold and shock?"

Ben shook his head, having no answer, and continued to drive in silence.

"Holy shit," Phil exclaimed when they reached their street, waking Annie who sat with a small shriek and grabbed her husband's arm. She moaned and dropped his arm to cradle her stomach, but she stared out the window and smiled for a moment before she began to cry.

"I knew it couldn't be everywhere. Oh, thank God."

"Honey," Phil said and kissed her temple. He gave a Ben a desperate glance, and Ben again shook his head. What could he say? He drove faster, knowing the roads here were cleared of debris. Annie was clearly in labor and he wanted her out of the truck and someone else's problem.

Phil apparently decided it wasn't worth bursting her bubble

and let her ramble, and Ben couldn't blame her for thinking the devastation had only affected a small area. His street remained perfect. The storm damage was much lighter and the roads intact. Lights twinkled in house windows, and if he hadn't seen, he too would've believed all was normal. But the lights would soon go out when they ran out of gas for the generators, and the houses would be cold and hard to heat. The clothing they had was the only clothing left and it was already stretched thin with just the few survivors they'd found. He didn't even want to consider the food.

The lights at his house were off, but Helen's house right next door was brightly lit. His tractor was parked in the drive, so he pulled in to see what to do with his passengers.

Sue opened the front door and gestured him inside. "Everyone in!" she called. She lowered her voice to say," Jill is awake and waiting, and Anne is in Helen's room."

Ben Returns Home

Friday Morning 1/19

The normality of Helen's kitchen felt like a blow. Warmth and the smell of freshly baked bread enveloped him and the normalcy of it felt surreal. How could they have this bounty when the rest of the town had nothing at all?

His mother glanced up from the kitchen table where she was rolling meatballs and gave him a strained smile. She'd aged ten years since he'd seen her last. Deep lines bracketed her eyes and mouth and she looked small and frail. But the pale mask of his daughter's face shocked him.

"Jill," Ben said and scooped his daughter into a tight embrace.

"Mom!" she wailed. She began to cry and held him hard.

Helen made a tsking noise and patted Jill's back. "Anne will be just fine. My girl is tough. Ben, take her into my room. I'll send in soup and sandwiches. Use my shower."

"I brought over dry clothes for you," Sue added and put her arm around Jill to kiss her temple. "We'll get through it," she whispered and kissed her again. She stood on tiptoe to kiss Ben's cheek. "Rest and be with your family."

Ben lead his daughter to Helen's room, nodding at the scared people he passed who sat on the couches and lay on the floor wrapped in sheets and wearing an assortment of ill-fitting clothing.

Anne lay on Helen's bed and his heart thumped hard at the sight of her. It had always been that way for him. The very first time he'd seen her, his pulse had begun to race. The graceful way she walked and kind way she spoke, her smile, her laugh, her frown— everything about her captivated him.

She had a way of being still and listening that had won his heart on the very first date. Her stillness now horrified him.

Someone had cleaned her and dressed her in a pair of her flannel pajamas. She was warm to the touch, but she didn't respond when he called her name.

"Mom," Jill said in a heartbroken voice and began to sob louder. Ben left his wife's side and hugged his daughter, holding her until her tears slowed.

"You should shower and change," she said through her tears. "I'm okay. It's just— "

He pulled away to see her better, and she rubbed her face with both hands. "I don't know what it was. Everyone keeps asking me, and I don't know." She took a deep tremulous breath and whispered, "I think it was God."

She began to cry again and clutched his wet shirt in both hands. He could feel her shaking and stood speechless, not knowing how to comfort her.

"God?" he finally asked.

"It knew everything. Everything, Dad! Anything I looked at it knew down to the atom. I could see the cells, the structure, the meaning!" Her voice rose as she released him and began to pace, taking short sharp strides and slapping her fist into her palm, the mannerism was so like his father's that he smiled in spite of himself.

"I saw it," she continued in a voice laced with hysteria.

"What did you see?"

"Everything!" she half yelled, sounding angry and exasperated.

Ben sat on the side of the bed and took Anne's hand in his. He patted the bed beside him. "Slow down, honey, and take a deep breath. Start at the beginning. When did you see the everything?"

She didn't sit but she spoke in a calmer voice when she said, "That morning, when Mom and I went out to set up the tent."

Ben made a small amused sound, and she grimaced and wrinkled her nose at him. "We meant to set them up, but the storm was so powerful, we just had to watch it. We could feel it coming. Not like a regular storm but like— Santa Clause."

He rose an eyebrow in surprise.

"You know— that feeling you get on Christmas Eve, when you know in just a few hours Santa will come and he'll have gifts and it will be so amazing?"

"Yeah," he said doubtfully. The storm had been anything except amazing as far as he was concerned, but he knew what she meant, the excitement of the unknown gift.

"Well, it was like that," she went on, oblivious to his tone.

She was talking to herself, he thought as her words slowed, and she stopped pacing to stare blankly at the wall. "It was like knowing something great was coming but more than knowing. I could almost feel it, even when it was hours away. And when it got closer, I saw but couldn't believe it."

"What did you see?"

She glanced at him, then at her hands and frowned as if what she expected to see wasn't what she saw. "Everything I looked at, but I wasn't looking here, I was with the storm."

"With it?"

"I was in Boston and saw what it did. I saw the houses crumble and the apartment buildings, but I was also in Maine and in Florida and everywhere in between. I had but to think of a place, and I was there, and I couldn't bear it, Dad. It was like God was showing me the end of the world, and I didn't want to see it." She took a deep trembling breath and sounded guilty when she said, "But the knowing... I wanted that. So, I focused on beauty and stared at an orange tree, and I saw the leaves, the bark, the flowers, the roots, the ground— all of it, and it was so beautiful, so beautiful..." She covered her face with her hands and began to cry again.

"Honey..." He trailed off and just hugged her. He didn't know if she was delusional or had experienced a real event, and he supposed it didn't matter. Real or not, she believed it and was beyond upset.

He held her until she pulled away to grab a tissue from Helen's nightstand. She blew her nose twice before saying. "I saw Mom. She's a brilliant splash of white in the green. She's huge, Dad, much bigger than normal people. You're all little sparks of light barely bigger than the animals and she's a bus-sized ball of energy. And she was using the knowing. I wanted to use it too, but you took me away."

She said the last angrily and glared for a moment until the glare melted into a lost expression. "And now she won't come back. I think she's still in that storm, but it's too far."

Ben's heart pounded hard. It was clear Jill believed what she was saying. "How was she using it?"

"I don't know," Jill snapped, then grimaced and grabbed another tissue to blow her nose again. She spoke in a softer voice when she said, "She could use it though. I saw the changes. It was wrong, and she knew it. I knew she knew, and she unmade it, but I didn't see how."

"What was wrong?"

"The changes Mom made."

Ben took a deep breath and tried for patience.

Jill gave him a rueful smile. "I'm not being difficult. I really

132

don't know. I was looking at the light that was her and saw the change, but I don't know what it was changing. It was happening so fast and the knowledge was so distracting. There was so much…"

Ben was suddenly exhausted and thumped back onto the pillows on Helen's bed. His daughter had seen God. He couldn't get his mind around it.

Jill winced and reached for him. "Go shower. If you ruin this quilt, we'll never hear the end of it."

The normalcy of her worry soothed him. He allowed himself to be pulled to his feet, and Jill followed him to the bathroom door. "Doug told me about the dome and the storm and the balls. I can sense them out there. I know exactly how many and where they are. And the storm… I feel that too. It's moving away from me. All the knowing is moving away."

She said the last so sadly it nearly broke Ben's heart.

"I think it was Mom," she said in a firmer voice, giving him a fake smile. "Mom would fight God himself for us." She shivered and rubbed her arms, spinning away and heading for the door. "I'll get your soup."

Enough Problems

Friday Noon 1/19

Raised voices right above his head brought Ben from a sound sleep. It felt as if he'd just fallen asleep, and he groaned as he glanced at his watch. He'd slept less than four hours.

He rolled onto his side and sat up on an elbow to examine Anne. A swath of dim sunlight cut across her face. She lay exactly as she had when he'd fallen asleep. His heart stuttered until he felt the pulse beating slowly in her wrist and his breath left him in a relieved whoosh.

"Just give her to me!" a man yelled angrily.

"Damn it," Ben mumbled as he threw the blanket back.

Helen gave him a relieved glance when he appeared, and he took the stairs two at time.

"He's just visiting," a woman said as Doug said, "What's your problem?"

"You're my problem, asshole! She's *my* wife!"

Ben recognized Phil's voice. He hadn't realized Annie had delivered the baby and he hoped they were both well.

134

"He just wanted to congratulate me," Annie said.

"Dude, get a grip."

Ben entered as Doug laid a swaddled newborn in Annie's arms.

"She's as beautiful as you are," Doug said. "I'm so glad you're both doing well."

Phil grabbed Doug by the shoulder and drew his arm back.

Ben grabbed his fist and squeezed.

"Fucker," Phil snarled and turned. His expression changed from fury to chagrin.

Ben snapped, "What's going on here?"

"Doug was just visiting," Annie said fearfully.

Her anxious eyes stayed on Phil, and Ben tightened his grip.

"Sorry," Phil mumbled and released Doug's shoulder. He glared at Doug, avoiding Ben's eyes, and smiled when he turned to Annie. "She needs to rest."

"I'm sure Doug didn't mean any harm." Ben pushed past Phil and bent over Annie to see the child she held. "She's beautiful. You're both doing well?"

"Yes. I'm so relieved it's over. I never want to do that again." Her expression softened as she gazed down at the baby she held. "You were worth it though, weren't you?"

"What's her name?"

"Meredith, after my mother," Phil said.

Ben nodded and gave him a considering glance. He'd thought Phil's hostile attitude was panic induced from the storm but maybe he was just an ass.

"Can we come in?" Jill asked from the doorway. She held out a tray covered with a dishtowel.

Phil glared and opened his mouth as Annie said happily, "Jill, come meet Meredith. Isn't she beautiful?" Annie gave Phil a nervous glance and held out the baby.

Ben stepped from the bed and placed his hands on hips, his glare at Phil daring him to kick his daughter out. Phil snapped his mouth shut and gave Jill a fake smile that she returned.

Jill entered saying, "Annie, this is Johanna, Doug's fiancé. She brought tea and diapers and a book she thought you might like."

Doug and Jill exchanged quick grins, and Doug turned away smothering a laugh in his closed fist.

Ben wondered what that was about, but Phil's hostile attitude distracted the thought. He scowled at Phil, and Phil snapped his mouth closed. It was clear Annie appreciated the visitors even if her husband didn't, and the girls were clearly excited about the baby. As far as Ben was concerned any good news was to be treasured and his glare ratcheted up a notch.

Annie smiled sweetly at Johanna. "Oh, I was hoping you'd stop in. Doug told me you were here. Come see Meredith."

"Phil, can I have a private word," Ben asked and grasped his shoulder, making it clear he'd drag him away if he had to.

Phil followed him into the hallway as the girls entered and bustled about Annie, exclaiming over the baby.

Doug followed, and Ben gestured him away, pulling Phil out of earshot of the doorway.

"I'll go check on Mom," Doug said, flinging a dark look at Phil before running down the stairs.

Ben waited until he was out of sight before saying, "Your wife and daughter are guests under our roof and welcome here, but you won't be if you're rude to my family again. Keep your voice down and speak civilly or get out."

"I'm sorry—"

"Don't apologize when you don't mean it. I didn't realize you and Doug had history, but he isn't one to hold a grudge, so I suggest you let it go too. High school was a long time ago, and he has no designs on your wife. Frankly, I think it's bullshit to make her feel bad about greeting an old friend. Don't we have enough to worry about?"

"You're right. It's just…" Phil scowled and slashed his hand through the air. "She means everything to me— everything! And Doug was always mister popular. But you're right, we *are* guests, and you saved our lives. It won't happen again." He glared down at his feet, then glanced back through the open door. "She loves me," he said, but Ben thought he was saying it to convince himself.

Ben's anger faded.

"She does and you're a lucky man to have such a sweet wife, one who'd give you the clothes off her back and freeze to keep you warm. One who gave you such a beautiful daughter, but I promise you, unreasonable jealousy isn't the way to a woman's heart."

Jill came to the doorway and darted a questioning glance at Phil. "Dad?"

"Everything's fine. Phil and I are just chatting.

Jill hesitated in the doorway, clearly not believing that.

Phil said, "It was nice of you to bring up the tray, Jill. Tell your grandmother I said thank you. And thanks for the clothes."

Johanna stepped into the hall, holding the baby, and grinned at Ben. He smiled back, relieved to see a real smile on her face. She'd barely said a word since the storm.

Jill said, "You're welcome. Doug's boots don't fit anyone else; his feet are so enormous. We're asking around for baby things for Meredith. She's a beauty."

"She really is," Johanna said. "Look at those curls."

Abby climbed the stairs, saying, "Are you guys disturbing my patient? She needs rest." She kissed Ben's cheek in passing and grinned at Phil. "Everyone will be stopping in to see the baby. We're all thrilled, but Annie does need to rest."

Phil followed Abby into the bedroom. "I'll see to our daughter so Annie can sleep. I can go join a search party when she wakes."

Annie's anxious glance traveled from the window to Phil. "No, go. But can you at least stay and have lunch with me?"

Phil smoothed his wife's hair, his expression tender. "Yes. I wish I could stay all day, but they really need help."

Annie's eyes filled with tears.

"I'm sorry, honey."

"I know you should go. It's just..." She sniffled and ducked her head, her blond curls falling forward to hide her face.

Jill took the baby from Johanna, cradling her carefully. "My dad will watch out for Phil, and I'll be watching out for the baby. You guys eat, and he'll be back before you even wake."

She placed the baby into a laundry basket lined with towels beside the bed, grabbed Johanna's arm, and tugged her from the room.

"Come get me when you're done with lunch," she said to Phil in passing. "See ya later, Abby," she called back, and the girls clattered down the stairs, talking excitedly about the baby and who might have baby clothes.

Ben followed slowly. His bones ached, and he wanted to lay down beside Anne and sleep for a week. But he headed to the kitchen and reached for his boots that were drying beneath the table. It had started to snow while he slept, and an inch already covered the ground.

"Mom's still sleeping," Doug said as he entered.

Helen handed him a thermos and a buttered roll.

"Eat before you go back out," she said to Ben.

"I'll eat in the truck. That snow is coming down pretty good."

She wordlessly began making a sandwich while he shrugged on his damp jacket.

Doug followed him outside, juggling the thermos, a pack, two sandwiches and Styrofoam cups.

Ben took the pack and swung it over his shoulder and accepted a cup and sandwhich.

"He was always an ass." Doug glared over his shoulder at the house. "Annie's sweet though. She could do better than him."

Ben lifted an eyebrow. It occurred to him Jill must know Phil from school too, and she hadn't greeted him either. Phil must be a

138

real ass if Jill disliked him so much that she wouldn't give him a hello in this situation.

Doug waved his sandwhich. "Not me. I'll admit, Annie and I dated for about a week in eighth grade, and I still think she's beautiful, but she's also sort of dumb. You can't have a real conversation with her."

Ben snorted with laughter and glanced back at the house. "Well, stay away from her. Phil is a hothead, and we don't need any problems."

Doug gave him a sarcastic salute. "Yes, sir,"

"We have enough problems."

The smile fled Doug's face and they tromped through the snow to the barn without speaking. Ben forced himself to finish the suddenly tasteless sandwhich. He'd need the energy to continue the search although he dreaded what they'd find.

A Long History
Sunday Afternoon 1/21

Ben stared out from his bedroom window over the deceptively tranquil, snow-covered fields. For twenty-seven years now he'd lived here with his wife and family. His wife's family had owned this land for over three hundred years. Her ancestors had settled here with the Paugussett Indians after leaving the Isle of Mann in the Hebrides of Scotland. He'd felt this land was a part of him as well.

He loved the life he led here running the farm. Where others might've resented the long hours, he looked forward to the early mornings in the quiet warmth of the barns. He loved the orchards on the hillside, picking the fruit they'd make into the locally renowned pies they sold at the family's seasonal bakery and the berries they'd turn into wine. The satisfaction he received caring for the land and the animals that provided for them, and teaching his children the value of self-sufficiency, were payment enough for his long hours. He'd work long and hard to build up the farm into the thriving business it was now.

He placed his forehead against the cold glass and lightly gripped the pane. The scene looked so normal, so peaceful, until you noticed the lack of lights. There were no streetlamps, no car headlights or taillights going up the hill on the road across the river. There wasn't a plane in the sky. No house lights twinkled in the distance. The radio tower that had stood atop the opposite hill was gone completely, no lights, no silhouetted black shape, just gone.

He glanced back at the woman lying so still and silent on the bed and the small dog whining beside her. It was impossible for him to fathom what had transpired. He turned away to examine the deceiving peacefulness of the snow-covered hills beyond this land. Unthinkable, what lay silent beneath that serene blanket of white—the twisted ruckus of a face clinging desperately to life, the peaceful countenance of others who'd sat down and quietly fallen asleep, holding their families close. Huddled frozen corpses of men, women, and children found singly or together, but all equally dead.

He shivered at the sight and turned away after he pulled the shade down as if that would block the memories as well as the light. He went to his wife's bedside and stared at her familiar, beloved countenance.

"Doug, take Merlin!" he called.

The dog's whining grated. Every time they let him into the room, he cried piteously until they took him out. The sound was breaking Ben's heart.

Doug took the dog and glanced at Anne. Tears filled his eyes. "I'm going to Grandma's," he said.

Ben nodded and gave him a hard hug.

The door closed softly behind Doug, and Ben returned to the bed.

Anne Wakes

Sunday Afternoon 1/21

Anne woke and remembered. *It must have been a dream*, she told herself, but she kept her eyes closed while she relived her memories of the storm.

A soft sound drew her attention back to the present, and she reluctantly opened her eyes. Her eyelids felt weighted and dry and she wanted to go back to sleep but the scared, grim expression on Ben's face frightened her.

A headache throbbed behind her eyes, and she felt weak and shaky. The shakiness increased as she considered the idea that it hadn't been a dream.

She shivered in anticipation. She longed to feel that potential again.

"Anne…." He trailed off and hugged her hard.

"Are you okay?" she asked.

"Yes. God. You don't know. Are you?"

He pushed away and wiped his eyes. "I was so worried."

"What happened?"

"You tell me," Ben said.

His bright blue eyes were ringed with dark circles, and he looked very tired to her, tired, sick and sad.

She glanced toward the window, but the shades were drawn, and she couldn't see out. "Okay... but it's going to sound crazy..." she said warningly.

He nodded. "Go on."

"The storm wasn't a storm at all. It was the potential of everything, and I could call it." She laughed sourly at his dubious expression. "I reached out to it and it came to me, and it felt incredible, like all the good feelings you could ever feel all at once. It knew me and filled me with possibilities..., with an intensity I can't describe.

"It was like the first time you see your child," she continued. "The utter love you feel, the connection." She slumped when he stared impassively. "Words just can't describe it. Anyway, it knew me, it knew everything. It was everything."

"Like God?" he asked softly.

"No!" she replied with certainty. "It wasn't holy or sacred or even alive really. It just was." She frowned thoughtfully. "It was more like God's ideas then God, if that makes any sense."

"Not really but keep going."

"Well, I reached out to it, and we connected somehow, and I was trying to know what it knows, and I couldn't grasp it. It was like a really deep thought you have that skitters out of reach when you try to ponder it. I wanted to keep that cloud! I wanted to possess it forever. I remember thinking if I could, I would encase it with diamonds and store it with me forever—"

"Why diamonds?" he interrupted.

"I knew diamonds. The storm had shown me their essence. I pictured big, clear diamond-hard balls filled with purple clouds and they were there at my feet, but they weren't enough. I wanted all of it, all the knowledge or knowing or being."

She shook her hands in frustration at not being able to put into words what the essence of that cloud was for her. "I wanted to have the potential of it. Its essence.

"Everything the purple cloud touched it knew, and I could follow the knowing if I concentrated. A flick of red would outline a leaf and I knew it, the color, the shape, the flavor, smell, feel. Each cell connecting to another and another, how each worked, what each molecule was and what it did; what it had been; what it would be; what it could be. There was so much to know I had to pick and choose which idea to follow. The deeper I delved, the harder it was. A tree, a simple blade of grass held so much knowledge it would take me a hundred years to explore it.

"The lighter sparks of bugs were even more complex. I saw how a single cell made the delicate wings rounded and how a small change would make them pointed, but I also saw how pointed wings would require a wider wing base. The bug was perfect as it was. To change one would change the entire.

"But I could do it. I could shape that bug to my will, but I knew I'd do it wrongly if hurried. The possibilities were so endless and each one held a consequence."

"The wrong thing?" Ben asked.

Anne flushed and ducked her head, rising her hands to her burning cheeks.

"Jill said something you were doing was wrong, but she didn't know what it was."

Guilt seared her, roiling like acid in her stomach, and she had to swallow hard against the nausea.

"Anne?"

"I didn't' know, Ben." Hot tears dripped down her cheeks and she angrily dashed them away, angry she'd cry for herself when she'd killed so many.

"Know what, sweetheart?"

His kindness made the tears fall faster until she bawled like a baby, clutching his shirt and sobbing.

"*Shh.* None of this is your fault." He kept saying comforting things, but none really penetrated her misery.

"What was the wrong thing?" he asked again when her tears had slowed.

Her head had begun to throb hard, and she lifted a shaky hand to rub her temple. Ben handed her a water bottle that she took gratefully, and she drank the entire thing before saying, "I called it, Ben."

She cringed, waiting for his disgust and anger, but he snorted and looked exasperated, not angry and repulsed.

"Don't be ridiculous. At most you greeted it. It was well on its way here when you sensed it."

"But I called it to me, and it destroyed those houses. I killed them!"

She jumped to her feet and staggered as she lurched to the bathroom where she vomited the water she'd just drank.

"Anne, sweetheart…"

She vomited again, the sad despair in his voice crushing her soul.

Ben dropped to his knees beside her and rubbed her back. "I'm so sorry, sweetheart. Jill saw— I just assumed you had too. That wasn't your fault. It's like that everywhere. The purple cloud destroyed the houses everywhere it went. Jill saw, or thought she saw, I'm still not certain, but she claims to have seen the destruction all along the coast. You didn't cause it, sweetheart."

For a moment she felt relief followed by horror. She'd though it was the power of her call that had destroyed the homes, and while she was happy that wasn't the case, it didn't change the fact that they were destroyed. Her mind couldn't seem to grasp the thought that the entire coast was devastated. *And not just the coast*, she thought in rising horror. She could feel the storm out there, growing.

"Oh, dear God," she said and she retched until the room swam before her eyes.

When she opened her eyes, she lay on the floor. Ben hovered above her dabbing a wet washcloth against her face.

"Maybe I didn't kill them, but I would've. At the time, I didn't care, I just wanted the knowledge but that wasn't the wrong thing."

Ben sat back on his heels, and she pushed herself up to lean against the cold porcelain of the tub behind her. "The wrong thing Jill saw was me trying to hold onto the people I— the storm killed. I saw the bright sparks being snuffed out and tried to weave them together to make them brighter, like Jill. It worked but changed them. It was a wrong thing. So I undid it."

Ben frowned, and Anne closed her eyes. She sounded cold and hard to herself, but contemplating those deaths still unnerved her. When she'd called the storm, she hadn't cared who it hurt, not even herself. The power of it had overwhelmed her.

"I didn't think I was a greedy person, but I am." She flushed as she considered how greedy. She'd still be out there with the storm right now if she could reach it, but she'd captured the last bits that had wandered through and had fallen asleep while waiting for more.

He sat beside her and rested his head on the wall, putting an arm around her.

"I think you need to give yourself a break. I can't imagine how overwhelming it was."

"You couldn't sense it at all?"

"No one else could except Jill, and it scared her half to death. She's fine now, physically at least, but I thought it might kill her. I don't think humans are supposed to see that."

"It was terrifying and glorious," Anne said and closed her eyes. She could feel the spheres she'd made waiting for her. Contemplating the captured storm that was waiting for her in the lower field made her palms sweat with anticipation.

And the dome? Was that you?"

"The barrier…." She rubbed her throbbing head.

"*Hmm…*" he made an encouraging noise when she remained quiet and nodded at her to continue.

"The cloud hit the edge of the farm."

Remembered anger flushed her skin, leaving her shoulders aching and making her head throb harder. He took her hand.

"It's okay," he said. "We're all okay. What happened next for you?"

She leaned up to kiss him. "I love you," she said the anger melting away, grateful they were together. He felt strong and safe; he felt like home.

"I love you too!" He smiled and traced her cheek with a work-roughened fingertip. "But what happened next?"

She gulped back salvia that flooded her mouth, remembered fear making her nauseous. "It was terrifying. I felt the land scream. It was a like it was me. In that moment, I knew every inch of our farm and every speck of dirt and blade of grass was mine. The animals, the people, the bugs, everything belonged to me and me to them. I knew them…" she trailed off, realizing her voice had risen to shrill.

After a moment she continued in a calmer tone, "I reached out to the storm and somehow forced it over us. The dome was just seething with energy. And I could feel it— and I knew…"

"What did you know?" Ben asked when she remained silent.

"I have no idea. Someone grabbed my arm then and tried to drag me off." She shrugged and forced a smile. "It seemed to take forever or seconds, I don't know which, to pass over us. I was the dome— my lands protector, and even when I let it dissipate, I was guarding the land, forcing the storm away." Remembering her pain and fear made her tremble. Odd snatches of clarity had burst through her preoccupation where she'd felt Ben calling to her, but the lands pain had pulled her back. That and her greed to capture it for herself. She flushed as she considered how she risked her family's lives.

"Jill thought you were stuck in the storm," Ben said.

Anne grimaced ruefully. "I was, sort of."

Ben's eyebrow lifted and her flush deepened. "I had to stay, Ben. The storm .... It hurts the land so badly. I couldn't let it touch our land." She turned away, avoiding his gaze. She'd hadn't been able to pull herself away. It was only distance that had let her release her concentration. If the storm had been bigger, she'd have killed herself trying to know, trying to harvest the last scraps of storm that had wandered through.

"Is it gone now?"

"It is." The thought made her sob and she rubbed her eyes briskly. "And that's all I remember until I woke."

"And you're certain it wasn't God?"

"Yes."

"Jill thought it was."

Anne smiled slightly and rubbed her stomach. She hadn't really known God until she'd carried a child. "Jill has no experience and no real belief. Well, maybe now she does, but I know God. I've prayed and been comforted and felt his presence. The storm wasn't God. It was an act of God."

Ben was pondering, she recognized the thoughtful expression. She closed her eyes and rested her forehead against the cold porcelain of the tub, grateful the throbbing was subsiding. Ben rose and handed her two aspirin and a glass of water.

"The storm is over. It's just regular snow fall out there now," he said.

"Where are the kids?"

"They're fine; they're both over at your mom's helping out. A lot has happened. Almost everyone is over at your mom's house. When you're up to it, we should go too. We went out looking for survivors as soon as that green glow was over the hill." He shook his head as if clearing it. "The road was fine until it hit Dover, then it was suddenly rubble and covered with black slime. All the way down to the river was like that." He closed his eyes and swallowed convulsively.

"Doug was in hurry to get to Will's house. He was hoping to find them. It was getting colder out, and we knew without shelter... well..." he paused and shook his head again.

"Luckily we had the chainsaws to clear the road. Some of the older telephone poles hadn't totally disintegrated and had fallen and the storm damage was severe, and we needed to plow a few scraps of cars away." He shook his head again, shuddering. We'd already begun to see bodies. Checking each... I never want to do that again. Our son... well, I wish to God he hadn't seen, but I couldn't protect him from it.

He was quiet a moment before straightening and saying, "Anyway, we got there all right. It took us almost an hour to go that mile, but we did it.

"Are Will and Janice okay?" Anne interrupted.

"They will be, I think. We got them out. They were half frozen and in shock and Janice's arm is broken and Will has a concussion, and of course they're very upset about their families."

"Did you go to Will's parents?"

Ben didn't answer but his grim expression told her Will's parents were dead.

"We searched all that night and the next day. Teams are still out," He paused to blow his nose and clear his throat. "We only found two hundred and eighty people."

"Three hundred," Anne said in relief. "That seems like a lot."

Ben shook his head grimly. "No," he said "It's a nightmare! We went as far up the river road as we could until it was blocked by debris. Then we went toward Fairview all around the housing developments up there in Franklin. Wayne's been to his neighborhood, and I went with Pat to his, there's no one. The dead— they lay in frozen piles. I can't even begin to describe the horror of it."

"No one," she repeated numbly. The full horror made her shake.

"It doesn't look good," he said, "Everyone we found was naked; all their clothes had disappeared in the purple mist. The rain has turned to snow and it's still snowing. The survivors watched the storm from outside like us. There was nothing they could do. They saw it approach and what it did. The glow turned red when it touched them, and their clothes just melted away. A few had scraps let, hanks of wool or cotton but even pure cotton clothes bubbled away on contact with the mist, leaving just thin gossamer-like strands behind. The lightning killed so many…..

"It's freezing out there, and with no shelter the survivors aren't going to do well. Some people were seriously injured from their fillings or contacts dissolving. The only hope people will have is if they were underground and not in concrete. Most of our survivors so far had taken shelter like that, or just ran out of their houses when they saw them collapsing and we found them before they could freeze to death. We only had about twenty people show up on their own.

"We're keeping the fire on the point lit. People should be able to see it for miles around. There is no other light except the stars at night, but really," he said sadly, "I don't think we'll get many more. It's too cold. The ones who came here all lived close. And they were all frostbitten just getting here."

He started to cry again, tears running unheeded down his cheeks. "So much tragedy! Houses just collapsing on people and there's no way to get help to them." He put his face in her hair and cried.

"All our families," she sobbed. "Our friends? We have to keep looking!"

Ben cried harder. Horror made her shake.

"Your brother? Ricky, Maggie— Molly? Oh, my God, Ben, the babies. We have to try to get to them." She turned desperate, imploring eyes on her husband. The thought of her small nieces and nephew dying in the storm, freezing, trapped under rubble was just too much.

"Sweetheart" –he turned her to face him— "We won't give up, but we can't go out in this storm. Only two of our trucks have plows on them and we need them here right now. The best we could do was leaving signs saying where we were and small packs of supply's every few miles. "Rich is just too far away. There's nothing we can do."

Anne started to sob. "I should've made them come!" In her heart, she knew they must be dead already. They'd lived in the city in a ten-story apartment building.

"My Grandma?"

"We couldn't get anywhere near there," he said. "We can't cross the river. There are no more bridges, and she was on the third floor," he continued softly.

"Oh…, no hope then." She said it calmly because she couldn't grasp the magnitude of her loss.

"No," he said and stroked her hair. "I don't think there is."

"Johanna's family? Oh, my God! Did Andrea and Dean show up?" she asked, hoping they'd turned up at the last minute.

Ben heaved a heavy sigh and rubbed his face. "No. Andrea didn't make it. Dean is here with Julie though, thank God. Thank God." he said again. "There's at least hope for the Martinez's though. They had a root cellar; if they took shelter there, they would've been okay. And they have the chickens and goats for food if the buildings collapsing didn't kill them. We won't know. We can't cross the river to go there. Johanna's pretty upset but she has hope. Hell, everyone's pretty upset. Andrea…" he trailed off, shaking his head. "Last we heard she was on her way here, but she had to cross a river to get here and without shelter in this weather…

No, Andrea is most likely dead." He looked away and cleared his throat. "Dean and Julie— Well, I don't know, Anne. How do we get through this? Half our family gone just like that, and we'll never know—" He stopped speaking abruptly to clear his throat again and blew his nose.

"There's so much to do," he said in a brisk no nonsense tone. "We have to figure out what we're going to do now. There's almost five hundred people counting on us to get through the winter. We're the only ones with any supplies at all."

"No hope for rescue then?"

"No, we're on our own. The government must have known," he said with anger in his voice

"You think the government knew?" The idea shocked her.

"They must've," he replied, "how could they not have? Those pictures we saw must have been fakes. The rumors they assured us were hoaxes...."

Anne had no answer. She hadn't believed the rumors. She'd believed the assurances of the newsmen, that although severe, this was a normal storm. The president himself had come on television and assured America the rumors of the storm destroying ships sent to investigate it where a hoax. They'd shown clippings of storm ravaged boats. And it had all been a lie. Anne's anger grew as she contemplated the depth of that betrayal. Her family would've come. The children would be alive and safe with her.

Ben held her, rocking her gently as she cried. Grief burned like acid. It still felt unreal, dream like. Her emotions whipsawed back and forth from grief to denial to a scorching anger. Any moment she expected to wake and see homes and lights on the hill across from them.

A knock on their bedroom door interrupted Anne's reflections.

"Come in!" she said briskly, wiping her eyes.

"Mom!" Her daughter rushed into the room. Merlin barked and struggled to be released. Anne took him and kissed his nose, clutching him as she hugged Jill.

Jill said, "Oh, my God, Mom, I'm so glad you're okay! Did you see? Did Dad tell you what happened?"

With her long, dark hair in a ponytail, Jill looked fresh and young, a grownup version of Molly. Anne was overcome with gladness at the sight of her child and sadness for the one she'd never see again. The conflicting emotions tore a moan from her. Both started crying.

"I'm okay," she sobbed, "You're okay. We're okay." Jill's tears were warm on Anne's cheeks. Merlin frantically licked them both, wagging his tail so hard it shook his small body.

Jill sobbed, "We we're so scared. It's so awful. Everything is gone! Everything!"

"We're here. We have each other."

They clung to each other crying.

"What are we going to do now?" her daughter asked when her tears slowed.

"I don't know." Anne straightened and wiped her eyes on her pajama top. "But, first things first. I'm hungry," she lied. "Any food made?"

"I'll make sandwiches while you dress."

In the kitchen, Ben motioned her to a chair, saying, "If you're up to it, there's supposed to be a big meeting at six tonight at your mom's. Who's there now, Jill?" he asked while reaching into the fridge. He pulled out the mayo and pickles and set them on the counter. "You want mustard?"

"I do," Anne said.

He grasped the ham and cheese and two bottles of soda. "Jill, grab the rye bread, please."

"And the chips," Anne added, wondering if they were forcing themselves through the motions too.

Jill set the chips down on the table where they all settled to make sandwiches.

153

"You know, these could be the last chips on Earth," Jill said sadly as she listlessly took a chip from the bag.

"They're not," Anne said smugly. "I have twenty-three bags downstairs."

"Twenty-three?" her daughter said, sounding much happier.

"I bought a case," Anne said proudly. "Besides, we should give up chips anyway. They're bad for you."

"No point." Her daughter stuffed a handful of chips in her mouth, speaking with her mouth full. "You never know how long you got."

They all quietly ate for a few minutes. The two bites Anne took felt like lead in her stomach. "Should we bring some sandwiches or something to grandma's house?" Anne asked Jill after they'd pushed the food on their plates around for a few more minutes.

"Nah, Grandma's got it covered. She and Grandma Rose have been heating the soup we made and making bread all day to feed everyone."

Anne nodded and headed to the office. "Let me just grab my notebook and my notes, and we can head over."

Her office appeared the same as it always had, she thought with surprise.

Her world had changed so drastically so fast that she couldn't grasp it. There should be some sign, but it all seemed so normal. She firmly pushed thoughts of missing family away. Picturing their faces made tears well and she needed to be strong now.

She grabbed a notebook and her favorite pen from the top of the desk, then rummaged around in her filing cabinet, pulling out papers and placing them in an empty folder she took from the drawer.

"One minute!" she yelled as she headed back upstairs to grab her parka from the closet in her room. She slipped on her bright blue coat and pulled on a pair of fleece lined boots from the bottom of her closet, put on her mittens she kept in her coat pocket, grabbed up her papers, and headed back down the stairs.

"Ready!" she said in a determined voice and gestured for them to precede her out the door.

Jill handed Merlin to Anne and zipped her jacket.

"You better stay her, little man," Anne said and closed Merlin into the kitchen.

Snow had been churned to mud in her mother's front yard from the cars parked on the lawn. Light flickered from all the windows and cast long shadows on the snow drifts.

"Is everyone staying here?" Anne asked as they approached the door.

Ben shrugged. "That's what we are here to decide."

"Some people are up at Aunt Angie's already," Jill piped in, "and I think a bunch more are at the Russo's."

They walked into the warm kitchen, fragrant with the smells of cooking bread. "*Mmm…* something smells great," Anne said and gave her mom a hug.

The women in the kitchen gave her teary smiles and headed to the living room where low talking could be heard.

Her mom started crying. "We were so worried"

"I'm fine," Anne said and gave her another hug. "What's cooking that smells so good?"

"Are you hungry?" Helen asked, heading to the cabinet where she kept her soup bowls.

"No," Anne said stopping her with a hand on her arm. "We ate before we came over."

"I made soup and bread," Helen said. "I figured that was easiest to make in bulk."

"It's delicious," Sue said as she ushered her daughters to the door. Anne smiled, happy they at least had been spared. Horror sank its claws in and tried to overwhelm her. She firmly pushed her thoughts away. Crying again would help no one and she had information to share.

"Has everyone eaten?" Anne asked.

"I think so," Helen replied, looking vaguely around the crowded room.

"We were just clearing the table," added Sue. She patted Helen's arm, giving Anne a worried glance from red-rimmed eyes.

The First Meeting
Sunday Evening 1/21

Anne greeted neighbors she knew and nodded at people she didn't know. The living room was crowded, every chair taken, and people sat against the walls and in the center of the floor. Most held cups or bowls. Some wore odd combinations of ill-fitting clothes while others wore scraps of fabric. The majority of them had very short hair or burnt looking wisps. With horror Anne realized the patterned marks left on some of the women's faces was caused by holding their hands up to cover their eyes. Makeup had boiled away, scarring them, some so severely it made Anne ill to contemplate the pain of it.

Rashes and weeping wounds covered them. Her gaze caught on a small group of men who all wore blood-stained bandages on upper arms and forearms and the damage looked so severe that Anne worried the scouring of the tattoos from their bodies would lead to permanent disability. Crusted scabs covered angry looking welts on almost everyone. The wounds were sure to be painful and they had no supplies to treat them. Only the people who lived on her street appeared unscathed.

Kate gave her a relieved smile, but Anne gestured her to stay with Dave.

Kate answered with a glance that warned she'd by later to get the full scoop, and Anne spent a moment being grateful her best friend had accepted her invitation and that she'd talked Sue into coming. Sue and Pat weren't just Kate's in-laws but Anne's treasured friends.

She examined the faces of friends family and strangers. Everyone looked worn and sad with tear-stained faces. Most spoke quietly with a hysterical edge in their voices. She'd known a lot of these people for years. They all suddenly looked older to her. Stress had aged them overnight.

We need direction, a clear goal, something to give us hope.

"Okay, then!" she said loudly and clapped her hands twice. "Let's get down to business!"

Everyone peered around in confusion and a few people started to speak at once.

"Hold on." Anne waved a hand. "We won't get anything done like this. I know everyone wants to talk, and we all a have questions, but we need to straighten out what we're doing first. I propose that everyone who has a house standing takes a seat at the dining room table and we discuss who gets to stay where." She gestured to the crowded dining room off the living room and people rose, taking their cups and plates with them.

A table that could seat ten comfortably sat in the middle of the dining room. Someone had removed the hutches that normally lay against the wall and placed folding chairs around the perimeter of the room and crammed more chairs around the table.

Anne nodded apologetically to those who lost their seats, but no one complained. They moved slowly and hesitantly as if grief and shock weighed them down.

"Mom, you sit there at the head of the table. Roger" –she

beckoned her brother-in-law to the table— "Dan, you and Abby have a seat." She paused as she counted. "We definitely need more chairs."

She made a note in her notebook. *Need a place to meet we can all fit.*

"Where's Judy?"

Silence descended.

"I think she was at the church for the storm," Helen said. "There's been no sign of her at her house, its empty."

"Okay." Anne gulped and angrily wiped her tearing eyes. "Mr. and Mrs. Brooks take a seat, please. Who am I forgetting?" Anne said uncertainly.

Ben called the rest of their neighbors forward and arranged seating for them.

"Did we forget anyone?" Anne asked, gazing around the crowded room. People stood against the wall and filled both doorways, craning over shoulders to see. "Let's get started then," she said and smiled over at Jill who sat on the floor behind Ben. "Jill, honey, could you take some notes, please? In case there's anything we need to look at or forget about."

"Sure," Jill said and took out her cell phone. "All set."

Anne cleared her throat nervously and began, "We all know why we're here. We have to make some decisions about what to do now."

"Can't we just wait for help to come?" Mrs. Brooks asked.

"Help isn't likely to come," Ben said, looking grim. "From what we've seen, this is likely the condition all over. Here in the North we have it rough because of the weather, but I'm sure the South has its own problems."

"Like what?" Sue asked.

"What kind of problems?" Lorraine asked at the same time.

Anne held up her hand. "We can't afford to all talk at once. I propose we use Roberts's Rules of Order for meetings. I'll have them printed up for our next meeting, but in general, one person runs the meeting. If you want to talk, raise your hand and wait to be called on."

"Just like school." Mike snickered.

"Yeah." Anne laughed with him. "I'm going to run this first meeting as I have information you'll need."

Most nodded but some stared blankly. Anne turned her gaze from their stricken faces, staring at her notes.

"First, we need to work out shelter and food for everyone." She straightened in her chair. "Does everyone here have a generator at their house?"

Twelve people said no we don't, all talking over each other.

"Wait a second. Only one person from each house respond, please. I'll make a list and let's check you off. Starting at the top of the street with the Wards; Mike, do you guys have a generator?"

She went down the list of standing houses and was encouraged by the response. Most had a generator or some sort of wood stove.

"Does anyone know if Judy had a way of heating her house?"

Finally, Helen said, "I don't think so, but she does have a fireplace in her living room."

"Okay." Anne wrote it down in her notebook. "That just leaves you, Kevin."

"We have one, and a wood stove with a very small supply of wood. But I do have a chainsaw and that's a big forest back there" he said, pointing to the back of the house.

"Gas for the generator?" Anne asked.

"I have three hundred gallons in the big tank we use for the backhoe as well as a mostly full oil tank in the house," he replied. "We used quite a bit of the gas clearing the roads, so I'm not sure how much remains. I'll have to check it.

"I think road clearing needs to stop until we're a bit more organized," she said, rifling through her papers. "Ah, here it is. Okay, folks. The farm has nine hundred gallons of gas; both our tanks are full, and there's twelve hundred gallons of oil down at the greenhouses. They're still standing, aren't they?" she asked, suddenly anxious.

Ben said, "The bars were still there but I haven't had a chance to examine them. I know we lost the plastic on two and we've used one of the backup rolls to make shelters. Hell, I'm not even sure our gas tanks didn't explode from lightning."

"We need to check that out first thing," Anne said. Ben nodded, and she continued. "Shelter and food are our top priorities."

"What about the winery? That's a big building. Couldn't some of us stay there?" a man Anne didn't know asked.

Before she could answer, Ben said, "Sorry, Phil, but no. It isn't heated. We'd talked of adding heat and staying open all year, but we liked having our winters free with the kids."

"Maybe we could build a wood stove there or something," Anne said.

"We'll need to do that for all the homes by next year. As it is, we're going to be cold this year. There's nowhere near enough fuel to keep all the houses warm until spring.

Anne said, "Set a schedule to ration the gas out so no one freezes to death but use as little as possible for heat. We'll need it in the spring for the tractors unless we all want to be planting by hand."

"Speaking of planting," Helen said. "We should round up all of the potatoes we can. If we plant them now in our houses, we can harvest come... let me think... Juneish, and then replant them outside. We should have enough to make a decent crop come fall."

"That's sounds like something we could do," Anne said and made a note. "A few pounds of potatoes right now won't make any difference and it's our only way to get them."

Helen said, "Everyone, bring your potatoes to the meeting tomorrow, and I'll get them ready to plant. We can start planting in say a week?"

"How do we know you won't just eat them?" Henry Brooks asked with a faint sneer.

Helen gave him a withering glance. "Why would I bother? You heard Anne. We own most of the supplies we'll be sharing. I certainly won't starve, but you might if you annoy me."

Anne stifled a giggle and said, "Collect them and you prepare them, and then we plant them. Where exactly?"

"The Russo's have a sunroom and so do I," Helen said. "I'm sure almost everyone has room for a few pots somewhere?"

Anne glanced around as her neighbors nodded or mumbled agreement. They looked shocked and very worried and cast measuring glances at the strangers in their midst as if debating the merits of feeding them.

"Fine, we plant them as soon as Helen says they're ready and we'll work on getting a greenhouse going. We can plant vegetables and use it for shelter." She pursed her lips as she considered. "Ben, if we can manage covers for all three by splitting the last roll of plastic, we should do it. It would be better to keep it double hung for insulation but even a single pane of plastic would hold in heat during the day. We could use the space to work in.

"I'll see if it can be done."

"I'll need to do some calculations, but we could also heat them with wood if we can scavenge piping from somewhere."

The amount of work that needed to be done suddenly hit her. She could no longer just order the supplies they needed. It was make it themselves or go without.

Ben seemed to sense her distress, he smiled crookedly and took her hand.

"We can do this. There's plenty of helping hands available."

Nervous laughter erupted, and the crowd began to speak in whispers. She let them talk as she examined her notes.

"I'm putting you and Pat in charge of heating and repair."

Ben nodded agreement and jerked his chin at Pat who gave him a two-fingered salute.

"Aren't we overreacting a tad?" her neighbor Mrs. Wilson asked. "I mean, sure, ration our food and gas but help is sure to come before we have to plant food. For Christ's sake, I'm an accountant, not a farmer!"

Anne was silent thinking of how to explain it as she understood it when Ben said, "I'm sorry, but help will never come. This is a worldwide event. They tracked that storm for over a week, and it didn't deviate in the slightest. If it keeps going like this, everything will be gone. It'll cover the entire world within a year. There'll be no way to rescue us. People on the west coast might have word of its advance and might not, I couldn't say, but they couldn't get to us through the storm even if they wanted to. Any plane entering it would just… dissolve. Only things in natural caves would survive. There won't be any rescue."

"But my daughters?" Mrs. Wilson said in growing horror. "They're at school in Florida. It hit there already... How will I get them home?"

"I'm afraid you can't right now. We have no way at all to contact them. If they were outside away from big buildings when the storm hit there, they could've survived it," he added reassuringly. "But I'm sure they'll assume you didn't, that the cold killed you if your house falling in didn't. There's no way they could know what Anne did to stop it from hitting us. Hell, she doesn't even know how she did it."

Their neighbor Carl Perez stepped forward from his spot against the wall. "What exactly did she do?" Is all we heard are rumors."

Ben explained what Anne had told him and passed a purple ball around for them to examine.

Anne eyed it with longing and clamped her hands together to stop herself from reaching for it.

"We don't know how or what she did," he said, "or what this

stuff is. We do know we're stuck here with no way to communicate or leave. That won't change even after the snow clears. We need to plan for our future food and shelter needs as best we can."

The look of disbelief and dismay deepened on many faces as the severity of the situation sank in.

"How are we setting up living arrangements?" Anne asked.

Ben said, "Well, right now, I think everyone has ten or so people sleeping on their floors and spare rooms. I know Dan has a bunch of hurt people at his house." Ben turned to Dan. "How bad are they?"

"Abby's been taking care of them." Dan smiled fondly at his wife. "We have five broken legs, three broken arms, and a lady with what we think is a badly dislocated shoulder. There's a few men and women with very serious frostbite. So serious that Abby had to do amputations. We have a few with what we think are internal injuries from collapsing buildings and a few blinded by the disintegration of their glasses and contacts. Almost everyone was injured in some way by the gas and we're running out of pain medication. Angie has a few with severe frostbite at her house," he continued, "and Mike and Mary have a few that are deeply disturbed." He shrugged helplessly. "I think there's about fifty people or so in the barn too." He glanced at Ben for confirmation.

"Last I checked," Ben agreed, "They're packed in like rats, which is good for heat but not hygiene." Ben leaned back in his chair. "We need to do something about that and clothes. Right now, they're all huddled together under blankets and hay; we need to do better there."

Anne nodded and tapped her pencil again as she thought. "I'm assuming everyone went through their closets and such?" she asked the table in general. A round of nodding assents and murmurs went around the table. Anne saw some flushed faces and guilty glances at the strangers in their midst and assumed they had clothing they weren't sharing, and she couldn't really blame them.

They had no way to replace it.

"Well. We'll have to think of something. Anyone have any ideas?" Again, her gaze went around the table.

"The curtains!" her daughter said suddenly.

"*Hmm,*" Anne said as everyone turned to look at Jill.

"The curtains," Jill repeated haltingly, suddenly shy at the attention. "We could use the curtain material to make some clothes."

Anne smiled at her in approval as everyone turned to look at the big windows framed in the heavy curtains.

"That's a great idea!" Sue exclaimed. She got up to run her hand down the fabric. "This would make a great thick robe. How about you guys? Do you have curtains at your houses we could use?"

There were nods again, and general sounds of assent.

Anne smacked her hand down on the table. "So moved!" she said. "Bring all our curtains here tomorrow and see what we can make. Also, if you have a sewing machine or any skill at it, come then too. Is tomorrow at nine good for you, Mom?"

"It's fine," Helen said, "but I haven't used my old machine for years."

"We'll see what we can do with it tomorrow," Anne said, then turned to her husband. "We'll have to set up some kind of shower rotation as well. Make sure everyone has access to hot water on a regular basis. We need a list of names and where they are," she continued. She looked up and asked the room in general, "Any volunteers?"

Her eyes narrowed, and she pursed her lips as she examined the silent crowd. "We need someone, well probably two someone's, to go around and make a list of who's where so we can organize this mob."

Sue said, "I'll do it. I was a secretary. I'm good at lists."

Jill said, "I'll help too."

"Great," Anne nodded approvingly at her daughter. "Jill will meet you here at nine tomorrow. She can bring some pads and pencils."

Sue nodded her head in agreement, smiling at Jill.

"Karen, you come home with us tonight. We'll work out something about heat at your house as soon as we can." She squinted down at her notes. "The Peters, Judy's, Wilson's, and Henry Brooks' homes will need wood delivered tonight.

Pat said, "I'm on it. I'll meet up with Kevin and Todd and we'll work something out."

"That's good for tonight, but we need a better housing situation," Anne said. "We also need to move the cooking to the bakcry and arrange for work shifts there. Ben, do you think we can build a few outdoor hearths? We could use the propane at the greenhouse to cook with but eventually, no matter how frugal we are with it, we'll run out. We'll need some sort of wood stoves to cook on."

"Speaking of kitchens," Helen said, "How's the food situation?"

"Well, there I think we have some good news." Anne turned to her husband. "Are we still getting about a hundred and fifty gallons of milk a day?"

"One hundred and sixty today," he said with a real smile.

The sight eased her, and she smiled back.

"The eggs?"

"A hundred and ten. Production was down a bit, but I think they were stressed. I threw them some extra feed. We'll keep an eye on them and I'll set some hens to laying and we can move the brooding pens inside."

She nodded and drew another paper from the pile in front of her. "This is a list of the supplies we bought for the bakery season. We usually don't have nearly this much on hand, but I stocked up early." A flush heated her cheeks and she avoided her mother's gaze. "I've been on a shopping spree as my kids will tell you. When we first heard about the storm, I started buying stuff. I never expected this degree of isolation though. I just bought our regular supplies early because I thought prices would rise, not that we wouldn't be able to get them."

She cleared her throat and continued, "We have five hundred, fifty-pound bags of pastry flour and granulated sugar at the bakery. There's eight hundred pounds of shortening…" Anne continued to read the list and tense faces relaxed.

Anne laid her lists aside and turned to her mother. "Mom, do you remember what's left on the shelves?" Anne grinned as Jill giggled. It was a running joke that Helen knew the merchandise on hand for their farm market and who'd bought what for ten years back.

"We have a thousand jars of apple jam, four hundred of peach and six hundred of blueberry for the shelves in the shop," Helen said promptly.

She rose an eyebrow when Doug chuckled but continued, "Three freezers are filled with a variety of pie filling and one freezer is full of beef pastries."

She paused a moment and looked thoughtful. "Did you buy all the potting soil we needed for planting season too?"

"Yes. I also bought the seed corn and rye and eight tons of fertilizer. There's Marathon pesticide and a new kind of fungicide they recommended to me as well as all the packaging. It's in the winery."

Her mother's eyes widened. "There can't be any money left in the account."

"No." Anne coughed and rose a hand to cover her flaming cheeks. "We have sixty-two dollars left, not that it matters now," she said sadly. "I should've talked to you about the purchases," she went on, "and I was going to after the storm, but here we are now." She spread her hands out on the table and stared down at them, unable to meet her mother's eyes.

Ben took her hand, and she gave him a grateful smile.

"I ordered all the supplies we use regularly and as much extra as I could afford."

"The canning jars?"

Anne heart lightened, glad her mother wasn't upset that she'd acted so precipitously. "Three thousand empty canning jars for making new jam and five hundred empty honey jars are in your basement."

"How much honey do we have left from last year?" Ben asked.

Anne flipped a page from the stack in front of her and thumbed through them a second.

"Sixty, one-pound bottles," Helen said before Anne could find the answer.

"How much did we get last year?" Doug asked.

Anne glanced back down at the paper. "Just over three hundred pounds," she said. "We lost one hive completely and set out two new ones but it's too soon to know if they'll take," she continued.

"What about sap?" she asked her husband.

"We made fifty-six gallons last year; I bought enough tubing to put in two hundred more taps. I was going to ask Mr. Myer if I could tap his lot. Guess I don't have to ask him now," Ben said sadly. "We need to do something for the bee's too. The hives there will be destroyed."

Anne reached over and squeezed his hand. "He was a good man," she said and looked around the table. "We lost a lot of good friends."

Nods and teary eyes followed that statement.

Anne cleared her throat and asked briskly, "Did you buy the packaging for the syrup?"

"I did. We have assorted sizes of syrup containers, from two-ounce glass containers to one-gallon plastic ones."

"Okay," she said and cleared her throat again. "Let's see,

what's next on my list here…," She stared down at the top sheet of paper until her eyes cleared.

"The walk-in freezer has twelve hundred pounds of assorted beef and a small amount of pork." She laid her paper back down. "We have the twenty milk cows, fourteen more are pregnant, four heifers too young to breed, and six steers we were raising for beef sales. We have no bulls." She let that sink in a minute.

"So, basically," Ben said grimly. "We have fourteen chances on a bull or no milk next year."

"Exactly!" Anne said.

Everyone looked concerned.

"We'll just have to go find a bull," Doug said. "I mean someone somewhere must have had one."

Anne said "Well, there were two small farms across the river, but we can't cross it."

The crowd began to murmur and expressions darkened.

"There's Glen Down Farm, over the hill in Fairview," Doug said. "We can check there."

"Good idea." Anne gave him an approving smile. "We should make a list of all the possible sources of livestock around."

"It will be a cold stone bitch getting them back here though," Ben said quellingly. "We'll need to make some kind of cart Lightning and Thunder can pull. Our horse trailer will be too heavy for them and the roads are unpassable for the truck."

"Will and I will work on it," Doug said. "Hey, Uncle Roger, you still have that trailer you used to move the pellets with?"

"Yeah," Roger said, "we could probably remake that."

Anne tapped her knuckles on the table. "You two meet after this and talk about it."

"This is so surreal," Dean said. "I can't believe we're sitting here talking about finding cows— I mean, two days ago I was planning a vacation to New Orleans and today I can't cross a river."

169

Both Jill and Julie hugged him briefly. Julie started to cry softly and put her head on her father's shoulder. Anne knew she was thinking of her mother stuck somewhere across the river.

Anne wiped her eyes and cleared her throat, then continued determinedly, "We also have a hundred pounds of rice and two hundred pounds of assorted dried beans at our house."

She glanced nervously at Ben, then pretended to be absorbed in her notes as she said, "I bought a bunch of dried foods; those emergency ration things you see advertised. I have no idea how they taste but they claim to be nutritious. And twelve rechargeable battery lanterns and ten walkie-talkies." She looked up from the paper and smiled slightly, "they also have rechargeable batteries."

Ben snorted with amusement, and Anne sighed with relief.

She spoke with renewed confidence when she said, "Now, onto the next item of business." Anne looked down and continued to read from her paper. "We have two pregnant sows as well as old sugar, who is a pet and past breeding, and Jill's four pet goats," She said as an afterthought, "The boys are neutered though."

"We're not going to eat our pets?" Jill leaned forward to grab her father's arm.

"Honey, I don't want to, but if comes down to them or us…" and she gestured around the table.

Jill gulped and nodded.

"There's plenty of game," Ben said and half stood to touch Jill's cheek. "It won't come to that."

"I'll go hunting, Princess," Kate said and gave Jill a reassuring smile. Dave nodded his agreement and Jill's tight shoulders eased.

"I'm sure we all have personal supplies at our homes," Anne continued as she glanced around the room, nodding thankfully at Kate. "I want us all to go home tonight and think about what we have extra to share. No one is going to come and take anything that's yours. We need to be frugal, but no one should starve. We have enough for everyone. If you could all come back tomorrow with lists of what you have, hopefully Sue and Jill will have lists of what we need by then, and Pat and Ben can work out the fuel needs. My Mom and I will work out cooking arrangements. It'll be a lot of work to cook for this mob, so we'll need volunteers for that. Tell Jill or Sue if you're willing to help and if you have any experience."

"Jill, remind me to print out the Robert's Rules for tomorrow's meeting" she said, turning back to her daughter.

"Will do." Jill gave her a mock salute.

Anne said, "I think that does it for tonight. Anyone have any concerns we should be aware of?

Ben stood. "We need to begin rationing immediately. Your cars, your supplies, are your own, but once the fuel is gone, we have no way to replace it. We'll never have a way to replace it ourselves. The cars are destined to become museum relics."

Ben waited for the low muttering to die down before continuing. "I won't tell you not to drive to the meetings or anywhere else. It's your own business, but please, think first and be frugal." He sat, and Anne stood.

No one said anything, so she slapped her hand on the table again. "Meeting adjourned."

"Jill, remind me to get a gavel," she said as she wrung her hand.

"Writing it down now."

Anne stretched and gave an exaggerated yawn as she turned to the kitchen. Mr. Brooks frowned but stopped his advance.

She said, "I don't know about you guys, but I'm exhausted. I say we call it a night." Again, there were nods and murmurs all around. Everyone stood and milled around in small groups, some heading for their coats, others going off to look for a bathroom.

"Who's coming home with us?" Anne asked Ben.

"Fifteen strangers are in our basement. Dean and Julie are staying with us. Pat, Sue and their girls, Chloe and Emily. Wayne and Marie and the kids are with us too. David, Kate, and Edward," he stopped and pursed his lips. "Well, Edward was," he corrected "and will when he returns. He left to go search for his wife. She wasn't feeling well and stayed home the night of the storm."

Tears rose to Anne's eyes, and she gasped and hunched as if from a blow. She didn't want to acknowledge her friend Barbara was dead. The manner of her death made her shiver, and she pushed the thought away again.

"Will and Janice?" Anne asked, turning to look for them.

"No. They're staying here in your old room. We took them here the night we found them. Abby came and set Janice's arm, but she hasn't left the room since. Will is really worried," he said, looking worried himself.

Anne laid her hand on his arm. "Let it be. We have enough worries tonight. I'll go see her tomorrow. Maybe having a plan will help," she added.

"Maybe," he said skeptically.

Ben headed to the kitchen to kiss his mother goodnight. "See you tomorrow," he said as he smoothed back Rose's salt and pepper hair.

Anne smiled after him. He dwarfed his mother's five-foot frame. Her smiled died as she examined Rose. Rose looked pale and fragile. Tears burned Anne's eyes again. Rose had lost a son and three beautiful grandchildren as well as Andrea who she loved like a daughter. Reminded, Anne turned to look for Ben's sister, Angie, surprised she wasn't by her mother's side.

Angie stood in a group of women by the drapes, already removing them. Anne turned back to give Rose a hug in time to hear Ben ask, "Are you okay?"

Rose patted his cheek and began to cry. "I've lived too long! I shouldn't outlive my children."

"Don't say that!" Ben said angrily. "Don't ever say that! Look at them." He pointed to Jill and Julie who were handing out coats by the door. "They love you and need you to be strong for them."

She wiped her eyes, "Yes," she agreed in a quavering voice. "They've lost so much," she said sadly, but she straightened up a little and gave Ben a tremulous smile." I'm okay. I'm staying here tonight. Angie has a full house and it's easier on my knee's here. Helen and I are sharing her bedroom downstairs, and I like to help with the cooking."

"Mom—" Ben's voice cracked and he cleared his throat. "We love you. I'm so sorry. We loved them too." He stopped speaking and fished out a tissue and blew his nose before saying, "We'll get through it." He kissed his mother's pale cheek again and stepped aside to let Anne hug her. Rose cried quietly on her shoulder.

"Doug!" Ben yelled across the room. "Mom and I are going home. Make sure your sister gets home okay."

"Julie and I'll come with you," Jill said and handed them their coats. She started crying as she hugged Rose. Helen patted her back, looking stricken. Her gaze traveled the crowd and tears filled her eyes too.

Everyone would be crying in a minute, Anne thought and released Rose, gave her mother a quick kiss, and pulled Ben to the door.

"Doors unlocked whenever you come home," Ben said as he slapped his brother on the back.

Anne hadn't even seen Dean arrive. She began crying when he turned away and rose his hands to his face. He dropped them and straightened quickly but his eyes were red and puffy and his cheeks sunken. Andrea's loss had hit him hard. Anne couldn't imagine the hurt. She didn't want to imagine it. Pain radiated from everyone. Tears began and stopped, and voices rose and fell in forced cheer and burning sorrow.

"Where did Pat and Wayne go?" Ben asked, looking around the room.

"They headed out to see about moving wood around while you were talking to Grandma," Jill said. She passed them, pulling Julie outside with her.

"Night, Mom; night all!" Anne yelled back through the door. A chorus of good nights followed them out into the night. Snow fell softly. A sight she normally found peaceful but tonight it made her shiver.

How many people stared up into the sky, praying the snow would stop, praying for warmth as their families died? She angrily pushed the thoughts away and snatched her gloves from her pocket, trying not to feel guilty she was warm while others froze. She told herself again that Ben was right; it wasn't her fault. The storm had been coming whether or not she'd called it.

She forced the gloves over her trembling fingers. *Not wearing them would help no one,* she told herself forcefully and reached for the zip-tab on her parka.

"I should tell you now," she said as she zipped her coat. "I maxed our credit cards on those new fuel tanks and the dried food and the extra feed I ordered. And we have nothing left in our savings at all."

Ben glanced down and gently tugged on a lock of her hair that had come loose from her ponytail. "Well, it's a good thing for you the end of the world came, isn't it?"

The joke made them both tear up again.

"Sorry," he whispered as he brushed the tears from her cheeks with his thumbs.

She wiped her face with her mittens and tried to speak normally. "I never expected this. How could I? But I did think the prices would rise, and I figured it was a savings in the long run what with the price of gas going up so fast." She shrugged and gave him a sickly smile. "I should've asked you, but I didn't want you to say no. I'm sorry, but I didn't know how to explain the urgency I felt. I could feel it out there." She shivered and took Ben's hand. His hand in hers warmed her soul. "I knew it was different from anything that had ever been before, but I couldn't explain it."

Ben stopped and turned her to face him. "You can tell me anything. Admittedly, I would've had a hard time believing or understanding, but I trust you. Hell!" He went on in a lighter tone and continued walking, tucking the hand she held in the crook of his arm and pulling her along with him. "I still don't understand it. So, you're the expert, and I'll listen. Besides, I bought that new harrow and all those attachments, and I knew we couldn't really afford it with Jill in collage, but I did it anyway. I took advantage of your willingness to spend money, so I'm just as much to blame, but we aren't broke— we're the richest people in the world."

They were both quiet for a second. Anne squeezed his hand.

"So, what are we doing with all the milk?" she asked as they crossed the yard back to their house.

"Well, so far, it's fine in the holding tank, but we need to decide soon. No more milk pickups," he added.

"Yeah," she said glumly. Tears again threatened, and she angrily rubbed her eyes, wondering if these mood swings would be a permanent part of her life now— if every thought would trigger memories of deceased loved ones.

The deaths still didn't feel real. She knew they were but felt it for fleeting moments as if her brain itself was in denial. She glanced at the silent girls following, wondering if grief overpowered them in waves too.

"No more a lot of things," Jill said.

"I guess it's just something we can work out tomorrow with the food committee," Anne said in a tone of forced good cheer. "Hey, Jill, speaking of committees, tomorrow, when you're taking names, get the former addresses and occupations."

"Occupations I understand, but why addresses?"

"Because, hopefully, someday someone will show up and say, do you know John Doe, the guy who used to live over on Main Street? And we can then say sure, he lives on New Main now and won't he be happy to see you." She turned to glance at Jill, caught sight of Julie's face, and could've kicked herself. How could she forget, even for a second, that Julie's mother was one of those missing people who would hopefully show up?

"I'm sorry, Julie," she said. "I didn't mean to be insensitive."

Tears glittered on Julie's cheeks. Anne put an arm around her niece's shoulder.

"Oh, honey," she said and then they were all crying and hugging and trying to comfort each other.

The wind kicked up, sending stinging pellets of snow around them. Ben took Julie's' hand and put an arm around her shoulder, murmuring to her as he led her to the house. Jill and Anne followed. The crying had mostly stopped by the time they reached the back door. Anne gave Julie a big hug. "We love you, honey. This is your home now. You and your dad will always be welcome here, and we'll never stop looking for your mom, I promise."

Julie hugged her back, then she and a very subdued Jill headed to Jill's room.

As soon as they opened the back door, a berserk, little, black-and-white dog ran out, barking furiously. "Well someone didn't like being left alone." Anne laughed as she bent to pick him up, rubbing her face on his soft fur. "That's what I call devotion," she said and winked at Ben. "His little heart is beating so hard, and I've only been gone a little while."

"He's a faker." Ben took Merlin and rubbed his ears as Anne removed her coat. He handed the dog back and hung their coats on the hook by the door.

"Never!" Anne said fervently. "He adores me."

"*Hmm*, he adores doggie treats," Ben said discouragingly, and headed off toward their room.

She was laughing as she followed until she spied the purple sphere on the counter.

It felt slick and warm and full of potential in her hand.

"Silly dog," she said when Merlin licked it. "It isn't a treat for you." *It's a treat for me.* She stuck her head in the living room. "Everyone all set in here?"

Sue glanced over from the air mattress she leaned over, tucking her girls in.

Both girls called, "Goodnight, Aunt Anne."

Anne entered to kiss their cheeks. They smiled sunnily, not at all affected by the tragedy, too young to understand their world had changed forever, too young to understand they'd never see their home or missing family again. The thought made tears spring to Anne's eyes again.

Sue understood though. Her hands trembled as she smoothed their hair and resettled them. Anne said nothing. What was there to say. Words wouldn't ease a hurt this big. Sue's entire family would be dead by now. She'd lost everything— home, family, friends.

The girls giggled and hugged their mother and Anne's dark thoughts lightened. Sue still had them and Pat and that had to count for something.

"Sue…"

"We're good," Sue said. "See you tomorrow."

It was clear she didn't wish to speak of it. And truthfully, Anne didn't want to either. Acknowledging the loss made it real. She wanted to pretend, to unthink it, for this terrible weight to lift, to see lights out her living room window and to watch television. A sob caught in her throat and she hurried her step, calling good night in a tight voice and running upstairs.

Ten minutes later, she and Ben were all snuggled in their bed. Ben's eyes were already closed. Merlin curled up in a little ball between them, and Anne clutched her purple sphere.

"Night," she whispered.

"Love you," he mumbled back.

He was almost asleep already. *Poor man,* she thought. *I bet he hasn't slept at all since the storm.* She was still very tired herself and she'd slept for days. *Tomorrow is another day.*

She let darkness claim her.

That night, her dreams were filled with confused images. She dreamed of the storm and purple lightning hitting the barn, turning the cows into little flocks of flying cow fairies that swooped around in a purple sky. She dreamed someone was calling her, but she couldn't answer them, all her words turned to purple smoke. She dreamed she stood on a high mountain overlooking a little village that looked like a fairytale toy, but it got swallowed up in purple swirling smoke. She dreamed she saw her grandmother walking down the street with her face all crushed in on one side. It scared her so much, she woke.

"What! What's wrong?" Ben asked, as she sat abruptly.

"Nothing. Its late. Go back to sleep. Just a bad dream."

He reached over and hugged her close, kissing her sleepily on the forehead. He fell back asleep in seconds. She was awake for a long while before she snuggled into his side and slept. She didn't dream again that night.

The small black and white dog slept curled up with the purple ball and had doggy dreams, his little feet twitching, but Anne slept on undisturbed.

Impossible but True

Monday Morning 1/22

The next morning they rose at five-thirty, their usual time, to milk the cows. Anne groaned as she heaved herself from the bed. She felt like she could sleep for a week, but Ben's normal helper wouldn't be joining him ever again.

Sam Percy had lived across the river and kept his family home for the storm despite Anne's pleadings for him to join them. And now across the river might as well be Africa. They had no way to cross it.

Her breath hitched in a sob, and she stumbled, having to catch herself on the sink. Sam and his family were likely already dead. The thought filled her with horror, and she rose shaking hands to rub her face.

"You should rest," Ben whispered and frowned when she reached for her toothbrush.

"Can't, too much to do."

She smiled sadly and shook her head when he tiptoed to the closet. Ben usually didn't care how much noise he made in the mornings. In fact, she sometimes thought he tried to be noisy to wake the kids. But now, with all their house guests, he was trying for quiet.

They both dressed warmly in jeans and sweatshirts over thermal underwear and headed down to the kitchen.

"Breakfast?" she asked.

"No, just coffee," he said like usual. He normally returned to the house at nine or so, after the morning chores, to eat. But he looked thinner to her as if he hadn't eaten in days.

The normality of the moment felt surreal. They both stared at the coffee pot as it brewed.

What was there to say, Anne thought as she silently handed Ben a Styrofoam cup. *Life did go on. The cows needed to be cared for. Crying over Rich and the babies...* a sob caught in her throat and she hastily cleared it.

Sue entered the kitchen.

"How did you sleep?" Anne asked.

"Bad dreams." Sue shrugged irritably. "Pat's up. He's in the bathroom. Dave and Kate left hours ago with their bows to go hunting. Everyone's up, I think, except the kids. They're all still sleeping."

"Let them sleep," Anne said. "You want anything?"

"Just coffee." Sue waved Anne away and headed to the coffee maker on the counter.

Wayne and Pat entered the kitchen together. "Where to, boss?" Wayne asked.

"The barn to milk the cows," Anne said.

"*Hmm...*" Wayne quirked an eyebrow and headed to the pile of coats on the hooks by the backdoor. "Let Pat and I go. We need to earn our keep around here, and you and Sue can start on your lists."

"You sure...?" Anne asked, "I mean, you've never milked a cow before, have you?"

"How hard could it be?" Wayne snickered and slapped his

gloved hands together. "If Ben could do it...." And he trailed off meaningfully.

Pat laughed. "True." He slapped Wayne's back. "I'll eat when we get back," and he leaned over to kiss his wife, "Just coffee for me now."

Sue handed him her cup and started another as she pointed to the jug of milk on the counter next to the sugar bowl. "Help yourself. I'm going to go get a shower," and she headed off to the bathroom.

"You sure you can handle these guys?" Anne asked her husband.

"Not much choice." He winked and kissed her forehead. She pulled him down for a real kiss. The tight expression, his pale face, the deep lines by his eyes all worried her. He looked sick and still so tired it hurt, but he was trying to be cheerful. She reluctantly released him and gave him a fake smile that he returned. She wondered if she looked so grief sick to him and tried to put the smile into her eyes.

The three men headed out into the bright winter morning.

She peered out the door after them and saw it was a beautiful day, clear and bright but bitingly cold.

At least the snow has stopped, she thought and shivered.

Imagining the bodies beneath the snow made her feel sick. Horror made her step unsteady as she went to grab a cup of coffee for herself and she spied the purple sphere. It looked harmless and inconsequential, but she could feel it's potential from across the room. She slipped it into her pocket, then poured herself a bowl of Cheerios and headed into her office to eat it, setting the bowl on the ring made from countless other bowls placed in the exact same spot. She stared at it, not at all hungry. She'd taken it from habit.

She forced herself to eat it, not wanting to waste the last bowl of Cheerios on Earth. Her hand trembled badly, and her stomach squirmed, but she finished the bowl.

The printer whirred to life as her computer booted up. While she waited, she swiveled in her cheap black chair as she examined the purple sphere she took from her pocket. She was still looking at it, her dirty dishes next to her, when Sue popped her head in.

"Want anything?" Sue asked, peering curiously at the sphere Anne held. "The kids are up now. I'm going to make them pancakes. I'll feed the guests downstairs too. I'm sure the kids rattling around up here will wake them."

"Thanks. I'm all set, just thinking." Anne had forgotten they had a basement full of people. The house had been so quiet it was easy to forget it was bulging at the seams.

Sue nodded and reached for the dirty dishes.

"I can do them," Anne said and started to rise.

"So can I. You keep thinking." She laughed a harsh bark of laughter as she plucked the bowl from Anne's hand and headed back out to the kitchen.

Anne spun slowly side-to-side in her chair. There was so much to do today. She should make a list of her household assets, and go through the closets, and she shouldn't forget the curtains, but the sphere grabbed her attention.

She rapped it lightly on her desk.

She was still sitting there, staring at it, when Jill poked her head through the doorway. She eyed the sphere Anne held and paled, quickly averting her gaze. "Morning, Mom."

"Is Julie up?"

"She's just finishing breakfast. Sue made us pancakes. We were going to head over to Grandma's and see if she wanted us to bring some food over to the barn when we did our count. Want me to bring anything over there?"

"Yeah, be a doll and get the curtains down, would you? And maybe sometime today you and Julie could take a quick count of the canned goods downstairs for me too?"

"We can do that. Hey, Julie!" Jill yelled over shoulder, "Let's get the curtains down for Mom and head over."

Anne couldn't hear what the reply was but assumed it was affirmative because Jill turned and left, and she could hear them running back up the stairs over the low murmur of voices from the kitchen. *What good girls,* Anne thought. *God, we're so lucky,* and she shivered a bit at the thought of the loss of them. She'd have to find time to talk with her daughter and compare experiences, but it was clear the storm still unnerved her.

Sue poked her head inside the doorway and said, "I'm taking off too. Cole is headed to the barn with Emily and Chloe. Alicia is doing the dishes. And I've asked our, *um,* guests to go next door to Helen's. Anything else you want Alicia to do before I go?"

"No, have her go next door too and see if they need help when she's done here."

"Will do," Sue said and left.

Alone again, Anne lifted the ball into her hand. It practically pulsed with potential. *Hmm...* she thought, *if I could make you, maybe I could make something else.*

"Be a chair!" she commanded the purple ball. She glanced to the door to be sure no one had seen, an embarrassed flushed heating her cheeks. They'd think her mad if they caught her talking to the sphere.

The ball felt cool and slick and so full of possibility she again said, "Be a chair!" The purple cloud within the ball swirled faster but her words had no effect.

"It wasn't words, was it?" she said thoughtfully and placed the ball down on her desk. *Come to me,* she thought as she pictured what she wanted and held out her hand.

A thin vapor of mist seemed to leak from the sides of the ball. The paper on her desk where the ball sat glowed red and disappeared. There was suddenly more purple haze on her desk.

"Oh no you don't!" She grabbed the ball up. The purple haze and red glow vanished, leaving behind a hole in the desk. The ball she clutched was bigger now and warmer.

"Oh, my god!" Anne said and sat staring at her desk in shock.

"Mom," Jill said as she came to the door, holding up a sheer drapery panel in front of her. "You want us to take these over? They're awful thin."

Anne scowled at the decorative sheer panels that had been on the living room windows.

"I guess. Maybe they can be used for ties or something. They're not much protection from the cold, are they?"

Jill shrugged and turned to go.

"Oh, wait a sec." Anne flicked a quick glance to her desk. Jill hadn't seemed to notice the damage. "Give me one of those, would you?"

Jill wordlessly handed one over and left.

Anne stared at the cloth in her hand, a sheer piece of beige fabric with small brown and green vines embroidered on it. The material was so thin she could see her hand through it. Bunched into a ball, it hardly weighed anything. The potential in the sphere mocked her. She could feel its longing to be, but she was afraid to release it inside the house. She grabbed the sphere and the curtain up and went out to the kitchen.

"I'll be back in a bit," she said to Alicia and grabbed her coat. Outside, her breath plumed in the frosty air and cold nipped at her nose. Merlin followed her out and danced beside her. She absently bent to pet him as she debated where to go. She wanted privacy and somewhere it wouldn't matter if the purple cloud got away from her. She headed to the west field.

Rock walls, built hundreds of years ago by her ancestors, surrounded the western fields. Only forest and ledge remained behind the walls. The housing development beyond the forest was already destroyed. Even if her purple cloud got away from her, it would likely just float west on the wind, doing no damage because the bigger cloud had already obliterated everything.

The thought gave her pause. What she held was deadly dangerous.

With a last glance around to be sure no one was in sight, she placed the sphere on the rock wall and thought, *Come out.*

Immediately a haze formed and flowed to her hands. Red mist boiled up on contact, and she jerked away. The mist hovered and spun, then settled to the rock wall exactly as her panicked mind thought it. Her glove was ruined, and an edge of her sleeve had melted away, leaving rough edges and feathers poking out. Her heart still pounded, and she lifted a shaking hand to wipe her sweating brow. The rock beneath the purple mist glowed green.

Green is good, she thought, *green is go,* and she laughed nervously. When her heart resumed a normal rhythm, she stepped closer, and by thinking of it, moved the purple haze around the rocks. Potential blazed from it. It took willpower not to touch it. With another nervous giggle, she removed her coat and remaining glove, setting them ten feet away in the snow, and pushed up her sleeves.

Purple smoke curled around her fingertips bringing with it the sensation of almost knowing. She felt like with enough she could know everything. Merlin licking her hands jerked her back to the present. He'd climbed atop the rock wall and pranced in the cloud. She'd released the entire ball and hadn't realized she'd done so. It hovered above the rock, wafting gently from the dog's movements but always returning to form a blob before her. Released, the essence had expanded to ten times its size and was much lighter in color.

She stared at the fabric in her hand and tried to picture the haze sinking into the rock and forming the fabric

The haze sank as she intended, but she couldn't visualize the changes needed. She didn't know the fabric.

She ripped off a hunk and set it on the rocks, but the storm essence disintegrated the cloth so fast she wasn't able to learn much.

"I need a more natural fabric than this," she said to Merlin who woofed, happy for the attention. She laughed at her dog as she jogged back to the house.

No one was home to question her as she ransacked drawers and closets for cloth samples.

She stuffed her purloined cloth into a plastic garbage bag and went to get herself another purple sphere.

Mounded snow covered the smaller orbs, but she stared in awe at the bus sized ones she'd created. The entire field was littered with varying sized purple spheres. The sight filled her with giddy excitement. She wanted to release it all and stand it until she knew everything.

"It would take a million years," she said to Merlin and scooped up a handful of the smaller balls.

Back at the rock wall, she laid small pieces of fabric in a row and released minute amounts of storm essence, staring hard, trying to see the cloth, to know it.

Sweat dripped from her forehead and between her breasts with the force of her concentration.

A cotton ball remained cotton longest before the red mist overtook it and she was able to grasp its essence after going through an entire bag of them.

"Here goes nothing," she said and spread the storm essence over the rocks, picturing the cotton in her mind.

The haze sank into the rock, which flared bright green. Before she could see what happened, the haze was gone, and the rock had transformed. In its place was a thick, dense ball of what appeared to be wadded up cotton.

"Eureka!" she exclaimed and pumped her fist in the air, then darted a quick glance around to be sure she was still unobserved.

Amazed and excited, she examined it closely without touching it. It appeared to be an enormous ball of cotton much bigger than the rock had been. She poked it gingerly, not knowing what she expected. She felt nothing from it. It lacked potential. It felt inert, lifeless, normal. Her glance flicked to the purple cloud, and she pursed her lips. A fingertip placed inside the cloud confirmed she could still feel its potential.

"So, once used. That's it," she murmured and daringly gathered the wadded fabric. This time the storm essence remained green when it coated it and she was able to stare to her hearts content. Mass," she said thoughtfully and hefted a rock from the wall.

I need something thinner, less massy, she thought as she scanned the ground. *Or maybe better visualizations?* She glanced back to ensure she was still unobserved, then rubbed her hands together. The gold wedding band on her finger caught her eye.

"Let's try this again." She released another whiff of purple haze and settled it on her finger. Gold was surprisingly easy to learn. It had a very simple structure that she was able to duplicate on her first try.

"Holy shit!" she shouted and slapped a hand to her mouth as she turned to peer guiltily over her shoulder.

The gold ball she'd made glimmered in the winter sun. Her hands were cold, and it was hard to judge but she didn't think the metal felt either hot or cold. It lacked potential, but she was pretty sure her guess about mass was correct, the ball of gold was much smaller than the rock had been but weighed about the same. *Is this really gold?* She thought half hysterically.

The sheer impossibility of what she'd done staggered her. She slid to her knees in the snow and cradled her head in her hands.

"Maybe I'm crazy," she said.

Merlin licked her face. She'd forgotten all about him. He licked her again, then ran around her in a circle. The action was so normal she burst into hysterical laughter. Merlin had no idea the world had changed. He wanted to play. She cuddled him a moment and stood on shaky legs.

They didn't need gold, they needed cloth and not wadded and useless but thin sheets they could form into clothing. It took her two trips to the eastern edge of the field to sneak back more of the balls that littered the ground. No footprints marred the snow except hers. No one had come since, and she supposed she couldn't blame them. The captured storm essence awed her too.

After another hour of trial and error she managed to produce a lumpy cloth. Moving the haze, releasing and encasing it she could do now with a bare thought. Forming it was harder. The barest break in her concentration gave her mangled results. She had to picture each step, the release, the essence sinking into the stone, and the formation into a new shape. Long thin strips were easiest. Making shapes more difficult. Changing color was tricky but she could do it. It was easier to just apply more essence and saturate the object to change the entire color. She learned to never let the purple haze touch the grass or trees. Touching any plant with haze made the land scream out in agony that pushed her to her knees with pain. Merlin whined, and she realized she was cold when she noticed him shivering.

Rough piles of varying colors and density of fabrics littered the ground. The more she'd made, the easier it was to do. He huddled on a mound looking very unhappy.

"Sorry, boy, I got caught up. I'm cold too."

As she rubbed her hands and stamped her feet, she had a thought. Excited by her idea, she coaxed a nickel-sized glob from her ball and let the haze settle into the palm of her hand. Heat, she thought at it. *I want a round hard hot ball.* It took her over thirty minutes to learn the nature of heat. She could see the heat radiating from Merlin as he gamboled in the purple haze but capturing and condensing it was difficult. She strained to understand what she saw but finally gave up and just visualized the pattern, replicating it in the haze she held in her hand.

Pain seared her palm, and she screamed and threw the glowing ball from her. It sizzled as it sank into the snow. Merlin began barking and then whined as Anne cried and clutched her burned hand to her chest.

"Jesus, that was stupid," she moaned and plunged her hand into the snow.

Where the small ball and been there was a perfectly round circle burned deep into her hand.

"Well damn!"

The ball still smoldered, melting the snow around it. She cautiously approached and held her uninjured hand above it. Warmth tickled her fingers. A thought directed more haze to the glowing white ball. She closed her eyes and pictured cold, which was much easier to do because she didn't try to learn it, she just visualized what she saw when she examined the cold radiating from the snow. When she opened her eyes, a dull blue orb had replaced the glowing one and heat no longer radiated from it.

Eyes squinched and a grimace on her face, she tapped it. It felt cold. Not burningly cold. Just cold like metal that had been outside in the winter. She crouched down on her knees and prodded it. Nothing, it was still just cold. She passed her hand over it, then picked it up, placing it against the burn on her palm. It chilled her flesh in moments, and she let it fall to the ground. She squatted to examine it closer.

About the size of a marble, it resembled the larger purple ball she'd made it from but had no sense of anything about it except cold. It lacked the potential of the bigger ball. A swirl of purple appeared to be trapped unmoving inside like a cats-eye-marble.

"But you do have potential, don't you," she murmured, making Merlin woof and wiggle in delight. She rubbed his ears while gathering her thoughts. Warmth would be literally lifesaving if she could make balls that didn't burn on contact. There was a field of trapped storm essence she could use to form to her will. Her gaze

189

shifted west. More storm essence than she could ever use drifted a few days ahead of her. The thought excited her. Merlin whining to be released distracted her.

She set him down, the small movement sending a flare of pain through her injured hand, and she smacked herself in the head.

She didn't need more storm essence. She needed to learn to control what she had. She shivered and hunched, drawing her coat closed and resting on her heels. The potential of the storm held more danger than she liked to remember. Just contemplating it made her long for it.

"It's addictive."

Merlin put his paws on her knee.

She scratched his ears.

"We really need this stuff though."

Merlin licked her hand. She placed the injured one into the snow and held the purple ball to her chest.

Realizations

Monday Noon 1/22

"Hello?" she called out as she entered the back door of her kitchen. No one answered except for Merlin who capered around her feet.

She headed to the bathroom on the main floor, where they kept the medical supplies, and washed her hand good with antibacterial soap before applying a thin coating of antibacterial gel. Yellow pus leaked from the black flaky skin, mixing with the blood that still oozed. Angry red surrounded the small black spot and her entire hand throbbed in time with her heartbeat.

She awkwardly wrapped her hand with gauze, cursing to herself as she fumbled one-handed. She cleaned up the bathroom as best she could with one hand and headed into the kitchen to fix some tea and toast to take with the aspirin. What she wanted to take was a nap. She felt as if she could sleep for a week but so much remained to be done, she forced herself to go into the kitchen instead of her bedroom.

She was just finishing up when Jill came in followed by Boomer.

191

"Can I use the computer to print up my list?" Jill asked as she was hanging up her coat on the hook by the door.

"Sure," Anne said. "But could you go get your dad for me first? Oh, and any kids you see, send them back here, would you? I have a small job for them."

Jill heaved a deep sigh. "I guess I can," she said not at all happy to be sent back out into the cold. "I just got back in," she added petulantly.

"I know, but it's important, hun."

"Fine! Jill heaved a dramatic sigh and added, "Grandma was looking for you. She wants to talk about the bakery kitchen."

"I'll go over as soon as I talk to Dad."

Jill grabbed her coat. "What happened to your hand?"

"It's just a burn."

"A bad one. It's bleeding right through. I'll hurry for Dad."

"Don't hurry, love. That's not why I want him."

But Jill was already running out the door with Boomer at her heels.

Ben and Wayne came hurrying in a few minutes later followed by an anxious Jill and a hyper Boomer who thought all this running around was the best thing ever.

"What happened?" Ben asked, worry in his voice.

"It's nothing" she said, waving her hand airily, then winced, ruining the effect she was going for.

He grabbed her hand, being careful of the bandage. "Ouch. That had to hurt. How'd it happen?"

"Burned my hand." She gave him an insincere smile as she stood. "Maybe you could help me change the dressing? I'm fine," she added as Jill started to follow. "Did you find any kids around for my chore?" she asked as an afterthought.

"No," Jill said, "I didn't see any."

Wayne shrugged and said, "I'm not busy. What do you need done?"

"Could you take the quad down to the lower west field. Not the side where we stood, the opposite one. There's a stack of cloth there you can bring to my mom's."

"If they all haven't softly and silently vanished away," she said under her breath.

"What was that about?" Ben asked as she closed the bathroom door. "And how did you burn yourself?" He reached toward her hand. "Let's see it."

"First, I want to show you something." She reached into her jacket pocket, pulled out the cold ball, and placed it on the counter.

His eyes narrowed as he leaned closer. "What's that?"

"Careful," she said but his hand was already slowing.

Proudly, she withdrew another ball from her pocket. This one glowed faintly and gave off a pleasant heat.

"What is that?" he asked again, eyeing her suspiciously now, not the two balls on the bathroom sink.

Without answering, she reached into her pocket and handed him the lump of what she thought was gold.

"*Errgghh!*" he said, making a surprised sound when she released it.

"I think that's gold," she said, a trace of hysterical laughter in her voice.

"Gold?" he asked dubiously, holding it up to the bathroom light. "Where did you get it?"

"I made it."

His eyes widened, and his mouth dropped open, and she giggled at his expression.

"You what?"

"I made it," she repeated firmly.

"You made it— and you think it's gold?" His amazed expression changed to a concerned look, and he held a hand to her forehead as if he were checking for a fever.

She batted his hand away. "That's why I said I think it is, I'm not sure. I don't know how to tell gold, I mean real gold, from a fake. Do you?"

"No idea." He held the ball up again, turning it slowly.

"I really think it's real though. It looks exactly the same under the storm essence." Anne tapped the cold orb. "Then I made these. The hot one took some experimenting." She waggled her injured hand ruefully.

His eyes widened as she spoke, and he poked the two balls on the sink with a fingertip.

"Holy cow!" He slid to a seat on the toilet.

"I know," she said, while unwrapping the bloody bandage from her hand. "I could hardly believe it myself and I was there."

"So, what do we do now?"

She held out the gauze and sat on the edge of the tub for him to rewrap her hand. "I don't know."

He was quiet while he finished, then he kissed the back of the bandage and said, "Okay, all better."

The familiar words made her smile. She'd heard him say that to Doug and Jill a million times after bandaging scrapped knees and elbows.

Both turned to stare at the orbs. Ben tapped the gold with his finger, then gouged a divot with his nail.

"It's soft."

She nodded.

"It really could be gold."

She nodded again. He looked as amazed as she felt.

"And you made cloth?"

"I could make anything."

"Anything?"

"Maybe." She removed the remains of the last ball of captured storm essence and held it out. "There's lots more in the field. I'm getting better at using it. I can feel it want to be… it's the pure essence of being. The base of everything."

She shrugged and handed the ball to Ben. "I know it sounds crazy, but I *feel* it."

"Oh, I believe you. It just scares the crap out of me." He fell silent and stared at her while rolling the ball in his hands.

"What are you thinking?" she asked.

"I don't know. I have a million thoughts racing through my head."

"Tell me some." She took the ball from him and tucked it into her coat pocket.

"I'm thinking you should go out there and turn that whole wall into gold. Hell, turn every wall into gold until we run out of purple balls." He snickered and said, "We need a better word for those."

He clasped her good hand and sobered. "I'm thinking, what else can you make, and if I can make purple stuff too? Or if anyone can? I'm thinking, I hope you aren't an evil witch we need to burn at the stake."

At that one she jerked a bit. "A witch!" she said indignantly.

He hugged her. "I'm really worried people will say that. Hell, your mother is one of the people I'm worried about saying that!"

She leaned back to meet his eyes. "I'm not a witch. I cast no spells. There was no voodoo. It's all the purple stuff."

He hugged her again, nodding against her hair. "What are we going to do?" he asked, his voice muffled in her neck.

"We can't keep it secret." She leaned away to see his expression.

His expression said yes they could and had better.

"Wayne," she said, "he has the cloth by now."

"*Hmm...* we could make up some kind of story."

"We could," she agreed "but we shouldn't."

His worried gaze pierced her. She rose to sit in his lap.

"Look what happened before when secrets were kept. The government kept the storm a secret. They so confused the world with their fake pictures and reports that no one was really prepared for this storm. Do you think they didn't know what we know about it now? They must have had satellite images. They must've known. Claiming all those reports were just hoaxes…. They're murderers. They murdered every person who believed their lies and followed their advice and stayed in their homes."

"I agree, sweetheart," he said, "but we're not the government."

"We're going to have to be," she said.

The shoulder she leaned on tensed. "What?"

"Think about it." Anne knelt before him, taking his hands in her good one. "What's going to happen if everyone just does what they want? Are we going to let people raid the bakery and take whatever they want or kill our cows?"

"No," he said, "that won't happen."

"Maybe not with our friends, but we don't know half these people. We need law and order. We need to be able to protect what's ours."

"Okay, I see that. We can vote and set up a governor or something."

She tightened her grip. "No! We can't do that now. What's going to happen if we take a vote? Say someone we don't know is voted governor of our land. People will always vote themselves bread and circuses. I'll be a slave if we aren't in charge. I'll have no choice but to do what the people in charge want, and they'll want to control what I can do completely."

"So, what are we going to do, declare ourselves kings?"

"Exactly."

He sat back, looking dumbfounded. "This power went right to your head."

"I guess," she said sadly, "but I do have a power, and I'm not letting anyone else tell me how to use it."

"Not even me?"

"Well, of course I'll listen to you, don't I always? I'm just saying we need to protect ourselves."

He exhaled a long, drawn-out sigh. "Okay, but kings?"

"We are already." Anne rose and absently rubbed her knees, wincing as she banged her burned hand. "This is our land. There is no government. We are the king and queen of it. We say what goes on here, on our land. It doesn't matter what they call us, king, boss, president, laird, none of that matters, it just matters that we're in charge.

Ben slowly nodded.

"We aren't tyrants," she continued, "no one has to bow to us or call us his majesty. I'm fine being called governor or whatever, but we need to set the rules. No votes on us being in charge."

"No votes," He agreed hesitantly. "*Umm...* how are we going to do that?"

She shrugged and wiped her brow, then grabbed the cold ball to chill her hand. "Not sure. But we have too if I want to stay free. I won't let anyone make Jill a slave."

Ben's expression hardened, and he nodded vehemently.

Boomer and Merlin began barking. Ben rose and headed to the kitchen. Anne followed slowly. His expressions had been hard to read. He was already so drawn and pale she wasn't certain how upsetting he'd found her revelations.

All the kids had returned and clamored noisily for Jill to make lunch. They were cheerful, happy to be there, and she knew it hadn't sunk in yet that they'd never go home.

"The cloth was a big hit!" Wayne said. "Where'd you get it?"

"Tell you later," Anne said before Ben could reply. "I'm starved," she continued, "let's make lunch."

The kids eagerly agreed to that, and they set about making sandwiches. Jill went downstairs to get more chips. "Twenty-two more. Go easy on these," she said when she placed the open bag on the table.

"What's being served over at the barn?" Anne asked.

Jill said, "Grandma sent over some big pots of stew and like fifteen loaves of bread. She's making rolls today at the bakery. Well, she's supervising roll making. There's a bunch of people helping her."

"Hamburgers tomorrow," chimed in Cole, his mouth half full of sandwich. "She had us take a butt load out of the freezer in the garage."

"Watch your mouth," Wayne said sharply to his son.

'Sorry," Cole mumbled. "She had us take ALOT out of the freezer," he enunciated.

Anne laughed and turned to Jill. "What do the supplies downstairs look like?"

"Didn't do it yet, been busy," Jill said through a mouthful of sandwich.

"Try to get it done before the meeting. I want to set a good example. Did you print out your lists?"

"Going to, soon as I'm done here."

"Print me out twenty copies of Roberts's Rules of Order, please. I have a copy of that in with the Girl Scout books."

Jill snatched another handful of chips and stood.

"Dishes" –Ben jerked his thumb at the sink— "we don't have a maid."

"Right," Jill grumbled and put her dish in the sink.

Anne said, "I'm going to go lay down a few minutes. I'm exhausted, and my hand hurts."

"What about Grandma?" Jill asked.

"Tell her I'm sorry, but I'll have to meet with her tomorrow about the bakery."

Jill shrugged and headed to the office.

"You okay, sweetheart?" Ben whispered as he kissed her cheek.

She pulled him back to kiss his lips and patted his chest. "I'm fine, just tired." She pushed him away when he hesitated. "Really, I'm fine. Go do whatever it was I pulled you away from earlier and think about what we were talking about."

"I will," he promised and kissed her cheek again.

"One of you kids do the dishes," he said. "Come on, Wayne, let's get back to the barn.

Cole rose to follow them. Ben gently turned him around. "Not until the dishes are cleaned."

* * *

"Wow!" Wayne said as Ben finished filling him in. "That's amazing. I mean the possibilities."

"Yeah." Ben rubbed his aching head and stretched, trying to ease his sore shoulders. "We're going to tell everyone tonight at the meeting."

"That's one meeting I'm not going to miss," Wayne said right as the walkie-talkie that was sitting on the workbench crackled.

"Hello!" a man said. "Hello, can anyone hear me? Hello! We need help! Please, for the love of God! Hello!"

Ben rushed over and grabbed the headset. "I can hear you. Quiet!" he yelled as other people came on the line. The line hushed. "We can hear you. Where are you?"

The line crackled again. "I'm sorry but I'm not familiar with the area enough to know road names. I followed your signs and found this tent here. I'm about a half a mile from where the train station was. There's a group of people a bit down the street aways. They're freezing and won't last another night."

Ben turned to Wayne. "Get the trucks and whatever blankets we can grab from the barn. Make sure we have two of the emergency packs we made. Grab whoever is around and dressed, I'll meet you in ten minutes."

Ben returned his attention to the radio. "Help is coming. What's the number of the tent you're at? It should be on the sign outside it."

"Oh, hold on..., three," he said.

"Okay. We're headed there now. How many of you are there?"

"Eighteen."

"We'll be there in twenty minutes."

"Thank God!"

"Hang in there. You're not alone; help is coming."

He'd reached the truck while speaking with the man. Wayne sat in the driver seat, leaning out the window.

Ben said, "Eighteen people. We better take two trucks. I'm going to run home and get Doug's. Let Pat know where we're going," he continued. "Put some bales in the back. It'll be a cold ride back here."

The Weight of Responsibility
Monday Afternoon 1/22

Snow concealed the debris and corpses but left the landscape looking unfamiliar and hid the road. It was hard to stay in the cleared lane, and Ben worried they'd puncture a tire, then he wondered if Anne could make tires. He couldn't seem to wrap his head around what she could do.

It took them twenty-five minutes of white-knuckled driving to get to station three, a distance that had taken less than ten minutes in the past.

A group of people were huddled together in a clump of bushes under the plastic tent made from greenhouse covering that they'd left behind.

Two men wearing regular clothing stood in front. On closer inspection Ben realized the people inside the tent weren't sitting in brush but wore plant clothing like Phil had.

"Get under the hay," Ben said. "If you need medical attention, get into the green truck. Our medical facilities are really limited though, so cuts and bruises will be taken care of at the barn."

"You have houses?"

Ben nodded and helped the older man who'd sounded amazed that they had houses into the back of the truck. "The storm missed the farm with a little help from my wife. It's a long story that I'm sure you'll get sick of hearing."

The bush people exclaimed and spoke excitedly amongst themselves, and Ben let them chatter. They'd learn soon enough how unlikely it was that the storm had left other untouched pockets.

He paused as he considered maybe there were lots more people like Anne. Maybe this town had few who could use the storm but elsewhere there were thousands. He supposed it didn't matter though as they had no way of knowing or contacting them.

Wayne handed out tablecloths from the winery, the only thing they had left for coverings, and helped them into the back of the trucks. "We have more clothes at home and food."

Ben examined the dressed men. "There's a story here but can it wait for later?"

The older of the men nodded.

"Can you drive the truck?"

"Yes."

Ben handed him the keys and gave a pregnant woman the passenger seat.

"We'll follow you, Wayne. Drop your group at my mother-in-laws house. I'll drop the injured at the Russo's, and take the rest to the barn," he said as he climbed into the back of his truck.

"Follow him exactly. There's only a small cleared lane," he shouted to be heard through the closed window of the truck cab.

The man nodded he understood, and Ben sat, feeling guilty he had a warm coat and thermal underwear while they shivered with cold.

His passengers huddled miserably in the hay, and he wondered what they thought, hoping they didn't believe the disaster had just affected them. He hated to see the hope die in their eyes.

He said, "I know you all must have a million questions, and we'll answer them all after we get you checked in. I'm Ben Windsor, and we're going to the Carmichael Farm

"Joe Conrad," the younger dressed man said and offered his hand.

"It's still standing?" another man asked.

"Yeah, our entire street is still intact." He held up his hand as they started to ask questions. "It's a long story, and I'm sure you'll hear it more than you want to, but right now let's hear about you guys. Is anyone hurt? There's a first-aid kit under the front seat."

The woman in the front seat started to sob. The man next to her reached over and patted her shoulder. "It's okay, honey," he said, but his tone told Ben that the man was just as upset as the woman. He turned to look out the small window in the back of the cab. "Our little boy died. He was only three. He froze to death that first night."

"We tried to keep him warm," she said, sobbing louder. "We were freezing too. There was nothing we could do."

Ben winced. It was clear she felt guilty for surviving when her child hadn't. They all felt guilty and angry and scared.

The man leaned closer and murmured something too low for Ben to hear.

Joe whispered, "Al and I found them huddled under a pile of rubble, but the boy had already died. We took them back to our shelter and shared what we had."

Ben examined Joe closely, wondering if he was able to use the purple cloud like Anne. "How'd you have anything?"

"Al and I'd been hopping trains, living rough. We didn't even know about the storm until that first bad lightning storm hit, and then we began looking for a place to hole up. And we found a good one, an unfinished culvert under old Route Four down there by where the train tracks were." Joe gestured back the way they'd come. "We made ourselves a snug little camp with an old freezer and some packing crates. But we hadn't counted on the rain being as damned hard as it was. We got buried beneath a mud slide and it saved our lives. But I tell you, when we dug ourselves out, I about died of fright. There wasn't a building left standing, and the worse lightning storm I ever saw was passing overhead."

He shook his head and stared into the distance. "We didn't have much, but we were millionaires compared to the folks we found. Our little hideaway was crowded as hell, but so many bodies packed in tightly made it warmer for everyone. But it was clear we needed a better spot and more food. So, Al and me fashioned the leaf clothing for them and went hunting. We'd the snares and fishing lines and some experience with using them." He gave Ben a cheerful grin, clearly not embarrassed about his vagabond existence.

We caught some game and began making clothing. There were twenty-four of us, but we lost two the next night and four more the night after that. Al has their names written down; if they have family out there, they'll want to know what happened to them." His sad expression lightened, and he grinned again as he shook his head. "I was getting despondent, you know. The deaths, the weather, I knew we couldn't take care of all of them much longer, that more would die, and then Al found one of your signs and here we are."

"Thank God," the crying woman said. She turned but couldn't really see into the back, her bulk and the close confines kept her from turning all the way. "Thank you," She sobbed, "Thank you," she repeated, and her husband patted her again. She held her hands out to the heat coming from the dashboard and cried quietly.

The passengers exclaimed in amazement when they reached the outskirts of the farm, as Ben had known they would, and he guided Al to the Russo's where he left the pregnant woman and her husband along with two others with bad frostbite.

The rest he brought to the barn. Chairs and tables taken from the winery had been set up in the main room, and although it wasn't heated, the animal's body heat kept it warm. He gestured to the tables and a bowl of apples sitting on it.

"Help yourself. Someone will be by shortly with hot food and, hopefully, better clothing. The hayloft is warm if a bit scratchy, and you can go wherever you like. We're asking that this room be kept clear for new arrivals and scheduled meals. There's a bathroom through that doorway there, and the water from the tap is safe to drink. If you want to look around, just close doors behind yourself. We're asking the men to urinate in the manure piles downstairs or outside to save the septic system, but this is just temporary. We're working on better accommodations for everyone. My daughter will be around, asking for names and occupations and setting up shower schedules. She can answer your questions, but I'm afraid you'll be stuck in here for a few days at least."

"Warm and dry with food will be like heaven," one of the men said.

Ben gave the woman with him an apologetic grimace. "We're prioritizing families with small children into the homes, and then elderly and single women, but—"

"I'd rather stay with my husband," she said, clutching her husband's arm.

"We're not forcing anyone anywhere," Ben said reassuringly. "There's cards and some books in the hayloft and lots of sewing if you have any skill with that but the lighting is bad up there with just the crank lanterns. We don't allow any fire inside the barn." He gestured to the radio chained to the workbench. "That's for emergencies. We don't have very many radios, so be careful with it."

"Is there anything we can to do to help?" Joe asked.

"I'm headed to the greenhouse to see about repairing the

plastic. I could use a hand with that, or you could help with the farm chores here, or, if your good at cooking, I'm sure they could use a hand at the bakery."

"Greenhouse it is," Joe said while Al laughed and slapped his back.

Al said, "I'll see about helping with the milking. I've done that a time or two before."

Ben pointed to the back stairs. "Someone will be down with the cows and can tell you what needs doing. I appreciate the help."

"And we appreciate the hospitality," Joe said to murmurs of thanks from the rest of the crowd.

Back outside the cold felt bracing.

"You sure you're up for it?" Ben asked Joe. "If you want to rest a few days?"

"I'm good and glad to be of use. I can't tell you how relieved I am that we found you." He stuffed his hands into his pocket and gazed up at the sky. "It'll be a cold one tonight, and we'd have lost some more for sure."

"If we can get the plastic on the greenhouse, and the furnace going, we can bring down a load of bales and make some beds up to ease the crowding in the barn."

"How are we going to dress them all?"

Ben smiled and shot a glance at Joe. He liked the man's attitude. *This man was a doer.* Ben thought Joe would've been a survivor even without the cave in. He wasn't the type to wait for help to arrive.

"My wife is a woman of many talents." He told Joe his story as they walked down the hill.

"That's some tale. There must be more to the story," Joe said when he'd finished.

Ben shrugged. "Nope. It's that simple. She had no idea what she was doing, but she can use the purple cloud. She says it's the essence of everything and with enough of it she could know anything."

"And they fucking knew…"

"Well, maybe not about it being the essence, but about the effects, yes, I think they did. All of our electronics worked. There was no EMP."

"Those fucking bastards."

"I agree."

"What are we going to do about them?"

Ben stopped and stared. It had never occurred to him, but Joe was right. They had known so had likely prepared. They were probably all snug and cozy in some mountain hideout waiting for the storms to dissipate. He was suddenly consumed with fury. He'd never thought himself a vengeful man, but he longed for vengeance. *There would be an accounting,* he promised himself.

"Your wife is a dangerous woman," Joe said thoughtfully.

"I suppose she is." *Anne could use the storm essence on them.* For a moment he wanted to grab a bag of her purple balls and rush home but the thought of Anne at war sickened him.

"I can't think about it now. Now is for recovering, not for war."

"If you say so, but aren't we already at war? That was a hell of opening salvo they threw. What will they follow it up with?"

Ben glanced over the snow-covered vines. "Why would anyone bother with us?"

Joe shrugged and began walking again.

Ben followed at a slower pace, craning his head to peer back up the hill. *Anne,* he thought in mounting dread. *They would bother for Anne.* Before he could really contemplate the thought, Pat hailed him.

"I've lined up twenty-five men who have some clothing, and we're ready when you are, boss."

Ben put thoughts of vengeance and worries of war away. He could worry about it later, he told himself firmly and began directing his helpers in rolling out the plastic.

A Witch or a Saint?

Monday Afternoon 1/22

When Ben returned home, he found Anne asleep with her head on the kitchen table.

Merlin danced around his feet, neither the dog's antics nor his arrival woke her. He frowned as he considered the paleness of her cheeks and woke her with a kiss.

"What time is it," she asked as she rubbed her face, wincing then glaring at her bandaged hand.

He took it and kissed it. "What's got you so tired you fell asleep at the table?"

"That." She pointed to the office door.

Ben's eyebrow rose as he peeked inside. Thick stacks of material covered the floor. He bent to feel the closest, a brown canvas like material that reminded him of his barn coat. He picked it up and shook it out, surprised by the weight and size.

"I'm getting better at it," she said and reached past him to grab a handful of dark blue fabric. It was surprisingly thick and soft and reminded Ben of their comforter.

"I made this one in layers and used essence to fuse it together. The inner layer is cotton ball."

"Cotton?"

"I took some cotton balls and replicated it. I want to see if Jill can do it too."

"What else can you make?" he asked as he let the new blanket fall to the floor. Her tiredness worried him, and he went to pour her a glass of water.

"I have no idea." She accepted the glass and drank the entire thing.

"Well, don't make anything else today. You need to rest."

"Yeah," she agreed, rubbing her temples. She glanced at the kitchen clock and frowned. "Where is everyone?"

"Jill, Julie, Chloe and Sue are at the sugar shack using the tables there, making something. Doug and Will are down at the greenhouse starting it up. Wayne is at your Mom's and I saw his daughter there but not Cole. I have no idea where he is. Marie was at the barn earlier, but I haven't seen her in a while. She's probably at the Russo's helping Abby. There's still no sign of Edward, I'm starting to get worried," he admitted.

"Go look for him tomorrow."

"I'm not sure I can. Maybe Wayne or Pat can. I've been showing people how to do the milking and feeding, but I have to stay close in case they need me."

"Doug can do it," Anne said.

"He can," Ben agreed, "but he's busy too. Speaking of busy, I've got to go finish up the milking for the night, it's almost four-thirty."

She started to stand.

"No! You rest! I have enough help over there."

"You sure?"

"Yes," he said and leaned over to kiss her. "Go up to bed. I'll wake you when I'm done, and we'll go to your Mom's for the meeting."

"Okay," she agreed. "Sorry," she added in a small voice.

"There's nothing to be sorry for." He smoothed her hair back, wishing he could smooth the worry lines from her face. "Using the storm essence like you're doing is tiring. Who knows how you do it or what it costs you? Go to bed."

She mumbled agreement and plodded upstairs, and his worry grew. He couldn't remember the last time she'd napped like this.

He gathered a stack of the new cloth and headed back to the barn. The canvas material would be perfect for keeping the hay from poking them. *This is surreal,* he thought bemusedly. *I can't believe I'm carrying around cloth conjured from thin air. What's next, leprechauns?*

The cloth Anne had made was greatly appreciated as he'd known it would be. He didn't mention its origins and let them divide it up as they liked.

"We'll have more tomorrow, I think, but this is it for tonight."

Joe held up a piece of cloth and examined it in the dim light cast by the crank lanterns. He said nothing, but Ben knew he realized the material had been crafted by Anne.

Joe nodded slightly and spread the material over the hay, gesturing for a woman who looked on with interest and a bit covetously to sit there.

"This is great. Real helpful. We're lucky your wife is so kind. She's a saint to put us all up like this."

Ben said, "She's a kind woman. A good woman. I'm sure you've all heard the story of how we came through the storm, and I can assure you she had no idea how she did it."

No one responded but most looked thoughtful, not afraid or hostile, and he supposed he'd have to settle for that.

"We're working hard at accommodations," he continued. "We have some ideas and hopefully we'll move most of you to better places soon. Are you all getting enough to eat?"

"Its fine," someone in the back said, "we appreciate all you're doing for us. I wish we could do more for ourselves but without shoes we're stuck here. Maybe we can make some with this canvas though. It looks pretty sturdy."

Another said, "Is it true what they say about your wife? She's some kind of witch or something?"

"No." Ben stiffened. "Anne isn't a witch or a saint. It's true she was able to use whatever was in the storm to make a shield or something over this street, but it wasn't magic."

"Sure sounds like magic" someone else said. The hayloft was too dim and crowded for Ben to see who spoke.

He said, "Well, so does a radio if you didn't know about radio waves, but it isn't magic, we just don't know how she did it. More cloth should be coming soon," Ben said changing the subject. "I'll leave a walkie-talkie in here tonight so you guys can hear the meeting. I wish you all could go but there's just not enough room for everyone. How about if you pick someone to attend who can fill you in on anything you can't hear through the walkie-talkie?"

"Sure, we can do that," Joe said and there were nods all around.

Ben glanced at his watch. "I've got to run, it's milking time."

Joe joined Ben as he was flushing the last line.

Ben said, "We'll have to start milking by hand soon. Production will go down while the cows get used to it.

"Ham-handed klutzs will be giving these beauties mastitis if we aren't careful," Al said as he dumped his pail of fresh milk into the tank. He slapped the side of the tank. "Storage will be a problem. We don't have nearly enough small containers. Without refrigeration this here will be worthless."

Ben grinned ruefully, "We might have a solution for that.

Joe lifted an eyebrow. "Anne?"

"Yeah… Tonight's meeting should be enlightening."

"Well, then, I'm glad to be the barns representative."

"You both better get going if you're going to be on time," Al said, making a shooing gesture. "I'll see to the cleanup."

Ben nodded gratefully and gestured Joe to follow. "Come meet Anne and the family before the meeting. I just need to make a quick stop first."

No one was at the sugar shack, and he pursed his lips as he considered where they'd all gotten to. He'd been hoping to speak with his daughter privately before the meeting.

The two men headed to Ben's house.

"Make yourself at home," he said, as he led the way inside. "I'll just be a few minutes."

The house bustled with activity when he arrived. Every seat at his dining room table was full. All strangers, he noted as he nodded a greeting.

The kitchen table was empty except for Alicia who jumped up and scurried to the stove.

"I saved plenty for us," she said. She lowered her voice to a whisper. "Sue said I'm to stay here and guard the kitchen and not allow anyone except family upstairs."

Ben took the bowl of pasta she handed him and gestured with his chin to the kitchen Island. "Joe, this is Wayne's daughter, Alicia. Have a seat here and I'll be right back. Alicia, honey, make Joe here comfortable. I'm sure he'd appreciate a big bowl of pasta and some of those delicious rolls." Ben took a few rolls and headed upstairs, calling over his shoulder, "We might be a few minutes late. Let them know, we'll meet you over there."

A sliver of light leaked from the partially open door of his bedroom. Anne was awake and siting up in bed with a notebook on her knees.

"Still at it?" He handed her the plate and one of the rolls, keeping the other for himself. "Did you get any sleep at all?"

Anne slid her legs over so Ben could sit down.

"Some."

She did look a bit better, Ben thought as he kissed her temple.

"Yum. This is delicious. Who made it?"

"No idea." Ben took her fork and a big bite, "but it is good."

Anne handed him the plate after taking two more bites and picked up her notebook. "I made a list of people I think we should have running things for a while," she started to say.

"Eat!" he commanded, taking the notebook from her and handing back her plate.

She meekly picked her plate back up and started eating.

He read over the list she'd made and said, "Looks good, if they all agree."

Anne shrugged and swallowed. "They will, I think. They're the best choices we have. They're all good people, and they'll see that they're needed."

"*Mmm hmm,* so when are you going to spring our surprises on them?"

"I'm thinking I'll clobber the housing first. Then I'll bring it up as new business."

"It's your show." He shrugged.

Her eyes narrowed anxiously as she scanned the list. "You don't think I should tell them?"

He said, "I think they need to know. I'm just worried about the response."

"I have faith in them. It'll be fine." She wiped her plate with her last piece of bread. "Sorry, dog," she said as she ate it and licked her fingers. She ruffled Merlin's hair and said, "You have to stay home again tonight, little man. Too many people there for you."

She jumped out of bed and headed to the bathroom. "I'll just be a minute," she added and closed the door.

"Meet you downstairs," Ben said, gathering up her plate and heading to the kitchen.

Sue and Pat sat at the table chatting with Joe. Alicia took Ben's empty plate and handed him a full one that he ate standing.

"Hello," Anne said when she appeared.

"Anne, this is Joe. He's just arrived and going to be the representative for the barn folks."

"Nice to meet you." Anne offered her hand.

Ben watched anxiously but Joe shook it with no hesitation.

"We should get going," Sue said, and handed Pat his coat.

"Girls!" she called and went to the living room doorway to talk with her daughters.

"Listen to Alicia. When she says it's bedtime, you're to go directly to bed!"

Ben and Anne exchanged grins as Chloe and Emily complained. It eased Sue's heart too, Ben was happy to note when she turned and gave him her first real smile in days.

Sue's smile faded when she took her husband's arm.

"Let's get this done," she said and marched from the house.

Ben followed. He dreaded this coming talk too.

Revelations

Monday Evening 1/22

Hi, everyone," Anne said when they entered her mother's kitchen. Butterflies danced in her stomach, and she regretted eating so quickly.

Strangers and neighbors glanced up from the papers and plates before them, nodding or murmuring greetings but avoiding her eyes as much as they could.

The house was even more crowded than it had been the previous night. A karaoke machine sat on the dining room table alongside one of Doug's old walkie-talkies. There were notebooks and pencils before each chair with a bigger stack of loose-leaf paper and four, three-ring binders before the chair Sue sat in.

She immediately began flipping through the papers.

Anne stopped to kiss her mother's cheek. Helen sat at the head of the table with a half-empty cup of tea before her.

She headed over to Jill and gave her a quick hug. "Hand out those printouts you made to the heads of the houses, please."

Jill grinned at her. "Way ahead of you, Mom. We already did

this afternoon."

Anne grinned back. "You're a smart kid." She gave her another hug and promised herself to make time to speak with both girls.

"Come look at what we did today," Jill said proudly, pointing to a big map of the street. "We made it this afternoon"

Anne leaned forward to read the small printing beneath the drawing. Jill had drawn in the entire farm, including all the trails and roads and labeled each house with little slots beneath them with removable pink and blue name plates inserted.

Anne picked one out of the slot by her house. Sue Foster thirty-nine, it read on the front of it. She flipped it over, secretary, basic first aid, basic cooking. She put it back in the slot and grabbed a blue one. It read Patrick Foster thirty-nine on the front. She turned it over to read the back; it read, market research, welder, hunter, basic first aid, basic carpentry, mechanic.

"Nice," she said to Jill when she put it back. She noted that there were some tags paper clipped together and pinned to the board. "What's this?"

"Those are family groups or people who requested to stay together," Jill answered. "You see the empty slots there?" and she pointed at one of the houses. "We figured on at least twenty people per house at the homeowner's discretion. That gets most of the families in a house. We'll let the heads of the house choose who they want from the people up on the board here. Everyone else can go down to the greenhouses. It'll be easier on them and us that way," she added.

"Great job, Jill!" Anne said enthusiastically. "This will be a huge help."

She turned to Doug who was listening. "You guys are a great help," she said giving him a quick hug, "but I need another favor." Doug sighed. "It's just a small one," she added.

He nodded.

"I need the biggest block of fresh chopped wood we have, and a few rocks of varying sizes. Nothing too big or small, about two to five pounds."

His eyebrows rose as she spoke. "What for?"

"You'll see." She smiled and shooed him out.

"What's it for?" Jill asked.

"You'll just have to wait and see too," Anne said, pulling lightly at her daughter's ponytail.

"Attention!" she said loudly. "This meeting is being called to order. There has been a revision of the seating plan. We want one person representing the house to sit at the table. Take ten minutes to decide who it will be, and then take your seat at the table. Thank you!"

She sat and gestured for Ben to sit. "Karen, you too." She said to the woman who lived alone two houses down the street from her.

"Joe," Ben said, "take a seat here, please. "He's representing the barn," Ben said to the room in general.

Anne examined Joe as he exchanged greetings and introductions with her neighbors as they took their seats. He was taller than Ben and maybe a bit older, rangy, with dark hair and eyes. His hair was slightly curly; he needed a trim but had recently had a shave. His eyes were sad but his jaw firm. She liked him immediately.

She beckoned to Abby. "Have a seat by Dan, please."

Abby rose an eyebrow but took the indicated seat.

Anne waved Wayne and Marie over. "Please take a seat at the table. Dave, can you please take a seat here?" She scanned for Kate but didn't see her. She pointed at one of the chairs behind her against the wall in front of the windows of the dining room, "And Dean, could you please come over too, and save a seat for Doug," she added.

Anne stood. "Thank you for coming again. It's going to take us a while and a bit of trial and error to get organized. I see a lot of people I don't know and a lot of good friends here. I hope we can all be patient. This housing situation is temporary, but it's also very serious. I would appreciate it if you'd all bear with me for a minute as I make some introductions."

Ben depressed the button on the radio and handed Anne the microphone from the karaoke machine.

Anne cleared her throat and tried to sound confident. "I asked Abby to sit at the table as the new head of our medical division. She knows our entire neighborhood and has a wide experience in the field." She gave Abby a small apologetic shrug. "I'm sorry I didn't get a chance to talk to any of you about this, but everything has been happening fast." Abby nodded, and Anne continued. "Jill made a list of everyone and their prior jobs. Get together with her after the meeting to pick out your staff. I don't need to tell you all how serious this is. We have a lot of sick and hurt people here who will need care for a while. Most of them Abby is already looking after. Any medical questions should be brought to her. I'm sorry, Abby, I know it's a lot to ask, but we need you. I'm promoting you to doctor. As a surgical nurse, you're the closest we have."

"My next appointee is Sue Foster." Sue looked surprised at this but then nodded as Anne went on, "Sue is going to be in charge of personnel. Any of the house leaders needing anything, see Sue. She knows we're everyone is. If you don't know who to ask about something, she's your girl. She'll find it out for you."

Sue stood to wave acknowledgement at the people crammed into the living room. "I can be found at the Windsor house or reached by radio if anyone needs to speak with me."

She resumed her seat as Anne said, "Okay, next we have Ben Windsor. He's in charge of the barns and all our current domestic livestock." Ben nodded in acknowledgement.

"Dean, I'd like you to be the representative for our house. Anyone living at Windsor should go to you if they have questions or problems," Anne said.

"Okay," he said, looking puzzled.

He was probably wondering why I'm not doing it, Anne thought.

"Next, we have David Foster. You've been hunting here with your brother for years. You know the area really well. I want you and Kate to be in charge of hunting fishing and gathering. That means you keep track of who's going where for what and you pick hunting teams and make sure they can use the weapons safely."

"No problem." Dave said

"Anyone wanting to be on a hunting or fishing team, speak with him. He can be found at Windsor house as well."

"Next we have food production." She looked down at her notebook and picked up some loose pages and tapped them to neaten them up. "You all know Helen has been doing the cooking and supervising most of the meals. She's been doing a great job, and I'd like her to stay in a supervisory position, but she needs someone to run the bakery.

"I'll help out when I can," she went on, seeing the surprise on her mother's face, "but I'll be doing something else most of the time, so we'll have to find someone else to run it full time. I suggest we find a few people and see who works out. I'm sorry I didn't get a chance to talk to you about this earlier, but I've been busy."

Her mother nodded, her perplexed expression deepening.

Right then Doug and Will entered, carrying a thin hunk of new cut wood and a bag of rocks. "Nice timing," Anne said. "Just place the board on the table here."

She smiled at Will who smiled sadly back, and she promised herself to make time to talk with him.

"Sure thing," Doug said in the tone of voice you'd use when humoring a mental patient.

"Okay, one last appointee. Doug, I want you in charge of buildings."

"Me?" he exclaimed in surprise.

"You're an engineer and you know the area; you'll be fine. Anyone who wants to build anywhere on the farm has to ask you first. We don't want sheds going up willy-nilly all over the place."

"I'll do my best."

"Sit in one of these chairs here." She pointed at the chairs lining the wall behind her. "Last, but not least, is our house leaders. As you know, Judy Young's house is vacant. I'm sure if she were here that she'd want to help all she could. She was a good woman and a good friend to us. We need a volunteer to organize the Young house."

No one responded. Anne sighed with exasperation. She stood to stand in the doorway. "Any one of you could do it. I'm sorry I don't know any of your names yet, we'll have time to get acquainted later, but right now we need someone to take charge of Judy's house."

A woman raised a hesitant hand.

Anne gave her an encouraging smile.

"I'm Rachel Bernstein," she said, "I'm a realtor, or I was a realtor. I'll do it."

"Great," Anne said. "Get together with Pat Sue and Doug after the meeting and they can help you get what you need. Some of you people that haven't got anywhere to stay talk to Rachel please.

"If everyone here at the table could state their name and house for the record, we'll get started. She pointed at Todd who was sitting next to her.

Anne introduced her neighbors, gesturing them to seats and was heartened to see the small activity brighten them.

"That's everyone." Anne rapped the hammer on the board in front of her. "This meeting is called to order. On to old business. As you can see, we have this lovely board behind us made for us by Jill Julie and Sue. Take a bow, girls. What you see here is a beautifully made drawing of the houses on this street. These tabs are people who need to be in a house," and she pointed at the papers pinned to the board, "these tabs are empty slots. If you could please try to pick at least twenty people for your houses tonight before you leave, that would be great."

"Twenty!" Henry Brooks exclaimed, and his scowl deepened. "That's outrageous. I can't feed twenty people."

Anne banged her hammer down. "You're out of order! Please save questions for the end." Anne turned back to the board. "As you can see, some houses are almost full already. If you want to make any changes, please talk to the head of the house where you'll be swapping, and keep in mind, please" –she rose her voice as the crowd began muttering— "this is just temporary. Any supplies you need, please see the appropriate division head. If you don't know where to go, or who to ask, ask Sue."

Sue waved around the room again.

"We plan on moving the people from the barn to the greenhouses as soon as possible," she went on. She turned to Joe, "There's lights, bathrooms, and hot and cold water there. We can rig a shower of some sort and try to make it more comfortable, but we don't have enough gas to run the fans, so it might be too warm during the day. The sides roll up and the doors can be opened but we plan on planting too, so you'll have to be careful not to let it get too cold. The furnace will keep it warm enough at night.

We want to make everyone as comfortable as we can, but everyone will need to compromise a bit. We're hoping you'll share the warmer clothes so that people can get outside a bit to stretch their legs. The winery is just a short walk from the greenhouses. It isn't heated, but it does have big windows that should keep it warm enough to use during the day. We're moving the sewing machines there, but there will be space for other projects or just to sit and visit. If you have an idea that needs space, talk to Sue. She'll know how to get you set up.

"The greenhouses share a common storefront with the bakery. We plan to move some tables and chairs there too. All public cooking will be done there starting tomorrow. Helen will be making a menu and overseeing the distribution of food supplies. When you have a count of your house's occupants, inform Helen and she'll insure you get the correct amount of food delivered. We need at least ten volunteers to clean the kitchens and eating areas. Please speak with Helen if you're willing to be on the cleanup crew. If we don't get enough volunteers, we'll implement a rotation and assign everyone hours. Any questions on housing?" She asked, looking pointedly at Henry.

He waved irritably at her.

She exchanged a quick grin with Ben who winked.

"On to the next item of business. Since we'll be opening up the greenhouses, we need some volunteers to oversee the planting we're going to be doing. If you have any skill with plants or just want to learn, find time to see me. I'll be looking for someone else to put in charge of them, so I'm really hoping someone else can manage it.

"On to new business. First, our rescue attempt has been successful. We've retrieved eighteen more survivors. If you have any ideas for finding or helping survivors, please see Wayne," she added.

Jill rose her hand.

"Yes, Jill."

"We could leave cars parked with directions and keys, so people could bring themselves here,' she said. "We have more cars than we need or have any use for."

Anne nodded her approval. "It's a great idea if people want to volunteer their vehicles but those vehicles are all private property. Carmichael Farm is volunteer only. What's yours is yours. You're not required to do anything or give anything away that you don't want too. Anyone can feel free to leave at any time. We have to choose the kinds of neighborhood we want to be. Keep in mind that if you leave your car out there with a note and full tank of gas, you might never see it again. There would be nothing stopping someone from driving off anywhere they wanted in it although I don't think anyone would get very far at all in a car with roads being like they are."

Anne noted some of the them looked as if the thought leaving was a new idea. "Any of us could leave whenever we wanted too," she said again.

"Where would we go?" A man in the back of the room cried out.

Anne held up her hand to quiet the growing mummers. "I don't know," she said. "That would be up to you. We're safe here, warm, with food to eat. I don't know how true that would be anywhere else. I'm sure all the cities are a disaster with all the buildings collapsed." She stopped talking to clear her throat. Picturing the cities sickened her. "Well, I wouldn't want to be there, but down south where it's warmer, I'm sure there are lots of survivors. Maybe not with our benefits— we probably have modern convinces they don't, but it's an option. And I don't want to start rumors, this is just my own opinion, but I personally think our government knew about the effects of the purple cloud and prepared for it so there could conceivable be a big contingent of them somewhere.

"I know for sure I want nothing to do with people who'd let this happen with no warning. But, again, it's up to you as individuals to make up your own minds. If you do want to go, talk to the head of your house, and we'll see what we can do about supplying you, but if you steal supplies and sneak off, we'll track you down and leave you naked where we find you." She straightened back up, realizing just then she'd been leaning forward with her hands braced on the table. Her burned hand started to throb as soon as she noticed it.

An embarrassed flush burned across her cheeks as she cleared her throat. "Anyone else have any new business they want to bring up?" she asked.

Helen stood. "I'd like to propose a day of mourning to take place this Sunday out on the point by the big bonfire."

"I second it," a woman in the crowd said.

"All those in favor?" Anne asked.

The entire room said aye.

"All those opposed?"

She waited but there was no opposition just quite sniffles.

"Motion carries. Sunday is officially a day of mourning; coordinate within your houses please as to what sermons we want to perform. Anyone else with new business?"

The room seemed to grower tenser, and she hoped it was her imagination.

She took a deep breath and paused to gather her thoughts. The microphone in her hand trembled, and she used both to steady it, staring at her clasped hands as she said, "This is hard for me. No one likes to be different and the unknown can be scary, but I promise you all that my word can be trusted." She glanced up to gauge their response and was encouraged by the interested expressions. She relaxed her hold a bit on the microphone.

"I will *always*," and she put as much emphasis on always as she could, "tell the truth as best I can. I want you all to trust me" — she gestured around the table— "to trust each other. I don't think anyone should have to be a completely public person, to have to defend their every thought and idea, but I do think you should mean what you say, that your word is your bond. Without our words spoken in truth we have no honor and without honor we're worthless. A poor man who speaks the truth would be a better friend to me than a rich one who lies." There were nods and some looks of confusion.

She took a deep breath." Okay, this is the truth as I know it. I know there are rumors of what happened on the night of the storm, but this is what happened from my perspective."

She proceeded to tell them what she'd told Ben when she'd awakened. "That brings us to my purple balls," she said, placing one on the board in front to her. "I really need a new name for them."

Nervous laughter erupted, and she was happy to note most still looked interested and not afraid.

"First, let me show you what happens when an item comes into contact with my purple haze." She turned to Jill. "Hand me a piece of garbage from the can."

Jill quickly returned from the kitchen with a discarded Styrofoam package from the hamburger they'd made earlier; it had a couple of peels from what looked like a cucumber sticking to it.

"How's this?" she asked.

"Perfect." Anne placed the Styrofoam on the board in front of her and moved a drop of the purple haze over it. "Watch closely," she said.

Everyone leaned over and watched intently as a red glow covered the Styrofoam. Before you could blink there was nothing left of the Styrofoam but a black sludge puddle, a few cucumber peels with newly marred skin, the faintest whiff of ozone, and a greenish glow. "That glow" —she traced her finger over the green, being careful not to touch it— "means there's active essence there."

"Active essence?" Sue asked.

Anne shrugged. "I don't know what else to call it. It feels like it's made up of potential or the essence of things. I'm sorry I have no good words to describe it."

"Essence is as good as anything," Sue said with a shrug.

"I'm not sure who else can do this, and I'd like for you all to try at some point, but I'm going to show you where the cloth came from."

Everyone sitting at the table leaned forward, and she hid her smile.

She picked up one of the bigger rocks, placed it atop the freshly cut piece of wood, and thought about cloth. This was a quick easy process for her now and before you could really see what had happened, a gray swath of fabric unfolded across the table in front of her.

Shrieks and cries of disbelief mingled with awed exclamations, and a woman yelled it's a fake in a shrill voice over a louder cacophony of how did you do that?

Anne glanced at Ben who gave her a reassuring nod.

"I'm sure you're wondering how I did that, and the real answer is I don't know, but my explanation is, I move some of the essence over onto the rocks and will it to be cloth."

"Move it?" Dean asked, "I didn't see you move it."

"Will it?" Sue asked at the same time. "What's that mean?"

"Let me try again slower." She picked up the purple sphere and handed it to Sue. "I can sense that the same way you can smell things. Like if I made a pie and left it on the counter, I could it smell it better the closer I came, and then, if I took a bite, I could taste it— sort of like the smell is realized."

Sue nodded along.

"The essence reeks of potential to me." She darted a glance at Jill who watched with wide eyes and nodded slowly.

"It feels like it's straining to become something as if it has the possibility to become anything. When it's loose, not constrained inside the sphere, it knows everything it touches down to the smallest molecule, and I can see what it knows. To make the essence become something, I picture the item as exactly as I can. Not a physical picture of it, but the essence of it."

"I understand your words but not how you're doing it," Sue said.

Anne shrugged and grinned ruefully at the intent observers. "I have no idea how I do it either."

"It looks like magic to me. You make the rock glow green and then it's cloth." Sue picked up the gray cloth as she spoke and rubbed it between her fingers.

"You can't see the purple haze when it's released from the sphere?"

"I can," Jill said as Sue shook her head.

"Can anyone else?" Anne asked and glanced at the frowning faces. She placed another rock atop the board and let a dollop of essence coat it.

No one admitted to being able to see the purple haze. Anne released another small amount and formed it into a ball that she sailed around the room, being careful to keep it from touching anything. Only Jill watched its progress. Everyone else stared at her or the line of green phosphorescence on top of the rock.

"You all see the green glow?" she asked and waited for the crowd to shift as people in the back pressed forward to peer into the doorway. There were nods all around and low comments about what they saw. Some sitting at the table were leaned closer to watch in fascination while others were leaning back to get as far away as possible.

"I'll come around to each house so everyone gets a chance to see up close," she promised.

"I'm filming this with my phone," Doug added. "You can talk to me later if you want to see."

"Here's how it works so far," Anne said. "I think to the essence inside the ball— go there." She pointed at the rock in front of her. "It goes where and how I will it. Jill and I can see the essence still, not just the green glow. Then, I try to let its potential make it into something I want by thinking of the thing as clearly as I can. I'm going to try to make a gavel. I never made anything like it before, so it might take me a few tries. I know rock pretty well. I learned that this afternoon, and I'm not trying to change its essence just it's shape, so I'm not even certain it can be done but I think I can do it." She closed her eyes a second to better visualize what she wanted, then opened them, picturing a gavel and the rock in front of her shimmered as if hot and reformed too quickly for the eye to follow.

The gavel she'd made wasn't perfectly formed, it was more like a bad copy, but it was clearly a gavel. It hadn't taken much essence to change the shape. Most of the essence remained on the new gavel. She directed it back into the ball.

"Tada!" she said and picked up the gavel as the crowd exclaimed. She let the talk go on for a minute, then banged her new gavel on the piece of wood.

"Magic!" A woman said loudly and with derision.

"Witchcraft," another said, and the tone of the exclamations changed.

"No," Anne said firmly and stood. "It isn't witchcraft or magic. I'm not casting a spell or making deals with the devil. I'm accessing the potential in the purple essence."

"You're what?" Helen asked.

Anne shrugged helplessly as she tried to explain it. "These purple balls are pure potential, unformed matter. They have the potential to be anything. Well, anything naturally occurring as far as I can figure. During that storm, when it was swirling all over, I think it made me a little drunk— too much input, too much...," and she trailed off, frustrated at not being able to put her impressions into words. "I don't know how to describe it."

"Is it alive?" Dave asked.

"I'm not sure." Anne considered it. "It could be alive like a plant but isn't alive like person. It has no thoughts or at least none that I can tell."

"How do you control it?" Helen asked.

"I just tell it what I want. I think at it," she went on helplessly. "We're connected somehow. I can feel it out there."

There was dead silence at this, and she looked up, startled. "What?"

"You can feel it out there right now?" Ben asked.

"Yes. I can feel were the balls are and the storm moving away from here."

"The storm's still moving?" someone asked.

"Yes." Anne turned to stare out the dining room window. "It's steadily getting further away. It hasn't diminished in size. As far as I can tell, it's getting bigger."

Jill was nodding in agreement.

"But that means it'll come back," Abby said in a small voice.

"Probably," Anne said and shivered in anticipation.

For a moment the room was completely silent before it erupted into loud shouting as everyone began talking at once. Anne banged the gavel down hard a few times. "There's no need to panic," she said, "We're safe here."

"Safe?" a woman shouted, her voice thick with scorn. "We're not safe! It's just a matter of time until anything we make turns to dust."

Anne banged the gavel again. "Not true," she said. "We know now that anything we make with non-natural products needs to be underground or under a shield."

"A shield," Joe said thoughtfully.

She nodded at him, grateful for the support. "I did it once. I can do it again."

The loud talked died to quieter comments.

Henry Brooks said, "You won't live forever though, and you can't shield the whole world."

Anne pointed at Jill. "I'm not the only one who can sense it. There must be others besides us. I did learn to harness some of it too. We're just learning what can be done with it. Let's not panic before we have too," she finished.

She reached into her pockets and pulled out the other balls she'd made. "I also made these earlier today." She placed them on different ends of the board with the gold ball in the center.

Essence of the Storm

"What are they?" Mike Ward asked as he leaned closer.

"This one emits cold." Anne pointed at the purplish ball, "and this one heat." She pointed at the orangish ball, "and that one is gold, I think."

There were some sharp intakes of breath at this. Mike reached toward the gold ball.

"Stop!" a man shouted urgently from the back of the room.

A tall, thin, black man Anne and never seen before pushed his way to the front. "Don't touch it!" he said, his voice high with urgency.

"What, why?" Anne jerked back, instinctively clasping her hands to her chest.

"How do we know it's not explosive or radioactive?"

"*Umm...*, we don't." Anne leaned away from the table. Her sense of accomplishment switched to dismay so fast it left her slightly breathless. Just seconds ago she'd been proud she could make something so helpful and now she felt sick with the thought that she might've made something deadly dangerous. It had never occurred to her there might be danger it. *But it should have*, she thought grimly, exchanging worried glances with Ben.

Everyone at the table leaned as far back as they could.

"Why would they be?" Ben asked.

"Daryl Santire." He held out his hand for Anne to shake. "I'm a science teacher. "If it emits light," — he pointed at the glowing orange ball— "that means it's producing rays. What we scientists call electromagnetic radiation. We don't know what kind of radiation it's producing though."

"What kinds are there?" Anne asked nervously.

"Let's put these somewhere outside while we talk," he said.

"I'll do it," Anne said when Ben reached for them. "I've been carrying them all day. No sense in exposing you." She gathered them up, and the crowd moved away to let her through.

She could hear them questioning Daryl and Ben as soon as the door closed behind her and winced at the accusing tones. She placed the balls on the rock wall in front of the house and lingered a few minutes to give them time to vent without her present. The quiet when she entered told her they hadn't been kind in her absence. Ben's furious scowl and Jill's scared expression firmed her step though.

"My family had nothing to do with it." The silence seemed to deepen as she glared around the room. She took a breath and tried to smooth her face as she turned to Daryl. "How do we tell if they're safe or not?"

"We can test to see if it's explosive although testing has unknown risks. By your description of how you're making things, you condensed the essence of heat into a sphere and programmed the sphere to release the heat at the temperature you wanted. Who knows what would happen if that sphere releases the heat all at once? But I'm more concerned with radiation. It's obviously producing some sort of radiation, unless the laws of physics have completely changed, which I admit might well be the case. As far as I know, no one ever postulated the existence of an element as you describe."

He shook his head and rubbed his neck with both hands, giving her a crooked smile. "I'm sorry, I'm getting off topic. What you and everyone else wants to know, is if the things you're crafting are harmful."

Anne darted a glance around, and everyone was staring at Daryl with hopeful eyes. She hoped he'd have good answers too.

He continued, "Well, everyone has heard of X-rays, but there's many more types, alpha, beta gamma and so on." He waved his hand in the air in a dismissive gesture. "I won't go into the science of it, but basically, we have harmful and nonharmful types of radiation. Light, like the type emitted by lightbulbs, is ultra-violet radiation. In large doses it's harmful, but a light bulb doesn't emit enough to bother us. Sitting under a lightbulb all day is about the equivalent of sitting in the sun for a minute. Not all radiation is deadly. What we need is a Geiger counter."

"We don't have one," Anne said.

Daryl said, "I can make a crude version. I'll need some supplies, and it won't tell us what kind of radiation it's emitting, it's entirely possible that it's emitting a new kind of radiation. I wish I had access to my lab, but I can jury-rig testing equipment that can tell if the radiation is harmful." He gave Anne an apologetic glance.

She nodded back numbly.

"What do you need?" Ben asked.

Daryl thought a second, "Well, first, I'll need some 10K resistors, two percent or better, and some Darlington transistors."

Anne sighed and exchanged doubtful glances with Ben. "We don't have any of those things."

Doug said, "Actually, we might, Mom. We just need some old electronics."

Marcus and Henry Wilson both raised their hands.

Doug said, "We have an old boom box in the broken-down truck in the woods out back and the broken radio in the dash."

Daryl nodded approvingly. "Get those. And I'll need a nine-volt battery, a tin can of some kind, some wire, and a soldering tool. I'll make a device to check for ionizing radiation. I can explain in more depth later to those who are interested."

Ben stood. "We have those things in the workshop."

Helen handed over a decorative tin box that had once held chocolates "There's batteries in the junk drawer," she added.

"How long to make this?" Anne asked.

"Say, an hour or so," Daryl said. "You understand it's just going to measure ions; it won't tell us what kind they are. I'll need to do more testing to determine the dangers."

Anne nodded. "What about the cloth?"

"No idea." Daryl shrugged, and his rueful scowl deepened.

"We should probably place it outside away from us for the time being. It isn't emitting heat or light, and no one appears to be affected, but better safe than sorry. Sorry about that," he said to the dismayed cries of the people already wearing it. "You all might want to shower off too," he added. "I'll check everything as soon as I can. Don't make anything more until we know."

Anne stood at the table in shock. She banged the gavel with a shaking hand. "Please, all return to your homes and remove all formed cloth items and shower as soon as possible. We'll send someone to notify you as soon as we learn anything. The next meeting will be on Thursday at the greenhouse. Everyone should fit inside so everyone can attend. If we need an emergency meeting, let Sue or I know, and we'll notify everyone to gather. Also, Sue, if you could find some kind a bell or have the building committee make one, we should put it out on the hill by the fire to ring in an emergency."

"Good idea," Sue said. "I'll get right on it."

"I move to adjourn the meeting," Anne said, proud her voice sounded steady when she wanted to burst into tears. "All those in favor," Everyone agreed. "The ayes have it. Meeting adjourned." She stood. "I'm going to go move my stuff; you all go to your houses."

The talk grew louder and the sidelong glances she received were speculative as if they couldn't decide if she were a blessing or a curse. She tried to pretend not to hear or see the disparaging remarks and glances and turned to Joe.

"Joe, wait a minute. Abby!" she called out, "can you fit some extra showering in at your house?"

Abby nodded as she stood and grabbed her jacket from the back of her chair. "The showering isn't a problem if they don't mind cold water, but what will they wear when they get out?"

Helen pushed herself to her feet. The slow hard way she moved worried Anne. Her revelations seemed to have aged her mother and her feelings of guilt intensified.

Helen headed to the stairs, saying, "The sewing crew has stacks of drapes they haven't gotten to yet, take them. It isn't clothes but it's good enough for modesty's sake."

"Roger and Terry, how about you guys? Can you fit some people in for showers?"

Dean gave her a quick hug. "We can fit some too. Don't worry so much. It could be perfectly safe. Let's go split those curtains up. We'll make do."

Terry and Roger nodded agreement and headed off with Dean.

"Joe, go back and split your robe wearers into four groups and send them to these houses." Anne pointed on the map Jill had made. "They're the closest houses to the barn. You got that?" She waited for his nod, knowing Joe hadn't had much time to get accustomed to where everything was located.

"No problem," he said, "Where can I get a map?"

"Ask Sue. I'm sure she could make you one."

"Thanks, it'll be a big help for us in the barn."

Anne nodded and glanced around for Daryl, but he'd already left with Ben. "See you tomorrow at the greenhouse!" she called in a vague goodbye as she scurried for the door to get her balls that she hoped weren't balls of death.

Daryl the Physicist

Monday Night 1/22

Ben led Daryl to his workshop at the barn.

Daryl examined the work benches and cabinets with interest.

"You have a nice little shop here," he said as he eyed the big air compressor. He trailed a hand over the lever of a small hydraulic press and a hydraulic air jack. "May I?" he asked as his hand hovered over a battery powered drill.

"Be my guest," Ben said, making an expansive gesture. "There's welding supplies in that back cabinet."

Daryl opened the cabinet and eyed the contents with interest. The top shelf held neatly stacked boxes of nails and screws. Spools of soldiering wire, a can of flux, tip cleaner, and a soldiering iron on a stand sat beside a bigger portable welder on the bottom shelf. Daryl rifled through the electric tools and battery packs, his eyes lighting when he spied the digital multimeter.

"Perfect." He held up the multimeter. "Can I use this?"

"Use whatever you'd like," Ben said anxiously. Anne's expression haunted him. She'd never recover if her cloth had harmed them. He felt sick with nerves and cursed himself for not being more cautious.

"Your workshop is well stocked," Daryl said approvingly as he set his chosen items on the center work bench.

"You never know what you'll need to fix around here, so I've learned to keep an assortment of repair tools on hand. "That back cabinet has varied weights of welding wire and a MIG welder." Ben took the thick leather apron he wore when welding from the smaller cabinet beside the door and handed it to Daryl.

Anne entered, and Ben gave her a hard hug. "Sweetheart…"

She sobbed once and clung to him, and his words lodged in his throat. He didn't know what to say to ease her.

"I really think the cloth is harmless," Daryl said encouragingly. "The balls are likely emitting only small amounts of radiation if you've been holding them all day with no ill effects."

Anne sniffled and straightened. The tears on her cheeks glittered in the barn light. Ben wiped them away with his thumbs and kissed her. "Sweetheart, let's not worry until we have too. Leave them on the wall beside the barn and go home and rest. You're so tired…" He pursed his lips and shook his head at her stubborn expression.

"Go home," he repeated and nudged her to the door. "Jill will be worried, and you should shower too."

"Jill— God, we need to talk. I've been so self-absorbed…"

Her guilty expression deepened, and Ben sighed hard. "That wasn't what I meant."

"I love you," she mumbled and left, almost running.

He followed to the edge of the barn parking lot to watch her go. When he returned to the barn, Daryl was already hard at work.

"Your wife is a fascinating woman."

Ben grunted acknowledgment.

"I have a million theories I'm dying to test. Hand me that spool of wire, would you?" He absently held out his hand, his gaze intent on the small metal box. "Do you think she'll mind answering my questions or doing some small experiments?"

Daryl glanced up and laughed ruefully. "Sorry, I realize she's upset about this, but it is important to learn everything we can about this phenomenon."

"Oh, she'll cooperate and be glad of the help. I just wish it hadn't happened."

Daryl frowned and nodded. "We all wish that. But it did happen, and we need to look past the immediate effects and prepare for the long terms ones."

"Long term ones?" A feeling of dread infused Ben.

Private Plans

Tuesday Morning 1/23

The next morning Ben arranged for a private meeting at his house. Coffee cups and slightly stale Danish littered the surface of his dining room table, scattered among samples of items Anne had made, including an assortment of varying sizes of the purple spheres.

Sue had shooed their house guests away, and it was just his friends and family in attendance. Ben sat beside Anne and took her hand.

Word had been sent around last night to all the homes that the created items were presumed to be safe as they had passed all the tests Daryl had been able to devise, but his wife still looked guilty and worried to him.

He gestured Jill to the seat beside him and pulled her closer, putting his free arm around her. Dark circles ringed Jill's eyes and she hunched as if she had a stomachache. He hated how scared she looked and wondered if she'd had as restless a night as Anne had.

Pat and Sue sat beside Pat's brother Dave and his wife Kate. They spoke of their kids in low voices. Dan and Abby entered and exchanged greetings with Dean.

Johanna offered them coffee and circled the table, refreshing the cups. The tension in the room was palpable, *but at least no one was glaring at his wife.* He hadn't liked the mood of last night's meeting at all. It had shocked him how quickly the interested expressions had changed to accusing ones.

Ben waved Doug to a seat beside Anne. Johanna sat at the kitchen island beside Julie and the two girls spoke quietly until Daryl cleared his throat.

He held up one of Anne's purple spheres, then tapped the ball lightly on the table.

"What we have here is a type of element I've never seen before in a plasma state. Anne here is a real live alchemist."

"Alchemy?" Ben asked. "I thought that was made up."

Daryl grinned with delight at Anne, and her expression eased. He said, "As far as I can tell, what's happening here is transmutation. She's apparently rearranging the atoms, adding or taking away electrons or neutrons, hence changing the elements."

Ben grinned at the blank expressions of his friends, glad he wasn't the only one having trouble following.

"It's plasma to a solid, or more correctly, sublimation that's taking place here. The gas that makes up the sphere and storm cloud is visible in a spectrum we can't see until enough is present to refract light or it's in a different state as the spheres here are," Daryl went on. "I believe Anne's eyes are a bit different than ours, allowing her to see into different spectrums. There are tests I'd love to run to map the spectrums she sees, but that can wait. We're unable to see this gas until Anne places it in these balls and changes its state to plasma." He frowned thoughtfully. "Or maybe the act of encasing it is enough to change its state. I'll need to study that more."

"Can that be done— transmute one thing into another?" Ben asked doubtfully.

Daryl said, "We've seen it done right in front of us. She can obviously do it. The question is, how is she doing it? If you mean could we do it before this, the only transmutations I'm familiar with are nuclear transmutation, which is the conversion of one chemical element or isotope into another. Not all radioactive decay or nuclear reactions cause transmutation, but all transmutation is caused by either decay or nuclear reaction. Or at least that was the theory." He paused again, deep in thought. "There are forms of natural transmutation that we know about, but they're rare and the cause of the decay is unexplained."

"Like what?" Ben asked.

"The natural decay of potassium to argon is one example." Daryl shrugged lightly. "Artificial transmutation can occur with a machine that is very powerful, like a particle accelerator. Obviously, Anne's transmutations should be taking a lot of energy. At this point, I'm unable to determine where that energy is coming from. It could be the process itself is its own fuel. Although, I think it more likely the purple cloud she sees is made up of a form of electricity that we're unfamiliar with which powers the transformation." He leaned forward and placed his hand on the table. "It's obvious that this plasma in its natural state isn't radioactive or we'd all be dead now. Most of us spent over thirty minutes standing in this stuff, breathing it in as the storm passed over us, and we've shown no long-lasting ill effects, but I lack the tools to identify what the element is or is made up of. It appears to be a previously unidentified element with properties I can only hypothesize about."

"But how's she changing them?" Pat asked as he handed one of the purple balls to his wife.

"Well, that's another process altogether. My hypothesis at this point is that she's somehow interfacing with it like a computer and changing the phases of it. She inputs commands with her thoughts I.E. brainwaves, but I really have no idea how she's accomplishing it. We know that electrical bio energy is evident in the brain. Scientists have mapped that energy and tried to identify the source with limited success. And the storm seethed with electrical energy. It could potentially be an enormous repository of information as Anne sensed. In effect, an enormous brain. It appears as if her brain and the storm are on the same wavelength, allowing her to access the information and use the stored power, power we have no familiarity with, to change the state of matter of the storm essence. I'm just guessing, but it happens all the time. Molecules can move from one physical state to another and not change their basic structure, like water to ice."

"*Um*—" Ben laughed when Pat snorted. It was clear no one understood what Daryl was trying to say.

Daryl pursed his lips and tapped his fingers on the tabletop a moment, then started again, "Think of it like this. Atoms and molecules are all composed of matter. Everything is. The gas we saw and the plasma in this ball are the same thing. Anne is able to change the phase of her essence with brain waves I.E. electric bio-energy; she doesn't need to boil or freeze it."

"A phase?" Dave asked in confusion.

"Phase describes a physical state of matter." Daryl explained. "When molecules move from one phase to another, they're still the same substance. Water vapor above a pot of boiling water is still H_2O. That vapor or gas can condense and become a drop of water in cooler air. If you put that liquid in the freezer, it would become a solid piece of ice. No matter what physical state it was in, it was always water. It always had the same chemical properties. He grinned at Anne. "Its essence remains unchanged."

There were nods all around.

"What Anne does is she takes the essence of the storm in one phase and places it inside these balls in another. She can change its phase at will." He tapped the ball lightly on the table for emphasis. "I wish I could see the essence as she can to see her perform a transmutation and see if there are even more phases for it." He shook his head, looking so put out that Ben laughed.

His laughter eased Jill who relaxed into his side. He kissed the top of her head.

Daryl said, "The next stage of what she does is different in that she's not only changing the phase, but the molecules, and apparently, the very elements themselves. We're able to do that as well, but we make tools to do it. Think of oxygen becoming helium, but she can do it with just this plasma," he pointed at the purple ball. "I have no way to measure the neutrons and protons making up this plasma. I measured its temperature and weighed it, but that's about all I can do without better tools. I wish I had access to a mass spectrograph, or a particle accelerator and a fully stocked lab and my books," he finished wistfully. "But those things are gone."

"That's a lot of information from a science teacher," Ben said.

Daryl cleared his throat, "I taught physics at M.I.T."

"*Ahh…*" Ben nodded. "So, you're a doctor?"

"Yes, I hold a doctorate in physics," Daryl said and fiddled with the papers before him.

"What were you doing here in town?" Anne asked.

Daryl glanced around the room, a red flush climbing his cheeks, then stared down at his hands. "I went home to get my mother. I grew up here in town. There were rumors flying all over the school. I knew something bigger than we were being told was up. My department head had been whisked away to work at the pentagon the day the storm appeared. Then, he emailed me Thursday and told me to get myself and anyone I cared about underground for the storm."

"Those fucking bastards!" Wayne said angrily, "They did know!" He clenched his hands and glared angrily around the room.

"I have reason to believe they did," agreed Daryl. "My boss wasn't the only expert in their field who was missing from school last month." Daryl took a deep breath. "I read that email and just knew I'd better prepare, so I immediately forwarded it to every contact I had with a note to pass it on and headed home. I'd been so involved in my work that I hadn't really realized how the world was reacting. We had internet at the school. I was able to reach my contacts in Switzerland, and it wasn't until I'd left that I realized the net was down for private communication. But the phone lines were down. I had no way to tell anyone what I knew. So, I paid an exorbitant fee to rent a small backhoe; dug a hole in the backyard; threw in some supplies; made my mother go in it, and believe me, she didn't want to. I buried us alive right before the storm's estimated arrival. We sat in the dark, in that hole, counting the minutes until I could start to dig us out."

"Wow," Anne said.

Daryl nodded. "I should've done more, warned more people, but there wasn't any time, and to be honest, I was scared. We'd been warned that breaking our non-disclosure contracts would lead to severe jail time and cautioned we weren't to speak about our findings, but that wasn't the really worrying thing. We didn't just have professors missing to work in Washington. There'd been a rash of accidents. Some fatal and some not, but the non-fatal ones led to dismals for 'health' reasons. And once off campus, you were effectively cut out of the communications loop. Communications were crap on campus too. Our servers took minutes to boot up, and more sites than not gave a 404 error, but we we're still in touch with our compatriots in parts of Europe, and they reported missing doctors and a rash of fatal accidents too. It couldn't be a coincidence. We all knew it but speaking of it was sure to get you sent home on one pretext or another or you'd suddenly suffer from a heart attack or something. We were all scared. The conspiracy of silence was so blatant that everyone knew there was real power behind it. The rumor was the dead weren't really dead but on some super-secret mission and communications were down to prevent civil panic."

Daryl shrugged and rubbed his forehead. "I didn't really believe it. I wanted to believe it, but the deaths were mounting, and I'd attended funerals and seen the corpses. I knew whatever they were keeping secret was big. This wasn't a ploy to prevent civil unrest over a dangerous storm. NASA hadn't lost their satellites; we still received footage. My department was still working on analyzing graphs I now believe to be samples of essence. None of us knew a thing. I realized the storm was much more dangerous than they were letting on, but I never suspected this. How could I?"

Ben glanced at his friends, and they all looked as horrified as he felt.

Anne patted Daryl's hand, and he gave her a wan smile.

"Anyway," Daryl continued after clearing his throat. "My mother and I crawled out of that hole filthy, but with our supplies and clothes. The small excavator I'd rented and our cars were gone, and the house was a pile of rubble, but we were fine. We headed down the road, looking for others. It took us a few hours to walk to the nearest major road. My mom is old, and we had to go slowly. We found a few people wandering naked by their homes and shared our supplies, and we were headed to the center of town when Doug found us and drove us here."

"Is she here now?" Anne asked.

"Yep," Daryl said. "She's at your mother's, helping with the cooking."

"So, what does this mean for us?" Sue asked and rolled the sphere to Daryl.

"Well, I'd like to keep studying this." He held out the ball. "If I could keep the microscope for a while longer, it would be really helpful."

Abby nodded. "Keep it as long as you like. It's our grandson's, and I'm sure he won't mind. He might come bug you for lessons though. He's a real science nut."

"I'll be glad to talk with him. I'll need a space to set up in, the workshop really isn't practical. Ideally, I'd work away from anything in case the plasma gets loose. There's much more to learn about this process and its long ranging consequences, but right now, in the short range, in our everyday lives, it seems safe enough." He glanced over at Anne. "When I say safe enough, I mean the end product." He tapped the cloth on the table. "Making these things…" and here he shook his head, "We can't foresee the consequence to you. It's obviously using energy from you, and as you apply this" –he held out the ball in his hand—"to bigger and bigger projects, we can't foresee what the energy released and consumed might be. I suggest you work far away from others and go slowly."

He stroked his chin meditatively. "It would probably be very helpful to have a volunteer taking notes and observing the process so we can get a better understanding of it." He rose his hand and smiled. "I volunteer."

Anne grinned at him. Ben smiled too almost giddy with relief that there was no harm done from her creations.

"The other things I made?" She gestured questioningly at the two balls.

"I'd like some time to study them further, if I may."

Anne nodded, and Daryl went on, "I'd also recommend you don't try to make any more of them until we've had more time to study it." He looked over at Ben. "If I could have two or three smaller animals to monitor the effects, that would be helpful too, and a place to keep them isolated away from others." He leaned back in his chair and sighed. "This gets complicated; I really need my own workshop away from everyone. Somewhere Anne could work as well."

"Don't forget Jill," Anne said. "She should be there too."

"Jill?" Daryl asked.

"So far, she's the only other one who sees the essence, *err*, plasma."

Daryl waved an airy hand in the air. "Call it whatever you want. We have to name it sometime."

"I vote, hair of the dog," Pat said dryly.

Daryl lifted his eyebrows while Anne laughed. "Hair of the dog that bit you," she said.

Ben snickered, glad the pinched haunted expression had faded from her face.

"Aren't discoveries usually named after their discoverers?" Ben said, grinning crookedly at Anne. "We should call it Annium."

Again, there were chuckles, but Anne grimaced. "I want no part of that disaster named after me," she said seriously.

Daryl smiled, but Ben thought he wasn't paying much attention to their quips. He still stared intently at the spheres as if trying to decipher the contents. He said, "No point in worrying about it, things have a way of naming themselves."

"Agreed." Anne gave Ben a quick kiss on the cheek. "We have more than enough to worry about as it is."

Daryl nudged a scrap of cloth laying on the table. "The cloth is safe, but it isn't quite cotton. It has a much tighter crystalline structure than cotton does. The gavel you made is the same. It's not really rock. It's as if you condensed the rock and cotton to make it stronger."

"I might have," Anne said sheepishly. I was trying to make it stronger. What about the wooden forks?"

Daryl picked up the sample fork and turned it slowly in his hands. "It isn't quite wood either. It's also a tightly crystallized cellulose structure formed with much more precision than naturally occurring organics. The power of that microscope won't let me tell much, but it shows that. They should wear much better.

I predict you'll be able to transmute single elements much easier than complex ones. This cellulose is a pretty simple compound, elementally speaking. As for this," he said, rolling the gold ball across the table. "As far as I can tell, it's twenty-four-karat gold."

Ben laughed at Dean's amazed expression.

Daryl said, "I tested it in every way I could. I checked its density with a mass-volume displacement test and got a result nineteen grams per milliliter, which indicates either real gold, or a material with a density similar to gold. We then used some nitric acid on it that Ben uses for cleaning the milk tanks. It passed that test too. It's physical property's match in every particular. I'm unable to assess its atomic weight, but for all practical purposes, it's gold." He passed the gold over to Anne. "I really can't wait to see what else we can learn," he added with a grin.

After the gold had been passed around and examined by everyone at the table, Sue tapped the pages in front of her. "If the cloth is safe to wear, let's have someone go tell Joe down at the barn, please. We have over a hundred people in there now sitting around in sheets and curtain scraps."

Ben said, "I already told Joe. I'm sure they're making the cloth into clothing as we speak."

"They're not at the greenhouses yet?" Anne asked in concern.

"Not yet," Sue said. "They have no footwear."

Ben said, "Once Doug okays the greenhouse setup, we'll drive them down. How long will it be until the greenhouses are habitable?"

Doug said, "Will is down there right now with a team of fifty or so people laying out the hay and hooking the hoses to the new showers we put in. It shouldn't take too much longer."

"What are we doing down there," Anne asked worriedly. "We still have to use it for planting season."

Doug said, "The rolled plastic on the front greenhouse came through mostly intact. We patched it with duct-tape and used the remaining roll of plastic on the other two houses by separating it into single ply. I don't think it will hold up that well, we won't be able to roll the sides up, but it was warm beneath it. We're moving the benches out of the back greenhouse and using the bags of potting soil as furniture for now."

"Don't worry," Doug added, when Anne frowned. "We told them all to be careful. We can expect some breakage, but it's easily cleaned up from the floor."

"And the first house?" Ben asked.

The benches in that house were much more heavy duty, not meant to be moved. They often reconfigured the back house as that one was usually filled last with vegetable plants and had no set configuration. They decided on what vegetables to grow based on what had sold best the previous year and what their customers asked for. The front two greenhouses were usually filled with bedding plants and hanging baskets.

"We left the front greenhouse alone to use to grow crops. I moved an assortment of pots inside so Mom can start planting whenever she's ready. The furnace started right up. I figure with body heat it shouldn't take much oil to keep the back houses heated at night.

"Assuming we skip all the decorative flowers this year and only plant useful ones, we can put off our planting season by a whole month," Anne said.

"Really?" Doug asked.

"Yeah. We usually start March first, but that's so the hangers have time to become pretty for Mother's Day. Safe planting can't occur outside here until the end of May. So we should begin planting the outdoor crop in April. But we'll run out of fuel before then if we start heating now. We need to make sure we can heat at least one greenhouse until the end of April."

"Kevin has a wood stove that we could move down there. There's a huge forest behind us," Ben said. "It'll be hard to get wood out by hand; its rough terrain in there, but there's plenty of wood."

Daryl said, "Anne might be able to craft a stove if we can get her some metal samples."

Anne said, "They'd need to be pure metal, or I'd use a lot of it to learn to replicate it."

Ben pursed his lips. "*Hmm*, we need to take into account what you can do when making plans. We could build ovens with stone."

"I think worrying over the heat can wait," Daryl said. "If she can form the essence into balls that give off a safe heat, we won't need to bring in wood. Let's make everyone as comfortable as we can. I'll know more in a few weeks, and we can reassess our situation then."

"We should plan for expansion," Sue said. "We'll need to put in more garden space than we currently have available. I'd like to send out some scavenging groups as soon as possible to round up livestock and search for survivors but any livestock we find will need to be fed."

Anne said, "Ben can use the hay fields from the Myer's farm. Those lots are much bigger than ours."

"And it all has to be harvested by hand," Ben reminded her.

"We have Thunder and Lightning, maybe we can find some more horses?"

"And we'll need to make plows and rakes and harrows... We need so many things that we don't have.

"We have more than most." Dean rose to go to Julie. "Don't worry, honey, we can make any tools we need. And with Aunt Anne able to make us base material, it won't even be that difficult."

"I hate this," Julie muttered and began to cry.

Dean closed his eyes and bowed his head over his crying daughter, and Ben's eyes filled with tears. A life working on a farm wasn't what Julie had planned, but it was all she had left.

Johanna patted Julie's back, but her face was so sad Ben had to look away.

Anne stood to hug Julie too. "We've lost a lot but there are still things to look forward too. We can be happy, Jewels. I promise you, it'll get better. We'll make a good place, a safe place, and you'll have friends and play and laugh again. Your mother would want you to be safe and happy. God knows we all miss her, but she'd want you to look forward, not back. You can still be a vet. We'll need them too."

Julie sobbed and her tears escalated. Ben hugged Jill as she began to cry.

"*Shh*," he said and rocked her. "Your dreams for your future can still come true. All your dreams. This isn't the end just a strange new beginning."

Sue said, "We'll be busy doing important work. What we do over the next year will shape the future, and we get to be a big part of that."

Ben gave her a grateful smile as the girls quieted.

"Our new town will need laws, Jewels," Doug said and stood to hug her. He kissed her forehead and hugged Johanna. "A vet, a lawyer, you can be whatever you want." He hugged Johanna hard. "As soon as we can, we'll go see about your family."

"It won't be soon," Ben warned, shaking his head at his son.

Anne resumed her seat and cleared her throat. "Ben and I have discussed this and decided Carmichael Farm won't be a democracy. What I can do makes that impossible. I won't put myself or my skill under someone else's power. At the next meeting, we plan to inform everyone that if they choose to stay here, they agree to live by my rules."

"You're appointing yourself mayor?" Dean asked in a teasing tone.

Anne nodded. "Yes, I'm appointing myself mayor for life."

Everyone laughed, and Ben winced. They thought she was kidding.

"No, I mean it, this is our land the only reason we're all here talking about this is because it was my land. I couldn't have saved it if it weren't."

"You're sure about that?" Daryl asked with interest.

"I'm sure," she said firmly. "I can't describe the connection to you, but it's there."

Kate said, "But what about what's not on your land?"

"If they want my protection and our goods and services, it's our rules or get out."

"That's harsh" Pat said, exchanging a glance Ben couldn't read with his brother.

"There have to be rules," Anne said. "We don't want anarchy. I think I'm capable of setting out as good of rules as anyone."

Sue said, "Can't we just adopt the constitution?"

"We could," Anne said thoughtfully, "but I think we'd need some changes."

"Like what? Pat asked in a suspicious tone.

"Well, taxes for one thing," Anne said, and Wayne groaned.

Ben exchanged amused glances with him. Both had heard Anne's complaints on the tax system countless times.

She gave him an annoyed glance and said, "Government spending was out of hand and half the population was paying more than others. Our constitution should have one clearly defined method of income tax. One that can't be changed later. No weird air tax or random tax method put in. No rules for some people and not others."

"But what if we suddenly need more money for something important for our town?" Pat asked.

"Then we ask for private donations." Anne shrugged. "If enough people think it's important, then it'll get done. If not, then we shouldn't do it."

"I don't know," Pat said doubtfully. "That seems awfully idealized."

"Where are we getting this money from?" Sue asked practically.

Anne laughed and pointed at her gold ball in the center of the table. "How much are we going to need?" she asked.

A weighty silence followed as they considered the implications of unlimited gold.

"Holy crap! I forgot about that," Sue said.

Anne smirked. "We can go on the gold standard again."

"We'll need a bank," Sue said thoughtfully.

"That isn't how it works," Daryl said but his words were drowned under an excited babble.

"And a hospital," put in Abby.

"And a police station," Dan added.

"What about a fire station?" Dave asked.

Anne held up her hand as the suggestions kept coming. "This is a complicated project, and we aren't going to settle it in a day. Let's table it for now. We can all think about it. I'll bring it up at Thursday's meeting. We can form some kind of town planning committee. Until then, we have a lot of people to settle." She turned to Sue. "What are our priorities for the move?"

Sue examined her notes. "With your crafted cloth we're in much better shape. I'll need some time and more information to decide on the best way to proceed."

Anne rose an eyebrow, and Sue said, "For instance, how much and what types of cloth can you make? Can you form clothing or just bolts? I was considering tents but after I saw you make the gavel I started to wonder if you could make homes? There's a million things I think we could use but I don't know what you can do."

Daryl was nodding along and said, "We'll need to measure the essence and Anne's stamina. Our priority needs to be survival and that means we need to prepare for the storm's return. If Anne can craft stormproof clothing, everyone needs a few sets, including bedding. I hadn't considered, but you're correct. If she can also fashion us shelters that can withstand the storm, we'll be in a really good position when it returns."

"Are you sure it will return?" Dean asked.

Anne said, "No, but it *is* growing and still moving. It could disappear as quickly and suddenly as it arrived, I have no way of knowing, but it feels to me as if it won't die out."

"It'll be back," Jill said in an odd tone.

Ben tightened his hold on her.

"It won't be so overwhelming next time," Anne said and reached over to take Jill's hand. "We'll practice with the smaller trapped bits. It's already easier for me to let it go and concentrate on other things while using it."

Jill nodded and withdrew her hands from Anne's, ducking her head and pulling away from Ben to fiddle with her hair.

She was clearly embarrassed, so Ben let her be.

Dean said, "One of our priorities has got to be rescue, especially if the storm will return. It isn't just the essence or whatever that's dangerous. That lightning killed. It won't matter a lick what kind of clothing the survivors manage to make themselves if the storm returns and they don't have safe shelters to go to."

Doug said, "I agree."

Sue said, "We're working on that as we speak. Every vehicle has been donated to the emergency except four. And they're already being positioned. I was hoping we could use Anne with that. If she could use essence to clear the roadways, we could go much farther."

"Of course," Anne said. She exchanged a laughing glance with Ben as she added, "Let me guess, Henry Brooks is keeping both of his."

Sue laughed. "You got it. What he thinks it'll be good for when his gas is gone, I have no idea."

"Who else was a holdout?" Ben asked.

Doug held up his hand. "Me. I love my truck. If you want to use it, you got to ask."

"Fair enough. Who else didn't volunteer?"

"The Wilson's are keeping one too. They donated the husband's, though," Sue added fairly. "I think they're planning on heading out in the spring."

Anne looked surprised. "How come?"

"Their two girls were in school, in Florida."

"Well, God be with them on the search," Anne said softly into the sad silence Sue's words generated.

Ben said, "Amen."

Sue cleared her throat. "Back to the move. Our most critical need is foot protection. Even socks would be a huge help. We have no shoemakers, but we do have two amateur taxidermists. Maybe they could make leather? And if we could make some glue, we could glue leather on Anne's canvas-like material?"

"Make a note to ask for ideas at the next meeting. I know I can fuse my crafted material together with essence, so maybe I can make something like pull-on boots if we cut out the pieces and lay them out."

Sue made a note and flipped through her notebook.

Ben asked, "Has everyone taken in at least twenty people?"

"Everyone except Henry Brooks," Sue said without glancing up from her book.

"How many does he have?" Anne asked.

Sue sighed and flipped some pages, stopping and running her finger along a long column. "Six, including him and his wife."

Anne frowned. "Remind him later, please. Maybe he just forgot in all the radiation excitement," she added doubtfully.

Sue made a note in her notebook.

Anne asked, "Is the bakery kitchen running yet?"

Kate said, "I was down there this morning to organize

breakfast. I was thinking we could remove the glass cases and use that space to put in a buffet table, but I didn't want to make any changes until speaking with you and Doug."

"I'll stop by later and we—"

The walkie-talkie on the counter crackled and everyone turned.

"This is Mark Potter out on the hill monitoring the signal fire. I can see smoke coming from across the river. Something in Ashland is burning."

Ben grabbed the receiver. "Is it a lot of smoke?" he asked as they all got up and rushed to the windows.

"Not too much. It's a steady plume like ours is."

"People!" Anne gasped.

"Maybe," Ben said, "but we have no way to get them. We can't cross the river. And it might just be a forest fire."

Everyone looked deflated at this.

"Keep an eye on it, Mark. Let us know if there are any changes."

Daryl said, "Maybe try to signal, a smoke signal," he clarified.

"*Ahh*! Good idea! Doug, grab a towel, wet it down and go out there and give it to Mark. Let's see what he can do."

Doug ran from the room and they could hear a door slam. Ben got back on the radio. "Doug is coming out. See what you can do about making some smoke signals."

"I'll do my best," Mark said doubtfully.

They returned to the table.

Ben said, "Our second priority is figuring out how to safely cross that river. The current has slowed down some but it's very wide with a lot of debris and ice forming."

"Anyone have a boat?" Pat asked Sue.

"One small power boat, a rubber raft, and two kayaks," she answered after looking at her notes.

Pat said, "The power boat has possibilities. Think the owner will let us use it?"

"Probably. It's Mike Ward's fishing boat."

"Couldn't we make a rope crossing like they did for the Mississippi? You know the kind where they had a rope and the raft was pulled over?" Anne wondered aloud.

"Two things wrong with that idea." Ben held up two fingers. "No rope and no raft. Well, three things," he amended "No knowledge of how to do it safely."

"I'm sure I could make rope," Anne said.

Dean snickered. "Ben, your face…" he laughed again, and Ben grinned when Julie joined him.

"I keep forgetting that," said Ben, "but it still leaves two problems."

Anne said, "Or, maybe I could make a bridge with enough essence."

Pat stood to peer from the dining room window again. "*Hmm…* assuming Anne can make us something, a bridge or boat or whatever, where do we cross? We can't go upstream; the roads are flooded there and there's too much debris to get a boat through. Even assuming we had a bridge, a car would be useless. There are too many trees down. Downstream would be better. The damage from the dam's collapse is much less severe but it has the same problems. We could launch a boat, but that wouldn't help get to the people on the other side. We'd be across the river, but it could take us weeks of walking to find anyone."

Everyone looked discouraged at this.

Johanna said, "We need a way to get the quad and dirt bike across.

"Maybe Rogers's jeep would work?" Ben asked. "Those things are made for rough terrain."

Pat said, "Assuming we take it across somehow. Where do we go though? There is no road across from us."

"The best spot would be downstream where the bridge was," Ben said firmly. "We'll probably have to clear out a bunch of trees or rubble, whatever looks easier to do once we are over there, but it has the best connections to major roads from there."

In one way they were lucky they were in a very thinly populated area of their state, in others it wasn't so good, Ben thought.

Anne glanced over her shoulder at Johnna and said, "We'll need someone to organize this."

"I will." Pat returned to his seat at the table. "How long until we can get some rope or word on a bridge or boat that can cross it?"

Before she could say anything, Ben said firmly, "Not today! She needs to rest. No," he said firmly as she opened her mouth to talk. "I mean it— you make nothing today!"

"Okay," Anne agreed meekly. "I'll try to get some shoes and rope tomorrow though." She turned to Sue. "It would be a real help if I had samples of what's wanted."

Daryl said, "We should organize a trial of items that Anne can make. Let's get together a bunch of different materials and see what ones she can copy."

Sue nodded and wrote it down.

Ben frowned. There was something about her eager guilty expression he didn't like. "Don't overdo it. You get tired, you rest, and no skipping meals.

"Cross my heart," Anne said and did.

"I nominate Pat as the head of search and rescue," Sue said.

"I second it," Ben said.

"All in favor," Anne asked jokingly.

Pat rolled his eyes and Sue laughed.

"The ayes have it!" Anne sobered. "Any word on Edward?"

Ben's mirth died. "He came in last night while you were sleeping. He's at the barn now."

"His wife?" Anne asked softly.

Ben shook his head. "He found her, but too late. He doesn't want to talk about it."

Anne's eyes welled with tears. "What will we do?"

"The same thing we've been doing." He kissed her hand, then clasped it in both of his. "We go on."

Loose Ends

Tuesday Afternoon 1/23

The meeting broke up and everyone turned to their own pursuits.

Anne said, "Jill, come with me and Doug to the greenhouse, and we'll see if we can get that straightened out. Let me just nip downstairs to grab the seeds."

She stepped carefully around a small pile of blankets at the bottom of the stairs. Jill's easels and paints had been moved and the craft table taken down. Anne wondered where they'd gotten to. She hated to think her daughter would lose the paints and then felt guilty.

Everyone else had lost everything and she was worried over paints. She pursed her lips as she examined the sleeping conditions in her basement. The old couch and chair were still there but they'd been pushed up against the shelves that held her canned goods to make room for the loose hay that now filled the center of the floor.

It was better than sleeping on concrete, she mused but those sleeping here were sure to resent the ones sleeping in beds right above them. She hadn't given these house guests much thought, hadn't even asked their names.

Doug ran down the stairs. "I'll get this all cleaned up once they move out, Mom."

"I wasn't mad about the mess, just worried about the living conditions down here. Maybe we should take turns—"

"Don't be silly. You start thinking you owe people just because you have something they don't— you'll never work toward anything."

Anne laughed. "Your dad does give a powerful lecture, doesn't he?"

"And he was right. It applied when I was twelve and it applies now. We earned everything we have. Yes, we were lucky our ancestors were so smart and frugal, that they worked hard to build something worth handing down to their children but that's exactly why they worked so hard. We owe it to them to pass it on to our kids in as good of shape as we received it. The storm wasn't our fault. It isn't our fault that they lost everything. We're doing our best to help, but we don't owe them the shirt off our backs or our beds."

"Johanna?"

Doug grimaced ruefully. "I had to give her the same lecture. She has a soft heart just like you and felt guilty too. But honestly, if the tables were turned, would you expect the homeowner to give you their bed?"

Anne shook her head and gave him a quick hug.

"I came down to say we moved the seeds to the hall closet. I was worried someone would leave a door open or something and we wouldn't notice until they were frozen and it would be too late."

The lie was apparent, but Anne let it go. She should've been worried to have strangers near the priceless seeds too, and she vowed to be more careful. Her children's lives depended on her. And not just her children, she thought in sudden worry when she heard Chloe call for Emily. Everyone on the farm depended on her.

The weight of the thought felt smothering and she trudged back up the stairs, tired to her soul.

* * *

I'm sorry we haven't had a chance to really talk," Anne said as she walked along the path to the greenhouse with Jill and Doug.

Someone had plowed or shoveled the snow and it lined the narrow road, forming a windbreak from the sharp gusts. It was slippery though, and Anne stepped carefully.

"I'd meant to, but it all sort of got away from me."

"Are you recovered from—" Doug made a broad expansive gesture and wrinkled his brow.

"Mostly. I don't think I'll ever forget it. Just describing it can't do the feeling of knowing justice."

Jill said, "It's sort of like my art, when I paint a really great picture that comes out exactly as I envisioned it."

Anne nodded thoughtfully. "The potential realized."

"But it's much more overwhelming. It sort of rolls you over and smothers you. You want to know, but there's so much…"

Anne tuck her hand and into the crook of Jill's arm. "The trick is to just concentrate on a tiny bit at a time. The essence in the spheres isn't nearly as overwhelming as the storm was. The storm was like a billion men shouting what they knew at you while the spheres whisper it."

Doug said, "I have no idea what you guys are talking about."

"I wonder why you can't see it too," Jill asked thoughtfully.

"I'm glad I can't. It must be terrifying."

"It is, but it's also incredible."

Anne exchanged smiles with Jill, relieved she seemed more open to the essence now.

"You'll need to practice. Hell, we both will."

Jill's smile fled, and she pursed her lips as she considered the greenhouses directly below them. Thin plumes of smoke rose into the frosty air, and she turned to peer over her shoulder at the larger fire burning on the point.

Doug followed her gaze and rose his hands to shade his eyes. "Signals of a sort, I guess," he said as they watched the intermittent puffs that billowed into the sky in thick black clouds.

Jill said, "Will we even be able to cross the river? Look how fast it's running."

They all turned back to stare at the river. They were low enough now that trees blocked the view of their side of the river, but the shore opposite was visible. Uprooted and smashed trees had wedged themselves together along the length of the shore as far as Anne could see. White water she could hear from where they stood rolled over the trees, dislodging the occasional limb or tree that would float downstream until it became entangled again.

"Not in boats," Anne said. "Look at that current. It would be impossible to safely navigate it."

"We should wait for it to slow," Jill said.

Doug said, "It might never slow without the dam to hold it back. It'll thin though now that the rains have stopped, but that was a big lake. It'll take a while for it to drain."

"We can worry about it later." Anne pointed to a campfire right behind the closest greenhouse. "That's way to close. You'll have to make sure everyone knows nothing, not even fires, can be built without permission."

"How am I going to stop them?" Doug asked.

Jill released Anne to punch his shoulder. "Just put it out."

"And they'll just make another as soon as I walk away. I already asked them to put them out last night. And I felt like a shit for doing it. They just want a place to gather that isn't as constrained."

Jill furrowed her brow but before she could ask Doug sighed hard and said, "They need to be quiet in the barn and greenhouses because so many are inside, trying to sleep or read or whatever. There's nowhere for them to really move around and make noise or get away from the crying."

Anne winced.

Doug slung and arm around her shoulder. "Your cloth will help. Not only will it keep them warm, it'll keep them busy. They can make their own clothing and get outside. And maybe we can use some for partitions or tents. Privacy will be good for them."

"We need so much," Jill said in dismay.

"It isn't that hard to do," Anne said as reassuringly as she could.

Doug tweaked his sister's hair. "And you don't have to do it all. There's other things you can do to help out."

A flush darkened Jill's cheeks. "It isn't that I don't want to use the essence. I'm afraid I want to too much. I feel it out there like a giant magnet pulling me."

Anne said, "When we finish here, we'll go somewhere private and you can explore it in peace."

Doug's expression darkened. "Is that safe?"

"She needs to learn to manage it, Doug. When the storm returns, she needs to be ready for it. Or as ready as we can be." Anne sighed and straightened, taking a deep breath before leaving the path to cut through the snow to the fire behind the greenhouse.

Nine men held their gloveless hands to the flame, huddled in a bunch beneath a faded blue blanket. All wore t-shirts and sweatpants that didn't fit well and had bare feet that they'd wrapped in scraps of plastic. Anne wondered where they'd gotten the wood to burn and stand on.

"I'm sorry," she said as she approached. "Fires aren't allowed so close to the buildings. Doug will show you were you can make one."

"The parking lot is too far to walk to," one of the men said and turned away to hold his hands to the flame again.

"We can clear a path for you. And, hopefully, we'll have enough material soon to make some shoes, but you really can't burn here. There's too much hay around and one spark would light it. I have to ask you to put this out and not light any more."

"Tim, we should go in." An older graying man touched the first speaker lightly on the shoulder.

Tim batted his hand away.

The older man darted a quick glance at Anne and bobbed his head. "I'll have this out in a jiffy. Sorry, we didn't mean to be an inconvenience."

"No worries," Anne said, smiling a fake smile. "I'll see about getting you a spot set up you can get to. We want you to be comfortable while we work out what to do next."

"And we appreciate your hospitality."

Tim snorted and the two men on the opposite side of him laughed.

Anne laid a hand on Doug's arm as he stepped forward.

"Everyone is on edge and allowances can be made—"

"Allowances? Think you're the queen, do you?" Tim snorted again and turned to glare at her.

Anne returned his glare, hoping he didn't see how nervous he made her. She was glad Doug was with her but there were more of them. *They're just upset,* she told herself and took a deep breath. "Yes. This is my land. My home. If you're going to be my guest, you're going to be polite and that means you don't make fires when you're politely asked not to."

He snickered, and she took a step forward to glare at Tim nose-to-nose, placing her hands on her hips. "If you persist in being rude, I'll kick your ass out!"

"Tim," the older man said in a beseeching tone.

"Don't get your knickers in a twist, Fred. She can have her way. She holds all the cards now."

Anne frowned and shook her head, surprised at her angry

response. She stepped away and spoke in a softer voice. "This isn't a game. I'm not trying to score on you. The fire is dangerous. Maybe you don't have enough experience with farms to know how easily a hay fire can start. I'm not trying to throw my weight around but protect a priceless asset. If we lose the plastic on the greenhouses, where will the people inside it sleep? If the bakery burns down when the hay catches, how will we feed everyone?"

"You'll sleep all snug and warm in your beds."

"Don't be an ass, Tim," the man beside him snapped and began to kick snow onto the fire. "Sorry, Ma'am. We weren't thinking. It won't happen again. We were just trying to get some fresh air."

Tim said nothing as the rest of the men began to kick snow onto the fire.

Anne said, "I'm going to be planting and could use a hand with that if you have the time and energy to help."

"Sure," the older man said.

"Pussies," Tim said and stalked away.

"Light another fire, and we'll kick you out!" Doug called after him.

Anne winced when the remaining men exchanged grim glances. She pasted a fake smile on her face and led the way inside the building.

The shop had already been converted into an eating area. She stopped to examine the changes, surprised so much had already been done. Men and women eating at the tables glance up but continued eating in a listless manner.

"We boxed up all the candles and things and put the shelves in the Russo's basement to make way for the tables," Doug said.

"Anne!" Helen called and hurried from around the counter to hug her. She hugged Jill and Doug and gestured a woman forward. "Meet Claire. She's my top assistant. I've let her take over the meals completely."

Kate stuck her head from the kitchen doorway and waved but

265

ducked back inside before Anne could greet her.

"Nice to meet you," Claire said, offering her hand. "I ran Puffy's for years and was a cook there before that."

"I'm glad to meet you," Anne said with real sincerity, and she grinned with relief at Helen who smiled back.

Helen said, "Claire has been a blessing. She's taken over planning the menu's and overseeing the food deliveries. She tells me how much bread she needs, and I can leave the rest to her."

"Well, something smells great," Jill inhaled deeply and closed her eyes.

Helen said, "Fresh venison your Uncle Dean caught. Dave is dressing out three more under Kate's supervision if you want to give him a hand, Doug."

"Sure." Doug stooped to kiss Helen's cheek and handed the bag of seeds he carried to Jill. "Come with me if you'd like to learn how to butcher deer instead of gardening," he said over his shoulder.

Most of the men followed Doug, and Anne laughed.

Claire waved to a wooden counter that had replaced the glass case that usually stood in front of the kitchen door. "There's a pot of soup ready and a pasta dish— pesto and garlic, no meat." She made a face, and Anne laughed again although it worried her that people had complained about the food choices already. They'd need to eat meat whether they liked it or not. There weren't enough resources to have specialty diets.

Claire said, "We also have some sandwiches, but the stew won't be ready until dinner time."

"Ben said he'd see about making us another counter to serve at." Helen took a step away and called after a woman retreating from the table, "Excuse me, but if you've finished, bring your plate to the kitchen for cleanup!" She sighed hard when the woman continued without looking back and went to gather the used utensils herself.

Anne stared after the woman and then examined the rest of the diners. Most picked listlessly at their food. The crowd appeared dull and lifeless. No one spoke, and they ate as if it were a chore. Anne didn't think the woman had even heard Helen, she was so trapped in her misery.

Helen made a tsking noise as she scrapped the leftover food into a bowl. "Such a waste. We need a server. Letting them take their own isn't working out."

"I'll find us a few," Claire said.

Anne asked, "Did we get any volunteers for cleanup duty?"

Claire said, "A few."

Helen continued to neaten the serving station as she said, "It's clothing that's the issue. There just isn't enough of it to supply everyone. They're still wearing sheets and towels." She stepped closer and lowered her voice. "Resentment is starting to build for the people inside the houses. Henry Brooks came down early this morning and made a scene. He walked through the greenhouses as if he were at the store making a purchase, and questioned everyone, offering the comforts of his home if they had skills he could use. I threw him out and warned him not to come back, but it got the people here really riled up. The nerve of that man."

"I'll speak to Ben. Call Sue for me and have a work crew sent down here to clear a path to the parking lot and tell her I need firewood and some chairs brought out for it, and I need it as soon as possible."

Helen rose an eyebrow.

"I don't have time to talk now, but I'm glad the kitchen is under control. I'll be down here awhile in the greenhouses if you need me." She gave her a mother a kiss on the cheek. "Nice to meet you, Claire."

Claire lifted a hand and hurried back into the kitchen.

Anne headed to the basement door, beckoning for her remaining helpers to follow.

"We moved all the potting soil into the greenhouses already!" Helen called after her.

"You're okay here, Grandma?" Jill asked.

Helen's reply was cut off by the closing door.

"Grab a stack of the blue seed trays over there and three hoses…" Anne trailed off as she examined the empty shelf where her hoses should've been. Only two remained. The carboard boxes full of packaging remained as she'd left them, but someone had rummaged through the hose fittings and left the cabinet holding the pesticides open. Jill clattered down the stairs.

"Grandma said to tell you the potatoes will need the bigger pots, and she's asked Doug to make her some bins for them."

Anne knelt to check the mouse traps and frowned when she saw they'd been set off and not reset.

"Jill, remember to tell your father we'll need a lock on the door here." She reset the traps as she continued, "These traps need to be kept up."

"Mice are a problem?" the older man asked.

"I'm sorry, I didn't catch your name. I'm Anne Windsor and this is my daughter, Jillian."

"Fred Richardson, and this is my brother Barry and that's Frank Owens."

"Nice to meet you, Fred." She nodded greetings to the other two men. "And, yes, the mice are a problem. We store the paper goods for the bakery down here, and they can destroy it. And they're hell on the seeds, so if you see a tripped trap, reset it."

We should lock up the poisons too," Jill said as she closed the cabinet door.

"I think just locking the main door will be enough."

Fred was shivering and lifting his feet and Anne realized the floor here was probably freezing. "Let's get to the greenhouse. You must be freezing down here."

She led the way back upstairs and through the double doors

that lead to the greenhouse sales area. The sounds of laughter and children calling to each other eased her heart. *Jill's too judging by her sudden smile.* Even the men smiled, their tight expressions easing.

Boomer bounded into the room, and Jill crouched to rub his ears. "I'd wondered where you'd gotten too," she said.

Anne ruffled the dog's ears as she examined the changes already made. "He found some playmates," she said as a golden retriever ran into the room.

The long wooden sales counter still sat before the garage door but the decorative pots that were usually on the tiered shelves beside the door of the first greenhouse had been removed to make room for books and magazines. She peeked down the hallway that led to the back greenhouses and saw her missing hoses trailed along the floor from the men's bathroom, leading to the middle greenhouse.

The sliding barn doors that led to the greenhouses had been left open and the room was warm enough Anne removed her coat, laying it on the counter.

"I wouldn't," Fred said quietly and picked it up. "Clothing left lying around tends to disappear."

Anne flushed and took her coat from him. She glanced at Barry and Frank but couldn't judge their expressions. She nervously cleared her throat and stopped to examine the books, frowning as she held up a tattered copy of Hamlet she recognized as being Jill's.

"We should make a library. These are the only books we'll ever have, and we need to take better care of them."

Fred plucked the book from her hand and caressed the cover with his thumbs. "It's such a tragedy." His gaze flitted to the open doorway and tears filled his eyes. "Those poor kids, to never know the Bard's words. The sheer waste of it all...."

Anne laid a hand on his shoulder.

"They've got their lives," Barry said, hefting his stack of trays impatiently. "They can write their own stories. I never liked that crap anyway."

The men continued to discuss the merits of Shakespeare as Anne stepped into the front greenhouse.

A group of women wearing sheets looked over when they entered. Anne nodded hello and smiled at the children running through the aisles between the benches. She squatted to feel the floor and was relived it felt warm to the touch as the children wore nothing except scraps tied for modesty. They seemed to be having fun though, playing some game that involved balls of various sizes and a group of dogs. Boomer joined them.

"We can work in the second house," Jill said.

Anne grinned at her and followed her from the room. The second house was quieter.

Anne's neighbor Claire stood right inside the doorway of the greenhouse, speaking to a group of women wearing tablecloths from the winery wrapped toga style. Men and women wearing a motley assortment of castoffs, from gowns to sheets, sat on hay bales and the ground waiting their turn in the showers. Plastic sheeting, wet blankets and old shower curtains were nailed to boards, making a line of cubicles. It was obvious from the wet flooring that only three of the cubicles were actually showers, the others were likely dressing rooms bracketing the shower stalls. Music played softly and Anne wondered why they'd put the speakers right outside the shower curtains when the sound of the water would likely drown out the music.

Two women sat at a folding table right in front of the cubicles with a wind-up egg timer, a bottle of the industrial soap from the bakery, and shot glasses, some full of soap and some waiting to be filled. A smaller table made from empty milk crates was across from them manned by three of Anne's neighbors and surrounded by a group of people who were all examining the same notebook.

Claire was saying to the women, "Mrs. Russo will see you as soon as possible but we have limited medicine and limited hot water. You can wait here for an opening or schedule a visit with Terry at the milk crates. If you have an urgent problem, speak with Mrs. Ward behind me, and she'll direct you were you need to go."

Anne nodded a greeting to Mary Ward who nodded back. She sat a table with four empty chairs. Cardboard had been tacked to a wooden frame to make a partition that she could pull closed. An assortment of medicines and cleaning products lay on the table by her. A record player, the source of the music, was on top of a small stack of milk crates behind her with a box of records and a pile of towels. Two boxes of rolled fabric scraps sat by her feet.

Another empty cubicle beside her was obviously meant to be an examine room. It held the first aid kit from the barn, a table made from a door and sawhorses with an air mattress on top, two kitchen chairs, and ten cases of wine.

Abby exited the nearest cubicle, drying her hands on a kitchen towel. "Next," she said, holding the curtain back so her patient could enter. She shook her head minutely at Anne and waved her away.

The egg timer dinged and one of the women said, "You have one minute to rinse and two minutes to change cubicles."

Anne winced at a woman's painfilled gasp.

Mary turned the music up and Anne winced again. She'd thought the music was to give the waiting bathers something to listen too, but it was obviously there to muffle the sounds of the people cleaning their wounds. Privacy was an issue they'd need to do something about. As was soap. She'd only bought four gallons. They'd be out in no time at this rate.

Clair continued speaking to the people waiting, "If you don't mind cold water, you can take a number for one of the four bathing chambers but we don't limit the time in them so you might have a long wait. Help yourself to a bottle of wine. Feel free to drink it

271

but we recommend you wash all affected areas with it, despite how uncomfortable it is. If you don't have a friend who can apply the alcohol to your back, speak with Terry and she'll arrange for one of our nursing staff to help you. There are pails in the cubicles so you pour it and reuse it. We don't have unlimited supplies of anything, I'm afraid. Make sure you get a clean washcloth—"

Anne headed to the next greenhouse.

Men and women glanced up as they entered but didn't rise from their seats, a low row of cinderblocks that had held the benches up.

She pasted a fake smile on her face and turned away to examine the rest of the changes. The benches had been removed except for a row in the center of the aisle. Loose hay was scattered in piles, clearly meant for sleeping on while other bales were being used as chairs at the benches. Men and women, wearing a motley assortment of clothing from towels to gowns, played cards at the tables or reclined on the hay reading or sleeping. Most turned to stare curiously when they entered.

"Good morning," Anne called, smiling in greeting, hoping she didn't look as nervous as she felt. It felt odd to be so normally dressed when everyone around her wasn't. "We're going to be using the far bench to start the seeds. If anyone is interested, I'll explain as I go."

She led her helpers to the back and began explaining the process of starting the seeds.

✳ ✳ ✳

Anne dusted off her hands and straightened to face her audience. She was pleased to see most of the people had left their bales and had gathered to watch.

Their faces were more animated, and they eagerly questioned Jill as she finished covering the lettuce seeds with a light dusting of potting soil.

"And that's it," Jill said and carefully watered the seedlings in. "Keep them covered with these screens to prevent mice from eating the seeds but check them twice a day to ensure they're being kept moist. You'll need to keep the backdoor here closed to keep them warm; if the temperature varies too much the seeds can rot before they have a chance to sprout."

"Jill and I will be busy, so who am I leaving in charge here?" Anne asked.

Joe stepped forward, pushing through the crowd. "I'm in charge down here, so me, I guess."

Anne shook his hand. "Hey, Joe, I didn't see you come in. Some of the plants will use more water than others, so you need to check them all individually and keep them damp just like this." She handed him a seed tray to examine. "It's important they only be slightly damp. The key is to keep them warm. We should have some sprouts in four or five days."

"That fast?" Fred asked in amazement.

"We should have edible lettuce in less than a month. As soon as we have two root hairs, we can transplant them. I'll come back Monday and show you how."

Anne gestured to the haybales. "Joe, you'll need to make room for the plants, maybe at the foot of the beds? I'll get you a list of the containers we'll be using so you can plan it out but speak with Doug before building anything."

"We've talked about it already a bit. I'd like to leave the first greenhouse empty as long as we can so the kids can play during the day."

"Those benches can't be comfortable to sleep on. See if we can get more hay down here."

"This is all the bales Ben had. The rest of the hay is in bigger bales that we'd need to break up to use, and Ben is worried there won't be enough for the cows to eat." Joe's lips quirked and he shook his head. "It won't kill us to sleep on a hard surface. The hunting teams are bringing back game, and we'll have leather soon. We can gather ferns in the spring for bedding, it's just a few weeks away." He held up the plastic wrapping the potting soil came in. "Meanwhile, we use what we have. Every person we can dress is another pair of hands working to get us all back on our feet."

"Well, Jill and I have a lot to learn before we can be more help."

"The cloth is a godsend, but you look exhausted."

Anne rubbed her face. She felt exhausted, but they needed clothing. Her cheeks felt sore from all the fake smiles she was forcing, and she let the smile drop as she turned to Jill. "Let's go find Daryl and see what we can learn."

Learning

Tuesday Afternoon 1/23

Anne carefully stepped over the smaller balls of encased storm that she had captured that lay beneath the snow and placed her hand against the largest sphere.

"Can you feel it?" she asked.

Daryl shook his head, frowning at Jill who stood with her eyes closed and her fingertips touching the sphere.

"It feels like a cold rock to me. Inert and lifeless. I wonder what the casing is?" He ran his hands along it, walking the length.

"Diamond? Or diamond like. I was picturing rock-hard, clear facets like in my engagement ring. It was one of the first things I saw with clarity." Anne pressed her palm against the sphere. To her, it felt full of energy. "Can you see the swirling inside it? The little streaks of brightness?"

"Yes. It's fascinating. Look how the light gathers by Jill's hand." Daryl leaned so close his breath misted Anne's fingertips. "See the light flicker to your fingers? Are you calling it?"

"Not on purpose, but I can feel it want to be. The potential of the bigger balls is stronger than the smaller ones. I barely feel them unless I concentrate on them."

"Jill—"

Anne held up a hand and shook her head. "Let her be a few minutes."

Daryl nodded and reached for the pack on his back. "Can I have a few of the smaller balls?"

"Sure. Take as many as you want."

She scuffed the snow with her boot and revealed a mound of golf-ball-sized balls.

"You know right where they are?"

"I can sense them like smelling cookies beneath the snow. The bigger ones are easier to smell out than these smaller ones, but I can sense them all."

"Pick out a few to use and I'll measure them. I'd like to measure them all to see if they shrink over time, but we don't even know if handling them is dangerous."

"It isn't," Jill said in a faraway voice. "You won't be able to open it. I'm trying and it's resisting me. I see the lock but can't get around it."

Anne closed her eyes, resting her fingertips beside Jill's, and let herself examine the sphere. It felt open to her, as easy to move as breathing. In her mind's eye, Jill was a vivid spot of light with a million small tendrils waving about her. Daryl was a much smaller spec of brightness. And the sphere was speckles and streaks of brilliant white that roiled in patterns that drew her attention. She pulled her attention away, knowing if she followed the light the new knowledge would consume her interest.

"Touch the sphere," she said.

She knew when he touched it because he suddenly gained clarity in her mind's eyes. The brightness that was him took on definition and she was able to see the tiny tendrils of light leaking from him. She was examining the new brightness trying to figure out what it meant when Jill touched her hand.

She moaned and fell forward as Jill's brightness collided with her. She felt Jill's surprise and fear and laughed when she swore.

"That wasn't funny," Jill said, and Anne felt her anger.

"I didn't know it would happen."

"What happened?" Daryl asked.

"He's never going to believe this," Jill said.

Anne frowned at her daughter's disbelief. Her daughter thought she'd lied. "Sure, he will."

"He will what?" Daryl asked.

"Mom…"

Jill suddenly felt awed and terrified, and Anne jerked her hand from the sphere to hug her.

Jill skittered away and held up her hands as if fending her off. Shocked, Anne halted.

Jill said, "I didn't say it aloud. You were reading my mind."

"What?" Stunned, Anne dropped her reaching hands. "No, I wasn't. Well maybe a bit. I know you thought I lied, but I laughed when you swore. I didn't know it would happen."

"What happened?" Daryl asked again and pulled Jill away from the sphere.

Jill said, "She heard me, but I didn't say a word."

"Yes, you did."

Jill rolled her eyes and grabbed Anne's hand. She pressed it to the sphere and cocked her head and although Jill's lips didn't move, as clear as day, Anne heard, *I didn't say a word.*

Jill released her hand and stepped away, rubbing her hands on her jeans. "See?"

"Oh my God." Anne sat abruptly in the snow, her knees suddenly too weak to support her. Jill's annoyed frown changed to an expression of concern and she crouched to take Anne's hand.

"Are you okay?"

"You can read her mind?" Daryl looked intrigued and let his

pack fall from his shoulder to open it. He withdrew a notebook and began writing.

"Jill, can you read hers too?"

"I don't know. And I'm not sure I want too."

Daryl glanced up and pointed to the sphere with his pencil. "It's a transmitter of some sort. We knew that already but apparently if you're physically connected it makes a loop. I don't think you need to worry she'll be able to read your mind all the time. She'll need the essence."

"Well, I don't like it."

Anne reached a trembling hand to wipe her sweating brow. "I agree. I have thoughts I wouldn't want my daughter to overhear."

"I see how it could be awkward but think what we could learn! I wish I could use my tools. This is so frustrating."

"The sphere is safe to touch. You could use them on it."

Daryl bit his lip, his expression so conflicted Anne laughed.

"You want to measure the effects as it happens?"

"I'd like to use the voltage meter if you think it's safe, but I hate to ask you to do anything that makes you uncomfortable."

"It won't kill us. Jill, try concentrating on math problems or tell me the plot of your favorite book or something. But if you do think something you don't want me to know just remove your hand from the sphere, and I'll pretend I never heard it."

Jill snorted.

"Did you see how we were touching? I bet if we keep those tendrils away from each other we won't hear."

"Mom, those tendrils are always there. I can see them all over you when you're nowhere near the sphere."

Daryl said, "The sphere is a conduit. I think it's safe to assume it holds electrical energy, bio energy like you do. You and your mother produce more bio energy than most people so appear brighter. I don't have the right type of tools to measure the output, but assuming I'm correct, it means you'd need to be physically touching or using a conduit of some sort. And seeing as how you've touched your entire lives with no thought transference, I think you do it on whatever wavelength is contained inside the essence, so you'll need it to perform the connection."

He tapped the side of the sphere. "This is a big conduit. Jill says she sees millions of tendrils. All won't be your thoughts. So keeping the thought tendrils contained could be learned. Focus on the tendrils. If you can control them, maybe you could talk without a conduit. Think of the potential!"

Jill's scowl lightened. "You think we could learn to block it too?"

"If you can control the tendrils, if that's even what's transmitting, but it seems likely. God, I'd love to know what frequency you're transmitting at."

"Like a radio," Jill said thoughtfully and placed her hand against the sphere. She stared intently at Anne, and Anne knew Jill wasn't looking at her but at her essence.

I love you, she thought as hard as she could.

"I love you too." Jill grinned and removed her hand, shaking it and staring at it. "It was easy, and you didn't hear a thing I was saying in my head."

"Let me try," Anne said and reached for the sphere.

Handling It
Tuesday Evening 1/23

I'm glad to see the girls laughing," Ben whispered as he set a bowl of stew before Anne.

She ate it absently, her gaze on her daughter who sat at the kitchen island with her back to them. Ben chuckled quietly and stretched his feet out under the table. Seeing Jill smile relieved his soul. He hadn't realized how upsetting he found her wan face but hearing the girls giggle was a tonic.

He flicked a glance to his brother whose shoulders eased as he watched them.

"Daryl, eat before it grows cold," he said.

Daryl grunted but didn't glance up from the notebooks spread out before him.

"Mother!" Jill exclaimed and jumped to her feet.

Anne laughed so hard tears fell from her eyes. "That was a nice try, but I knew you were listening."

Daryl grinned and shook his head, turning his attention back to his books.

"*Aww,*" Julie said and nudged Jill's arm.

Jill held out her hand and a purple golf ball appeared on it. She clenched her hand around it, winked at Anne, and both girls broke into giggles and ran from the room.

"What was that about?" Ben asked as he watched them run up the stairs.

Anne wiped her eyes and said, "We discovered we can speak to each other using the essence and she was trying to spy on me."

"Sounds like you had a busy day," Dean said and grinned when the girls laughed upstairs. Music drowned out the laughter and Chloe and Emily ran from the living room and up the stairs.

"It's so nice to see the kids smiling," Ben said as Sue entered the kitchen.

"It really is," Sue agreed as she helped herself to a bowl of stew.

Anne eyed Sue's bowl, and Ben rose to refill hers. "Eat," he said when he placed it before her. There's plenty of food, and Claire makes a very good stew."

Anne took a big bite and made a face, swallowing quickly and blowing on the next mouthful.

"Did you know immediately?" Daryl asked.

"Yes, but I saw the essence in the air. So, I thought about that time Julie fell into the pigpen and how she smelled so bad we had to hose her down. Which made me remember the syrup incident of last year, and she got a bit more than I intended."

"She saw it?" Ben squeaked as an embarrassed flush heated his cheeks. It was one of his fondest memories but not one he wanted to share with anyone except Anne.

"It isn't pictures we share but words and feelings, it sounds to me exactly as if she's speaking, although, maybe we could think in pictures…."

"That's a great idea. I'll set up some experiments. Do you mind if I use the computer for a bit?"

"Go ahead."

Daryl gathered his notebooks, calling over his shoulder. "Don't forget to weigh yourself and keep track of your calorie intake. We need to figure out where the energy is coming from."

"You can use the essence like a telephone?" Sue asked.

"Just with Jill. Daryl never heard us, but we're just learning, so maybe someday."

Ben said, "I don't like her letting it loose in the house like that."

"I'll talk to her, but she knows how dangerous it is."

Sue said, "I'd been meaning to ask, are those spheres safe? The kids were running around in the snow, and I was wondering if we should move the spheres so they don't break them."

"No one could break one, not by stepping on it at least. We tried to break them today, and Daryl couldn't even scratch the surface. I somehow locked the spheres to myself and had to release and reform it so Jill could use it at all. I can make it any shape I want and was considering forming it into tents or something, but I thought it would freak people out to sleep under it."

Dean rubbed his arms. "You thought right. It would give me the willies and I didn't have to experience it eating the clothes from my back.

Ben frowned as Dean's smile died and he rose to begin gathering dishes.

Tears filled Anne's eyes as she watched him, and she pushed her bowl away.

Ben said, "So, what else did you learn about it today?"

"Do you want the technicalities or practical stuff?

"Practical," Sue said, and Ben laughed.

He pushed the bowl back to Anne. "Daryl can fill us in on the technical stuff later."

"Well, Jill can use it just like I can. She has an eye for detail and color I lack, but I'm better at sorting the information." She picked up her spoon and began to eat as she thought. "I can see past the extraneous quicker. Jill gets caught by the flow of information."

"Should I be worried? I have no idea what you're talking about, but it doesn't sound good."

To Ben's relief, Anne laughed. "It's just Jill being Jill, easily distracted by new ideas. She's learning, and I can yank her back. I think with more practice she'll be fine, but I do plan on releasing all the essence we have so she can practice withstanding it."

Sue said, "That sounds dire."

"It isn't. It's more like frustrating. Imagine you got online and there were fifty stories on the front page that all sounded interesting. So, you click on the first one and there are fifty more and for every story you read you see ads about other stories you want to read. You could get a hundred pages in, in seconds. The difference is when you're done on the computer, you're still in your desk chair. When you're finished with essence you have to find your way back. The farther you go, the harder it is to pull yourself back here because everything along the way is another enticing story to read. Our captured essence is here, so easy to navigate. But the storm is huge, and I worry if she follows the links too far, she'll get trapped there. So, she needs to learn to stick close at least until we know how it works."

"That must be so amazing," Sue said wistfully.

Dean said, "*Ughh*, I'd be bored. I could care less what makes a bug's wings rounded or why leaves turn brown."

"You think that, but I'm telling you, when you see it, it's so beautiful. It's the most beautiful thing you've ever seen."

"And when you make something?" Sue asked.

"That's boring after the first few like reading the same story over-and-over. It's hard to keep your attention on it because everything the essence touches is an intriguing new story to read."

She shot a guilty glance at Ben, and he shook his head.

"I only made a few things to show Jill how. Mostly we did

some small experiments Daryl set up."

"What am I going to do with you," he said, and the front door burst open.

Doug ran in looking excited. "Smoke signals from Chester! We've found people!"

"Jill!" Anne called as Daryl ran in from the office.

Ben stood and headed for the living room to look from the windows.

"What?" Jill called down the stairs.

"We should make more cloth. They'll need it."

Ben didn't turn from the window. Anne was right. If there were survivors out there, they'd need supplies and they had nothing left. They'd already given away almost all their clothing. They still had the sheets, one blanket, and one towel each but every scrap of fabric had been stripped from the house.

Starlight sparkled across the pristine snow, and if he squinted, he could barely make out the short puffs of black smoke over the hills in Chester.

"Wait!" Daryl called, the urgency in his voice catching Ben's attention. He strode back to the kitchen as Jill ran downstairs, followed by Julie. Both girls looked anxious, their earlier happiness had vanished.

"Mom!" Chloe called, and Sue stood.

"They can keep coloring in my room if it's okay with you," Jill said.

"I'll see to them." Sue gave Jill a quick hug.

Daryl said, "You should conserve your energy to make a bridge."

"I have no idea how to make a bridge," Anne said.

"Me either," Jill muttered.

"Bridges are simple structures," Doug said, but his brow was furrowed and he looked worried.

Ben shook his head. "Don't be ridiculous. We can't build a

bridge in that water; it's moving way to fast."

"They wouldn't need to go into the water. We should find the narrowest section or a wider one with lots of debris would work."

Anne headed to the junk drawer and opened it. "Up where the dam was. It was narrow there, and there's a natural ridge line that we might be able to use." She took out the small pad they kept to leave each other notes, and a pencil, and handed it to Doug. "Draw me a bridge and explain each part and what it does."

"Mom…"

Daryl said, "Getting the essence there will be tricky."

"It'll follow me," Anne said absently as she peered over Doug's shoulder.

Jill heaved a heavy sigh and thumped into a seat at the table. "It's too dangerous."

"What is?" Ben glared at Anne when she ducked her head.

"Anne Windsor, what are you planning?"

She grinned at him and stuck her tongue out, making Jill laugh.

Daryl said, "We did some small experiments this afternoon and found Anne and Jill can transmute the shape of wood at a small distance. The older it is the easier it is for them to manipulate. The finished product isn't quite wood. It has a much denser more regular crystalline structure, but it's quite strong. It burns hotter and longer than natural wood, and I'm testing the buoyancy and absorbency, which so far has met my expectations. I did some quick tests on tensile strength and haven't had time to reach conclusive results, but I'd be willing to cross a bridge made of their pseudo-wood, assuming it was supported sufficiently."

Jill frowned at Anne but spoke to Ben, "The only way we could support it would be to grow it in increments. And what's to stop a giant tree from sailing down the river and knocking it out from under us?"

Daryl frowned and turned to Doug. "Netting? Isn't that what's normally used?"

Anne said, "We need to cross that river!" She darted a glance at Johanna, giving Ben a pointed glance.

Ben recognized her stubborn expression. She'd try with or without help. He sighed hard and turned to his brother. "Dean, you and Julie go to the barn and put the oldest hackamores we have on Thunder and Lightning. Tell Dave and Kate we're going. We'll take a radio and two survival packs but don't put anything inside them that we can't do without. Anne and Jill can ride bareback and guide their essence while I lead the horses. Ask for a few volunteers to come but warn them it's a five-mile hike there and back and we might be gone a day or more." Ben gathered a loaf of uncut bread from the counter and opened the refrigerator.

"Doug, make me sandwiches and fill the thermoses with tea. Pack enough food for ten people for two meals and give us all the cookies. If you don't hear from us by noon tomorrow, send someone to come looking, but you stay here and oversee the farm. Make sure the morning milking is done properly and the livestock is fed and watered.

"Jill, go put on your snow suit and wear thermals under it" –he grinned as Jill opened her mouth— "and, yes, Boomer can come."

She snapped her mouth closed and rolled her eyes, but her eyes were laughing now. He watched her run up the stairs and waited for her door to close before saying, "Anne, it isn't pretty out there. If you think she can't handle it…."

"We can handle it. We have too." She kissed his cheek before running up the stairs after their daughter.

Ben clasped his son's shoulder. "You're in charge until we get back."

"Yes, sir," Doug said respectfully with no sign of sarcasm.

Ben heaved a heavy sigh and went to get a pistol from his safe.

A New World

Tuesday Evening 1/23

Snow crunched softly beneath the horse's hooves. Daryl spoke quietly to Wayne and Pat, discussing the best approach to bridge building with essence.

"Hold the reins," Ben asked Kate and jogged to the top of the hill to look for Anne.

She and Jill were easy to spot. The essence was so thick above Anne's head, Ben could see the swirling purple cloud. Light flickered in the cloud as if it contained a storm. The sight made him shiver, fear making his mouth dry.

"Holy crap," Dave whispered, and Ben darted him a quick glance. He'd been so entranced he hadn't heard the others arrive.

The cloud rolled through the air five feet above her head.

Daryl said, "She's keeping it closely contained to avoid touching the live wood."

Ben frowned at him.

Daryl said, "It doesn't spread on contact with live plants, but it does hurt them."

"It hurts the plants?"

"It hurts them, which hurts Anne. The essence works like an antivirus in the body that attacks impurities, and Anne can feel it. If you consider the Earth as a living organism, it makes sense it would develop something to counteract the damage done by pollutants."

"I guess," Kate said, her worried gaze on Jill.

"Good thing you're doing this at night with no one around," Wayne said.

Ben nodded agreement. He'd chosen this route because it led past the captured storm essence. This trail led to the lower lots and the main road, and he'd figured even if the essence got loose it wouldn't do much damage if they were past the winery turnoff. Not being visible from the greenhouses or winery was just a bonus. Now he worried the essence would brush the trees, and he frowned at his wife who'd made no mention that it hurt to touch them.

Jill left Anne's side and ran forward, calling out as she approached, "Mom says she'll go ahead of us and clear the road for practice and to see if she can gauge how much she's using. Once she gets the knack of it, I'll try."

Boomer followed, wagging his tail and prancing.

Kate asked, "She has it under control?"

"It's easy to control. Either of us could encase it again in seconds. You don't need to worry about it getting away from us but we might get distracted so hang back so we don't accidently engulf you."

"Right." Kate gave Jill a rueful smile. "Need a boost?" she gestured to Lightning's bare back.

"I'd rather walk a bit."

Kate shrugged and pulled herself to Lightning's back. Ben handed her Thunder's lead and took Jill's hand.

Jill leaned to pet Boomer. "No one walk in front of me. I have a small bit of essence going to Mom so we can talk."

Ben asked, "How come we can't see the green glow?"

"It's not touching anything. I can use it from about fifteen feet away," she answered absently. She frowned as her head scanned the lower lot as if she saw something he didn't. It rose the small hairs on his arms, and he rubbed them as he considered his daughter.

Anne cut through the vines, climbing over the wire to get ahead of them. The purple cloud followed, hanging over her head. Like the larger one that had decimated the neighborhood, this one roiled and flickered with lights.

"I see it," Jill said, and Ben turned to her.

"What is it?" She released Ben's hand to stride forward.

"What's what?" Ben called, but he knew she wasn't speaking to him. Awe and dread collided, weakening his knees. His daughter heard voices and saw God. He remembered stories of the martyrs and had to stop walking to catch his breath.

The others caught up to him. Daryl was explaining, making broad expansive gestures as he pointed to the cloud following Anne.

"Those flickers of light are information surges. When they concentrate on something, the flickers grow to a solid glow." Ben wanted to pay attention, he needed an explanation that made sense, but Jill ran forward, calling for her mother in a panicked voice.

He chased her, reaching her side as Anne yelled, "No!" and fell to her knees.

"Stay back!" she screamed, and Ben yanked Jill into his arms, turning her away from Anne who lay on the ground now. The purple cloud above her condensed and fell, encased in a clear sphere. It rolled when it landed, and Jill screamed again. The sphere was suddenly a cloud again, missing Anne's prostate form by a foot. It shot into the air and became a sphere that settled gently to the ground a few feet from her.

Jill trembled in his arms. She shook so hard Ben didn't know if he was trembling too.

"What's wrong?" he asked as Daryl reached them.

Boomer barked and snapped at the sphere.

Anne rose to her knees and shook her head hard, her hair coming loose from her ponytail and falling about her face.

"Anne?" Ben called.

"I'm okay. Keep Jill back."

Daryl stepped forward, his anxious eyes scanning the ground. "What is it?"

"There's so much." Anne stood and brushed herself off. "Sorry, I wasn't expecting it." She gestured to the trees before her. "I hadn't seen it before. Wait here."

"What is it?" Ben asked again, but his wife didn't answer or look back.

"Lights. A billion small lights," Jill said as she scanned the horizon. "Sorry, I will." She gave Ben an abashed smile and folded her arms.

"I can't see it anymore. Mom wants me to wait."

"You were using the essence to see it?" Daryl asked. He opened his pack and withdrew a notebook and began writing notes.

"Yes. I think I could see it without if I tried but Mom told me to wait."

"Describe what you saw."

"The trees and ground sparkled. Some more than others. Tiny little flecks of light."

"Have you left the farm before?"

"No."

"Been outside at night?"

Jill shook her head.

"So, this could've been here since the storm?"

"Yes."

Anne sank to her knees and leaned forward, thrusting her hands into the snow.

Daryl laid a hand on Ben's arm as he stepped forward.

"Give her a few minutes. If the light is information, she'll need a few minutes to sort it out."

"Wait here," Ben said to Jill and walked forward. To him the night remained dark. The trees blocked the starlight but gave enough light to make out shapes and hints of color. But he saw no sparkle. The hair rose on his arms again as he considered how different his wife and child were. They were touched by God. Chosen for a reason he couldn't fathom but dreaded. They saw the secrets of the universe, short glimpses that brought them to their knees, and it terrified him. He sank to his knees beside his wife. He was relieved to note her breathing appeared even. She was frowning but it wasn't painfilled or angry. She was concentrating.

They sat there long enough for his pants to become soaked before she straightened and stretched.

Ben was glad she wore snow pants. He could see she was just a bit damp. He stood and offered his hand, which she took with a grateful smile. She groaned when she stood, releasing his hand to rub her back.

"I don't know what it is." She linked her arm with his and stood on tiptoe to kiss him. "There's a lot of it though." She led the way back to Jill and hugged her before saying, "It isn't quite the same as active essence. I can pull it out and use it, but it damages the trees to do it. It's a wrong thing to do." She gestured over her shoulder without looking. "If you follow the lights in the ground, you'll see they're forming a web or circuit or something. Like their falling slowly through the dirt into patterns that I can't quite make out. Go look but go slow and stay close. Check in every few minutes so I don't worry."

Jill grinned and ran forward.

"Should we?" Ben whispered as his daughter sat cross-legged in the snow. She petted Boomer absently her hand slowly stilling until the dog saunter away to get more active attention.

"As opposed to locking her in her room?" Anne shook her head, giving him a rueful grin. "It would call her, Ben. It's best to let her listen when we can supervise."

"And if it doesn't let her go?"

"I'll pull her away." She glanced at their quiet friends. "Might as well make a fire. We could be here a while." She turned back to observe Jill. "I'll let her be a few minutes, then join her."

"Will it trap you?"

"I don't think so, but if we don't move by morning bring us home."

"Gee, that's reassuring."

She laughed and turned to kiss him.

He kissed her back, the familiar feel of her lips on his easing his tense shoulders. "You're an incredible woman, Anne Windsor."

"I love when you call me that," she whispered.

"I love you." He rested his forehead on hers and hugged her lightly. They stood in an embrace while his friends made a small fire and settled beside it to wait.

Daryl sat on tree stump Dave cut loose from a pile of storm debris and absently nodded his thanks as he opened his notebook. "Did it hurt to touch the essence inside the trees?"

"No. It's not like mine." Anne frowned thoughtfully and rose. "Or maybe they aren't my trees and I can't feel their pain."

She stood and stepped forward.

Ben laid a hand on her arm.

"Should you?"

"I have no idea."

The words did nothing to reassure him. He watched anxiously, wanting to drag his wife back onto the path.

Kate stepped up beside him and put her arm around his waist. He spared her a sympathetic smile. She loved them too.

To Ben's eyes Anne appeared to be doing nothing. She

crouched beside Jill in the snow and both remained unmoving for minutes. As one, they turned their heads and gestured.

"It freaks me out," Kate whispered.

"Me too," Ben said.

Daryl said, "I wish I had better tools. Imagine what we could learn if we knew the frequency they communicate on. The Earth itself has been speaking and we never heard it. It makes me wonder if some of the crazy people who heard voices really did."

Ben snorted as Kate said, "Anne never heard voices."

"Oh, I didn't mean her. I think she'd have told me, but in general. I mean, who's to say if it's only their minds that are different? Maybe the stars or trees or ocean or whatever also communicate in ways we can't hear."

"You think it's the Earth they hear?"

"I have no idea. Which is why I'd love tools to trace it to the source."

"Anne think's its God's ideas."

And she might be right." Daryl quirked a grin and gestured to the sphere. "God's computer virus. He's rebooting the system."

"Kate!" Dave called, and Ben turned as Kate's husband gestured her to the fire. "Stop worrying so much and come sit a bit and keep me company."

Ben shook his head, declining the offered canteen and turned back.

Anne had risen and held out her hand. A small sphere floated from the larger and landed on her palm. Jill nodded, and the sphere disappeared. A moment later yellow glowed among the top leaves of the shrub directly before them.

"Fascinating," Daryl said and began writing.

"Does it hurt?" Ben called.

"Can't feel a thing." Anne grinned over her shoulder at him. Her expression changed to fear, and Ben stepped forward as Jill fell face down in the snow.

"Jill!" Anne said and crouched to thrust her hands into the snow. She moaned and fell to her side.

Daryl yanked him back.

Ben glared and shook his hand off.

"Wait," Daryl said.

"Fuck that," Kate muttered as she ran past Ben.

Anne was already pushing herself up as Ben reached her.

"What happened," Kate asked as she reached for Jill.

"No. Leave her. I can get her back."

Anne closed her eyes and pressed her trembling hands to Jill's cheeks.

"Get her back? Anne, what's going on." Ben squatted and hovered, hating not knowing how to help them. And it was clear they needed help. Anne looked strained and scared, but Jill's expression made him groan. Whatever had happened had knocked the wits from her. She lay staring lifelessly before her, a small trickle of drool pooling on her chin and her wide-open eyes staring at nothing.

"Jilly," Kate said softly and clutched Ben's arm hard. "Come back, Princess."

Jill blinked, and Anne sat back on her heels, wiping her forehead with a hand that still trembled.

"I see it," she said, and Ben knew she spoke to Jill. "Don't."

Jill groaned and rolled, pushing herself to her hands and knees.

Anne hugged her, peering at Ben over her shoulder. Her glance flicked to Daryl, and she grimaced.

"The ground here sucks up our essence like a sponge. It's traveling fast, deep under the ground. Jill got caught up in a stream."

"I can handle it," Jill said.

Kate shook her head. "It didn't look like you could. Sorry, sport, I call them like I see them and whatever that was knocked you out."

"I wasn't expecting it." Jill sat and rubbed her forehead.

Anne stood and offered Jill a hand. "We'll need a few minutes. Maybe you guys should leave us here and come back in an hour or so?"

Ben said, "No. We'll wait. Do what you need to do. But, Anne, for heaven's sake, do it carefully. Your scaring the crap outa me!"

Anne laughed and released Jill's hand to hug him. He breathed in the scent of her hair and kissed her warm cheek. "Be careful," he whispered, wishing he could take her place. He knew without her saying a word that what they faced was dangerous and that it frightened her.

"We need to know what it is, Ben. It's more dangerous to not prepare ourselves, to let it take us unawares."

"I know, I just hate this."

"Me too," Kate muttered, and Anne laughed.

She released him to hug Kate.

"We'll be fine. Heat up some tea while Jill and I explore." She bit her lip and glanced over her shoulder. "If we do collapse leave us here. I'm not sure we could find our way back if our bodies are moved."

"That's reassuring," Kate said sarcastically, and Ben shook his head.

Anne hugged him again. "We got this."

He heard the lie in her voice and felt it in the tension of her body but said nothing when she released him to rejoin Jill.

The two women held hands and sat in the snow. A moment later the brush around them glowed green and they closed their eyes.

The glow faded and built again, and Daryl scribbled in his notebook, glancing at his watch and the large sphere.

"What do you think they're doing?" Wayne asked.

"Exploring," Daryl said. "I'm betting they're following the path of light under the ground. It must be fascinating."

"It is," Anne said without turning to them. "I can see specks I think are animals. See the small ones, Jill? If you follow the lights, there to the left, you can use the essence inside the trees to see them."

Jill laughed and gestured and the glow about her brightened.

"Careful," Anne warned, and the glow dimmed. "Don't let it touch you, or you'll be sitting here naked."

"We need better clothes. Imagine how much clearer it would be if we could sit in it."

"Look at the tone of the light on that one. I think it's a raccoon and that one is probably a possum."

"I can almost hear it," Jill murmured and leaned forward.

"I think's it's hunting. Look how intent it is." Anne frowned and opened her eyes to stare at the trees. "I'm worried we're hurting the trees. Don't use more than you need to and try to put it back."

You can pull it from the ground. It's much less spent. Look at that, Mom!"

Ben stepped forward, and Kate took his hand, dropping her free hand to her gun, then laughing ruefully, releasing both.

Ben didn't blame her. Jill had sounded excited and scared. Anne frowned in puzzled concentration and her eyes were closed again although her head was turning as though she was looking around. The sight unnerved him. He hated that she could see things that weren't there.

"I see it." Her expression eased into one of interest and Ben relaxed.

"It's big, whatever it is. I wonder… Daryl, step off the path and go into the trees."

Kate released Ben and held a finger to her lips. She eased off the path, stepping carefully through the brush, and Ben lost sight of her in moments. Daryl crashed through the brush, and Ben could follow his progress easily.

So could Anne who laughed as she pointed.

Jill turned her head and pursed her lips. Her eyes were still closed but she faced the direction Kate had gone.

"Aunt Kate!" she called and opened her eyes. She stood and walked forward, her fingers grazing the trees, and Ben knew she was using their essence to lead her when she changed direction and headed further into the woods.

Kate laughed, the sound muffled by distance and the two women spoke but were too far to make out more than voices.

Anne cocked her head. "We can use the essence here to talk or see if we're touching a conduit." As she spoke, she reached for a shrub and then a tuft of tall grass, then placed her bare hand into the snow. "The trees work very well. The smaller shrubs are more difficult. The roots...."

For minutes she leaned at an awkward angle, keeping her hand in the snow.

When she stood, her hand was bright red from cold and she rubbed it absently. "The ground is tricky, but we can go." She winked at Ben and slipped her glove on. "I called her. She's with Kate. There's a dangerous animal about half a mile away in the direction we're going. I wasn't able to get close enough to really see what it was, but it's big and full of energy."

"Great," Ben said and stepped forward to embrace Anne. He rested his chin on her head and peered into the dark.

"Jill knows about it," Anne said. "Kate will take care of her. Jill's better at sensing the animals' intent than me. She can look again when we get closer."

"Is it safe?'

"I have no idea. The essence in the ground has pockets and surges. We're being careful, but I suppose you could fall into one and be swept away."

You say that like it's a current."

"It is sort of. I wish I could explain but I don't understand it either. All I can say is the information is so enticing that it pulls you with it and before you know it, you're half a mile away and examining a family of badgers. I think it will get easier to guide ourselves as we gain experience but who knows."

"I don't know what to do here, Anne. Should you gain the experience, or will it make the addiction worse?"

Anne winced and flushed, and Ben knew he was right. His wife and daughter were already addicted to the essence. He glanced back up the dark path but couldn't see any signs of life from where they stood. No lights, no smoke, no noise betrayed the presence of the people who sheltered on their farm. And he knew it was Anne's power that kept them safe, and she and Jill could make their lives easier by using the essence. He also knew using it had consequences, and he couldn't imagine what they might be.

"We don't really have a choice," Anne whispered.

He kissed her hair and said nothing.

Knowledge is Power

Tuesday Late Evening 1/23

The dense trees lining the road dispersed the stronger wind that scoured the open fields of the farm. The snow on the remains of the road wasn't as deep, but it was just as treacherous, hiding the tree limbs and remains of the vehicles beneath a soft white blanket. The jingle of tack and swish of a tail merged with the louder murmurs of the men following and the tree limbs creaking in the wind.

The horses followed without fussing, trusting Ben would keep them safe. He wished he'd made more time for night-time rides with his family. It was peaceful beneath the spreading branches and the snow hid the remains and blanketed the ruins. He could almost pretend this was one of the rare stolen moments he'd taken with Anne when they'd sneak out when the kids were away and find a secluded spot to make love in the trees or just walk together beneath the stars.

He wished he'd done it more often. Jill was enjoying the ride and time spent with them, and he regretted not spending more nights with her and Doug exploring the mystery of the forests at night or riding like this.

Anne held up her lantern and the trees sparkled green.

"Woah," he said to the horses and stilled to watch in awe as the road before her smoothed. No matter how many times he saw it, it still awed him.

The men walking behind the horses quieted. The snow hid the downed trees that blocked the road, but he could see the snow rippling and shifting as she transmuted the wood and merged it into a smooth rock-like substance beneath the snow. The lantern she held casted a nimbus of light around her. Green phosphorescence lit the trees on the right side of the road, warning there was active essence there. He wondered what it looked like to her.

"Can you see it, Jill?" he asked.

"The road?"

"No, the essence."

"Yes. Mom has it under control, but I'm watching for stray bits."

"Have there been any?" Daryl asked, and Ben hid his smile by turning to brush his hand across Lightning's jaw. The horse whickered softly and bobbed his head.

"Don't fall off. You can take notes later," Jill said tartly, and Ben's laughter escaped.

"Proper notes are essential in research," Daryl said indignantly but with a hint of laughter in his voice. "I wish it were light out so I could see it better. Is it taking a lot of essence?"

"Not really, but there's so much in the trees and ground it's hard to tell."

"But it isn't leaking out... I don't understand why it isn't dissolving our clothes or the horses' feet."

"The shoes," Ben corrected and snorted with laughter at Daryl's dismissive shrug. It was clear he had no interest in the horses except as a means of transportation. He sat Thunder like a sack placed atop it, and Ben worried he'd fall off even at this slow pace.

"It should work like the storm essence if it's the same stuff, but it isn't."

"Don't look at it, Jill," Ben warned, shooting Daryl an irritated glance.

"He's right. Wait until Anne can explore it with you," Daryl said hurriedly.

"I can't help looking at it, Dad, but I'm being careful."

"If you need to go home, say something right away."

"I wish you could see it too. It's really pretty, like fairy lights in the trees, and the ground glitters with tiny lights."

"Jill." Ben grabbed her boot and shook it.

"I'm fine. It's just so pretty and interesting."

"You scared your mother half to death, and I'm still not convinced you should be out here."

"You're going to have to trust me."

"I do…."

He shook his head, turning away from her sad smile.

Pat called, "Ben, warn Anne that Wayne and I are going to go ahead! We'll make a fire and see if we can find a good spot for a crossing."

"I told her," Jill said. "She says to stay on the left to avoid the essence she's spreading under the snow."

"That's so freaky," Pat muttered, and Jill laughed. He smiled back and slapped her thigh, gesturing Wayne, Kate, and Dave past him.

"Don't get it too close to us," Ben warned.

Jill said, "It's under control. It isn't like smoke that can waft about."

"I guess it's just hard for me to envision it. It looks like clouds to me when I can see it, and I imagine it's blowing about in the wind but I just can't see it.

"It does look a bit like a cloud. It's almost transparent. I can see through it, but it doesn't move much unless I move it." She frowned, and her eyes got that unfocused expression that meant she was thinking at the essence. Ben watched anxiously but she smiled a moment later.

"I can release it and it wafts away like smoke. It responds as fast as I think it. I'm not saying I couldn't accidently touch someone with it but if I'm paying attention and see them coming, I could move it quickly."

Daryl asked, "How quickly? Is it traveling instantaneously or just responding instantly?"

"It travels fast but I can see it move so it isn't instant. But it's moving so fast it's hard to see it move. Not blurry exactly just too fast to focus on like lightning."

She gazed at nothing, her eyes following movement only she could see for another minute and then shrugged. "I can make it slower but can't speed it to instant."

"Don't try too," Daryl said, giving Ben a small apologetic nod. "Don't try to force it to do anything. We need to be very careful. We're dealing with an unknown form of energy that we know has a powerful effect, which means it's a powerful source of energy, so treat it with respect."

"Aye, aye, skipper." Her smile grew, and she slid from Lightning's back. "Mom says I can try now."

Ben watched her scamper through the snow.

"They're terrifying," he whispered, and Daryl snorted with laughter. "I love how matter-of-fact your wife is. If she were a nervous sort…" he grimaced and shook his head.

"Anne is tough and smart and a tiger when it comes to her kids."

"I see it and it's a good thing. Jill is distracted easier than Anne, but I think she worries a bit too much about that. Although, I suppose I'd worry too. She went all the way to Florida in minutes.

I think you're lucky she came back from that. It had to consume enormous amounts of power to do it. And any power source can surge and burn out receptors. Anne is Jill's surge protector."

"Who's Anne's?"

"Your wife is a sensible woman."

Ben snorted softly. He wiped the frown from his face as Anne approached.

"Talking about me," she asked as she reached them. She gave Ben a kiss and rubbed her shoulders.

"Tired?" he asked.

"A bit. I'm hungry. Is there any tea left?'

Ben rummaged in the pack Lightning carried and handed Anne a baggie of cookies and thermos of tea. "Should we make a fire?"

"No. Gimme a boost up and we'll follow Jill. Keep an eye on her pace. If she slows too much, I'll nudge her."

You sure she won't, *um*, wander off?"

"Pretty sure. It's getting easier to navigate. We need some time to explore although I suppose it's good to have a goal to keep us focused. It's just so frustrating to catch these enticing glimpses and have to ignore them."

"It doesn't seem to be taking much essence, but I'll admit it's hard for me to judge," Daryl said.

"It isn't. I'm using the leftover bits in the road sludge and downed trees. It's more inert than the stuff in the live trees."

"Inert?"

"The stuff in the trees is almost spent. The stuff in the ground is brighter but there's less of it lying about. I came across a few pockets of trapped essence caught in the road sludge. I think we can thank our lucky stars none of the vehicles has hit one."

"Great," Ben murmured.

"We'll have to adapt."

Daryl said, "I'd been thinking we could make tools and store them underground but if the essence is in the ground and sinking that won't work."

"It might work. We'll have to test it. But I think we'll have to be careful that anything we make in the future that's necessary for survival can withstand the storm."

Anne turned her head, and Ben knew Jill spoke to her. She said nothing, but her expressions told Ben she found whatever Jill had said interesting. She glanced behind her but remained on Lightning's back.

"She sees the animals around us. I'll look later." She grinned at Ben. "I hope she isn't making the road pink or something. She's finding something funny but hiding the thought from me."

"Could she do that?"

"She could do anything," Anne said, and Ben tried not to shiver.

Building a Bridge

Ben stood on a riverbank examining a bridge that hadn't been there an hour ago. Wayne handed him the binoculars and gestured to the left bank.

"They make it look easy."

Ben lifted the glasses to his eyes and scanned the new rock pilings that held up the bridge. He said, "Make sure nothing we need goes near that water. Anne says there's a lot of unspent essence in it. Keep three men on lookout for loose debris that could knock into it." The bridge filled him with unease. As sure as the sun rose, Doug would take Johanna across it to search for her family. Anne knew it too. It was in her eyes when she examined the plans Doug had given her.

Wayne said, "We have five men on it, but there could be trees we can't see under the water."

Ben's gaze flicked to the water as another section of bridge formed before his eyes. Anne stepped forward onto the new section. Ben's heart pounded and his palms sweat, but the new piece appeared rock steady. Jill remained laying on her stomach, staring into the water. She was supposedly searching for trees that might tumble loose and smash into them, but he doubted she was. She'd rolled her eyes when he'd asked her to check and assured him in a voice only a teenager could manage that she could catch any tree before it did much damage.

Ben asked. "Did Doug arrive yet?"

"Not yet, but they got the bigger tent up and a good fire going."

"Is the smoke still visible?" Guilt seared him. He almost wished the smoke had stopped and wishing that was wishing the death of strangers.

"Yes— and answering our bursts. Whoever is at the other end is alive and aware of us."

Ben lowered the glasses and handed them back to Wayne. "She's going to want to go."

"It would be quicker."

"She's going to kill herself. Look at her! She's so tired, she can hardly stand." He frowned as he examined the weary line of Anne's shoulders. She kept her back to the drop and frothing water behind her and faced the far shore. He couldn't see her face but knew she'd be wearing her stubborn expression.

She'd cleared the road in a much wider path than he'd intended. He'd thought they were smoothing out a car width, but they'd smoothed the entire width, and he hadn't realized until they arrived at the river head where it had once joined the lake.

Water had cascaded in torrents from the earthen bulwark that was all that remained of the dam. It trickled now from ten cutouts in the new rock wall that held the water back and formed the base of the bridge. And she and Jill had done that in less than an hour.

Both women had slept like the dead while Ben organized a base camp, and he thought they should still be resting but Anne wouldn't hear it.

"It must be scary as hell up there," Ben said as he turned to climb the embankment. "It terrifies me to just watch it. What if the wood they're forming breaks? They'll fall to their deaths. We should've made the bridge further up."

"Daryl says the woods structure is a much stronger than real wood, and they're almost across."

"Daryl is just guessing." Ben slashed his hand through the air in an angry gesture. "Not about his results. I'm sure he's reporting the facts as he knows them, but for all anyone knows, the things Anne and Jill make could rot within hours. We know nothing!"

"Science still works. And he sees nothing unusual in the woods' composition except the density of the cell structure. It isn't real wood but a facsimile of wood. He says it isn't something that would grow. It's a construct."

"And he can't see the essence either. Which means there could be a billion elements within that construct that none of us could see, and they could all be ticking time bombs."

Wayne rested a hand on his shoulder. "There's no reason to think it isn't exactly as Anne sees it. She can see the essence of things. Trust her, Ben."

"I do. It's just nerve wracking watching them up there on the edge like that."

Wayne laughed and shaded his eyes from the rising sun to peer down the river. "This is the logical spot. We think the smoke is coming from the Parkland district. We can take the quad and dirt bike, and Marcus will take his mountain bike. We'll find them while Anne rests."

"I'm not just being a worried husband here, Wayne. We need her. Without her and Jill, we won't have a prayer of feeding this lot."

"She is a miracle, isn't she?" Wayne frowned thoughtfully. "It gives me the shivers when I think about it. It's like God himself touched them and gave them gifts to save mankind while he cleanses the earth."

307

"I know. It freaks me out. And it scares the crap out of me that others will say her gifts are from Satan."

They were quiet, both watching the bridge take shape.

Wayne finally whispered. "Is this the End Times?"

Ben laughed although he'd considered it too. "The rapture? No. Daryl says it's a cycle. He's about having a fit he's so excited over his new theory, and it's killing him that he can't research and observe at the same time."

Ben tensed and grabbed Wayne's arm as Jill jumped to her feet, but she only stepped forward to Anne's side, and they stared down at the water together.

"Gives me the shivers," Wayne mumbled.

The rumble of a truck approaching made Ben turn and he hurried up the river embankment to the wider path that curved to the bridge to greet Doug.

"I left Johanna in charge," Doug said as he jumped from the cab.

Wayne held out his hand for the keys. "I should go back to oversee the new hands. One of us should be there."

Doug handed the keys to Wayne, his wide eyes locked on the bridge section rising from the tangled mass of debris and frothing water. "I brought more supplies and dropped them at the tent already… Holy shit! Is that safe?"

"That's why you're here."

Jill ran forward and knelt on the edge to stare down into the water. Another section rose from the water, this one much rougher than the other, and both women ran back. The purple cloud above them settled to the wood and the wood flowed like liquid, smoothing the roughness away. It happened quickly, and it wasn't until the cloud lifted that Ben noticed the height of the entire forward section had curved down toward the shore.

Jill reached into the water, yanking on a tree limb and Anne turned. They were too far to hear but it was clear by their expressions they were arguing. Jill shrugged and settled herself cross-legged and pointed. The limb she'd been trying to pull flowed across the water and onto the bridge where it rose and branched out into thin tendrils.

"Jesus Christ!" Doug exclaimed.

"Terrifying," Wayne agreed.

Ben said nothing as a rail formed and grew along the twenty-foot stretch before Jill. Anne watched for a minute before turning her back. She appeared to be doing nothing at all but a minute later another section of smooth bridge unrolled before her.

"She's transforming the downed trees," Doug said in awe.

"She'd better be careful," Ben said and rose the glasses to his eyes again. "If one breaks free…"

The men watched as Anne stepped from the bridge onto the opposite shore and held up her arms in a fist pump. She bowed with a flourish and walked slowly back, trailing the purple cloud over the surface of the bridge behind her. The wood smoothed and rolled, flattening and curving as she willed it. Another railing sprouted and grew along the left side and the entire thing turned gray, no longer wood but stone. Jill stood and began taking small steps backward, her eyes on the railing as it rippled free from the debris caught in the water and slithered into place.

"*Tada,*" she said proudly when they reached the shore.

"Oh good, Doug is here," Anne said and hurried forward to hug him. "We built it just like you said but added some more buttresses. It's pure rock into the bedrock. We both checked it for seams and cracks, and it looks good. Should we make it higher or thicker?"

Doug's expression made Ben laugh. Anne was so nonchalant as if she'd made a tray of cookies and wanted to know if he wanted another.

"*Um,* it is awful low. A big tree could roll over it if we get a storm surge."

Ben grabbed Anne's shoulder as she turned back to the bridge.

"It's good enough for today. You and Jill have been working too hard. Get something to eat and catch a nap in the tent while we work out logistics."

Anne frowned and opened her mouth, snapping it closed when he glanced meaningfully at Jill. He smiled when Anne nodded and hooked her arm in Jill's.

"He's right. We should rest. And I know I'm starving. I hope they made stew."

Ben kissed his wife and daughter's cheek and watched them climb the small hill they'd smoothed when they'd arrived.

"They're getting faster," Daryl said.

Ben glanced over; he hadn't heard him arrive.

"I need to run some experiments, but it looks like the cloud was even anticipating them or maybe storing their preferences. This is so exciting. Could I get a ride back and use the computer? I want to enter my notes while they're still fresh."

"Sure, go ahead. Use it whenever you like. It's your office too."

The quad and dirk bike roared to life, and Ben watched anxiously as the search team rode down the embankment and across the bridge. He held his breath, almost expecting the bridge to sink back into the water or disappear in a puff of smoke but it remained stable and unaltered.

"Freaks me right out," Wayne mumbled and slapped his shoulder, turning to get into the truck.

Lists and Rationing

Wednesday Afternoon 1/24

What's up guys?" Jill asked brightly as she entered the living room behind Anne.

"Homework," the kids said in irritated voices.

"We'll leave you to it then." Anne grabbed Jill and pulled her back into the kitchen. She'd been looking forward to kicking her feet up and relaxing, but the kitchen was comfortable too, and she'd been putting off this talk too long.

"Have a seat, honey," she said, pulling out one of the bar stools at the kitchen island and going to make tea. "We haven't had much of a chance to talk with all this going on."

Jill twisted her teacup and bit her lip.

"Doesn't it scare you?" she blurted, looking down at the table, avoiding Anne's eyes.

Anne returned the kettle to the stove and sat beside Jill. "Not really— I suppose it should." She held out her hand, turning it so they could both see the bandage where she'd burned herself. "But it doesn't."

311

"It scares me," Jill said.

"What part of it scares you?"

Jill looked thoughtful at this. "The part where people will think I'm a freak," she finally admitted.

"*Ahh*," Anne said softly, "I see." She spun her own cup around. "If I was nineteen, that would probably scare me too," she admitted. "It's no help for you to hear it won't matter so much to be accepted when you're older. It's true. But that doesn't help you now. The only thing I can say to you is don't judge yourself by another person's opinion. If you do the best you can, and act as honorably as you can, you can hold your head up high in any crowd."

She took Jill's hand. "There'll always be people who disapprove of or don't like you. That's true for everyone. Just make sure you like you! Be the type of person you'd want to be friends with. It's all cliché," she said with a laugh, "But it's true."

They sat there a while, quietly sipping their tea, thinking their own thoughts.

"Does the power of it scare you at all?" Jill finally asked.

"No." Anne shook her head. "Women have always been the creators. We create babies and homes and families. This is just more to make. Creating a good person out of a small baby is a much harder and way more important thing than creating a pile of cotton out of a rock," she said with conviction.

"*Hmm…*"

Anne smiled at the thoughtful expression on Jill's face that was so like Ben's. "One problem at a time."

"One problem at a time," Jill echoed.

Anne stood and headed to the door. "And we have plenty of those. I better go check on my mother and make sure she has the bakery under control."

* * *

"What should we make for dinner?" Anne was asking Jill when Sue exited the office.

"Kate's got it covered," she said. "She's bringing home soup and bread."

"Sounds good. What do you have there?" Anne added, noting the papers in Sue's hand.

"Lists!" Sue dropped tiredly into a kitchen chair. "I'm drowning in lists. I have lists of supplies, who owns them, and where they're located. I have lists of supplies needed. I have lists of people and where they're located. I have lists of professions." She was slapping the papers down on the table as she spoke. "I have wish lists of things people want. I have lists of things that need to get done. I have a list of my own lists," she said with irony, and Jill giggled.

Anne pulled the lists toward herself and went through them. There were indeed a lot of them. A knock on the kitchen door interrupted her perusal. A girl Anne didn't know, wearing a sweatshirt she recognized as Jill's, entered and handed Sue another list.

Sue read it and said, "Good job, Stacy. Can you go see if Carly has that research done? If she isn't done, you two finish it up by tomorrow's meeting, and remember it's been moved up to three."

Stacy agreed with a mumbled, "Yes, Ma'am," nodded to Anne and Jill, and was out the door.

"What was that all about?" Anne asked.

Sue sighed and handed her the new list. "We need to cut down on generator usage. At the rate we're going through our gas, we'll be completely out in five weeks. We have to initiate a conservation system."

Anne tapped the list in front of her of all households that currently had generators with the current supply of gas highlighted next to it. "*Hmm…*" Anne said thoughtfully. "We could cut down power consumption by moving all freezer items outside."

"We could." Sue rummaged in her pile of paper and removed one that she frowned at. "But I think it'd be better if we consolidated all food resources. We're going to go on a three hour a week allotment of electricity. Everyone's freezers and refrigerators won't work anyway. We'll make sure everyone has three days of food at their homes in case of snowstorms, but we should consolidate the rest."

"Three hours!" Anne exclaimed in dismay. "That's not a lot of time."

Sue shrugged, not glancing up from her papers. "No, it isn't. But it's the best we can do if we want gas for the tractors. Planting is our number two priority. Besides, it'll be no hours at all in six weeks if we don't."

"What's the number one priority?" Anne asked. "I would've thought gardening would've been it."

"No." Sue glanced up and Anne was surprised by her grim expression. "Our number one priority is rescue. Gas for rescue attempts, or medical needs, get an automatic okay. Another twenty came in while you were gone, and we sent out five new groups to search. People are still out there, and they need help."

"Makes sense," Jill said, examining the paper over Anne's shoulder. "How are you going to share the gas though when they all have different amounts?"

Sue pulled out another paper. "This is a list of the gas they started with for their generators; most have gone through approximately five gallons a day. We're issuing enough gas for six weeks, with two exceptions, the greenhouses and Abby's house." She tapped the list in front of her. "According to this list, Mr. Ward will need seven more gallons while Mr. Jones will need ten. You guys won't get any," she added with a smile.

Anne asked, "What about the people who already have more

than that, like us?"

"We won't take any away," Sue said. "But we'll strongly recommend they start rationing it like everyone else is. If they choose to volunteer their extra, it'll be gratefully accepted. We're going to recommend a three hour a week maximum. Enough time to do laundry and charge gadgets and fill water jugs. Showers, cooking, and lighting are going to have to be done the old fashion way."

"*Eww*," Jill said.

"I agree," Anne said. "What are we doing about heat?"

"Pat has organized the tree cutting crews; everyone will be supplied with wood. "Everyone except Harper house, that is. We're still working on that. There's no fireplace there," she finished gloomily.

"How many chainsaws do we have?" Anne asked.

"Thirteen," Jill said promptly.

"Are you sure, honey, that seems like a lot?

"Yep, I rounded them up." Todd has four of them. He used them in his business. He also has spare chains and parts too. And Dad has three. Kevin has two. He's been cutting wood out back for years for his house. A few others have one each. They were all donated. Todd's in charge of them. They have quite a big pile already at the back of Kevin's house. Fifty or so people can put a dent in things quick."

"Tomorrow's meeting will be interesting," Anne said.

Sue nodded. "We moved it up to three o'clock. We wanted to have people be able to attend while it was still light out. The bus will be leaving at two-thirty. If you don't want to walk down, be ready to go."

"What bus?" Anne asked, thoroughly confused.

"We're instituting public transit; Thunder and Lightning will be pulling a hay wagon and will make round trips for two hours starting at eight in the morning and from four to six in the evenings.

If you need to get there any other time, you're on your own."

Anne laughed. "It's not that far."

"It's not far but the entire thing is a steep slippery hill. It's too far for some. We don't have enough winter clothes and shoes for that long of a trek for most people."

Sue began rummaging in her stacks of lists. "*Ahh*! This one is for you."

Anne read it doubtfully. "I'll try, but we can't really make specific cloth types too well."

"Way ahead of you," Sue said. "We went around and asked what was needed. We then went around and collected samples from whoever we could get to give them to us. I still have ten people out doing that as we speak. It should all be in the garage for you when you're up to it."

"Holy cow, you're efficient!"

"I'm trying," Sue said. "I'm really motivated. Daryl asked me to line up as many samples of metal and minerals as I could as well. They're in the garage too."

"Jill, honey, can you go ask uncle Dean to make Daryl one of our housemates?" Anne asked. "It'll be easier on us if we don't need to track him down. We'll give him the garage as his temporary workshop. He can get some supplies from our office, and maybe we can get some from other people?"

Sue was rummaging in her lists. "Here you go— donated office supplies." She pursed her lips as she read. "Not much there, but I'll have it all gathered up and brought here. This is administration central, so it makes sense to have it all here.

"We'll have to move the books," Sue went on. 'We took those encyclopedias that were in your living room and put them in the garage for easier access, but that won't work if it's Daryl's space."

"Maybe we could—"

"Don't worry about it," Sue interrupted, rising to go. "I'll figure something out. I'm going to go shower now though before the hot water is gone."

"She is frighteningly efficient," Jill said, "but she's also right. I'm going to go use your shower, okay, Mom?"

Jill hurried for the stairs without waiting for an answer.

Chloe, Emily, and Cole entered the kitchen before Anne had time to do more than sip her tea.

"We're done with the homework Mom gave us," Chloe said. "Can we go play now?"

"Sure, what are you going to play?" Anne asked.

Cole said, "We're going to the barn. Our dogs are there."

Anne said, "Wear your coats and be back by dark."

Anne stood to watch them go and was heading for the stairs and a nap when the door opened and Ben and Daryl entered.

Resigned to spending the rest of the afternoon discussing the essence with Daryl, she headed to the stove to make more tea.

* * *

Anne glanced at Sue as she tapped her spoon on her glass. "Enjoy this meal. Our next one will be cooked outside. We go on power rationing tomorrow."

The kids began complaining but the adults exchanged grim glances.

"But, Mom, that's stupid. We need the lights and how will we cook?" Chloe continued to complain, and Emily chimed in.

Sue gave her girls a look that silenced Emily instantly. "It could be much worse than a little rationing."

"It is much worse for a lot of people," Ben said, giving Chloe a stern glance.

Chloe stopped whining and hung her head.

Dave broke in. "We saw some big cat tracks today on Myer's property where we were hunting and sent word around to the houses to be careful."

317

"How big?" Ben asked.

"A good five inches." David held his hands apart to show them.

"We have the occasional bobcat. And someone saw a mountain lion a few years ago, but nothing that big," Ben said doubtfully. "Are you sure?"

"I think it's a tiger," David said.

The kids began to giggle.

"Tiger?" Anne asked doubtfully and winked at Cole.

"There was a big zoo in Bridgeport," Dave said.

The kids continued to laugh, but the adults stilled. Ben's anxious expression worried Anne.

"That's not good. They had all kinds of dangerous animals there," he said.

Anne said, "They had a breeding pair of timber wolves. We went to see them three months ago." She glanced over at Jill and Julie. "You guys remember?"

The girls nodded.

"They had Bengal tigers too, and panthers," Julie said, starting to look scared. "And a lot of bears."

Ben reached over to smooth her hair. "From now on, no one goes into the woods unless they're armed. At least one, armed person per group," he corrected. "We don't have enough guns to arm everyone. "Pat, make sure the men who cross the river tomorrow have guns. The zoo was on that side. How many more are going?"

"Three men with three sets of skis, three twenty-pound packs and your heat ball, Anne," Pat said.

"I hope they're taking matches too," Anne said with an anxious glance at Daryl.

He nodded reassuringly.

She continued, "I would hate for it to give out just when they needed it."

Pat said, "We're sending them the freeze-dried food packs you had, some of the MRE, and two radios plus a flare gun, and, of course, matches. Marcus is bringing his lightweight pup tent, and a tarp and a map. He also has some good lightweight sleeping bags. Two of the skis are his too."

"Did you decide who is going?" Ben asked.

"Marcus, a guy named Jake Hansen, and Barry Richardson. Barry was a volunteer paramedic. Jake is older but in pretty good shape. He knew Marcus. They used to ride bikes together. They all have experience in cross country skiing. I'll tell Marcus to bring a gun in the morning, I know he has one. We'll need one more, I think. They can decide who carries it."

"How long do they plan to be gone?" Anne asked.

"Four days maximum," Pat said "They plan to check in every day. Hopefully, the walkies will reach that far. They're rated for eighteen miles, but we haven't gone nearly that far. We're moving ten men to the base camp upriver. We're taking one truck and Marcus's van. They'll have one walkie-talkie as well. That leaves two for here if the hunters still take four, but they need them more, I think."

Ben nodded in agreement. "We can leave one at the greenhouse and one here." No," he went on. "Better make that leave one at Helen's. Someone is always there. We'll make sure to have one of the younger, in shape, people there at all times so they can run for messages. What do you all think?"

They all agreed it was the best they could do.

"You know," Daryl said thoughtfully, "it wouldn't take much to fix these phone lines. If we had enough wire." He winked at Anne. "We could connect the severed ends. It would be an open circuit, but it would work. We could build some windmills too; get some power on this street."

Anne dozed as they spoke excitedly of repairing the phones and restoring power. Ben woke her and laughed as he pulled her to her feet.

"You're out on your feet," he chided as she mumbled apologies through yawns.

He ushered her up the stairs, calling goodnight to his brother who sat alone now at the kitchen table.

A Full Day of Making

Thursday Morning 1/25

The next day was cold but clear. Anne, Jill, and Daryl walked to the woodpile behind Kevin's house. They'd brought the boxes Sue had put in the garage and had packed a lunch.

Daryl carried his backpack and a stack of notebooks. A measuring tape was clipped to his belt and a gun stuck from his bag.

Anne glanced at him doubtfully. Daryl didn't strike her as a man used to firearms.

"It's a flare gun," he said sheepishly, following her gaze. "In case you guys keel over or something."

Anne laughed. "We'll be fine. I brought my twenty-two. So, you know how to shoot?"

"I do, although I haven't done it in years."

"You hold it then. Just in case I get some essence on me. The first thing Jill and I need to do is get some clothing that's essence formed so we don't need to worry about getting it on us. I really want some gloves. It gets cold keeping my hand's exposed like this." She handed him the small gun. "Jill got us two more purple balls," Anne added, holding hers up.

"We need a space to work," Daryl said, looking about him at the piles of wood stacked in Kevin's backyard.

"I got this." Anne winked at Jill and walked over to the pile of branches and concentrated for a few minutes. A slightly crooked pedestal table appeared among the pile of branches.

"That's so cool," Jill said, "Can I try?"

"One minute, honey. Let me finish this." Anne concentrated again, and a solid stool appeared. She quickly made two more. "That was super easy," she said as they dragged them out and placed them a short distance from the pile.

Jill said, "We know wood now, or at least our version of it. It's easier every time we do it."

Daryl placed his meters, a small scale, and the microscope on the table. "Let's discuss this before we have Jill try it. We need to have common terms for each action we take so we can communicate intelligently." He held up the purple ball. "What's this called?"

"A purple ball thing," Anne said, and Jill nodded.

Daryl laughed and shook his head. "We need a better, more precise name for it. Purple ball thing is two imprecise."

Anne examined the ball in his hand. "Essence?"

"No." Daryl shook his head again. "Essence is what it contains, not the container."

Jill nodded in understanding. "So, we call what's in the container essence and this" –she held up one of the purple balls— "Is a SEC— a small essence container." Jill giggled, her blue eyes alight with mirth. "We can call the large ones LEC."

Anne smiled approvingly. Jill seemed much more at ease with her new abilities since their small talk.

"Fine." Daryl nodded approvingly. "Let's try to learn a new element." He rummaged in the boxes and removed a handful of change that he began to sort.

"Try the pennies first. There should be copper and zinc in it. Let's see if we can gather enough to concentrate on."

Anne turned to Jill. "Try to remain focused because the essence of the man-made items is obliterated very fast and it can be confusing. Expect to go down some wrong lanes as you try to reproduce it. You'll hear the correct process. Well, not hear exactly, but I can feel its awareness." She paused, frustrated with not being able to put her thoughts into words "No, not awareness, its willingness." Anne sighed. "I don't know the word I'm looking for," she said with exasperation. "But when you get it right, you'll feel the rightness. Then the item manifests or transmutes rather." Anne glanced over at Daryl, hoping she was explaining it correctly.

"*A posse ad esse*," Daryl said.

Anne laughed. "Exactly."

Daryl rose an eyebrow.

"What?" Jill peered from one to the other, frowning.

"From possibility to reality," Anne said, laughing at Daryl's surprised expression.

"I work in horticulture," she said. "It's mostly in Latin. I went to school and everything," she added dryly.

Daryl inclined his head slightly. "Touché. Let's work on the metal samples and then you can explore a bit while I write up my notes. Stand as far back as you can and try not to inhale any of the gasses that release."

Anne mastered copper before Jill.

"Sweet!" she yelled and snatched up the newly transformed rock to hand it to Daryl.

He examined it, weighing and measuring it before running his meters over it. He handed her a pebble he took from an index card and Anne peered over his shoulder to read his notes.

"I've weighed and measured these." He indicated the line of

various sized rocks in front of him. "I'll just be doing simple tests here, but I'd like you to copy the essence of the metal as closely as you can. Don't try to make it stronger or condense it, just copy what you see. I need a good base of figures to start with."

He brought the microscope from his backpack and fiddled with it while Anne and Jill attempted to learn the metal in the coins.

The coins disintegrated on contact with essence in a rush of red gas and foul-smelling fumes that a wave of fresh essence sublimated, leaving the air pure and turning the red haze green. But only tiny specks of metal remained. A handful of coin actually left less remaining; the violence of the bigger batch being reduced to its base elements destroyed most of it and made the air flicker with tiny skeins of lightning.

Anne gathered her small specs and stared at her palm, careful to keep the loose essence contained. The spec appeared as a jumbled mass until she noticed a unique shape and tagged it a curled k in her mind and it suddenly took on dimension and definition. She wished they could release all the essence and stand in it. She was certain with enough she would see it clearly without effort, but she supposed, this way was better. It would be easy to be swept away by all the knowledge.

Excited by her progress, she mentally named the parts as she saw them and in seconds it was if the parts glowed, each unique and connected in logical ways that she mapped easily.

"Eureka," she said and applied her knowledge to a length of wood. The transmuting was harder than making cloth from wood, the changes she sought greater, but she could do it.

"I bet it would be easier to make rock into metal," she said as she handed Daryl the sample. "Jill, try color coding or naming the parts of it in your mind. As soon as I see a distinct difference, I tag it and suddenly I can see it much clearer. Metals don't have as much to grab onto as living things. They're a bit harder to see or maybe it's just I lack the knowledge to understand what I'm seeing. It just looks like splotches and squiggles to me without the potential bugs or grass has."

"Well, I suppose that makes sense," Daryl said. Metal is inert while bugs and grass are active. I'll see if I can round up some books that teach the different parts of metals." He frowned thoughtfully and tapped his bottom lip with his pencil. "You could probably use a course in physics. It would be much easier on me if we had a common language and think what we could learn if you knew the names scientist use to describe what you see."

Anne exchange amused grins with Jill and resumed staring at the metal in her hand.

"What is it?" she asked, gesturing at the sample she'd already handed Daryl.

"Zinc, I think." He picked up the chunk she'd handed him to weigh it as he said. "Use care with that method of reproduction though. If there's even a slight chance you might copy a dangerous element or isotope, don't do it."

"How would we know it was dangerous?"

"If the base material you're examining is made up of radium for instance. Granted it isn't likely you'd run into that but be cautious. Some chemicals that make up minerals could be dangerous like phosphorous, but we can take precautions. I'm particularly concerned with heat and light. Contracting either like you did into a small sphere could potentially be very explosive. We should approach it cautiously only after we've gained a greater understanding of the basics."

He handed Anne four coins. "They all have varying amounts of copper in them. Now that you know zinc, you might be able see the copper clearer.

* * *

Essence of the Storm

Anne lifted her frozen fingers to blow on them. Her stomach rumbled, and she glanced at Jill who sat in the snow, wrapped in hank of thick canvas-like material she'd made herself. She was surrounded by an assortment of objects, some so mangled Anne couldn't tell what they were supposed to be.

She eyed her own heap of mangled items and sighed. Learning the essence of an item was easiest. They had a handy chart Daryl had made with labeled samples they could reference if they forgot a pattern but transmuting one element to another while changing its shape took practice, and Jill was much better at it than she was.

Daryl laid her attempts at metal forks with wooden handles aside and said, "Let's try an experiment. I'll hand you something, and you both try to duplicate it."

He winked at Anne, who rolled her eyes, and Jill laughed. Daryl rummaged in one of the boxes and held out a piece of paper.

"See if you can make something resembling this by using any of the elements you've already learned."

Anne considered and said, "Paper is made from plants. And I read somewhere cloth. Making it super thin and square might be difficult."

Daryl said, "Don't worry about being exact. Have fun and be creative."

Jill giggled and gestured, and a roll of purple paper seemed to spill from the cut tree limbs before her. Anne picked it up and shook it out. It was surprisingly heavy but thin and relatively smooth. She let it fall and spread a dollop of essence on the branches, envision the pattern she thought of as trees but tightening and shrinking the structure like she did with the cloth. The essence lay on the cut branches almost quivering in its eagerness to become, and she laughed as she let it sink into the wood. White paper unfurled and tangled in the limbs. She ripped it pulling it free.

Jill stood to examine it closer and within minutes they could produce serviceable sheets of paper.

"It would need trimming," Anne said as she handed the samples to Daryl.

He laid them aside and handed her an inch-square piece of material.

"It's supposed to be one-hundred percent silk, but it'll have dyes and soaps in it."

They both produced something similar, but it wasn't exactly silk. Anne could see the difference in Jill's and remade hers.

"Cheater," Jill said in a laughing voice and guided her essence atop Anne's, remaking her length of silk into a smaller chunk of wood shaped like an X.

"*Hmm*, did you see that?" Anne peered at the mixed mass. "Make a new shape." Small tendrils of light reached from one cloud to the other and seemed to spark, lighting the essence almost too fast to see. Anne glanced at the crooked cup Jill had just made and formed her own, an identical match in seconds. "It's learning," Anne said.

"Not learning, remembering the pattern," Jill disagreed. "You learn a new element I don't know and see if it teaches my essence."

Daryl eagerly watched Anne. "That makes sense actually, but you should save a part of every SEC you use to merge into the next one. If the flickers are transmitted data, if you use it all, the gathered knowledge would be lost. Hand me the silk you made."

Anne handed him a new swath and took a piece of wool to learn.

While Daryl examined the silk under the microscope, she learned wool and passed the essence to Jill who was able to reproduce it on her first try.

"Brilliant," she said as she examined the pile of items left to test. "This should help tremendously." She handed Daryl the samples of wool. "What's the verdict on the silk?"

Same structure but tighter weave. I'll need my lab to do

chemical analysis and check the tensile strength. Take a break and then start on Sue's list, using what you've learned so far. If you're going to attempt a new element, let me know.

Anne sat at the small table she'd made earlier and reached for the lunch bag.

Daryl continue writing in his notebook, speaking without looking up. "Let me know right away if you have any ill effects, headaches, cramps, blurry vision, anything at all. And we shouldn't work too much longer." He glanced at his watch and pursed his lips. "It's twelve-thirty now so another hour or two, tops. That should give you time to get home and change for the meeting. I have some ideas on some simple experiments to do tomorrow, and there's still a ton of tests I want to do."

Daryl continued to chatter as she and Jill ate, and Anne exchanged amused grins with Jill. The food refreshed her, and she worked with renewed energy on the list Sue had given her.

"You know, we should be doing this on the road. Clearing and crafting all at the same time," Jill said as she yanked a swath of fabric from the woodpile. "We're wasting all their hard work."

"It's hardly a waste, but you're right. We'll need a truck and a helper or two to load it," Daryl continued as he gestured.

Anne followed his pointing finger and rose her hands to her face to block her startled exclamation. She hadn't realized they'd made quite so much. Daryl had been taking and stacking the items behind them.

A guilty flush heated her cheeks as she examined the remains of the once large wood piles.

"Wow!" Jill said, looking over what they'd done. "That's a lot of material."

Heaps of material in varying thicknesses and colors littered the ground. Daryl had spread out the bigger blankets and placed the smaller swathes atop them. Anne estimated it would fill the bed of the pickups and then some.

She said, "We'll have to get help moving this stuff."

"Gather the smaller items and toss them on this blanket but be careful of my samples. I'll talk to Sue about arranging a workspace closer to the bakery for you, but you'll have to craft it yourselves."

Anne held up a swath of pink silk and shook it out. "Pretty, Jill, is the umber effect intentional?"

"Yes, I think I could do patterns too. A workroom is a great idea. I'd love to try painting with it." She reached down and traced her finger an inch above the fabric. A darker pink line followed the curve of her finger and Jill clapped with delight. "This is going to be so fun. I could make it anything I want!"

Anne laughed and ruffled her hair. "Goose."

Jill's smile died, and she gestured at the mounded cloth. "I mean, if I had time. I know it's more important to make them clothes."

"You guys want some lunch?" Terry called, and Anne turned to wave.

Terry stood at the edge of her yard, wringing her hands together, her wide eyes locked on the piles behind Anne

"We'll eat at home. Thanks though. It's pretty amazing isn't it?" she said, gesturing at the transmuted wood lying around.

"I'll say," Terry said. "Is it safe?"

"Safe as houses," Daryl said.

"We'll move it to the front yard for you," Terry waved behind her in a come here motion.

Anne laughed as she rose her hands to shade her eyes and peered at the house where faces lined the second-floor windows.

"Have they been there long?" Jill asked.

"All morning," Terry said. "You guys are better than TV. It was really amazing to see. Scary and amazing," she repeated.

Anne said, "We'll explain more at the meeting today and, hopefully, that will take some of the scary away."

Daryl stood, gathering his equipment and placing it into his bag as he said, "I have some theories to talk over with everyone that I hope will help people understand it a bit better."

Terry nodded. "See you there."

Anne glanced back as she headed home. No one from the house joined Terry until they crested the hill between their homes. She flicked a glance at Jill who seemed oblivious.

"It'll take time for them to become accustom. It isn't as scary for us because we know we aren't doing anything. It's all the essence."

Jill nodded and picked up her pace. "Dibs on the shower!" she called back.

"This is hard on her," Anne said when Jill was safely out of ear shot.

"I can imagine. I see the looks but you're right, once people understand it, they'll take it for granted. She'll always get some sidelong glances, but I think most will be accepting."

"I hope so," Anne said and shivered.

What Will Come

Thursday Late Afternoon 1/25

Jill and Boomer had left before Anne finished her shower. She debated on what to wear. She still had two dresses. Both were gifts from Ben she couldn't bear to part with and a business suit her mother had bought her for Christmas. She'd only worn it one time, to a meeting at the bank, and she'd felt awkward in it then. She picked it up, intending to donate it, and then set it back into the closet. There was no point now, not when they'd have clothes in a day or so, and she'd look like a hoarder if she handed it over so late.

"I guess I am a hoarder," she said as she pulled out a pair of jeans. She'd kept three pairs and suddenly felt terrible that she had so much while others had nothing.

Ben found her on the floor of the closet crying, and she jumped to her feet, embarrassed to be caught.

"What is it," he asked, the tenderness in his voice making her cry harder.

"Look at all this! I'm an awful person. They're naked, and I kept all my pajamas."

"Sweetheart— it's one pair of sweats and three negligees. You really think wearing that pink teddy is going to keep someone warm?"

She dashed the tears from her cheeks and glared at her cowboy boots.

"Just stop. These are your things, and you have a right to them. Being generous doesn't mean you have to give everything away. Get a grip here." He kissed her forehead and held her while she cried. And she knew she wasn't crying over the clothes anymore but her family. She had them while others had no one and it was so unfair.

"Nothing we do will every make it right," she sobbed, and Ben hugged her tighter. "Not that stupid pantsuit or our sheets. No matter what I make them, how much I try, it'll never be right!"

"Hush," Ben kissed her temple, his warm breath a caress that made her cry harder.

"It'll be good again. Different but good. We have Doug and Jill, and, god-willing, grandchildren to look forward too. We're doing our best here, Anne. You need to slow down. You're exhausted."

"I could sleep for a week," she mumbled and straightened, pushing away to go to the bathroom and grab a tissue. Ben didn't need to be reminded of their losses, and she felt even worse for making him worry.

He said, "We'll come right home after the meeting."

She returned to kiss him long and hard.

His eyes sparkled when she finally pulled away.

"Right after," she said in the voice that meant she had plans for him, and he laughed.

They walked down the hill together and arrived to find the place milling with people. It looked to her as if almost everyone had come.

Someone had arranged the haybales in the middle greenhouse into long rows for seating. A hay podium and the karaoke machine waited as did Jill's map.

The house representatives sat before the podium, talking quietly amongst themselves. Sue carried a file box that she placed on a seat beside her, *saving it for Pat*, Anne assumed and hurried her step, there wasn't much room left in the front. She returned greetings as she edged through the crowd, tugging Ben with her.

Ben said, "You do what we talked about last night and you'll be fine."

Electric lanterns hanging from the braces overhead were already lit although the day remained bright enough to read. Anne hoped they wouldn't be here long enough to need them.

"No. Your family sits behind the podium," Sue whispered when she sat beside Sue's file box.

"She's right." Ben took her arm and escorted her to their seats before she could think of a demurral. He leaned close and rose a hand to block his face to whisper. "If we're declaring ourselves rulers, we need to remain a bit apart from them."

"A throne of hay," Anne whispered back just to see Ben smile.

He smiled but it didn't reach his eyes. She took his hand. He rose the other to beckon Doug and Johanna over.

"Jill!" he called and gave her a pointed glance when she held up a finger and continued to whisper with Julie.

"Jill!" he said again in the tone that meant right now.

Jill climbed over the haybales, excusing herself and giving Ben an annoyed look.

"The Windsor family sits here," Ben said firmly.

"But—"

"Here, Jill," Anne said, patting the bale beside her. "We're not here as citizens but as rulers. You can talk with Julie later."

Jill sank to her seat right as someone began to strum a guitar. The crowd quieted, more people entering and pressing into the aisles and sitting on the floor. The man playing began to sing and soon the crowd sang with him.

The country song was sad, about a man longing for his partner who was far away, and soon sobs could be heard over the singing. Anne's eyes teared, and Ben gave her an encouraging smile, but she saw he felt the crowd's sorrow too.

Anne stood and stepped to the microphone as the song trailed off. "That was beautiful," Anne said as the man let his fingers fall from the guitar strings. "I'm sorry; I don't know your name."

"It's Mike Hansen."

"That was really beautiful, Mike. Maybe you could put together some songs or a choir or something for the memorial Sunday?"

"Glad too," he responded, and stood to gesture to Terry. "And thank you, Mrs. Carrillo, for the loan of the guitar."

Anne took the microphone and announced, "Anyone interested in being in the choir, speak with Mike after the meeting." She cleared her throat and continued, "We have a lot to cover tonight, so let's get started." She banged her gavel that someone had thoughtfully placed on a hunk of wood atop the haybale and said, "This meeting is called to order. First, let's have Pat come up and tell us about the rescue attempt being made in Chester." She held up her hand as low mutters erupted. "I realize we're doing things out of order, but we have friends and family out there, and we want to know what's happening. We'll continue on to old business after this."

She resumed her seat as Pat went to the microphone.

Pat said, "As most of you already know, we've sent three men across the river toward Chester where we saw, and continue to see, smoke coming from. I'm happy to report our men crossed safely and reported they were fine and heading up old Route Three. We lost touch with them at nine this morning."

He held up his hand to silence the gasps of dismay. "We

expected to lose touch as the radios are rated for an eighteen-mile radius. We got approximately thirteen miles before we lost them but there's a huge hill between them and us. It's taking them time to explore the area. The damage is severe, the roads impassable in many places, meaning they need to backtrack often looking for ways around obstacles. They don't know where they're going and can no longer see the smoke. We have no idea how long it'll take to find people. But they've promised to be back in four days to report. Any questions?"

"How do we know smoke means people alive?" a woman asked.

Pat nodded and said, "It occasionally billows in three long and then three short puffs, which could only occur if someone were manipulating it. We're sending out the same message," he added. "Anyone else?"

There were no more questions, so Anne took the floor again. "Now, on to old business. Sue Foster has prepared a report for you." Anne sat down, and Sue took the mic, nervously clearing her throat.

"First," she said, "I'm sad to report we've had a death." She looked down at her notes. "Mr. Terrance Watin died today from wounds sustained from a collapsed building. He'll be cremated Sunday morning at the signal fire before our memorial service for those of you wishing to attend."

Sue pulled a sheet of paper out and glanced at it. "All houses are now clearly marked with a sign stating the name of the house. The one with the big Red Cross out front is our temporary hospital. That's the Russo house," she added.

"Now, on to the big changes— we'll be issuing enough gas to all homes with generators to supply electricity for three hours per week."

Gasps of dismay became annoyed mutters.

Sue held up her hand. "I know that's a real hardship, but we need to conserve our fuel for the tractors. Harvesting and plowing will take all our available resources. It'll be up to the house leaders how and when they use the generators. We suggest using it to get water and washing clothes as well as charging small appliances. If you're unhappy at the house you're currently in, you can ask another to take you in at any time or move down here to the greenhouse.

"We're also asking that food stuffs be moved here as these will be the only functioning freezers and refrigeration. We want every house to have a three-day supply of food for everyone in the house in case of inclement weather that prevents food dispersal. Bread and soup will be delivered daily to all houses, amounts varying depending on occupancy. A three-day supply of wood will also be delivered and kept for inclement weather. If you fall behind in wood supplies, report it immediately to Wayne Collins. Everyone will be assigned one bowl, which will be numbered. That bowl can be filled two times a day at the bakery here. But please, if you have food stuffs that will expire eat them before taking from the communal pot."

Also," she continued looking around the room, "if any of you have any manuals, encyclopedias, or how-to books, please bring them to the Carmichael house, which is going to be the new library. We'd appreciate any book or magazine donation but really need the manuals. Anyone wishing to borrow them will have to get permission to check them out, but we'd prefer to keep them in the house if at all possible. Mrs. Santire and Mrs. Lowed have agreed to be our librarians as they have some experience at it and will decide if a book can leave the premises or not.

"Lightning and Thunder are now our bus, which will make pickups and deliveries from eight until ten in the mornings, and four and six in the evenings. If you have a project that needs transportation, speak to Al at the barn to arrange a time slot.

"We need volunteers to teach the children. See me after the

meeting if you can volunteer. There are twenty-six school age children and school will be held at the Carmichael house."

She looked at her notes again. "You'll all be delighted to hear Anne and Jill have provided cloth for our use. It's being organized in the bakery sales area. The cloth needs to be cut and stitched but Anne thinks she can use essence to speed that along. We'll be working on that as time permits. If anyone needs anything that wasn't provided, see your house representative who will then see me. We're working to fix the bedding as soon as we can. I know it's uncomfortable for you sleeping on floors and hay. I'm not taking questions at this time, but I'll take them after all reports are in. Thank you," she said and sat.

"Thanks, Sue," Anne said, "You're doing a great job!"

A round of enthusiastic applause began. Anne let it go on for a moment before saying, "David Foster has a report he'd like to make now. Dave." She motioned for him to come up.

"Hi," he said and smoothed his collar, his eyes scanning the crowd. "I'm David Foster and I've been asked to lead our hunting and fishing crews. I've been hunting and fishing here on the farm and in the surrounding area for about twenty years now, so I have a lot of experience here. I'm here to report we've seen tracks several times now of a large cat that we're estimating is at least three hundred pounds by the size of its tracks. These are extremely dangerous animals. They can leap up to fifteen feet in one bound. The closest tracks were seen near the new bridge, right outside the camp there."

Nervous muttering swept the room.

Dave held up his hand. "They've been notified and are armed. The cat will probably leave the area when it smells them. I'm more worried about the wood cutters. Please make sure to stay in groups and have an armed lookout. Feral dogs have been seen and we've had reports of them acting aggressively. We recommend extreme caution when approaching unknown animals. Many non-native species could potentially be in our forest due to the proximity of zoos, so report any suspicious activity and keep in mind these aren't tame animals. Monkeys are cute but deadly."

He waited for the muttering to die down and said, "I do have some good news. We're averaging two deer a day as well as various small game trapped. These numbers will drop as we hunt this area out, so we can't count on those estimates, but it's enough that no one will be hungry until our crops come in."

The muttering grew louder and the tone happier.

Anne whispered, "Thank goodness," and Ben took her hand, squeezing for a moment before releasing her.

Dave said, "So far, we haven't had any luck fishing. We caught a few, but nothing to sustain us. The general consensus on this is that once the water settles back down and heats up it should pick up. Any questions?"

A man stood. "Hi, I'm Tim Arnault. How do I get on a hunting crew?"

Dave nodded and said, "For those of you interested in hunting or fishing, see me after the meeting. Are there any other questions?"

No one raised their hand or stood so he resumed his seat. Anne stood and gestured her mother forward. She smiled at Tim, glad he seemed to be settling in now and was willing to help. He grinned and winked, his expression somehow mocking, and she quickly averted her gaze.

Helen took the mic from Anne. "A lot of you know me. The Carmichaels have run this farm for generations and a lot of you have been customers. I'm sorry this tragedy has brought us here, but I'm glad to be working with so many good people. The kitchen crew has been doing a great job getting food prepared for everyone, but more help would be appreciated. If you have any cooking experience or would just like to learn, please see me after the meeting. We especially need people with butchering and cheese making experience and we could always use more dishwashers. Thank you." She handed the mic to Anne and resumed her seat.

Anne said, "That leaves Doctor Daryl Santire. He was a professor of physics at M.I.T. and has been studying what Jill and I can do. He has some insights and theories he'd like to share."

Daryl settled a stack of notes on the podium and took the microphone. "Hello again, everyone. There are a few things I'd like to cover quickly, then I'll take questions. To start with, I think it wouldn't take too much to get some windmills and maybe even some water wheels generating enough electricity to power our houses."

Immediately, the crowd began to talk excitedly.

"Also," he said, holding up his hand for quiet, "it shouldn't be that hard to run a wire and complete the circuit for our phones to work. It would be an open line, but it should work."

Again, a round of excited talk traveled the room.

"As some of you know," he continued. "I'm a Doctor of Physics. Basically, I deal with the principles that explain matter and energy. Specifically, I used to study nuclear energy.

"Anne has been letting me study what she does, and I'd like to clarify it a bit. I'm going to give a short speech about what I think has happened and what I've observed of Anne and Jill's abilities and how that pertains to the past and our future." Daryl glanced at his notes, then the crowd, and began to speak.

"Anthropologists break down the Earth into eons and count four major ones. During each of these time frames, the Earth had different conditions than it does today, sometimes being hotter, sometimes colder. There were different levels of CO_2 in the air. The proportion of elements in the water and land masses has changed. Scientists divide the eons and eras by the flora and fauna found in them. Are you all with me so far?" he asked.

The crowd nodded and murmured agreement. Anne took Ben's

hand and leaned forward.

Daryl continued, "Each of these geological eras has one thing in common. They all had events that triggered mass extinctions, causing the plants and flora to evolve. Sometimes, species were wiped out completely. Think dinosaurs," he said and smiled at the children who giggled. "Sometimes, the fauna wasn't wiped out and just gradually changed to suit their new environment, like birds. These changes generally took millions of years— we call it evolution." Again, most of the crowd nodded.

"Okay, let's skip the ancient history of millions of years ago and come to the closer events we know more about. Our encyclopedias are full of information on those early events for those of you who are interested in the details.

"Pliocene period two million years ago was attributed to a supernova that caused major changes in the land masses. It caused an ice age that wiped out many species of marine life. Now, over the past 740,000 years there've been eight glacial cycles. We've currently been in an interglacial period for about the last ten thousand years. After each of these eras, the life forms were different than they had been," he said with emphasis.

"You've all seen pictures of the evolution of man and horses and whatnot," he continued. "Sometimes, these changes happen faster than others. While in the past these events were spread out over millions of years, the later ones have come closer together. Seventy-four thousand years ago to as recent as thirteen thousand years ago, glaciation ended. Our current continents are in place and flora and fauna we would recognize is present. A major extinction event occurs, it has unknown causes, but something caused the extinction of large animals like wooly mammoths and sabretooths. The cause of this is still unknown and has been attributed to such things as the impacts of meteors, disease, and solar flares."

Anne wasn't the only one to inhale sharply at the word solar flare. The scientists had been calling the storm a sustained solar flare, explaining the electrical fields and lightning generated by the storm were caused by actions inside the sun.

Daryl said, "My theory is, the extinction occurred because of the release of what we're calling essence."

Ben's hand clenched hers hard.

"In our time, we know the event started small in the mid-Atlantic. The first reported disappearances occurred there. Within days there was a huge storm front tracked by NASA. We all watched it on television. Conflicting reports were made as to the cause. We all saw the different experts giving their opinions. No one was able to approach the area. All planes and boats sent in never returned. We know now that the essence probably disintegrated them within seconds, and the people on them probably drowned or were killed by the lightning that accompanied the storm. The disappearances weren't talked about much by the news. They blamed it on electromagnetic energy interrupting the ability of the people to report. There were wild rumors about aliens and every expert had their own theories." The crowd began to talk among themselves as Daryl spoke. "There's no reason that satellites couldn't get pictures of what was happening unless the storm event reached into space, which I find unlikely, and I believe they did have pictures. We'll never know the reasoning for not reporting what they knew and when." Daryl waited for the arguing to die down before speaking.

"I suppose it doesn't even matter why they did what they did. I only bring it up as a reminder that this is a world-wide event. If the eruption of essence from the sea also took place seventy-four thousand years ago, it could explain a lot."

"There were no manufactured items? How would that kill the bigger animals?" a man asked.

Daryl held up his hand. "I was getting to that. Suppose you have a gas that contains an unidentified element, which builds under the surface of the earth. We don't know what triggers the

341

release. Maybe its random; maybe there's a cause. Somehow, this element reaches critical mass, then erupts. It rapidly spreads over the earth's surface, breaking down all large mammals exposed to it or induces changes, again, maybe this is planned or random, we don't know. Now, suppose that we have an evolved version of the same element. The last version might've only affected organisms with a certain body weight. Or maybe there *were* man-made structures that were completely obliterated. After all, ten thousand years from now, who would recognize a home from the piles of debris we have left?"

Anne rose her hands to her mouth to stifle her gasp.

Daryl glanced over his shoulder and gave her a reassuring smile. "We do know this release of essence affects anything that is synthetic or manufactured or maybe it too would dissolve any large mammal to its basic elements." Daryl shrugged. "We have none to test it on. All of our animals were protected by Anne's dome.

"We do know essence reduces manufactured components to their basic elements, disintegrating them in the process. Natural cloth with dyes or detergents are destroyed when the essence releases the impurities, leaving behind unusable scraps. We've seen for ourselves the damage caused to teeth by impure metals being reduced to their base elements. The red rash-like burns were caused by the rapid disintegration of the clothing. Items composed either partially or wholly of synthetic materials like plastic or polyester disintegrate violently. The higher the concentration, the more damage is done to the natural elements within. Chemical compounds like those used to treat plywood or make paint are especially corrosive— the red glow we saw on the buildings. Anne and I have tested this extensively. My experiments are conclusive. The green glow we saw as the storm passed over trees and fields was impurities burning off. On already cleaned" –he made air quotes with his fingers— "organic material, the green glow is almost yellow and very slight unless large amounts of essence are present."

"Anne and Jill report microscopic specs of essence imbedded in the trees and seeping into the ground. This isn't raw essence but essence that is being used somehow. The raw essence Anne and Jill use is slightly different in that it uses itself up in the transmutation and leaves no trace of itself. Thousands of years from now there would be nothing left for scientist to discover except a mystery. They'd likely assume, as we did, that the changes in the flora and fauna were natural evolution. And I suppose, in a way, they'd be correct. The Earth has passed through many extinction-level events. Sometimes, these extinction events cause complete extinction of a species and sometimes it only kills eighty percent of organisms. It has never killed all life, or we wouldn't be here," Daryl said reassuringly when the muttering rose in volume.

"After every extinction event, there's *always* a change in the flora and fauna. In the later cycles, the change happened much more quickly. The pattern of events has drastically increased over time. Some scientist theorized that the evolution of flora and fauna happens very fast." Daryl rose his voice a bit as the muttering swelled to outright arguing.

The crowd quieted when he lifted his hand.

"Change can start to occur within one hundred years of the extinction event. This event, what we call the storm, has killed ninety-nine percent of the population where we are. Clearly this is an extinction level event."

There were loud cries of dismay at this.

"I have reason to believe much greater survival in other areas. Specifically, thirty degrees on either side of the equator should have a significantly higher survival rate," Daryl said reassuringly. "Although no area will be unaffected, I believe we can expect evolutionary changes to affect plants and animals in our lifetimes. Significant changes. I don't believe this was a man-made

343

catastrophe, but a natural event that has happened before and will happen again. The storm that we could see brought with it a plasma or gas we couldn't see. Most of us couldn't," he corrected himself and turned to wink at Anne.

"Anne and Jill are able to harness that gas and use it. The bio electricity in their minds must be appreciably different from yours and mine," he said gesturing expansively around the room. "The SEC they use to preform transmutations has the properties of a plasma, which when released reverts to a gaseous state. The plasma is acting as a computer interface between them and matter. What they're doing isn't witchcraft or magic— it's science. Just not science on elements we have words for yet."

"It seems like witchcraft!" a man yelled out from the back.

Daryl nodded. "And how many of you knew how your televisions worked."

The laughter that followed had a slightly hysterical edge, Anne thought and consciously loosened her grip on Ben's hand,

"I'll skip all the yada, yada, yada, and simplify it. Television worked by electricity and magnetism as well as the ability of our brains to convert small dots and still frames into moving pictures. These electrical waves travel through the air or cables and are converted into dots and we *see* pictures," he said, making air quotes when he said see.

"Anne does the same thing with the electrical impulses in her brain. In her case, it works like a combination of television and radio, the same way video chatting worked. She can see, hear, and speak. Radio is made up of two parts. The transmitter, which in this case is Anne, and the receiver, which is Essence. Radio transmitters generate waves in different frequency's that traveled through the air. We can't hear them without a receiver tuned to that frequency. That is exactly what I think Anne is doing. I lack the tools to discover on what frequency she's transmitting, but I have some experiments I want to run to verify it. The essence acts as a catalyst as well as an information delivery system. Anne sees what she wishes to make and transmits it to the SEC and the essence infuses the item in the way she specifies and *wallah*!" he said triumphantly. "We have a new item. The things they can make are limited and we're still finding out the limits. Any questions?" he asked.

"What's a SEC?" a woman asked.

Daryl smiled. "It's what we're calling the small purple balls Anne made. Small Essence Containers. S. E. C." Daryl spelled it out. He held his hand out palm up to the crowd, inviting more questions.

"How soon till we have electricity?" Henry Brooks asked.

"That depends on too many factors to go into now. Plans will have to be drawn and materials made and scavenged. Labor will have to be organized, but it can be done. The same with the phone. We'll rely a lot on Anne and Jill's ability to fashion us materials. Any other questions?"

"Who else can use this essence?" asked a lady in the front.

"We aren't sure yet. But we plan to have everyone try. It's just a matter of finding the time to organize it." The lady looked content with that answer, so Daryl asked again if there were questions. "I'd be happy to discuss this and talk over ideas for restoring our power with anyone who's interested. I can be reached at Windsor house." He gave Anne a thumbs up as he resumed his seat.

"Thanks, Doc," Anne said when she stood back at the mic. "Okay, folks, that just leaves my presentation, and it's a dozy. My department heads and I have decided that we need to plan for a town. We can't keep living in the greenhouse and basements. We need a permanent solution to this crisis." She took a deep breath and continued. "We'll have to lay out a town that will include stores, schools, offices and a bank. We'll have to decide on our laws and money. What we propose is that we reenact the homestead laws with a few minor changes. We want to get this done as quickly as possible so that at spring planting people can start working their own land. I have a list of people who I'd like to nominate for the planning committee."

Anne looked around the room to gauge the response but most just nodded thoughtfully or stared with no expression she could read. "This isn't the United States anymore. We're alone, but that doesn't mean we can't be civilized. I don't want us to descend into savagery with every man for himself, but I don't want to live in a welfare state with the few taking care of the many either.

"There aren't many of us. We should be able to reach a compromise with each other on how we go on from here. Let's make a strong foundation. I'll read the list of names, and then take any nominations. After every name is read, I'll ask for a show of hands. Raise your hands if you approve the nomination. I realize we all haven't had time to get to know one another and might not be able to work together. These places on the town board can be rescinded if the majority of the board votes you off."

This next part was the tricky part and she took a deep breath. Sue gave her an encouraging smile, and Kate gave her a thumbs up. The support from her friends strengthened her resolve and she spoke with confidence.

"I'm going to be chairman of this board. My vote will be the tie breaker vote if we have a tie. We're planning to have a constitutional monarchy with the Windsor family in charge."

The outcry was immediate but mostly of shock. Only a few protested. Anne held up her hand for silence. "I realize it isn't what we're used to, but times have changed. Think of it like the lairds of Scotland." She forced a smile, clutching the podium tightly with both hands. "The Windsor's will live by the same laws everyone else does. You can just come to us if your neighbor's goat eats your bushes."

The nervous laughter that followed eased her tense shoulders, and she smiled more naturally.

"Sounds like you're making yourself queen!" a woman shouted to murmurs of agreement.

Anne nodded. "In a way, I guess. But it's going to be a small town, so not queen of much."

Anne stood up straight, leaning forward. "This is my family's land. My power keeps us safe from the storm here. I *will* be in charge of this land," she said forcefully. "Anyone that doesn't like it can leave any time they want. We want this to be a good place to live, a safe place. We plan on forming a government body much like the one we were used too with representation and voting. An inherited leader is an accepted, or I should say, was an accepted method of government for many parts of the world. This town council won't be the ruling class. We'll vote for all positions, except mine. We'll vote on all laws. I'm making this sound terribly elitist," she said with dismay when the scowls grew. "This is just a small town trying to have rules so we can all get along. That's all."

She was happy to note some of the scowls eased, and she wiped her sweaty palms on her jeans to take the mic from the stand.

"I'll call my list of names with a short reason why I'm calling them, then wait for the show of hands. These names have all been seconded by my husband and mother. We're trying to keep this committee a reasonable size so we can come to decisions quickly."

Sue handed her the list, and she placed it on the hay before her, hoping no one had noticed how badly her hands were trembling.

"Doug Windsor, civil engineer."

Most of the people rose their hands.

"Helen Carmichael, food production."

Again, the majority rose their hands.

"Dan Russo, detective, police officer." He was voted in as was, "Roger Bennett, history teacher."

"Sue Foster, bank secretary."

All hands were raised for Sue. Anne smiled. Everyone liked

Sue. She'd been talking to almost everyone already, finding out what people needed and settling the minor disputes.

"Last, but not least, Mrs. Edwina Santire. She's been many things in her long life, a waitress, a mother, a writer, and a librarian— the list is long."

Again, hands were raised, and the vote passed. "Does anyone have any other nominations?"

A man in the back she didn't know said,

"I nominate Ben Windsor. He's a farmer and construction worker, and an all-around good guy."

"I second it," a bunch of people called, and the crowd laughed as they rose their hands. Again, the hands raised were unanimous.

"Any other nominations?" she asked.

"I nominate Joe Conrad, he's one of us," Fred said.

Joe's nomination was quickly seconded and passed, and Anne welcomed him to the planning committee.

"Any other nominations?" There were none, so she banged the gavel. "Those are your town planners. If you have ideas speak to one of them." The spontaneous applause that followed relieved her.

"One last thing before we finish up for the night. Public notices will be posted on the door of the barn and the door of the shop. Assuming we have no major changes or emergencies, the next meeting will take place here in two weeks' time. Does anyone have any questions or new business to bring up?"

She scanned the audience but saw no raised hands.

"The memorial service will be held this Sunday at three followed by a dinner served here. All are invited to attend. If you wish to speak or have some input into the service, please see Helen Carmichael. Those of you who are on the town planning committee, we'll meet Monday at three at Helen Carmichaels house. Sorry, Mom," she said, "but you have the biggest table."

Helen nodded in agreement.

Anne said, "I know our thoughts and prayers are with the men searching tonight in Chester for survivors, that they find many and bring them back safely. We'd like to have a moment of silence for them." She stood at the microphone for a minute, then banged the gavel. "I move we adjourn this meeting."

It was seconded and passed.

"Meeting dismissed," she said in relief and stepped down quickly. Jill melted into the crowd. Doug hailed Will and pulled Johanna after him.

"See you at home," he called over his shoulder.

Sue gave her a quick hug.

"All hail Queen Anne," Kate said in a British accent, giving her an extravagant curtsy.

"Loon!" Anne laughed nervously and rolled her eyes. "I'm the president."

"You're my liege, and I your faithful servant. You have but to crook your finger, and I shall endeavor to fulfill your wishes."

"Knock it off, clown. People will think you're serious."

Kate laughed and slung an arm over her shoulders. "I am serious," she said in her normal voice. "But I'll call you whatever you like, your majesty."

She snickered when Anne cuffed her. Anne shook her head, laughing as Kate began to spout extravagant promises of servitude in a fake British accent.

"Queen my ass," a woman whispered to her companion as Anne passed.

Anne shot her a surprised glance, and the woman glared, her smirk saying I dare you to say anything.

Ben pulled her forward before she could decide what to say.

"Thinks she's miss high and mighty," the woman said louder.

"Leave it," Ben whispered, tugging her forward.

The talk of the crowd swallowed up whatever further comments the woman made.

"Shall I propose a duel," Kate asked, glaring over her shoulder.

Anne laughed and took her friend's arm.

"Marge is an idiot," Ben said. "Don't worry about her. Now, who's helping with the milking you all made me late for?"

Anne laughed again as they trudged back up the hill. "We're the most pedestrian monarchy that ever lived."

She glanced back but there was no sign of Jill or Doug. She hoped Jill was handling this new wave of unwanted attention.

"She'll be fine," Ben said, tugging her forward again. But his eyes were worried as he glanced back at the greenhouses.

Princess Jillian

Friday Morning 1/26

Ben rode Lightning down the partially plowed road at a walk. The horse stepped easily through the six inches of fresh snow, bobbing its head and making the small bells lining its tack jingle with each step. The sled it pulled was an old one that Ben had been meaning to repair forever but had somehow never gotten around to. Al had fixed it and polished the tack until it shone.

There was a lot of things he'd let go, meaning to do them but never had. And he regretted every lost moment that he'd let his work distract him from his family.

"Hello!" he called when he spied the candle in the center of the road. Jill's idea to warn essence was loose in the vicinity.

"Dad?" Jill called back and a moment later she ran into view. She grinned when she saw him. "What are you doing?"

"Picking up the cloth and taking you to lunch," he added, not liking how drawn she looked.

Her smile grew and reached her eyes. Her mother's beautiful gray eyes in his daughter's face. Jill had inherited his thick brown hair and height and his father's strong nose, but the rest was pure

351

Essence of the Storm

Anne.

"Where's your Mom," he asked as he led Lightning around the corner and spied Jill's LEC, a pile of cloth stacked on a wooden table, and Daryl leaning over his notebook.

"She's home working on our workshop with Doug. The land screams when we work it, and she wanted me off."

Her tone made it clear she wished she were home too.

"Well, let's load it up and see what they're up to."

Daryl picked his head up and frowned. Ben lifted an eyebrow, and Daryl smiled ruefully.

"I can set up tomorrow's experiments without you, Jill. If Sue doesn't haven't any urgent items she needs, take the rest of the day off."

Jill asked, "What about the shelters on the road?"

"The tents in place will suffice for a few more days. I wanted to speak to Pat about that anyway. There's no point in clearing roads we have no use for. The essences would be better spent on the farm."

"Are we running out?" Ben almost wished they were. Then he could pretend things were normal, or as normal as they could be, he amended in his thoughts when Lightning whickered and stamped his feet, jerking his head away from the purple ball that whizzed past them to Jill's outstretched hand. It still boggled him that they were reduced to horse travel, and when the last of the fuel was gone, they'd have no running water or lights or power tools. He changed his mind and hoped they still had plenty of essence.

"They still have a large supply, but I've been doing some calculations, and if we want the essence to last until they can harvest more, we should be a bit frugal with it."

"You know when the storm will return?"

"My calculations are based on rate of growth and speed, all of which could be wrong. But Jill and Anne will know when it's close. It won't take us unawares."

"Make sure you figure in some lightning rods."

"Talk over storm preparations at your town meeting and have Sue prioritize the items you wish them to make."

"Good thing we've got Sue," Jill said.

"I know. She's been a lifesaver keeping us all organized." Ben grabbed a blue sack and grunted as he tried to lift it. "What's in this thing?"

"Metal nails and stuff. Lightning can't carry that or the pipes. We'll have to send a truck back for it." Jill placed a red sack on the sleigh and petted the horse's nose. "This is too hard for you, isn't it, beautiful? We need more horses, Dad. Draft horses. Lightning can't do farm work, and he shouldn't be pulling these heavy loads."

"I agree."

"The red bags are the cloth Sue requested," Daryl said and stood to help load the sleigh. "I'll wait here and help load the truck. And if you can meet me in your workshop later, there's some things I'd like to borrow for tomorrow's tests."

Ben nodded agreement as he said, "Speaking of starving, I'm starving." He eyed a stack of wooden bowls and pursed his lips. "Can you make food?"

"No. We can't shape living plants either."

Daryl said, "Actually, that isn't quite true, you can, you just see that it's wrong to do."

Ben lifted an eyebrow.

Jill said, "We see the wrongness of messing with living things. It's so complicated. Each change requires another to balance it, and you get a snarled mess, not what you intended. It'll take years of study before we can do anything with living plants."

"Can you make edible hay? That's dead."

"No. Daryl says our cellulose structure is too dense to digest. We can make a facsimile of hay but not real hay. It looks real, but it isn't. I can make flowers that look real, but they aren't alive."

"The spark of life eludes them," Daryl said quietly.

"Probably a good thing," Ben said in a massive understatement, tucking another red bag atop the others.

Imagining the people's reaction to Anne being able to manipulate life scared him. But he smiled at Jill, trying to pretend he wasn't worried a lick. "That should do it. Let's go eat."

✳ ✳ ✳

Both Ben and Jill slid from Lightning's back to walk him down the steep hill to the greenhouse. Puffs of smoke stained the cloud laden sky, marking where outdoor fires had been made, and he wondered if they were cooking now on Kevin's old stove.

Ben thought it would snow again soon and he spared a quick prayer for the men searching across the river.

He could see a crowd had gathered at the far end of the parking lot but was too far to see what they were doing. But a new wall stood there, and he assumed that was where Anne was working, and they'd gone to watch. Much closer, the sound of children arguing mingled with music and the excited barking of a small dog.

The arguing changed to a peel of laughter and the dog quieted.

"I wonder if Boomer is with them?" Jill asked.

"I wonder what's going on over there?" Ben pointed to a group of people gathered on the trail where it curved to the winery. He was surprised at the number of people out and about when the day was cold and the snow so high.

"Julie!" Jill called in a happy voice and waved at the red-coated figure. Julie's parka made her unmistakable in the sea of long cape-like clothing.

Ben frowned when his niece straightened but didn't turn. One of the boys with her glanced over his shoulder and smiled but he followed the rest as they ran toward the winery.

"What was that about? Did you two have a fight?"

"No. She's been avoiding me since the meeting."

Jill sounded angry and hurt but shrugged away from his hand.

"Honey, this is hard for her—"

"And it isn't for me? I never asked for this."

"None of us did. But she's lost so much. You need to be patient."

Jill snorted angrily and dropped her hand from Lightning's reins to put her hands on her hips and glare at him. "I lost just as much. And if she's going to be a jerk about it, who needs her!"

"Don't be like that, honey. This is hard on her."

"And it's not on me? I lost my mother too!" Tears trickled down Jill's cheek, and she spun to gesture angrily at the people below them. "I lost family, my friends, everything I thought I'd have in my future. Who's going to marry a freak like me? They all leave when I show up. And now Julie who I thought loved me…"

Ben dropped the reins to pull her into an embrace. "Oh, honey, no. She does love you. And Anne is still your mother. God, it would kill her if she thought even for one second that you didn't feel her love."

Then why is she doing this, Dad?"

"What else can she do? Should she have hidden what you can do and let them freeze?"

"No."

Ben smiled against his daughter's hair. "Your heart is just as kind as your mother's. But, Jill" –he stepped away to see her face, holding her by the shoulders— "With great gifts comes great responsibility and your mom saw that right away. She's right. There is no law, no courts, no way to keep you both safe except if we're in charge. So, we're making a place with law and courts. Everyone is afraid and floundering. Julie will come around. But you *will* be treated differently. It's inevitable and right." He waved after the kids who'd run from them. "They're still in shock, reeling from the loses. No one has had time to catch their breath. We haven't even buried our dead yet. Survival has taken all of our attention. The changes have come too fast and furiously for them to really sink in. It will be beginning to dawn on them how much they need you and your mother, and most will resent it. How could they not? But then they'll learn your mom is fair, that she doesn't intend to dictate their lives, and she'll be accepted, but you'll always be treated differently, hopefully with the respect your position deserves. But the Windsor's need to present a united front and act like leaders. If we aren't strong all this will be taken from us."

Jill lifted a SEC from her pocket and frowned at it.

"Not by force." Ben closed his hand around hers. "By making law that traps you. Your mom is a smart woman and making a world where that can't happen."

He was relieved to see she looked thoughtful now and he released her hand. "I better go make sure Julie doesn't let the kids into the winery cellar. Drop off the sleigh, and I'll meet you at the bakery in a few minutes."

He began jogging through the snow, cutting through the deeper drifts on the hillside to get to the cleared path that lead to the winery, the sound of sleigh bells following him as Jill led Lightning down the trail.

As he suspected, the backdoor of the winery was unlocked. They'd posted a sign on the door saying the backrooms were off limits and he was glad he saw no one as he headed to the stairs that led to the basement. Men and women spoke in the front room, and he could hear the whir of a sewing machine and light laughter mixed with the quiet talking. Lantern light lit the basement stairs with a dim glow when he opened the door, and he sighed hard.

"Julie!" he called and rolled his eyes when he heard the muffled footsteps and exclamations. The light wavered and went out.

"Look, I know you're all down there. Make it easy on an old

man and just come out."

A hissing argument broke out, and the light flared back to life. A few seconds later Julie appeared at the bottom of the stairs.

"I was just showing them around," she said.

"That's fine. But the alcohol is off limits to minors. If they want a glass of wine, they can ask their parents for it, but we're trying to conserve it. Drinking it to get drunk is a waste of one our most valuable resources. That wine could be used as an antiseptic on injuries, as fuel, and to store foods in when the refrigeration goes."

"Sorry, Uncle Ben. I didn't mean any harm."

"No harm done, sweetheart." He shook his head and said louder. "It's cowardly to let her take all the blame!"

She grimaced and glanced over her shoulder, setting the lantern she carried down at her feet. "It was my idea."

He stepped back, holding the door open, and she glanced behind her again but trudged up the steps.

"You're a Windsor and need to set an example," Ben said softly as he hugged her. "There's work to be done, and we need everyone to help. Gather your friends and find Doug. Tell him you need the truck to go pick up Daryl. There's supplies to be loaded and distributed, and Daryl has experiments he needs help setting up."

She grinned up at him with Andrea's smile, and he had to swallow back the lump that rose in his throat.

"I love you, kiddo. Never forget it."

"I love you too, Uncle Ben. Come on, guys, we're busted and there's things to do!" she called back down the stairs.

Ben kissed her forehead and turned away, turning back at the outer door to say, "These locks won't be changed because I trust you."

"You can. I *am* a Windsor."

He held up a hand in salute and headed back to the bakery.

Essence of the Storm

* * *

Jill's angry tone halted Ben in his tracks. He let the bag he carried fall to the floor and stepped forward to peer into the storeroom.

"I said no!" She slapped at the hand on her shoulder, and Tim took a step back, dropping his hand and reaching for her face.

"What's going on?" Ben asked as he strode into the room.

The relieved glance Jill darted him made his fists clench.

"Just making friendly conversation," Tim said and took another step away, letting his hand fall to his side. "I thought Jill might like some company for the movie tonight."

"Aren't you a little old to be keeping company with her?"

"Yes— he is," Jill said and pushed past Tim. "And I don't appreciate being cornered like that. You're old enough to have learned better manners."

Tim's smile faded to a glare. "Think you're too good for me?"

"Yes!" Ben and Jill said simultaneously and despite himself, Ben laughed. Jill grinned and shook her head, rolling her eyes at Tim as she stepped past Ben. "Let him finish the unloading. I'm starved."

"Sounds good," Ben said and turned to follow, saying over his shoulder. "Don't bother her again."

The delicious aroma of freshly made cinnamon rolls pulled Ben in the bakery door. Jill sniffed and grinned.

"Yum. Gram was cooking. She said yesterday she planned to come down. I hope Grandma was here and paying attention. Gram makes the best cinnamon rolls in the world."

Ben winced, hoping his mother had the necessary ingredients or Jill was going to be broken hearted. She sniffed again, grinning over her shoulder at him.

"And it smells like pork pasties. I'm so hungry I could eat ten."

The men and women sitting at the crowded tables nodded or called greetings. The talk was light and seemed more animated than it had just the day before he was happy to note as he returned the waves and said a general hello.

"Hey, Trish," Ben said in greeting to the woman wiping the new counter he'd installed yesterday. He eyed the trays of fresh pastry and winked at Jill.

"We're starving. What's for lunch?"

The woman stirring the big pot of soup in the electric kettle turned, and Ben's smile froze. Marge glared at him. He tried to keep his expression neutral but thought she'd already seen his dislike. He resisted the urge to rub his head. *First Tim and now her. Patience*, he told himself and offered her an insincere smile and a friendly greeting.

"Hello, Marge. I didn't recognize you."

She sniffed in clear disdain and said, "That's Mrs. Brochette, and you need to bring a bowl to be served."

"Don't be silly," Trish said, flushing.

People eating at the closest tables stared.

Ben winced. He'd forgotten they'd implemented the bowl system when they hadn't gotten enough volunteers for dishwashing.

Trish reached for a stack of bowls beside the soup, and Marge tapped her hand with the ladle.

"Ow!" Trish exclaimed and put her hand to her mouth. "That was hot."

"Sorry," Marge mumbled, then louder, "But they don't eat here. They eat at their own homes." She sneered the word home as if it were a swear.

"Do you have a problem with me," Ben asked, laying a hand on Jill's arm, worried she'd begin yelling and this would get out of hand.

"No. But rules are rules and should apply to everyone."

"For crying out loud," Trish said and snatched two bowls. "Don't be so petty. I can hear her stomach growling. And I bet Ben has been up since dawn. Just serve them already."

Small laughs and whispered comments grew to low voiced arguments in moments.

Claire poked her head from the kitchen and nodded a greeting but spoke to Trish.

"Problems?"

"No. Ben and Jill just stopped for lunch."

"Oh. Good, I'd been meaning to track you down." She exited the kitchen and offered her hand to shake. "Kate said as how you might have skinning knives somewhere and a good sharpener?" As she spoke, she gathered a bowl and filled it with pork pasties and placed it on a tray. She turned to the coffee urn and poured two cups of the weak milky coffee they served.

"Get them soup, Marge."

Marge dished the soup, but it was clear she didn't wish too. She dropped it to the tray where it sloshed onto the pasties.

Claire glared and made a tsking noise, dabbing at the mess with her apron, a simple piece of cloth Ben recognized as essence made.

"What—"

"It isn't proper," Marge said. "This is for us."

"Proper?" a woman Ben didn't know said in a disbelieving tone.

"Sharon…" Claire trailed off and sighed hard.

Sharon said, "You've got to be kidding me. How dare you talk about proper! This is his food we're eating, in his building, and you're going to climb your high horse and say it isn't proper?"

Marge turned bright red and glared so hard the rash on her face turned white.

"How dare you speak to me like that!"

"How dare I? Are you serious?" Sharon stood, and Ben could see her hands shook she was so angry. "I should've left you in that car to die! You killed my husband, took him from his children, and you have the nerve to act like you're better than everyone? Tell them what you were even doing in our part of town, Mrs. Mayor!"

Ben stared shocked. He hadn't recognized Marge even when she'd said her name. Without the hairdo, makeup, and fancy clothing she was an ugly woman. Or maybe it was the haughty angry expression. Her face had paled, leaving two red patches high on her cheeks.

Sharon said, "I saw you fucking my husband. In the fucking tool shed, down in the dirt where you belong. He should've been with his family. But no. You blackmailed him, or hell, maybe he lied, but I think that was true, No one would bang a skank like you if they didn't have too."

Jill giggled and slapped a hand to her mouth. Marge turned her glare on her. The red in her cheeks had grown to alarming proportions, and Ben thought she was so angry she might stroke out.

"That's a lie," Marge snapped. "I didn't even know the man."

A man sitting at the same table as Sharon began to laugh. "Who's the liar? We know you knew him. He worked at city hall and you were there every day. I saw you talk with him too many times to count."

Tears fell down Sharon's cheek now and her voice was tight as she said, "Don't you even care that you killed him? That he died trying to save you despite what you did to my family? You really are a cold, heartless bitch, aren't you?"

Marge took a deep breath and smiled an insincere smile.

"I'm very sorry for your loss. Of course, I'm sorry. I'm sorry for all the deaths, but I had nothing to do with him."

"Wow," Jill muttered, and Marge's smile hardened.

A man at the table behind Ben laughed and someone shushed him.

"But that has nothing to do with them," Marge went on, jerking her thumb at Ben. "We need to take a stand, stick together and demand our rights. Or do you like being their slaves?"

361

"Oh, come on," Jill said and the man behind Ben laughed again.

The room erupted into sound as everyone began talking at once.

"That woman," Claire muttered.

Trish shook her head and said nothing. She made a new plate, replacing the soggy pasties with fresh.

Marge waved her ladle. "Will you let them walk all over us? Or do we have rights too?"

"It's his house, stupid!" Claire yelled.

Marge said, "We're being treated like the basest servants, expected to wait on them while they dress us in their castoffs and make us sleep on their floors. And now they come eat our food and then go home to their hot meals."

Jill said, "Look, that's just silly. We eat the same thing you do and half the time it's cold by the time we get it."

"Delivered by us!"

Ben pulled Jill back as she took a step forward and he spoke in the calmest tone he could manage. "We don't make you sleep on our floors, we let you. I'm sorry you don't see the difference but it's a big one. The food and clothing you're wearing are ours, and believe me, it hurts to share it. It isn't a castoff. Al over there is wearing my second favorite shirt."

"And it's much appreciated, Ben!" Al held up his mug and saluted with it.

The men with him laughed and lifted their mugs.

Marge threw her spoon to the table and stomped to the corner where she sat with a small group of men and women who'd been nodding along with her. They all glared at Ben, but none said anything. He sighed hard and shook his head.

He said, "Where are we supposed to put you up? Our beds? Don't be ridiculous. We're doing the very best we can. The numbered bowls aren't to limit your food but to make sure you clean up after yourselves. If we get enough volunteers in the kitchen, we won't need them. I hope you weren't sending people away hungry."

She said nothing, crossing her arms and glaring.

"What's all the commotion? I could hear it out back," Kate said as she stuck her head through the kitchen doorway, wiping her hands on a dishtowel.

Ben eyed the bloodstains on her shirt and quirked his lips. Kate had been, and still was, he mused, a butcher. She'd worked in a local grocery store and for them butchering their cattle for as long as Ben had known Anne.

Her gaze narrowed at Marge, but Ben shook his head slightly. She shrugged and grinned at Jill.

"Hey, Princess. Ben, I'd been meaning to talk to you about Helen…"

"Princess," Marge scoffed loudly, then muttered, "Witch."

Before Ben could turn, Kate had leaped over the counter, scattering the wooden bowls and mugs, and ran toward Marge who jerked with surprise and tried to scramble away but she was too slow.

Kate grabbed her by the shirt and snarled, "That fucking does it! I've been patient! I've been the soul of fucking patience but one more word from you and I'll beat your ass and drag you out into the snow for the tigers to fucking eat! Anne is my best friend and Jillian the daughter of my heart! I've fucking called her princess since the moment of her birth and I'll call her that or any other damned thing I want!"

She grabbed Marge, by the collar of Helen's shirt Ben noted, and shook her hard, glaring at the woman next to her when she opened her mouth. Still yelling, she thrust her away. Marge stumbled back and rose her hands as if to block a blow.

"If you, or anyone else has a problem with them, then get the hell out!" Kate glared around the room a moment before whirling to lean into Marge's face. "Your fired! I don't want to see you back here!"

"You can't do that," Marge said nervously as her gaze darted the room, seeking reinforcement.

Ben glanced around too and saw most looked interested, amused, or annoyed with her. He turned back to see Marge lift her hand.

"I wouldn't" he said and laughed when Jill giggled. Kate was also a black belt as well as being a butcher and for a brief time had been a cage wrestler. Jill still giggled at those pictures.

"*Aww,*" Jill muttered, and Kate turned and winked.

"Marge, you're an idiot," Claire said, shaking her head. She waved the spoon she held at the door. "Just go."

"That's ridiculous." Marge tugged her shirt, trying to tuck it back into her too tight pants, which were also Helen's, Ben noted.

"I'm a volunteer just like her; she can't fire me or anyone else."

She glared at Ben as if daring him to contradict her. Ben almost admired her gall. It was clear to everyone in the room that Sharon had told the truth and her pain over her husband's death was raw. He couldn't figure out why Marge persisted in her denial when it would be kinder and smarter to admit a mistake and apologize. And now to face off with Kate when the dimmest-witted person could see that wasn't a fight she could win on any level.

Kate laughed and shook her head. "Sure I can. I just did. Now get out before I make you go."

Ben said, "Honestly, I find your rudeness unbelievable, but I'm willing to let some things slide. I understand that we're all stressed and tempers are high in this new scary situation but that doesn't give you the right to call anyone names. My daughter isn't a witch. She's a normal girl with a brain that has a higher electrical output than ours. There could be millions like her. We, those of us without that electricity, could be the anomaly. I for one am just glad she can use the essence. Without her help, half of you would still be naked. With it, we really have a good shot of not only survival but of making a nice place to live."

"You think there's others like her?" Trish asked, sounding intrigued.

"No way to know. Maybe." Ben shrugged and picked up the tray.

Marge took a step forward, flicked a glance at Kate, harrumphed loudly and stomped from the room.

"Good riddance," Sharon said, and Ben turned to her.

Some in the crowd applauded and the talk surged.

Sharon had stopped crying, but tears had left streaks across her face. The man beside her patted her back and murmured something too low to hear over the renewed talking.

Al waved Ben to his table, saying loudly. "I doubt there be too many. Druids were a rare and wonderous thing."

"Druids? Ben quirked an eyebrow as he sat and lifted the pasties. "Delicious," he said and took another big bite.

"Oh, aye. Me mum was from the isles and spoke the Gaelic and told stories she'd had from her mum and hers before her. The stories of drui were favorites. I'd always pester her for them stories and she'd laugh and call me an *aislingeach*, that be a dreamer for you-uns, but she'd tell me stories of the Drui and the beasts they fought and raised as guardians."

Drui?"

"Oh aye, it come to mean them who worship the trees and was changed to druid, but it started as being them who knew the trees. Those times were long ago but our people remembered the drui. They were the keepers of the machair, you ken, and revered.

"The keepers of the makers?" Ben pursed his lips and nodded. I suppose she's a maker at that."

The men sitting at the table laughed.

Al laughed too and shook his head. No— the land- the machair— but, yes, they were the makers, shapers of the machair, those who could use the lay lines to shape the plants and animals to their will. They'd bring in good harvests, and while they lived and prospered, so did their people."

"*Hmm*," Ben said thoughtfully. There was no denying Anne could shape things to her will.

"That's just an old wives' tale," Trish said as she sat beside them.

Kate straddled a seat backward, grinning at Jill. "Maybe, but even thousands of years ago there wouldn't have been much essence left if its sinking back into the ground, so maybe those maker guys had to work hard to gather it. For sure Princess here is a maker."

"What else could they do?' Trish asked, glancing at Jill from the corner of her eye.

Al leaned back in his seat and crossed his arms over his chest. Ben recognized the story telling position after a mere two days acquaintance and chuckled. Al loved nothing as much as telling a yarn.

Ben ate quietly while the rest of the room hung on Al's every word.

Jill laughed when he finished and rose to get another bowl of stew, saying over her shoulder," All that might be true, but I can't speak to animals or become a tree or any of that stuff."

"Not yet, but you're a brand new drui."

"Well, I hope your right. It would be cool as hell to talk to Boomer."

Trish laughed, and the crowd began talking excitedly about other things that would be cool to do. Ben exchanged relieved smiles with Kate.

"I've got her back, Ben," Kate whispered as she stood. "Hey, Princess! I put a bag of cinnamon rolls aside for you and Doug. Got any room left?"

Ben watched as Kate led Jill into the kitchen, glad his daughter had such a strong defender but hating that she needed one. He made a mental note to pull Kate aside and warn her about Tim. He planned to have a little chat with the man himself, but not today, he thought and grinned when he heard Jill laugh.

"Eases your heart, don't it," Al said and stood. "The sound of the young ones laughing— there's nothing better. I hadn't realized before all this, I'd thought I was happy as a hermit, living alone and on the move, but I'm right fond of hearing them laugh."

"Me too," Ben said with heartfelt sincerity, and the men at the table nodded agreement.

These are good people, Ben thought, turning away from the sour glances cast by Marge's friends.

Finding Trouble

Saturday Morning 1/27

Ben woke and stared at his sleeping wife. The sun hadn't yet risen and the house below him was quiet. He'd hoped to move the basement guests out soon, but the new refugees from across the river needed shelter and food.

The arrival of thirty more souls saved from the storm late yesterday had been cause for celebration for most but Ben felt it like a weight on his soul.

"And what do you feel?" he whispered, and Anne reached for him in her sleep.

He rolled onto his back and stared at the ceiling, mentally planning his day. First, he needed to track down who had the guns that hadn't been turned in last night. Dave thought the fifth team had them last, but they claimed someone had taken them back to the barn. Keeping track of where things where was becoming a fulltime job in itself, and he made a mental note to get Sue more help.

Then there was the livestock to care for, of course, and the rearranging of the greenhouse to cram in more beds. Which meant more hay used and he was already worried about running out. Anne could make bedding, but he hated to ask her. It felt like everyone turned to her and Jill for everything and the pressure had to be soul crushing. He knew it was exhausting and he worried she was trying to do way too much, that using the essence was taking an unseen toll.

Sue had implemented a shift in housing, allotting new arrivals house space and it made sense. They had no clothing and needed more medical care, but he felt as if the farm bulged at the seams and they still hadn't found the source of the smoke signals, so more where likely to arrive.

Guilt made his stomach roil.

"I'm a selfish bastard, aren't I?"

Anne mumbled, and Merlin picked his head up. Seeing Ben awake, he sauntered over and plopped down on Ben's chest, letting out a deep sigh as if the small effort had exhausted him.

Ben laughed softly and rubbed the dog's ears. Anne continued to sleep, and Ben frowned at her hollow cheeks. "Come on, pal, lets sneak out and warn them to be quiet so she and Jill can sleep." He kissed Anne's cheek and still holding Merlin, gathered his clothing and quietly left the room to dress in the hall bathroom.

Sue was already up and working in the office when he came down the stairs, and he wondered if she'd been up all night settling the new arrivals. Or maybe more had been found, and he tried to make himself feel happy about that but all he felt was overwhelmed. Not that he wished them dead, but everyone rescued meant another mouth to feed and clothe.

"Morning, Ben," Sue said quietly and stood to stretch.

"Did you get any sleep?"

"Some. I'm good. We got another small batch late last night. I settled them at the Carrillo's. I got up early to work out who's

369

being sent down to the greenhouses next. I figured it would be easier if they knew in advance that the next batch of incoming will be taking their housing."

"Problems?"

"Nothing I can't handle. Most are okay with moving, happy to help but there's always a complainer."

She grimaced and headed to the coffee pot. "I'll almost be glad when we run out although caffeine withdrawal might kill me."

"Maybe we should donate it?"

"No point. It would just cause more problems. Who decides who gets it? There isn't enough left to worry about. Claire is working on a substitute, but we'll just have to get used to going without."

She rested a hip on the counter as the coffee brewed.

Three men wearing toga-like garments fashioned from material Jill had made came up the stairs. Ben nodded a greeting, thinking the smell of coffee had drawn them but they barely glanced at Sue.

They walked through his house like ghosts, pale and silent, avoiding his eyes, avoiding everything, lost in their pain.

Sue waited until they were out of sight in the back hall and whispered. "It's hard on them knowing if we'd come sooner their families might've lived. I think they're in shock to find us so well provided for. They'd mostly given up hope." Her voice lowered even more as she leaned closer. "I shudder to think what they were eating to survive."

Ben's stomach flipped, and he turned to peer down the hall.

Sue laid a hand on his arm. "What would you do to save your family, Ben? We'll never ask. What's done is done. Our pasts, whatever we once were, we've become something new. It's up to us to make this new thing good."

Ben hugged her, having to lean down to kiss her cheek.

"Manhandling my wife," Pat asked without heat. He smiled

sadly at Ben as Ben stepped away.

"She's telling me how it is," Ben said.

Pat grinned and kissed his wife quickly before heading to the coffee. "What would do without her?"

"Thank god we'll never know."

* * *

Snow drifted down from the laden clouds and Ben pulled his coat closed as he turned, scanning the sky, trying to gauge whether this light dusting would become more. The gray skies gave him no sure answer, but he could feel the heaviness in the frigid air and assumed this was the beginning of a winter storm.

He hoped it would blow over by tomorrow's memorial service, but he figured the service would go on regardless of weather.

He grabbed a snow shovel and headed for the point.

Will was already there and had shoveled a wide path from the road.

"Good to see you up and about," Ben said and slapped his shoulder.

Will wiped his sweating brow and leaned on the shovel he held. "It's good to be about. I didn't get a chance to thank you." His expression darkened, and he bit his lip, casting a glance back at Helen's. "Janice won't thank you. She's so angry, Ben. She says nothing and does nothing. I don't know what to do."

"Give her time, son."

"Well, I thank you for her, Ben. I never thought I'd wake. I saw it and knew we were trapped, that we'd die there, and I let myself drift away and left her alone. I regret that more than I can say." He rubbed his face with his free hand, avoiding Ben's eyes. "No wonder she's so angry. I'm hoping she forgives me."

"Forgive yourself. Sue was just saying we all get a fresh start."

"And I mean to make the most of it. I'll never give up again."

Will straightened to gesture with his shovel at the pavilion. "I'll have this ready for the wake. I can't believe it's been over a week already. How did the world change so much in a week?"

He shook his head and turned to the east, lifting his hands to shade his face as he examined the sky. "The smoke dies out, but it always returns. It's taking longer though. They better find them soon."

"They will."

"I wish I could help look, but Abby says I'm not fit enough."

"Should you be doing this?"

"I feel fine.

Ben dropped it; it was clear from Will's tone he didn't wish to discuss his health. Ben stared into the sky too and surprised himself by really hoping they did find them soon.

"We'll find a way," Ben said.

Will flicked him a quick glance and grinned. "I believe in miracles now too. Who knows what Jill and Anne will do next? Maybe they can teleport them or something."

"Of course," Ben said and smacked himself in the head.

"I was just kidding!" Will called after him as Ben began to jog back to the house. "They can't really do that, can they?"

"No!" Ben called back but didn't stop. "It just gave me an idea!"

"Where's Anne?" Ben asked as he burst into the house.

"She's out making something," Alicia said, lifting her hands from the soapy dishwater to pat her chest. "You scared the crap out of me. What's wrong?"

"Nothing. I just have an idea. Do you know where?'

"Dover Street, I think."

Ben slammed the door and jogged back to the barn, slowing to catch his breath as he reached the upper driveway.

The barn felt deserted without the hustle and bustle of milking times.

"Al!" he called when he entered.

"Yo!"

"Get Thunder and Lightning saddled up for me. I don't care what they were scheduled for, this is an emergency. And see if you can round me up a radio! I'm taking the truck but should be back soon to get them!"

He ran out the door before Al had a chance to ask questions. His pace slowed as he slogged through the foot of snow that had drifted into the narrow path that led to the lower barn parking lot where he'd left the truck.

A woman stepped from his workshop and eased the door closed. Her furtive manner caught Ben's attention and he stilled to watch, his eyes narrowing as he recognized the pants.

"What are you up too, Marge?" he asked under his breath and pressed against the side of the barn. She scurried down the path, and he was about to follow when the door opened again. This time a man emerged, and Ben shook his head, lifting his lip to sneer.

He taken two more steps, intending to tell them to find somewhere else for their trysts when another man exited.

Ben's sneer turned to a puzzled frown.

"Can I help you!" he called, and the man turned, his gaze darting down the path before a fake smile formed on his face.

"Just seeing if Al needed any help."

"In the workshop?"

The man shrugged and waved, ducking his head and pulling the blanket he wore as a coat over his face.

Ben stepped into the workshop and halted in surprise. Four men glanced up from the tools spread on the main bench.

"Phil," Ben said, lifting an eyebrow when Phil flushed. His eyes narrowed at the next man. "Tim, what brings you to my workshop?"

Ben's gaze flicked to Tim's hand that clenched on Phil's arm as Phil opened his mouth. Phil snapped his mouth closed and titled his head, turning partly away as Tim said, "Anne. We thought we'd see about making her workshop more comfortable for her."

Ben lifted an eyebrow and crossed his arms.

"She could use a stove," Phil blurted.

"I suppose, but you need to ask Al before removing any tools. And, Tim, Anne won't be interested either. You're wasting your time." He dropped his arms and took a step closer. "Stay away from my wife. In fact, stay away from all the women in my family. If Jill comes to me again about you, you're out. Am I making myself clear?"

"Jill?" Phil said and glared at Tim.

Tim slashed his hand through the air, dismissing Phil, and said to Ben. "You made that crystal clear. I'm sorry we got off on the wrong foot. I meant no disrespect to her or you." He smiled slightly and half sat on the work bench behind him. "I admit, I'm a little old for her, but I thought she might want a man, not a boy, and it isn't like she has a ton of choices."

The other two men exchanged smiles and Ben's glare deepened. He didn't know if Tim were lying or what, but it was clear they thought they knew something and found it funny.

He said, "Everyone gets a clean slate here but only one shot to keep it clean."

Phil turned to glare at Tim. "You never said—"

The alarm bell began to ring, and everyone turned to the door. Ben ran outside, cursing as he waded through the drifts.

"Clean this up!" he called back over his shoulder.

He reached the back door as it opened and Wayne ran out.

He grabbed Ben's arm, yanking him forward as he said, "There you are. Let's go. That was the flare gun."

"Dover?" Ben asked breathlessly. The air froze in his lungs and his hands shook. Wayne released him to fumble with the truck door.

"We should've sent a radio with them," Wayne muttered as he

slid into the driver's seat.

"Go!"

Ben glared at Tim and Phil arguing by the workshop door and made a mental note to speak to Al about locking it but couldn't concentrate past his worry. If they'd used the flare gun it meant they were hurt and needed help, and he cursed himself for letting them use the essence. It was too unknown, too dangerous.

"We don't need it," he said. And Wayne shot him a dubious glance.

"We're messing with shit we shouldn't be."

Wayne nodded grimly and stepped on the gas.

Mrs. Ming

Saturday Morning 1/27

Anne screamed and fell backward, landing hard on her hands and trying to push herself up and back as the tiger pounced. Motes of fire drifted above the treetops that overshadowed the road, disappearing into whiffs of smoke. In a corner of her mind Anne wondered what Daryl thought the flare would do if anyone even noticed it. The tiger would eat them before help could arrive.

"Run!" she screamed at Jill and gathered the loose essence, forming it into a diamond hard barrier before her.

The cat snarled as it collided with the wall, razor-like claws slashing out but not marring the surface. It snarled again, and a bullet ricocheted from the barrier, the gunshot seeming to be right over Anne's head.

"Damn!" Daryl dropped the gun, grabbing Anne's arm and tugging her up as Jill shouted, "Don't shoot her!"

The tiger crouched, its tail lashing the air and its ears pinned back as it batted at the barrier. It found the edge and snarled again, pulling with its front paw while Anne and Daryl skittered backward.

"There isn't enough essence to stop her," Anne screamed as she frantically reformed the essence in the cat's path. Her gaze landed on the gun, and she contemplated reaching for it but the twenty-two would just make it mad unless she got lucky with a killing shot.

"Ming!" Jill screamed and swatted at the tiger with a tree limb she grabbed from the ground.

"No!" Anne reached for Jill, not knowing what she planned to do, and tried again to shift her small wall in front of the snarling tiger.

"There isn't enough!" Sobs caught in her throat as she yanked the essence from the nearby trees, whining from the pain of it but continuing, while forcing the small bits remaining from her SEC to block the cat as it leaped forward over the barrier.

"Jill!" she screamed and ran forward shrieking, hoping the tiger would go for her and let Jill get away. She'd taken just one step when the tiger grabbed at the limb Jill was poking at it. The limb flexed, and the tiger snapped at the air following the line of essence that flowed alongside the limb.

Before Anne could take another step, the limb had encircled the tiger's neck, and Jill released the wood, letting it fall to the ground where it sunk into the earth and became stone. The stone seemed to travel the branch until the tiger pulled frantically at the stone yoke that held it in place.

"Holy crap, are you okay? Jill lifted a shaky hand to rub her forehead.

"Jill..." Anne leaned forward to catch her breath, resting her hands on her knees and breathing deeply.

Jill turned and spoke softly to the tiger. "Calm down, Mrs. Ming. Who's a good kitty?"

"Jill?" Daryl pulled her back, shaking his head as his gaze darted from Jill to the still snarling tiger.

"She can't get loose, but I need a new SEC to make her a proper cage."

Daryl released Jill and reached for the gun.

Jill grabbed his arm, yanking him back. "No! We can't kill her. She's an endangered species. Mom, tell him! And she's pregnant. Remember – you took Julie and I to see her over Christmas break?" Jill's voice rose as Anne remained silent.

"Mother, we can't kill her!"

Anne pursed her lips and considered her angry daughter. "She's a tiger, Jill. Not a house cat. What are we going to do with a tiger?"

"It's a wrong thing to kill her!"

Jill glared at Anne but the tears in her eyes made Anne sigh. She slumped to sit gracelessly in the snow.

"She scared ten years off my life."

Jill grinned and turned back to Mrs. Ming.

Anne said, "I'm not saying yes, but I'll talk to your father."

"He'll let me keep her. I know he will. Thanks, Mom. I'm going to run back and get more essence. Don't let anyone hurt her. I'll make her a nice cage."

Before Anne could say more, Jill ran down the road.

"Great," Anne muttered, and Daryl laughed.

He gestured at the struggling tiger. "Are you sure that will hold her?"

"Jill was and she wouldn't risk my life. I don't have enough essence to do much unless I take it from the trees." She sighed hard when Daryl pursed his lips, and she stripped off her gloves to place her hands on the cold ground. She examined the woods about them for signs of life but saw no other big sparks. Small animals abounded but nothing was big or threatening.

The tiger loomed in her mind's eye and she could sense her vicious nature. Daryl saying her name brought her attention back, and she examined the stone holding the tiger in place. Jill had formed it deep into the bedrock. Mrs. Ming wouldn't be breaking free from it without help.

"Anne," Daryl said again in a more urgent tone, and she opened her eyes.

"It's fine. She's secure and there are no more."

His eyes widened, and he stared about as if just realizing a slew of tigers could be creeping up on him.

"Help me up." She accepted his hand and pulled herself up. "It didn't occur to me to trap it like that."

"Me neither. But I noticed something I should've realized right along. What happens to the diamond shell when you release the essence? Are you transmuting it or is the diamond-like shell really another stage of essence? And what's keeping it suspended like that?"

Anne frowned and reached for the remains of the wall she'd created.

"There's essence in it… let me examine it a bit." She grabbed the stool she'd been using until the tiger had leaped from the woods and paused as she considered the tiger's actions.

"I don't think Mrs. Ming was after me."

"It sure looked like she was. My heart is still beating too hard."

Anne plucked the other stool from the ground, set it upright, and motioned Daryl to take a seat. "She could've landed on me in one pounce. She pounced on the essence I was using. And I know she saw it when Jill was catching her."

"Really?"

Anne grinned at his interested tone. Curiosity had replaced his fear, and he now eyed Mrs. Ming as if she were desert.

"See if she still sees it."

"I don't have enough, not if I don't want to lose the information this SEC contained. We should make a backup every day. That way we'd only lose one day of knowledge if we accidently spend it all.

"Good idea," Daryl said and gave her an encouraging smile. "You could use some from the trees."

Anne frowned and shook her head. "You know it's wrong to do it."

"They're just trees…" he held up his hands and shook his head when she made an annoyed sound. "Sorry. You're right, you shouldn't do things you know are wrong. I wish you could see the wrongness better though."

"I see it just fine. I know it's a wrong thing to do."

"That isn't what I meant. And, again, I'm sorry. I shouldn't have asked when it wasn't an emergency but what exactly is wrong about it? I know it hurts them but…"

"It more than hurts them. It changes them. I can see the change but don't know what it does. It's dangerous to mess with it. I mean, what if I pull out the essence and somehow make the trees poisonous or something?"

Daryl flicked an anxious glance at the trees. "Do you see that?"

"I can't know what it'll do, and that's the point." She frowned pensively at the trees. "I know them as they are, not what they're becoming. I see glimpses but I can't grasp it." She waved a hand at the forest. "There's so much that no one could understand it all and to change one is to alter the entire tapestry of life. I can see that taking the essence is a wrong thing to do. I can see that changing the shape of a wing or strength of a claw is wrong, but I can't see all the consequences of doing it." Her frown grew as she considered.

'I'm sorry, I'm not explaining this well. I can see some of the consequences, but some elude me. I just sense the wrongness, and some seem fine but maybe I just don't know enough to see the wrongness. It's best if Jill and I stick to the shaping of dead objects."

"I agree. At least until you know more." He jumped when Mrs. Ming snarled again and began struggling with renewed vigor.

"Let's get these bowls gathered up and get back. Maybe Ben can talk her out of keeping it. "

Anne laughed and shook her head. "Ben doesn't have a prayer against Jill's tears."

A Rough Road

Saturday Morning 1/27

Wayne slammed on the breaks as Jill ran around the corner.

Ben grabbed at his pounding heart with one hand, using the other to stop himself from flying through the windshield.

"Jill!" Wayne called and stepped into the road.

"Dad! Wait till you see what I caught." She beamed at him but seemed nervous, almost afraid, and very excited. "Mom says I can keep her, but I need more essence to make a cage. Maybe I can get a lift back?"

"Slow down, honey. What did you catch?" Ben stepped from the truck on unsteady legs to embrace her. Relief left him feeling lightheaded. Her tone made it clear Anne was well. Sudden fear made him hug her tighter. "Wait, were you there when they sent up the flare?"

"Yeah. Daryl panicked."

He narrowed his eyes, and she flushed, staring down at her snow boots.

"What did you catch?"

Visions of gorillas and elephants wafted through his head. His daughter had always loved the animals, and who knew what could be in the woods now.

"A tiger," she said proudly, grinning at him as if that was the best news ever.

He sighed hard. "A tiger. Right. And I suppose you think we should keep it."

"Well, we can't let it go."

"Jill…."

"Dad, she's an endangered species! There's only like a hundred white tigers left in the world and the regular ones are going extinct too. We can't kill her."

"What will we do with her?"

"I'll make her a great cage."

Wayne said, "Being caged is no life for a tiger, and what would we feed her?"

"Please, Dad? Maybe we can release her far away someday, and I'm sure she'd be fine eating the scraps from the deer. I could hunt for her."

Jill stared at him beseechingly, and Wayne snorted and slapped his shoulder.

Jill said, "It isn't right to kill her. It isn't her fault she's here and not in her natural habitat. She's trying to survive just like we are. Don't we owe it to her to take care of her since we brought her here?"

Wayne said, "Just give in already, you know you're going to, and let's go see this tiger."

Jill squealed and gave Wayne a hug, practically dancing with excitement. "Mrs. Ming. She's beautiful." She glanced over her shoulder, releasing Wayne. "I better go get more SEC." She took a step away and turned back. "Why are you here, anyway? Is everything okay at home?"

"I had an idea that I need your mom for. We might be gone

overnight.

"Where are you going?"

"Across the river to search for survivors."

Jill bit her lip, and Ben could tell she thought she should go too but she wanted to stay with Mrs. Ming. He remembered how excited she'd been when they'd first gone to see her. Jill had spoken about white tigers endlessly and drawings of Mrs. Ming had covered the walls of her basement studio. She visited the zoo every time she came home from school. He groaned softly as he remembered the tiger was pregnant.

"Dad?"

He smiled to ease her anxious expression. "I'm okay. I just remembered Mrs. Ming was expecting. Go make her a cage that no one can fall into and she can't escape from. Somewhere behind our house so her scent doesn't terrify the animals. And, Jill, I don't need to tell you to be careful, do I? She isn't a tame animal. If she gets loose or becomes a danger, we'll have to put her down."

"I'll be careful, I promise!" The excitement had returned to her eyes, and she ran back to hug him again.

He kissed the top of her head and closed his eyes, whispering a prayer of thanksgiving in his mind.

"It's going to be fine!" she called back as she ran toward home.

"*Hah!*" Wayne said as he got back into the cab. He hesitated with his hand on the key. "Maybe we should walk."

"No. Drive. Let's get Anne. I want to get going. In fact, call the barn and have someone bring the horses to River Camp. And get us an overnight pack and emergency supply packs for, say, ten people. But I don't want the horses overloaded."

"Aye, aye, boss." Wayne lifted the radio, driving with one hand.

"A tiger," Ben muttered, then said louder, "And warn them she's coming home with a tiger."

Wayne laughed.

* * *

Marcus greeted Ben with a grim smile. "It's no use. We can't find a spot to cross safely. The water's just too deep and the hill too steep. We tried going around it but…"

"Anne can cross it." Ben turned to survey the deep gorge. At one time a highway had crossed it. He'd forgotten this tiny tributary was even here. It had been a bare trickling stream a week ago. Now it was a raging river that crashed through the tumbled debris that remained of the bridge. Trees had fallen along the southern edge and the bank had crumbled, leaving exposed roots and loose boulders that looked as if they'd fall at any moment.

"Jake went west, hoping he'd find a spot to cross it. We know the smoke is coming from beyond it." He sighed and shook his head. "It's amazing something like this can hold us back. I mean, I could almost jump across it, and it's keeping me back as surely as if it were a twenty-foot-tall wall topped with barbed wire and guarded by armed guards. When I think of the bridges, the buildings, the way we manipulated our environment to suit us, and now we can't even cross a gorge…"

It's shocking," Ben agreed. "I catch myself all the time thinking if we only had this or that and it's frustrating knowing we have the know-how but not the resources. Even with Anne we're going to barely eke by."

"Thank god we have her," Marcus said as the ground shivered and reformed, the boulders melting into a thin rock path that arched over the gorge. It happened quickly and it took Ben a moment to realize she'd used some of the downed trees, not just the rock.

"Wait a second," she said and squatted to place her hands on the ground.

The water suddenly gave off a green glow and the riverbed rose up and a minute later crude arches supported the rock above it. She remained squatting, but Ben couldn't see anything happening. He and Marcus waited until she opened her eyes and stood to speak.

"Is it finished?" Marcus asked.

"Better question, is it safe?" Ben lifted an eyebrow, and she shrugged.

"I think so. It's built like Doug told us, and the rock goes deeply into the earth. I could fill the gorge completely but then where would the water go?

"I'll go see if I can find Jake," Marcus said.

"You need any more supplies?" Anne asked, giving Ben a guilty glance.

"No. I have plenty. If I'm not back in two days…."

"Be safe." Ben offered his hand, and Marcus shook it, then saluted Anne. He was graceful on his skis and disappeared into the trees and whirling snow in minutes.

"*Brr*," Ben said. "I'd hate to be alone in this."

She stared after Marcus a moment before spinning and stomping across her new bridge, saying, "Me too. You lead the horses while I go ahead and try to clear a path through here." She lifted her face to the sky and frowned. "I think it's going to keep snowing. Night will come early. We have hours before we'll need to make a camp though."

He carefully folded the map and stuck it into the pack Lightning carried. "Follow this road but be careful. There'll be a steep drop on the right. We should take the first exit ramp and head as straight north as we can."

"It seems like forever ago Parkland was just a twenty-minute ride away."

"We'll find them, Anne."

"I hope so."

She said nothing else, picking up her pace and cursing softly when she stumbled on debris beneath the snow. He followed, hanging back so she could clear the way for him. He pulled his coat tighter and gazed up at the sky, hoping they'd find whoever was sending the smoke signals before they froze in this new storm.

Four hours later, Ben shivered and slapped his gloved hands together. Snow fell down in swirly sheets ruining visibility, but his wife wasn't using her eyes. She stood fifty feet away, resting her face against the trunk of a tree, and he knew she'd found their quarry by the tenseness of her posture.

"Fifty-three, Ben. And I think they're children. There's something unfinished about them."

He stared in shock. "How in the hell would fifty kids be able to survive this?"

"There's six adults with them, but we better hurry." She ran forward but had to slow within steps, the snow was too high to run through.

"How far, Anne?"

"At the edge of my range so maybe a mile and a half or so? I could try to see farther but—"

"No. Don't take any chances that you'll get lost. Wait a second while I look at the map. It won't help anyone if we get lost."

She returned to him and took the reins of the horses while he opened the pack to remove the map. The both leaned over it as he traced his finger over the paper, letting it rest on High Circle Road.

"If we're where I think we are, they're at the middle school," he said.

"Maybe," Anne agreed and took the map from him to hold it closer. She examined it with narrowed eyes. "We'll have to go a bit out of our way if we stay on the road."

"We stay on the road. And I'm regretting not marking our trail now. The snow will be covering our tracks."

Anne glanced to the left, her gaze following nothing that Ben could see. "I have enough essence to make a bridge if we need one. There's plenty that I could take from the road without doing much damage. As long as we can find the river again, we can cross it."

Ben patted Lightning's side as he reached for the radio tied to the saddle horn. Only Lightning wore a saddle. Thunder pulled a sleigh that held their supplies that he was glad now Wayne had talked him into taking. He handed Anne one of the energy bars and swung up onto Lightning's back.

He'd intended for the horse to carry Anne, but it was faster if she led from the front and cleared obstacles from their path.

He kept a sharp eye out, hoping he'd see the dip in the road where the turn offs had been but the white blanket of snow that covered the ground made spotting differences hard.

Anne squatted and straightened a moment later, turning more to her left and proceeding faster.

"The road in front of us is relatively straight. Roadways have a deader feel than the ground around them. I can't sense debris though, so I could be missing it beneath the snow. Maybe we should leave the horses?"

Ben said, "No. It's safer to keep them with us. I agree, we should've carried packs and used snowshoes or skis though. But I thought this would be faster.

Anne said, "I wish I'd thought of searching this way earlier."

Ben snorted. "You just realized you could even do it. Give yourself a break. And I think you should go slower, using it this way. It feels like we're rushing to me. And I'm worried we're getting over our heads, going faster than we can keep up with."

"The witch comments?" She glanced over her shoulder, grinning wryly.

"You've heard them?"

"Just from a few people, and I don't think they really even mean it. I think it's just bitterness."

"Marge?"

"Mostly. She was really rude. Nothing I can't handle. I guess we need to be prepared for troublemakers. Not everyone is going to be grateful. Especially when the horror wears off and they realize this is their life now."

"Marge hates the idea of being a farmer. She's never going to accept it."

"She's never going to accept any system where she isn't at the top. We can't worry about people like her. I think it'll sort itself out once we get more settled. An agriculture-based life will take some adjusting too, but it isn't necessarily a bad thing. We liked it well enough."

Ben snorted. "We had tractors and feed stores."

"I admit, I'm not looking forward to plowing and harvesting by hand, but we can raise horses. We do have knowledge. It won't be like living in the past. We can make electricity and motors. Maybe not cars and airplanes but it's possible to live a comfortable life with a lower level of technology."

"You sound like you're trying to convince yourself," Ben said.

"Maybe a little. I feel bad for the younger ones, like Doug. This is a big change for them. We're old enough to remember not having a television in every home or not having our own phones or even not havening lights or running water. They're so used to technology that doing without it will be a real blow."

He said, "I caught Julie sneaking her friends into the winery. We'll need to keep the kids too busy to cause problems."

"That's why we need the town set out as soon as possible. The quicker we get everyone supporting themselves, the better.

"This might be selfish of me, but I want our house back."

Anne laughed and squatted to place her hands on the ground. She was silent, her eyes open, not seeing what was before her, but seeing what she sensed from the essence embedded in the dirt.

"Left up here," she said as she straightened and began walking. "I have some ideas about that I wanted to talk over with Doug. Building isn't too hard with essence, but I'd rather do it off the farm. I made a building for Jill and I to work in, but I'd prefer to build as few as possible on the farm itself.

"I still can't wrap my head around that you can hear the ground scream. We don't need to build anything on the farm."

"We'll need to build some things, but most could be made elsewhere, and we can make wooden panels that can be used to build on the farm—"

A large brown dog bounded into the road, snarling as it raced toward them. Ben thought it might be a mastiff but Lightning neighed and pranced, half turning away from the dog, and he didn't get more than a glance.

"Bad dog!" Anne yelled.

Lightning jittered farther sideways, and Thunder reared, neighing shrilly.

Ben reached for his gun as another dog slunk from the trees behind them. Lightning saw it too, because he neighed shrilly and kicked out.

"Anne!" He lifted his gun and fired at the dog creeping up on them.

Two more dogs ran from the woods, and Ben fired again as Anne yelled a wordless sound of fear. The mastiff tumbled to the ground and batted at his neck with his front paws. The dog's low growl had changed to whines that cut off abruptly as he fell limp.

Ben turned in the saddle. "Easy, boy." He patted Lightning's neck as the horse pranced in place. The other dogs had run, and he couldn't see them anymore.

"Can you hold Thunder?"

"Let me see if there are more first," Anne said breathlessly and knelt to place her hands on the ground

"Running away from us. Let's see, I count four more but they're all moving away." She rose and took the reins from Ben's hand, speaking in a soft voice to Thunder as she pulled the horse to a shaking standstill.

"Hold Lightning," Ben said as he slipped from the saddle. "Wait here." The dog he'd shot licked at the wound in its side. He shot it again.

"Why would they attack like that?" Anne asked.

"Food," Ben said grimly as he checked the second dog.

The dog Anne had killed had a glass-like collar encircling its neck in the midst of spot bare of fur and he wondered if she'd used its own fur to choke the dog to death.

"Jesus, it wasn't neutered. Let's hope this beast didn't have time to breed. Thank god we didn't leave the horses behind. Feral dogs are going to be a real problem. They have no fear of humans."

"Food," Anne said weakly, and Ben hurried to her.

"Take a few deep breaths. That was fast thinking with the collar."

"Jill's idea. Oh, Ben…" She began to cry, and he held her tightly, consumed with horror himself at the idea of what the dogs had been eating.

When she stepped away, she looked angry. "I forget," she said as she strode away, speaking with her back turned. "I was enjoying this as if it were a walk in the park or something and I forget the world has become this horrible place."

"Anne, no… You can't think like that. Yes, what happened was horrifying and more horrible than I have words for but that doesn't mean we can't be happy or enjoy the beauty of nature. The world isn't horrible just different."

"And while I'm enjoying myself, people are dying. They're starving and freezing and afraid."

Ben said nothing. She wasn't ready to hear him, and he didn't know what to say to that truth. He followed her silently, leading both horses. She walked as close as she could get to the trees and shrubs, trailing her hand across them, only speaking to call directions to him. The storm continued, bringing an early twilight and Ben could smell smoke on the wind.

"Anne!"

She turned, and he gestured her to wait. "We're close," she said.

"I know. I smell the smoke. The people there might react badly at first. Be prepared to protect yourself. Don't hesitate. Panic can make people do things they normally wouldn't. We'll try to talk them down but if someone is being aggressive, you can't let them hurt us or the horses."

She nodded and swallowed hard.

"I'm so sorry, sweetheart."

"I know. Let's go."

She gestured with her gloveless hand. "I have a wall of essence in front of us. It won't hurt them to walk through it but stay behind me."

My wife the witch, Ben thought then wanted to smack himself for even thinking it.

"Hello!" he yelled as they rounded the corner and he could see the heap of snow-covered rubble in a wider cleared spot.

"Hello?" a man called back as a young girl said, "They have horses!"

"Lorrie, wait!" the man said.

An excited babble arose that distance muffled to indistinguishable sound.

"We have supplies we can share! I'm Ben Windsor and this is my wife, Anne. We saw your smoke from our farm and came to look for you."

"The storm didn't reach that side of the river?" the man who approached asked, sounding choked up.

Ben tried not to wrinkle his nose. He could smell the uncured hides the man wore from fifty feet away.

"It did. The homes are gone the same as here, but my wife is a maker and protected us."

"A maker?"

"It's a long story. Let's get our tent set up, and we can heat the food we brought. We have bread and soup and bandages."

"Knives? I'd kill for a proper knife."

"My wife can make you one."

The man jerked and swore when the air around him fluoresced Anne beckoned him forward. "It's harmless. I'll see about making some less, *um*, fragrant clothing."

The man laughed and held out his arms. "Dog skin, and we only have a few sets." He leaned closer and lowered his voice, offering his hand to Anne who shook it. "I'm Reginald Harlow. We've been surviving on dog meat and never believe it tastes like chicken."

She slapped a hand to her mouth, her horrified bark of laughter cutting off mid shout.

"I'll go see what I can make of the debris, if you'll be okay alone?" Anne asked.

Ben said, "We'll be fine. He seems a reasonable sort."

Reginald called, "Lorrie, let's help Ben here set up his tent. He brought bread."

"Bread!" the girl exclaimed and another babble of talking broke out.

"Don't get too excited," Ben yelled, but he couldn't contain his grin. "We don't have enough for all fifty-three of you here, but we have more than enough on the farm."

Reginald took a step back and his eyes narrowed.

"How did you know there were fifty-three of us?"

"My wife." He gestured, and Reginald turned, clenching his bone knife, and Ben wondered if other men had come and tried to steal the little they had. And it was clear they had little although it was also clear they were trying hard. The snow had been shapped into rough igloos from which branches poked, in what Ben assumed was the frame of the rough shelters. Smoke rose in light wisps from the nearer and thicker clouds from the bigger connecting one. A girl stood before the smaller shelter. She wore dog skins on her feet and across her chest in a sort of toga style skirt, and Ben thought she must be freezing with her arms and legs exposed

She'd started forward when he'd mentioned bread but had halted and withdrawn a bone knife when Reginald had stopped.

"Anne!" Ben called, and his wife turned.

"My wife is a maker and can use the essence of the storm to view the land at a distance. She sensed you here and was able to clear a path to you. We have others out searching." Ben gazed up the sky. "If we start back soon, we can make it home by morning. How much time do you need, Anne?"

"Say an hour or so?"

Time for what?" Reginald asked and shifted his grip on his knife to a two-handed one.

"This," Anne said and waved her hand.

The essence was suddenly visible as a purple ball the size of a Volkswagen. Light flickered in the constrained purple clouds within the sphere. The mound of snow before her shifted, and she reached into it and pulled out a swath of bright red cloth that she shook out and offered Reginald.

He remained where he was.

Lorrie called, "Ken, Brian, you better come out here!"

Two boys stuck their heads from the shelter. Both wore what appeared to be bark on their feet and moss or brush of some kind to protect modesty. Even from where Ben stood he could see them shiver.

Anne leaned down and withdrew another swath of fabric, this one bright blue.

"You're showing off now," Ben said, and she laughed.

Within minutes she had a pile of various colored cloth at her feet.

Reginal had lowered the hand clutching the bone knife but he didn't approach.

"It's perfectly safe," Ben said as reassuringly as he could. "She can transmute elements using the storm essence. That sphere there is captured storm cloud. She uses it to reshape the debris. She can make simple items, bowls, cups, cloth— things like that."

Lorrie walked cautiously forward as Ben spoke and squatted to feel the fabric.

"It feels normal."

"It is normal, or mostly normal. Our scientist says it's a tighter cellulose structure than real cloth, but it has all the same properties. Except the color…" Ben shook his head at the blue wooden spoon Lorrie held.

"I just learned that. Cool, isn't it," Anne grinned at Lorrie who grinned back.

"But how do you do it?" she asked and tentatively touched the sphere beside Anne.

"I have no idea… but it works. Take this to your friends, and I'll make some smaller pieces and some lengths you can use as ties. Back home we cut the cloth and then stitch it using essence, but it'll be quicker to just make crude boots that tie on."

Lorrie nodded eagerly and gathered the cloth.

"Mr. Harlow?" one of the boys asked doubtfully.

"It's okay, boys. Give Lorrie a hand." He slipped the knife back into the vine waistband and turned back to Ben. "You said you had food?" he stepped closer and lowered his voice to a whisper. "I'm relieved you found us. We haven't managed to catch much, and I was worried they'd starve."

"We have enough with us that everyone can eat something. If your group is up to it, we can start back to our farm. There's shelter and food there for everyone. The horses can carry the weakest, and we have the sleigh if you have any who can't walk. Or we could lead some of you back and send back more supplies, but I think this snow will continue. It's not going to get any easier to travel."

Reginald peered doubtfully at the small sleigh Thunder pulled. It only carried a small sack of grain and two packs.

"It's all food. Anne can make shelter and pots to cook in. We brought energy bars, condensed soup, and twenty rolls. The soup is pretty good and it's good for you despite being the kind that will last twenty years…"

"It sounds amazing."

"Anne, Make us a big pot!"

"Look at that, Mr. H! She just thinks it and it appears like magic." The two boys exclaimed in excitement and grabbed the metal pot that formed from a downed tree trunk in front of Anne and rolled to their feet.

"Fill it with clean snow," Lorrie said and bent to gather the large wooden spoons as Anne formed them.

"Will ten spoons be enough?"

"Yes." Reginald took the pack Ben handed him and passed it to one of the boys. "Follow the directions on the packaging," he said absently, his wide eyes glued to Anne. "The cloud forms the items?"

Anne said, "Sort of. It's a plasma and electricity and it has information stored in it, like a computer. I can see what it knows and reprogram the raw material to be whatever shape I want. I can change the type of material but that's harder to do and uses more essence. The sphere there lets me see the pattern, the molecules of the elements that make up matter, and I can coat the wood in the essence and impose that pattern on it."

"Like a printer," Reginald mused and ran a hand over the sphere.

Ben said, "We call her a maker. It isn't magic or witchcraft. It's science."

"It's amazing!" Lorrie held up one of the spoons, turning it slowly. She examined them all and then handed them to one of the watching boys. "They're identical. Can you teach others how to use the computer?"

"No. Sorry. To connect to it requires an innate ability. It isn't something you can learn. Daryl, our scientist, says my brain transmits data on a different wavelength than yours."

Reginald asked, "Has he found the frequency?"

"No. We lack the tools."

"I'd love to speak with him. It's fascinating. Can you affect living matter, or does it need to be certain types?"

"I could but it's much harder and it's wrong to do it."

"Wrong?" Lorrie asked but she turned and yelled over her shoulder. "Stop squabbling! There's enough for everyone. Take turns just like always!" She turned back and grimaced. "I better go take care of that."

Reginald waited until she was out of earshot to say, "That girl is amazing. Tough and smart with a big heart. There are four other adults with us but they're useless." He darted Ben a guilty glance and said, "Well, not useless. They just don't have any survival skills at all. They'd just sit down in the snow and wait to die. I had to lie to get them to eat. They'd rather starve than eat dog, and it was freaking the kids out listening to them." He glanced over his shoulder, a disgusted expression on his face. "We had to make two shelters. The kids were fine with sharing, but my fellow adults were scandalized I expected the girls to stay with the boys. I almost left it, they weren't interested in working out here in the cold, but it's easier to not have to listen to them whine and it keeps them from knowing what we're up to. Mrs. Larson almost pitched a fit when she realized we were wearing dog skins."

Ben laughed. He could sympathize. "Sometimes I think we're a little too civilized. I just got talked into keeping a tiger because they're an endangered species…"

Reginald laughed and winced. "Sounds like you have some good stories to tell."

Stories for sure. I don't know how good they are."

✳ ✳ ✳

Ben frowned at Anne. "Should you be doing that?"

Her guilty flush didn't reassure him, and he laid a hand on hers. "Anne?"

"Daryl says they're safe."

The false enthusiasm in her voice made his scowl deepen. "Safe to use maybe, but are they safe to make?"

"I haven't blown us up yet, have I?"

"For god's sake, Anne! It isn't funny. Don't make any more. We have no idea how these things work. What if they're time bombs?

"Daryl doesn't think they are. The heat output remains constant." She frowned down at the small pile of glowing orange balls. "I'm making them weak. Just enough to keep their feet warm."

He released her hand and shook his head. "I don't like it."

"You're not freezing."

He peered over his shoulder at the line of children hunched beneath their colorful blankets and he sighed hard.

"Just enough for their feet and not one extra!"

She saluted and resumed making. Marble-sized balls cascaded from the air and the kids passing them stopped to stare.

"Let's take a break, guys!" Ben called and began gathering sticks for a fire. "We'll rest here thirty minutes or so and switch out the riders." He turned to Reginald and spoke in a quieter tone. "The horses will need a longer rest soon but if we can go on for another hour, we'll meet up with some of our people who will have more supplies. Anne can make us a shelter and we can rest a few hours or even overnight."

"Two each," Anne said and held out one of the glowing balls. "I recommend putting them in your boots, but you can hold them if your hands are cold."

"Everything's cold," a boy said to laughing complaints from the rest of them.

Ben was amazed at how cheerful they were. No one had really complained other than cheerful teasing. The adults silently trudged at the back except for Reginald who walked along the line, checking on everyone.

"How much farther?" Mrs. Larson asked.

"About three miles until we reach the gorge and the temporary camp they're setting up. It's another five or so to the bridge and the trucks."

"I still can't believe you have trucks." she said as if questioning him, but he just nodded.

"It seems so unreal. All of this…" She trailed off and looked about her as if seeing it for the first time.

And maybe she was, he mused. *Maybe she'd hidden in the shelter without trying to look around.*

"We have running water and electricity. We'll run out of gas eventually, but we have the cows and the greenhouses. No one will starve."

Reginald said, "Thank god Lorrie saw the smoke. We didn't even know why we were signaling— we realized you were across the river— but it helped just knowing there were others alive out there."

"It's a miracle," Mrs. Larson said and began to cry, and Ben worried she'd fall from the horse.

A group of the younger girls gathered around her, patting her back and rubbing her feet.

"No crying!" Lorrie barked, glaring at Mrs. Larson. "Tears will make your face freeze and nose run. Shelia, Karen, grab that dead limb behind you. You boys give them a hand breaking it. Everyone get a handful of dead wood. Mark, Terrance, you two fill the pot with clean snow. Make sure it's clean!" Lorrie strode off, giving directions in a no-nonsense way.

Ben smiled after her.

"She's a treasure," Reginald whispered. "I couldn't have

managed without her. They admire her and take direction more easily from her than me. She has a real knack with them."

"How'd you guys happen to be at the school?' Anne asked as she handed two of the small glowing balls to Reginald.

"Science experiment," Reginald said bitterly. "The school has a fallout shelter in the basement. Or I guess I should say had one. Top students from all over the state were invited to participate in a group of experiments. We'd planned to make it a three-day event. It was a great idea, a special treat to encourage academics. We had games and prizes all lined up." He pursed his lips as he glanced at the children piling the branches to make a fire. "I had to fight hard to get permission. All the money goes to sports. They thought nothing of sending the football team away overnight, sent them to Florida, bought them all kinds of new gear, but ask for money for a science weekend and you'd think I'd asked for the moon.

"So, I set it up myself. I held fundraisers and begged for donations and got it done. It's all my fault they weren't home with their parents. To be honest, I thought we'd see some of the parents show up. It's why we stayed there. But then I realized the extent of the damage and knew we'd be on our own even if they did show. I don't know if I saved them or killed them…"

Ben said, "We've located a few other survivors on this side of the river and still have teams out. Maybe they'll find some of the parents."

"Doubt it." He shrugged and gestured at the trees. "The kids are from all over the state except for my class…"

"There's always hope."

"There is, but it's just going to get harder. I had a run in with a survivor who tried to steal the dog I'd killed. He'd have killed me to take it. He didn't give a shit that the kids depended on me or needed that dog. When survival is at stake some men will do anything. Lorrie and I had planned to try to hike up to Bensworthy to see if we could find a better spot. That was a big farming community and they might have enough to share but the kids needed us here, and I couldn't send her alone. Some men will do anything—" He clamped his lips and glared into the distance.

"They'll be safe with us," Ben said.

"And you can't know the relief I feel."

Ben snorted. "I can imagine it. I'd feel like a million pounds was lifted if I could pass you all on to someone else."

Reginald laughed. "You'll have help though and that makes all the difference."

"If your done chatting, I could use a hand!" Lorrie called, and Ben laughed and waved Reginald away.

* * *

Ben lifted his head and breathed deeply. The soft scent of smoke drifted to him on the frigid air. Snow still fell, faster now, in thick sheets that stuck to hair and exposed skin, and the kids were tired. They walked without the excited talk of earlier, plodding in a long line behind Anne. She led the way, letting the essence trail her in the thicker trees beside the road. The trees glowed a soft green as the essence passed over them, casting enough light to reveal Anne. Ben followed, bringing up the rear, leading Thunder who pulled the sleigh carrying Mrs. Larson and a young girl who couldn't be more than twelve and had fallen, weak from a fever that Ben hoped was just hunger induced. He turned to ensure they remained on the sleigh. Two other girls rode Lightning, their bare legs red from cold but they giggled and whispered together.

"Jill's here!" Anne called. The green in the trees rose and hovered, lighting the tips of the upper limbs as Anne walked back to speak to him.

"Here?"

"Going to the camp they're setting up about quarter of a mile away. She says she brought a LEC and will make tents for them.

She also says there's been a death on a hunting team, and we need to get back."

"Who?" Ben asked grimly.

"Phil Auburn. And Annie is hysterical. Doug wants us to come back. I don't know what he thinks we can do…"

"Jesus. What happened?"

Anne tilted her head, laying her hand on tree trunk. "Fell in the river. Jill doesn't know how. The team is pretty shaken up, and she says Dave is pissed. We should go home for the memorial anyway."

Reginald asked, "A friend of yours?"

Ben grimaced. "Not really but every soul counts, and I like his wife."

"The poor thing," Anne said and hugged Ben.

He returned the embrace. "I love you," he whispered, and she hugged him tighter.

"It would kill me, Ben."

"Me too. Let's not think about it. We'll get them settled in the camp and head home. How's Jill's new pet? Contained, I hope."

Anne wiped her eyes and released him to touch a tree. A moment later she said, "Contained but she has plans for a bigger cage. Kate offered to hunt for her. She spoils our daughter rotten."

Reginald said, "You can use the trees to communicate?"

Ben laughed when he glanced at Reginald who stared with his mouth hanging open.

Anne said, "Just to Jill. She's a maker too. But Daryl says it isn't the trees we use but the energy conduits between them."

"How many makers are there?"

"Just us two here. I guess there could be millions somewhere else."

"A million…" he walked quietly beside them for a few minutes before saying, "I don't think I like that idea. I'd hate to be one of the few who can't use the storm essence." He shot Anne a measuring glance. "Although, I suppose, being one of the few who can has its drawbacks too."

"It's a skill like any other. We're just people. But I better go lead this crew, their veering from the road." She kissed Ben's cheek and hurried back to the front of the line.

"Just like the pied piper," Reginald said.

I hope not, Ben thought. *They'd all fallen off a cliff.*

Frenemies

Sunday Dawn 1/28

Merlin's low growl woke Ben from a sound sleep. Moonlight trickling in the bedside window revealed the small dog stood on Anne's shoulder with his feet braced and mouth open in a snarl. She didn't stir.

"It's okay, boy," Ben said and reached to pet him. The dogs had mostly stopped fussing when people moved about at night, and Ben seldom heard the toilet or talking upstairs, and it was easy to ignore the quieter sounds from downstairs. He heard nothing at all now, but Merlin's growl ratchetted up a notch and he leaped to the foot of the bed.

Ben sat as his door eased open.

"Whose there?" he asked as Merlin barked once, then lunged.

"It's me. Call him off and keep quiet!"

"Phil?" Ben asked in amazement and reached for the lantern on his bedside table.

"Turn it off," Phil said urgently, as Anne said, "What's going on?"

"Get off, dog! Call off the mutt!"

"Merlin, come!" Anne said sharply as Ben got out of bed and reached for his bathrobe. Merlin continued to growl, but he returned to Anne and hunkered in her lap.

"We thought you were dead," Ben said.

"Yeah, Tim thought so too. He tried hard enough to kill me." Phil closed the door and stepped closer. "If he knows I'm not dead, he'll finish the job."

"What are you talking about?"

Tim and his pals plan to make a try for the farm."

"Try for the farm?" Anne asked.

She sounded confused, but Ben understood the danger instantly. "When?" he asked urgently as he dropped the robe and reached for his jeans.

"Ben?" Anne asked.

"Get dressed and get Jill," Ben said.

Anne jumped from bed, and Merlin began barking again.

"Quiet," Phil hissed.

"Merlin," Anne said sharply as she scooped him up. She halted beside Phil and rose a hand to his face. "What happened?"

"We don't have much time." Phil pushed her hand away.

Anne grabbed a blanket from the bed and handed it to him. "You must be freezing."

Ben said, "Get Jill! And wake Doug. Tell him to dress in dark clothes and wake Pat and—"

"No. That won't work." Phil wrapped himself in the blanket and sat at the edge of Ben's bed, and Ben realized how exhausted Phil was by the way he slumped. He stepped close enough to see the dried blood crusted on a jagged cut on his cheek.

"I'm not sure how many are involved, and if they know you're ready for them, they'll wait. It's better to let them gather and catch them at the same time."

"What's their plan and who's involved?" Ben continued

dressing.

Anne gave him a desperate glance but ran from the room.

"Twelve I'm certain of. I think he might have another crew lined up I don't know about."

How do you happen to be so privy to their plans?"

Phil curled his lip and gestured about the room. "Look, it's no secret I don't like Doug. I've never liked him. He was always a privileged little prick who got everything handed to him. When Tim approached me, I thought it was my chance to even the field. For once I'd be the guy with the nice house— the guy in charge. I had no idea that they planned murder until I was in, and then I knew it was a death sentence to get out.

"Tim's a bad dude. A real bad dude and when I heard he'd been sniffing around Jill, I got the chills. Jill's a good kid. Hell, no one deserves what he has planned."

Doug stuck his head in the door and glared at Phil. He carried his rifle and was shirtless and shoeless.

"Round up the guys— and Kate." Ben turned to Phil. "Are Joe or Al involved?"

"No. Everyone knows they're your men. Kevin, Marcus— none of the guys who went to Chester are involved. Tim had no chance to speak to any of them, but I doubt he'd have tried. He was careful and targeted the complainers and unhappy assholes like me," Phil finished bitterly.

"Get Al and Joe, make up an excuse, tell them we've got a downed cow and need help rolling her or something."

"Where do I bring them?

"The workshop," Ben said grimly, remembering he'd seen them meeting and done nothing. And he'd known they were up to no good but hadn't wanted to deal with it. He shook his head hard, angry with himself for letting things get so out of control so quickly. "We'll need more men we can trust but if we gather too many, we'll give ourselves away."

Phil said, "We have a few hours. Call in the Chester crew in the morning. Send in replacements. Tim doesn't plan to hit until right before the memorial service. He figures everyone will be gathered together and unarmed and he'll be able to walk right in and take the guns."

Doug's glare ratcheted up a notch, but he closed the door softly, and Ben couldn't hear him run back to finish dressing.

Ben said grimly, "It would've worked… the hunting crews would've turned in their guns and we don't have a guard on them or anything. But we do have Anne…"

A cold chill brought out goosebumps on his arms. Anne was more dangerous than twenty guns and Tim knew it.

"What did he have planned for Anne?"

"He—"

Phil stood as the bedroom door opened again. Anne entered followed by Jill who turned scared eyes on Ben. Ben's stomach tightened, and fury made his voice harsh as he said, "Jill, get your mom's pistol from my safe. You go nowhere without it!"

Anne placed a hand on Jill's arm. "She doesn't need a gun. She needs a LEC. There's only two small SEC in the house though."

"I'll send someone for one. Get the gun for now, honey."

Anne's face tightened, and she turned a fierce expression on Phil who held up both hands in a warding off gesture.

"I'm on your side."

"Now you are," Ben muttered, and Phil flashed him a rueful grimace.

"It wasn't personal…" He slashed his hand through the air and then rubbed his face gingerly. "I was an ass. I know it." His expression hardened, and he half smiled. "But you're lucky I was. I should've been smarter though. If I hadn't argued about Jill…" he flushed so dark Ben could see it in the dark room. He didn't want to know what Tim had planned for his daughter. A glance at Anne's face revealed how sickened she was. Sickened and furious.

Fury practically lit the room around her, and it occurred to him they'd angered more than a mother and wife, they'd angered a maker and she was going to make war. The thought made him feel sick.

He asked, "How were they going to stop Anne?"

"Poison. Marge said she could get it in the stew for your lunch. The timing and method were all her idea. And Tim got excited when he realized how easy it would be if Anne were dead."

"How'd he plan to get Jill away?"

"I'm not sure but it wouldn't be hard to do. I can think of a billion things that would get her out of the house at lunch time, and it isn't like she'd be hard to subdue."

"*Ha!*" Jill crossed her arms and glared.

"Sorry, Jill, but it's true. You're a strong girl but Tim's a strong man. Without essence you'd be defenseless, and it wouldn't be all that difficult to take a SEC from you. Hell, Steve could lift it from you, and you wouldn't even notice until you reached for it. The man is a genius at sleight-of-hand."

Ben said, "The missing guns?"

"Yes. They have the four guns already."

"God damn it!" Ben took a deep breath and gave Jill a reassuring smile he didn't feel.

"Jill, take Phil to Doug's room and get him some dry clothes. Give him Doug's parka and take him to the workshop. If anyone stops you, make excuses. Don't let anyone see he isn't Doug."

"My wife…"

"Thinks you're dead. Abby had to sedate her. Janice is looking after Meredith. We'll tell her but not tonight."

Phil nodded grimly.

Ben kissed his daughter's forehead and hugged her a moment, his angry eyes locked on Anne's. She'd been right, but he hadn't thought anyone would make such a blatant attempt. He'd thought they were all still reeling with the shock and had imagined it would take years to build enough discontent before anyone tried to take over. And he'd never imagined they'd do it by force, not from his people.

It shocked him that he thought of them as his people, but when he'd considered they might be attacked for what they had, he'd thought it would take years until survivors in other areas heard of them and by that time they'd have established such a strong foundation they'd be able to withstand groups of bandits. But the bandits were already here, and he'd been weak.

Anger clenched his jaw. He'd known Marge was no good, had known it from the moment he'd met her. He should've smacked her down hard then and never given her a chance to dare. And now she thought she could kill them all and take everything that was theirs. She thought he was weak, unable or unwilling to protect his family. His breath came in harsh pants he was so furious. He should've kicked her out when she'd insulted Anne to his face. He *had* been weak and unwilling. *Never again*, he vowed and pushed Jill away.

"Get the gun and don't hesitate to use it!"

She bit her lip and nodded.

Anne gazed after her as Jill grabbed the lantern. Jill closed the closet door before turning on the light, revealing only a thin slice of brightness that Ben doubted anyone outside would notice.

"Johanna went to wake my mom," Anne said. "No one will think it odd. She's on the medical detail."

Ben nodded and hugged Anne. "We'll be ready for them!"

Anne kissed him briskly and spun away, saying over her shoulder, "God help them, they'll never be ready for me!"

Anne Prepares for War

Sunday Morning 1/28

Daryl folded a black length of cloth and placed it on the pile beside him, reaching for the next piece without taking his eyes off the small flame heating the tip of an iron knife Anne had made.

"That one looks good, Anne. I think it's the best were going to do in the time we have. I wish we had more time to really research this. Pat's notes help, but…" He used a thick mitt to lift a knife from the flame and tried to pierce the fabric. "It's heavy. Too heavy to wear for long. That last sample would be better for clothing. Make long lengths of this for cloaks. We won't be able to sew it. You'll have to use essence to cut and form it.

"We don't have time to sew anyway," Anne said grimly. She glanced at Jill who stared at a swath of fabric that sat beneath a dark purple cloud of essence.

Metal and cloth samples littered the rock table of their workshop. The essence cloud filled the entire room. It was both easier and harder to make things in the dense cloud. Seeing to the essence of an object was easier but staying on track harder. Her anger and fear kept her focused and she realized how lucky they'd been that the storm hadn't swept them away. The land's pain had saved her life, but they could still lose everything.

Anne grasped the rough hank of material she wore and tightened the cord that held it above her breasts as she leaned closer to the fabric Daryl held out. Jill and Daryl were similarly attired.

They'd been working for four hours now and Anne was starving. She committed the pattern to memory before grabbing an apple and eating it absently as she arranged lengths of fresh cut wood across the smaller work bench that lined the back wall. She was an expert at gauging mass now and it was much easier to start with the correct mass than cut off a smaller chunk.

She peaked from the window to gauge the time she had left. Sunlight sparkled through the window and she laid her hand against the cold diamond panes. A light snow gusted outside that she thought was mostly the snow from the ground being whipped about by the wind. She could see the trees waving but no stray breezes seeped through the rock of the workshop walls. She was tempted to make Jill wait here. No one could enter or harm her here. Bullets passing through the essence infused diamond-like panes would turn to harmless mist if they could even breach it.

"We need to build a house," she said as she turned from the window.

"Humph, we need clothes first—"

A knock at the door interrupted Jill. Daryl peeked through the small window beside the door and motioned Anne back. "Let me answer it," he whispered.

"Hi," Marge said cheerfully when the door opened. "I saw you were already hard at work here, so I brought you some breakfast. Will you need lunch here too?"

"No. We're going home for lunch," Anne said as she pulled the door further open. "Tell everyone to stay away though. We're making new clothes for the service and the essence inside will dissolve the older clothes."

Marge's eyes hardened as she glanced down at her borrowed shirt, but she smiled and handed out the tray. The smell of the fresh bread made Anne's stomach growl loudly.

"Thanks," Anne said, hoping her fury didn't show in her eyes.

"No problem. I meant it as a peace offering. I'm sorry about...." She waved her hand airily.

"For being such a bitch?" Jill asked, and Anne turned to glare at Jill.

Jill pursed her lips and put her hands on her hips.

"Jill—" Anne said warningly.

Marge said, "No. She's right. I was very rude, and I'm sorry. Someone does need to be in charge, and it is your farm— I think it all made me kind of crazy."

"Stress can make us do crazy things." Anne considered Marge's smiling face. If she didn't know her plans, she'd never think this woman capable of murder. The heightened flush in her cheeks, the bright eyes, she'd have assumed were from embarrassment. And maybe she was in over her head and really was sorry but didn't know how to get out of it.

Anne said, "Sometimes we make choices we regret. We get pulled into the wrong crowd and don't know how to get ourselves back on track. Ben saw you talking with Tim. He isn't a nice guy. If you're afraid of him, if you need help..."

"Ben told you he saw me talking with Tim?"

Marge's expression sharpened, and Anne realized she wasn't as dumb as she seemed. She'd thought Marge's rudeness was spontaneous, that she couldn't help saying stupid things, but her expression changed so quickly Anne realized she wore it like a mask. Goosebumps rose on her arms, and she had to resist rubbing them.

"He wondered what you two had to talk about."

"I ran into him while looking for your husband to apologize for my behavior. I wanted to clear the air, make a fresh start."

Anne smiled, trying to project innocent acceptance and excitement lit Marge's eyes again.

She's looking forward to killing me. She couldn't stop the shiver that followed the thought.

"You must be freezing," Marge said, nodding at the tray Daryl held. "Enjoy it. Stop by if you're still hungry. We're making tons of food for after the service. That memorial service is just what we need."

Marge's smile brightened, and Anne thought she might giggle. She must've realized she looked too happy because she turned away and said, "It's all so sad…" She hurried away, and Anne watched her out of sight, wondering if she'd burst into laughter as soon as a door closed between them.

"That woman…" Daryl held the tray at arm's-length.

"I think she's crazy. Maybe she was always crazy. I wonder if there were any mysterious deaths in her past?"

Jill said, "Sharon said Marge forced her husband to have that affair, that she threatened him."

Anne examined the innocent seeming bread. If flared red as Daryl entered the essence but mildly, leaving behind a softly glowing green loaf with jagged edges and holes.

"It's still green," Jill said thoughtfully.

"We're not eating it," Anne said flatly and tossed it into the small metal brazier that heated the room.

Daryl leaned closer to examine the loaf as it burned. "Processed flour. I wonder if all poison would fluoresce?" Daryl mused as he opened a crude wooden basket, one of the first Anne had ever made, to remove the food he'd brought.

Anne grinned as she accepted the sandwhich. One of Daryl's jobs had become feeding them. They ate twice what they used too and had still begun losing weight. Anne wasn't sure it was the essence though. They were also getting ten times the exercise they were used to. Everyone had lost weight.

"Some poisons would burn off but if she used a natural one…"

"Where would she get it from?" Jill asked around a mouthful of sandwhich.

"Hemlock is very poisonous and readily available. Leaving meat out to spoil would do it although not quickly. You'd get very sick before dying."

Daryl examined his sandwich and replaced it uneaten into the box. "My point is— let's take nothing for granted and be careful. Jill, hand me that saw, and I'll cut some lengths of the correct weight."

✳ ✳ ✳

Anne stacked the new clothing on the dining room table. Her hands still shook from hearing the ground scream when they'd infused a perimeter around the house with essence and she still felt it like a dull ache in her bones although that was fading.

She already wore a new gown of dark purple. Jill had fashioned her a matching cloak and used rabbit fur to line it, mixing the real thing with her facsimile so cleverly Anne couldn't spot the seams. But the cloak was hot to wear, and she'd left it draped over a chair, hoping it would be enough to duck behind if men with guns came. But she wasn't too worried about guns. Essence would destroy the bullets before they'd gone a foot, a fact they'd tested.

As soon as they took their places at the table, she planned to put a thin wall of essence between the kitchen and dining room. She was confident it would be enough protection from gun wielders. She hoped they would come here first, a fact she hadn't mentioned to Ben when she'd talked him into splitting up. She worried about catching all the men involved. It terrified her to think they had hidden enemies among them who'd be so ruthless as to poison an entire household to kill two.

"But, Mom," Chloe said, her voice gaining volume as she drew closer.

"We were just there," Emily chimed in.

"And we're going back as soon as you thank your aunt. Aunt Anne made you these clothes special. Now go say thank you."

Sue shook her head and sighed, smiling down at her girls with a tight smile as she ushered them into the room.

"Thanks, Aunt Anne," Chloe said doubtfully as she examined her new clothes.

Anne laughed and crouched to tighten the silver belt on the bright red cloak Chloe wore. Jill had fashioned the belts and made them matching headbands.

"You know what this is?" she asked as she lifted the end of the belt, running her fingers lightly over the small beads.

"Marbles?" Emily asked as she examined her own clothes.

"Essence. It's worth more than gold or silver."

"Is this silver?" Chloe asked.

"Yes. Silver and diamonds and essence. You're wearing a fortune in clothing. No one else in the entire world will have such magnificent clothing as those Jill makes you. Talk to her later and help design your new wardrobe. We made these to match ours."

"You'll have cloaks too?"

She sounded interested and a bit excited now, Anne thought and kissed her forehead before rising. "Yes. Wait until you see them. Jill made us some super fancy duds. Uncle Ben, Doug, and your daddy will all be wearing them."

"For the funerals?" Emily asked and tears filled her big blue eyes.

"Oh, sweetie," Anne leaned down to hug her.

"Come on, girls, Aunt Anne has things to do. We'll go help Helen."

Sue gestured the girls to the door and took Anne's hand. "Be careful. Don't take any chances. I really wish you'd take the gun."

Anne closed Sue's hand around the pistol tucked into the silver sash that cinched her new dress. Sue also wore essence crafted clothing. A simple floor-length dress in black cinched with the same type of belt that held the cloaks closed. Jill had wanted to embellish them but had lacked the time, but Anne knew the simple links would be decorative soon. *If they won...*" the thought tightened her hands on Sue's. "Don't hesitate."

"You either." Sue kissed her cheek and hurried after her daughters.

Anne returned to sorting the clothing and was just finishing when Doug stuck his head in the door.

"Dress and take these to the barn. Daryl doesn't think it'll stop a bullet, but he thinks it'll slow it. A knife can't puncture it, but it'll still hurt, and they're flame retardant but not fireproof. The shirts and pants are equivalent to thick leather but hopefully soft enough to be comfortable. We need more time to design better ones."

"These are great, Mom, and we won't even need them. They'll walk right into us, and it'll be over in minutes with no shots fired."

"Don't get cocky."

"I still think you and Jill should—" Doug broke off, grimacing as steps sounded on the cellar stairs. Two men came through the cellar door.

"Tell Dad not to be late for lunch." She glanced at the pot on the counter and winced, quickly wiping the expression from her face and trying to look bored.

Doug said, "That cow still isn't on her feet. I'll bring him some." Doug headed to the stove and ladled a generous portion into a waiting container. Anne tried to project an air of innocence as she began to set the table.

The two men passed Doug, heading to the bathroom.

"I'm so hungry, I can't wait for Jill. She'll just have to heat up her own when she gets back from taking care of Mrs. Ming.

"She'll probably skip lunch and just eat after the service," Doug said in a falsely cheerful tone that Anne could hear the lie in.

She cleared her throat and gave him a hard glance. He rolled his eyes and gathered the bags, balancing the stew on the top of the pile.

Nerves made her palms sweat as she turned her own false smile on the two men. "Will you be joining us for lunch?"

They exchanged tight smiles and the older of the two shook his head. "We'll take ours to go too if we can, ma'am. Stan and me volunteered to watch the kitchen fires during the service."

Stan said, "You get more proficient forming the cloth all the time. That's a pretty outfit."

"We made plenty of cloth for everyone and will be holding office hours to join the seams. Helen can help fit you. She'll be holding office hours to teach sewing for those who wish to learn. We'll be offering personalized colors and fabric weights— this could be a really good place to live."

"It already is, ma'am." The two men exchanged amused glances.

"Well, tell the others downstairs lunch is ready, please."

"Yes, ma'am" he said cheerfully, offering her a mock salute. They ran down the stairs, and Anne held a hand to her pounding heart, releasing the edge of her silver belt she hadn't realized she'd grabbed. They hadn't taken any lunch with them, but she didn't call them back. She carried the stew up the stairs and put it in her shower.

Jill grabbed Boomer's collar. The dog wagged his tail, giving Jill a confused glance.

"Stay!" Jill said, and Boomer crouched with his tail between his legs. Jill grimaced and ruffled his ears. "Stay," she said again in a kinder tone and leaned over Anne's shoulder to peer into the pot.

Before Anne could stop her, she dabbed her finger into the food and the food flashed red, disappearing in a cloud that Jill captured and put back in the small SEC she clutched.

"Could be additives from the spices," Anne said.

"You know it isn't." Jill stomped back into the bedroom and petted Boomer who whined softly, *likely scenting the tension in the air*, Anne thought and rubbed his ears a moment before kissing Jill's cheek.

"Keep Merlin with you too."

"I should—"

"No!" You're backup. You'll remain here, and if we lose, you'll go hide."

"Mom…"

"You'll do whatever you need to do. We have enough essence you could engulf the farm in fire. Jill, I hate this, but I love you. You owe it to Daddy and I to live. Use whatever you have to. Be as hard as you need to be!"

She kissed Jill's forehead and stared into her teary eyes. "God willing you won't need to do a thing."

Jill bit back a sob and pressed her hands to her mouth.

"I love you," Anne called back as she strode from the room. Back in the kitchen she opened three big cans of soup and had it heating when Wayne entered followed by his wife and Edward.

"Marie—" she broke of not knowing what to say and finally settled on "The kids?" She exchanged sweaty hand clasps with Marie.

"With Sue." Marie took a seat and laid her cape along the back of her chair. Anne couldn't see the pistol she carried but she knew she had one. She wore the exact same dress as Anne.

"I'll be in the hall bath," Edward said brusquely and strode down the hall.

Wayne held the door of the cellar open, his expression darkening when a young boy entered.

"Ten fucking children," he muttered as he spooned up a bowl

of soup and placed it before the boy.

The dining room was soon full. The newest arrivals took the bowls Anne offered and sat to eat without speaking much. Most of the soft talk centered on the upcoming memorial service.

Anne watched them eat. Most picked listlessly at their food or ate hurriedly without seeming to taste it or care what they ate.

A man Anne didn't know didn't eat and watched them like Anne did. She wasn't sure if he just wasn't hungry or was part of the plan, and she shook her head at Wayne when he dropped his hand to his hidden pistol. She placed a basket of bread before him. "Eat before it gets cold."

She took a bowl and ate it standing at the counter, her attention on the essence she was directing around the room.

The man glanced at the clock, and she struck. He had time to gasp once before the shirt he wore turned bilious red. The gas had barely formed before Anne captured it, forming it with a thought into manacles. Wayne lunged across the table and grabbed the man as Marie rose and drew her pistol.

"No one moves!" she barked in a trembling voice.

Edward ran in from the hall.

"Take him upstairs. Jill can bind him." Anne said to Edward and took the man's seat. "You're all going to lay your heads on the table and stay still as stone."

"What's going on," one of the men asked, his nervous glance darting to the woman and child next to him.

"We expect some bad people to show up any minute. They think we're all dead by now." She poured the man's full bowl of soup across the table and closed her eyes, releasing more essence until a thin coating hovered inches from the floor and the kitchen ceiling.

'*I've got him contained,*' Jill said. '*He's not giving anything up.*'

"*Wait there,*' Anne thought back.

"He didn't eat," Marie said grimly.

"Jesus," the man said and snatched the spoon from the boy's hand.

"I switched the food. It's fine. But we want to catch them all."

The man nodded and cleared his throat. "My son…"

"Edward!" Anne called, then turned to the boy. "What's your name, sweetie?"

"Alex."

"Edward, take Alex and the other kids upstairs to wait with Jill. They shouldn't care if the kids aren't here. Marie, go turn the television on and start the DVD and maybe they'll think we let them eat in the living room.

'*Mom, five men just crossed the seeded ground.*'

"Hurry. They're on their way. Edward, take care of my daughter…"

He nodded grimly and took Alex's hand to lead the crying boy upstairs.

The parents urged their children to go upstairs as Anne said, "Five, Wayne. Jill will take good care of them," she said to the worried adults.

"Please put your heads down. Anne can handle them," Wayne said.

Anne said a quick prayer for her husband and laid her head on the table, using her body to hide the ragged edge of table her essence had touched. Warm soup wet her hair and face as she closed her eyes to slits. *They wouldn't make it two steps inside*, she vowed.

A Fight for Freedom

Sunday Afternoon 1/28

Silence reigned in the barn with only the distant sounds of the cows muffled by the walls to break the stillness. Ben hunkered in a half-closed storage cabinet, fingering the grip of his pistol and sweating beneath the thick folds of his cape. He peaked from the crack and scanned the room but couldn't see anything out of place.

Picking men to help had been harder to do than he'd originally thought. He had no doubts that the four people inside with him could be trusted but the men outside were mostly unknown to him.

Doug and Pat hid in the cabinet opposite his. The tools normally housed in the cabinets were stashed under loose hay in the mow over their heads.

The floor above them creaked slightly and Ben examined the ceiling. Motes of dust drifted in the sunlight streaming through the windows but that was the only thing that gave away the presence of the fifteen, armed men hidden with the tools above them.

He'd ended up leaving Dan in charge of setting out the rest of the men, hoping experience would win out if any of the men Ben had chosen were secretly working with Tim. He knew none had time to speak with Tim but that wouldn't stop a double cross if the men were ruthless enough,

Dan will know how to handle it, he told himself and nudged the door a bit wider to scan the rafters but didn't spot Kate or Dave although he knew they were laying atop the thick beams with the rifles. He regretted letting Kate stay with him now. She was the best shot he knew but there was sure to be violence. They had at least seven guns, maybe more if the other hunting team was in on it.

She volunteered, he told himself, but it didn't help the guilty sick feeling in his stomach. It still hadn't really sunk in that someone planned to kill them to steal their home. *And not just kill them,* he reminded himself and wiped his sweaty hands on his pants one at time. Jill would never be safe; this could only end with Tim's death.

He rose an arm to wipe his sweating brow. *They'll come here first,* he told himself for the millionth time. Worry for Anne and Jill built every minute, and he was cursing himself for agreeing to her plan. But it had seemed logical. They'd want the weapons before going to confront her in case the poison hadn't worked. But they also knew two of the men who lived in the basement worked for Tim and would likely show up.

Doug's assurances that they'd walked through and had seemed to believe Anne, hadn't lessoned his anxiety. They might be better actors than his son. They could walk in again and shoot her dead before she had time to do a thing. Wayne and Edward would do their best and likely be able to stop two men, but she'd still be dead. Only the memory of how fast she'd subdued that dog kept him inside the closet.

Time ticked by and the muscles in his shoulders began to ache from his tense posture. It was too dark in the closet to reveal his watch, but it felt as if he'd been waiting for hours although he knew it hadn't been. He'd be able to hear the bell on the point ring to gather them for the memorial.

The barn door slid open, and Ben stiffened, his gaze scanning the ceiling, but he still didn't see either of the Foster's in the rafters.

"Hello!" a man called. "Hello! Anyone here?" he walked down the hall as softer footsteps approached the open doorway of the main room.

"Told you this was a great time," the first man said.

"Marge told us, and she was right," Tim said. "As a reward for being right, you can have her, Josh."

Josh snorted with laughter as he walked in front of Ben. "Like I want that skank. I got my eye on the little Latino hottie."

"I already got dibs on her," another man said angrily.

Tim said, "Shut the fuck up and get the guns. We can worry about who gets which woman when we got them!"

Tim stalked past the two men who'd stopped to glare at each other and headed to the cabinet they kept the guns in. It had a simple combination lock on it meant to keep out children, not really protect from thieves.

"Holter, you got the bolt cutters?" Tim called.

"Yo, right here, boss. Let me through."

Five more men entered followed by a man Ben remembered being with Al's group. Holter slapped the shoulder of a man he passed, grinning as he offered the cutters to Tim. Four more men entered as Tim snipped the lock. Ben hoped he'd been right to trust Al. If he was in on it, they were about to be in some serious shit.

Tim said, "Get your gun and get into position. We'll shock them. I doubt they'll offer resistance but kill any fucker who looks like they'll be trying something." He swung open the cabinet door, peering over his shoulder to say, "Mike, stop for the chainsaws with Roberts and give them to Jesit and Meyers. But save me a small one. Chainsaws are fucking terrifying. We'll have all the girls wetting their panties and throwing themselves at us!"

"I fucking doubt that," Kate said. "Make one fucking move, and I'll blow your fucking head off!"

She'd no sooner said it then her gun roared, and a man screamed shrilly, grasping at the spreading stain on his stomach and falling into the man next to him.

No Turning Back

Sunday Afternoon 1/28

Gunfire sounded in the distance and Anne jerked.

"Wait," Wayne said grimly.

She laid her head back down, tensing as the door opened, and peeking through the strands of hair covering her face.

The man who entered walked softly and clutched a knife as long as her forearm. He held a finger to his lips and turned to gesture over his shoulder.

"The television is on," one whispered and headed to the living room. He carried a knife too but sheathed at his hip.

Anne debated and let him go. She needed them all to come inside.

"The kids are probably dead in there already," the next man said in a normal voice and the first gave him an irritated scowl.

He grinned and pushed past. "Anyone home?" he called in voice that sent chills down Anne's spine. He strode forward and the last two entered.

"I'm home," Anne said as she sat. The clothes the men wore

bubbled and the essence surrounding them thickened into wood as they shrieked and tried to turn.

"Fuckers!" Wayne snapped.

She jumped to her feet and ran for the living room almost running into the man in the small hallway. He had the knife out now, but he hesitated, then drew his arm back as if he'd throw it.

Anne hadn't hesitated. She'd willed the essence in the hall to lower and coat him and transformed his sweatshirt into metal manacles. The knife fell from his hand, turning to red mist that billowed past his face. She managed to catch the essence before it could reach the floor, leaving him in the tatters of his borrowed jeans before her.

Wayne yelled at the captives in the kitchen and she could hear clunking and cursing and breathless pleading to be released. More gunfire sounded in the distance; a quick flurry of shots too close together to count. Tears sprang to Anne's eyes.

"Anne, I think it might be too tight!" Marie yelled.

"Who else was involved?" Wayne asked roughly.

Anne didn't glance back. She didn't care if they smothered.

She said, "Were you going to slit the children's throats?"

The man in the hall paled and shook his head, rising his hands to rub at the red rash the shirt had made on his face as it disintegrated.

"Just me?"

He took a step back and licked his lips, his gaze darting to the doorway and then looking behind him.

"You're all caught. My husband was waiting for your pals."

"Anne!" Marie called again and came into the hallway. "Two of them are down and not breathing!"

"We got them, Edward! Stay with Jill!" Anne called up the stairs, then warned Marie, "Don't get too close to him."

She ran back to the kitchen. It was clear the two men motionless on the floor were already dead. She'd crushed them in her haste. It surprised her that she felt nothing for them, no guilt or sorrow just thankfulness that the threat had been ended. Her eyes narrowed as she examined the remaining two and they stopped thrashing and stared with panicked eyes at her.

"They won't talk," Wayne said and glanced to the door.

Marie spoke to the man in the living room, the sound muffled by the walls.

"Find out if he knows anything!" Wayne called loudly.

The others at the table gaped with wide eyes. Most hadn't seen Anne make anything at all and would've only heard rumors or maybe not even that. They'd just arrived the day before and appeared shocked.

Wayne shook his head, glaring at the two captives. "I guess we can take them to the greenhouse. Ben can have them hung like the traitors they are...."

"He can't hang us. We didn't do anything," one gasped out.

It would hurt her husband to do it, Anne thought with growing sorrow. She'd been so consumed with worry that she hadn't thought past it, but now she realized the hard choices would fall on her husband. Without conscious decision she surrounded the men with essence, but halted, shocked by her impulse.

She hesitated, she could kill them with a thought, smother them in the wood as she'd done to their companions.

"Anne!" Wayne said sharply, and she jerked and wiped her suddenly sweating brow.

"Are you okay?" he asked.

"Fine. I didn't mean to kill those two,"

"And no one blames you. You were attacked. It's their fault, not yours. You have a right to defend yourself."

"This is going to kill Ben."

Wayne's angry expression faded to worry. "I know." His gaze traveled the softly glowing wood and his eyes widened as he realized her intent. She saw him make the realization and the

427

myriad of expressions that followed.

"I don't know either, Anne," he said and laid a hand on her shoulder.

"It isn't fair to put it on Ben."

Marie entered the kitchen trailed by the man from the living room while Anne and Wayne still stared at the captives on the floor.

"You didn't release them," Marie said and fell to her knees to feel for a pulse.

Wayne pulled her up. "They're dead and good riddance."

Anne said, "I should go and see if Ben needs help."

"What should we do with them?" Marie asked.

Anne gathered the essence again.

"This is help I can give him," Anne said to Wayne, then turned to glare at the captives when he nodded slowly. "You've been found guilty of attempted murder, and I sentence you to death!"

"Anne!" Marie said in shock. She grabbed Anne's arm. "You can't! That's horrible!"

"We didn't do anything!" the manacled man said.

Wayne pulled Marie's hand from Anne's arm, his expression grim and angry. "He'd have murdered our children, Marie. If given the chance he'd rape our daughter and terrorize her for the rest of her life."

The manacled man, who'd followed Marie into the room, wide eyes fastened on the dishtowel Anne grabbed, and he ducked as she threw it.

"No. I would never—"

His words cut off in a strangled groan and he clawed at the metal encircling his neck with his manacled his hands. Marie screamed and the people at the table surged to their feet as the body thumped to the floor.

"You killed him!" Marie cried, darting Anne a horrified glance over her shoulder.

Anne infused the wood on the other two with essence and willed it to tighten. Their mouths opened in soundless screams, and she doubted anyone had even noticed she'd done it, they were so fixated on the other corpse.

"I executed them."

"She did the right thing," Wayne said and crouched beside his sobbing wife. "She did the hard thing. Poor Ben…"

Anne walked from the room in a daze. She'd just killed three men in cold blood, and it scared her to her soul that she wanted to kill the rest.

A babble broke out behind her as they realized she'd killed all three. The radio on the mantel remained silent and she couldn't see the barn from her window, but she had essence. She opened the window and let a tendril of essence out as another gunshot rent the air.

* * *

Ben pushed open the door of the cabinet and hollered, "On your knees!"

Kate fired again and a man reaching beneath his coat fell face down without making a sound. The man beside him screamed or at least Ben thought he did, his mouth was open and his eyes were wide and terrified. The ringing in his ears made it hard to hear.

"Get down," he yelled again and fired as Dave did. His bullet took his target in the shoulder and spun him. Dave's target crumpled, grasping at the blood gushing from his throat, but Ben couldn't hear if he screamed or not. Blood pounded in his ears in time to his heartbeat. Everything seemed to be happening in slow motion. He had time to notice the oddest details, the expressions of shock, anger, and fear, the pattern of new spray although he hadn't heard the shot. Doug was suddenly standing beside him, hitting a man with the stock of his rifle. Sound returned with a roar that staggered him.

Kate yelled, "I'm shooting the next man who isn't on the ground in two seconds. One, Two!"

Most of the men dropped, cowering on the floor with their hands over their heads.

Holter tried to reach into the cabinet past Tim's shoulder. Another burst of gunshots temporally deafened Ben. A wave of blood flowed from Holter's disintegrated head and over Tim who rose both hands as he fell away.

Kate swung down, landing on the table surefooted as a cat. She spun and kicked with one foot, knocking Tim all the way to the floor.

"Stay down, fucker! We want to talk with you! Anyone else want a piece?" She strode the length of the table and prodded a cowering man with her rifle. "Gimme the gun!"

He threw it to her with two fingers, then vomited.

He's probably as horrified as me, Ben thought and fought back his own vomit. *I bet he never imagined anyone would actually get shot. He probably thought we'd fold like cowards the second he pointed the gun at us.*

Men shouted, and guns fired outside the barn door.

Pat crouched, holding a radio in one hand and peered through the doorway as Kate ran for the hall. She was as familiar as he of the barn, maybe more so. She'd grown up playing here with Anne.

"Keep them covered, honey!" she called back, and Ben glanced at the ceiling.

Dave said, "I've got them covered. Start tying them but don't break my line-of-sight. If they twitch, shoot them!"

"Al!" Pat called.

"We got four out here! Two ran but we saw their faces! We'll catch them!"

"Stay here and oversee this," Ben said to Doug as he ran after Kate.

She was much faster than him and was already outside by the side corral by the time he reached the door.

"Kate, wait!" he yelled, but she ignored him, grabbing a handful of Lightning's mane and pulling herself up. She yelled and kicked the horse's side, urging him into a gallop and had jumped the far fence before Ben had gone half the distance.

"Damn it! You're going to get yourself killed!" he yelled.

He hesitated, debating trying to grab Thunder and follow but he doubted he could even mount the riled horse. Thunder ran around the corral, neighing and shaking his head, clearly upset by the noise and confusion.

"Damn it," he cursed again as he ran along the narrow path in the snow that led to the point. She galloped ahead of him and he could see the men she chased. They saw her two and spread out, running through the snow, trying to flank her.

She rose the gun and fired. Lightning screamed and reared, and she slid off, landing gracefully in the snow and striding through it. It reached past her knees, slowing her, but Ben slowed his headlong rush and took gasping breaths as he lowered his gun. The other man had thrown himself face down and risen his hands.

"I've got you covered," he yelled more to keep the man down than he thought he could pick him off at this distance.

He hoped they all thought he could shoot as good as Kate. She made it look easy when he knew it was anything but. She'd spent countless hours at the range, mostly with her bow but she'd given classes in gun safety there. He'd thought to be sure his kids were safe, but she'd kept it up even after they'd finished the course, claiming to like working with the kids, and he was glad she had.

The bell on the point began to ring and a group of men and women had gathered on the edge of the path, staring into the field but Ben was too far to hear what they said.

Kate said, "Take this fucker back. I'll go find Jesit and Meyers."

"Wait," Ben said and grabbed the man by his coat, a coat made from material Anne had made, and he shook the man so hard his teeth clacked together. "You have one chance to save your life. Tell me the name of every man involved right now or I'll hang you with the rest of them!"

Kate gave him an approving nod and cradled her gun.

Al and Joe ran up followed by five men Ben didn't know.

"Is this all of them?" Al asked.

Kate said, "He ain't talking, Ben. Hang his ass. We'll give them all one chance—"

"Tim Arnault was in charge. Him and Marge made the plan. Holter was supposed to get the bolt cutters. I wasn't there but I heard Tim was the one who killed Phil. That's why I stayed. I knew he'd kill me! I'm not like them— I swear it."

Ben listened impassively, counting in his head as the man babbled everything he knew.

"Eight are still loose somewhere," he said grimly to Kate, but she was already running toward his house.

The crowd behind him exclaimed, and Ben turned to look, his heart thumping hard at the sight of the red mist that rose from the hilltop.

"Go!" he yelled and waved at his house.

Kate hesitated another second then turned and began running again.

Good Riddance

Sunday Afternoon 1/28

Another gunshot made Anne jerk as if she'd been the one shot and she leaned as far out the window as she could. Wayne ran into the room and grabbed the radio.

"Pat?"

Pat said, "We've got them. How's things on your end?"

Wayne said, "We caught six, five of which are dead."

"Good riddance," Pat said.

Anne spied Kate and Ben standing over a man on the ground and sagged. She held her suddenly trembling hands to her hot cheeks. She'd forgotten the man upstairs

"Any injuries?" Wayne asked.

Pat said, "Not on our end. Ben and Kate ran off. But I'm sure they're fine. Kate's a bad ass."

Anne laughed a sharp bark of half-hysterical laughter.

"Let's see if he's more talkative than his friends," Wayne said grimly and led the way upstairs.

Anne's blood froze when she saw Jill gone. It boiled when she realized she'd snuck out from Doug's room. She gazed out the open window above the garage at Jill and Edward's footprints marring the pristine snow of the roof.

Anne examined the distant figures of people milling on the hillside. A large group of people had gathered by the emergency bell they'd installed, and it began to ring.

She'd probably gone to ring it, Anne thought.

"That girl," she muttered and caught her breath hard as the sky above the point turned a villainous red.

"Wayne!" she called as she ran back to the stairs.

Wayne said, "He's not admitting to anything. I have no idea if he was involved or not."

Jill's on the point, and she's destroying the pavilion!"

Wayne shouted, "Marie, lock the doors and don't hesitate to shoot! Anne, wait!"

He caught up with her on the stairs.

"I'm going to my mother's to make sure they're safe. Call Pat and send him to Jill!" she called back as she raced out the door.

✳ ✳ ✳

"I've got to get into better shape," Ben gasped out as he and Joe ran up the hill to the point. Joe outpaced him and reached the milling people before Ben did.

"Everyone, get on the ground!" Joe hollered and fired a shot into the air.

Women screamed, and men exclaimed. Most dropped to their knees although some tried to run.

"Stay still and you won't be hurt. We're chasing a group of criminals. Only the guilty need to fear anything." Joe cast a dubious glance at the cloud forming on the hilltop but continued to yell reassurance to the crowd.

Ben slowed and waved the yelling crowd away, his eyes on Jill who stood beneath a swirling storm of essence. Fire trailed from her fingers and encircled two men who knelt on the bare dirt in the rubble where the pavilion had stood. Edward stood five paces to her left with his gun out but not pointed at anyone.

The fire swirled in an intricate pattern about the men on the ground before it disappeared as if it had never been.

"You even twitch, and I'll burn you were you stand!"

She sounded so like Kate, Ben laughed, giddy with relief to see her alive and well.

"Your mother?"

"She's fine and at the house. So I came to make sure they were safe here. I was afraid they'd try to take hostages. Mom's going to be pissed I left the house." She glared at the men at her feet. "I caught these assholes though."

Ben said, "Can you make me something to tie them with?"

She picked up a small rock and threw it at the men. It unfurled into white cord midflight and landed short of them.

Ben took a deep breath trying to still his wildly beating heart and scooped up the rope. A small part of his brain yelled sorceress and cowered from her, but he knew she wasn't casting spells. *A lifetime of conditioning would be hard to overcome*, he thought as he tied the men. Her clothing didn't help matters. The dark purple gown and black robe were pretty and practical in the cold and easier to fashion than trousers, but they added to the impression of magic. As did the jewelry she wore, ornate pieces that held small SEC, and knowing his daughter as he did, he was sure her clothing and jewelry would get more ornate as she honed her craft.

Wind caught and tossed strands of her long dark hair across her face and silver cuffs studded with purple spheres flashed on her wrists as she pushed it back and held out her hand. A SEC dropped into her palm, appearing as if by magic, and even though he knew she was just encasing the essence that floated in the air, it still gave him chills.

435

The men at Jill's feet stared with fearful eyes and it both worried and relieved him. It would be easier to convince people Jill used magic, they were conditioned from millions of hours of television and video games to see what she did as mystical and maybe she'd be safer if they thought it was magic. But his gaze caught on the now mostly silent crowd standing before Joe and he knew a lie wasn't a strong foundation to build an empire on.

"They'll believe what they want anyway," he muttered, and the man he was yanking to his feet gave him a quizzical glance.

"I wasn't—"

"Shut up!" Ben barked and dragged the man to the crowd. "Claire!"

"Ben?" She eyed him fearfully, her gaze skipping from him to Jill who still stood beneath the cloud of essence.

"Gather everyone at the greenhouse. We're holding a trial. Set up a table and invite Marge and the men and women she normally eats with to sit at it. Invite them forcefully if you have to. Anyone who declines my invitation will be banished!"

Claire licked her lips and nodded.

Ben took one step forward and gestured with his free hand, not releasing the collar of the man he held. "This is Windsor land, and I'm the king of it!" he yelled, feeling foolish but equally angry.

He wondered how Helen would take the usurpation, but Anne was a Windsor, and this was their home. The crowd whispered together and shifted, the whispers growing as he spoke.

"If you live in my kingdom, you'll respect my laws and obey my commands. If you plot against us, we'll treat you as an enemy! And the Windsor's kill their enemies! Those involved in the attack on my family will be executed this afternoon!"

The crowd exclaimed. The man he held jerked, and Ben tightened his grip. "The memorial service will be put off until four this evening. It shouldn't take long to dispense justice! Do whatever you wish, attend the trial, the memorial, or not, as it pleases you. But if you won't accept us as your rulers, you better get off my land!

"And that means being polite to my wife and daughter! I won't tolerate anyone speaking ill of them, calling them witches, or whispering behind their backs. What they can do isn't magic, it's science and it's dammed hypocritical of you to make use of their gifts yet belittle them for it!" He flushed as he said it, feeling a hypocrite for warning them against thinking things he sometimes thought himself.

"You go, Dad," Jill whispered and took his arm.

He kissed her temple, his gaze locked on Pat as he ran down the path.

"Anne has gone to Helen's!" Pat shouted as he ran up the path, clutching his side and breathing hard. "Sue said it's quiet there. I think we've got them all."

Relief made Ben's knees weak.

"Take them to the greenhouse and question them. They get one chance to confess everything they know. If they're caught in one lie, they hang with the rest!" He shoved his captive to Pat and turned for the house, pulling Jill through the now quiet throng that parted respectfully to let them pass.

Anne met them at the door. She looked as sick as he felt as if she'd aged ten years in the hours they'd been parted.

"Thank God," she whispered and hugged him tightly.

Jill began to cry, and Helen bustled out the door followed by Sue who grasped Jill's arm and led her inside, saying over her shoulder. "She'll be fine. It's the shock. I'll take good care of her. You two figure out what we're doing next.

Anne said nothing. The stood silently in an embrace. They already knew what they needed to do next.

It wasn't until he used the bathroom that he realized his face and clothing had been liberally splattered with blood. Vomit burned his throat, but he swallowed it back and clenched his shaking hands hard. He'd be awash in blood. Those men would be a threat to his daughter if he let them live. He had no choice.

The Consequences

Sunday Afternoon 1/28

Let get this over with," Pat muttered as he thrust Tim through the greenhouse door and pushed him against the wall where the other captives were guarded by Kate and Dave.

Amen, Ben thought but didn't say it. "If everyone could take your seats."

The greenhouse was already crowded and grew more so as men and women entered from the front and back doors, jamming together behind the two long lines of haybales used for seating and talking excitedly amongst themselves.

There were too many people to fit inside, so they clustered outside the plastic greenhouse behind the hay podium and table Ben had ordered set up.

Claire finished escorting his invited guests to the seating and lifted an eyebrow in inquiry but didn't ask questions. The measuring glance she threw at them told him she suspected why he'd asked for them to be brought before him. They knew it too. They glared and spoke in heated whispers between themselves.

Rumors had been flying since the alarm bell had rung, and Ben was certain everyone had heard some version of what had transpired.

His hands still shook from adrenaline, and he felt as if his eyes had been ripped open, forcing him to see the hard truths that he didn't want to see. He wanted to live in a civilized society where everyone pulled their own weight and treated their neighbors decently, but that society had never existed. It was only the law that kept chaos in check, and he didn't have law now.

And they'd suddenly realized it. He could feel them tottering on the cusp of all out fighting where the strong would subjugate the weak. It shone from the measuring glances they gave each other.

He straightened and clenched his fists. He could be the law; he had no choice— not if he wanted his children to be safe.

"You all know why you're here," he said harshly, jerking a thumb at the bound captives. He stepped back to let Doug place a steaming pot of stew on the podium.

Doug glared at the bound men and stood with one hand resting on the butt of his pistol. Jill entered, carrying a full tray.

Marge paled and licked her lips. Her eyes darting from the pot of stew to the bowls Jill handed him.

Jill set the tray she carried beside the stew, straightening the plastic cups before grabbing a SEC from the tray and going to stand beside Doug.

Boomer bounded into the room and accepted the pets and head scratches as his due. The crowd began to talk in low voices that quieted when Anne entered.

"Hello, everyone," she said and hurried to Ben, placing the water she carried on the tray beside the bowls. She hesitated, then gave him a tight smile and kissed his cheek before sitting on the bale behind the podium.

Ben said, "The bound men you see before you are guilty of

attempted murder."

The crowd quieted as soon as he spoke.

"They've given statements implicating a few others and those few will be tried by me. In the future, we hope to implement a more formal court system, but we'll never have the sort of system we were used to. But that's all for later. For right now is all you need to know is that I've declared them guilty and sentenced them, and anyone else who had a hand in the attack, to death.

Loud talk erupted, and Ben let them talk while he turned to Doug. "Have any of the men they implicated admitted their guilt?" he whispered.

"Two of the three. The last protests his innocence but five of them claimed he was part of the group and he was on Tim's hunting team until he asked for a transfer onto the team with the missing guns."

"Bring him in and sit him at the table."

Doug nodded and hurried away, pushing through the crowd to reach the door.

Ben banged the gavel and the crowd began to quiet. He began speaking and a man yelled angrily for quiet.

Ben said, "These men were caught red-handed trying to steal our guns. Others were killed at my home when they attacked armed with knives. I'm offering one chance for a full pardon. If you were involved in any way, speak now and we'll send you on your way with food and supplies. If we find later you were involved, you'll hang like them!"

"You can't hang them, you haven't the authority," Marge said.

"I've given myself the authority. If you don't like that you can pack up and go!"

Marge looked confused and a bit scared for a moment before her expression changed to contempt as if he what he'd said was the stupidest thing she'd ever heard and not worth considering.

He glared at the crowd, silencing the mutters.

Doug entered and waved a short man to a seat at the table. He stared down at the table avoiding Ben's eyes. Marge stiffened and tried to look nonchalant, but Ben could see the sweat beading her brow.

She was certain now she'd been sat with the suspects, and Ben could practically see the wheels in her head turn as she debated the best approach.

He said, "I thought we could live here together peacefully. But I see now I was wrong. But I'm a fast learner, maybe not as fast as my wife" –he smiled when she snorted and those nearest laughed nervously.

Marge exchanged quick glances with the man who'd just sat, and Ben said, "This is your last chance." He stared pointedly at Marge, willing her to confess. The thought of executing a woman made bile rise in his throat, but she stared back with a slight smirk, either not believing he'd carry out his threats or thinking he knew nothing about her involvement or maybe thinking she could still turn the crowd against him.

"Let me be crystal clear here. These men have already been found guilty. If you're thinking there'll be a long trial and evidence given and cases pleaded, think again. We have no way to house criminals and no supplies to waste on them."

Marge stood and half turned to face the crowd behind her, speaking to him but at them. "Just because we don't agree with your policies, you'll make an example of us! You plan to murder us, is that it? Use their violence as an excuse?" her tone made it clear she didn't believe he really was. She was trying to rile them, get them to turn against him.

The woman sitting beside her jerked back and turned a horrified gaze on the man sitting next to her.

"Not at all," Ben said mildly and ladled a spoonful of stew into a bowl that he set before her. "I plan to serve dinner. Eat up."

She crossed her arms and glared but her face had paled two

shades. He grinned at her and placed a bowl of stew before the man to her right. "Eat before it gets cold."

The five women and three men sitting with Marge exchanged confused glances as Ben continued to place bowls. The short man looked as if he might faint and stared at Marge. Ben thought he was waiting for a sign from her on whether or not it was safe to eat it.

Ben reached for the water pitcher and began pouring drinks. "Go ahead. This was my dinner, and I want to prove to you all that we eat the same things you do."

"Who cares what you eat," Marge said and pushed her bowl to the floor.

The short man dropped his spoon while the rest of them halted with their spoons raised.

"Boomer, no!" Jill yelled, glaring at Marge as she grabbed at Boomer.

"You have no manners at all," Ben said as he squatted to wipe up the mess.

Trish yelled, "What is this farce! I can't believe I'm going to say this, but Marge is right. Who cares what you eat? We need to decide what to do with them."

Ben straightened. "There's only one thing to do with potential murders."

"That *is* murder," Marge spat. "They didn't kill anyone!"

"That's justice and common sense. If we kick them out, what's to stop them from sneaking back and robbing us? You think they won't try this again? That they won't kill you for your clothes or food? Don't be stupid, although I suppose you can't help it."

The crowd laughed, and she turned to glare over her shoulder.

She sounded furious when she yelled, "This is what's in store for you too if you don't kiss his ass! See how he belittles us? How he treats those who don't agree with him? That's why we need rules that everyone has to follow. We need to be a true democracy, not his peasants! He has no right to judge us!"

Ben dished up another bowl of stew and placed it before her. "Eat!"

She clenched her lips and shook her head, darting a hate filled glance at Tim who glared back. The gag in his mouth prevented him from speaking but his angry expression said volumes.

The woman beside Marge lifted her spoon again.

Ben rose an eyebrow when Marge turned away. "Will you let her eat it?"

Marge licked her lips, and the woman halted with the spoon halfway to her mouth.

"What? Did you put something in it?" she asked Ben.

"Ask Marge."

"He did. He's trying to poison us!" She shot Ben a triumphant smile, and he wanted to slap the smug expression from her face.

"But you knew? You somehow knew I put poison in it? But you were still going to let her eat?" Ben gazed at the suddenly quiet crowd and spoke to them. "You think I'd poison the food I give, kill them for disagreeing with me?"

"She poisoned it?" Trish pressed both hands to her mouth, her horrified gaze locked on Marge.

"Yes."

Silence met his answer, followed by a wave of sound as the crowd erupted into loud talk and Marge yelled, "He did it. He just wants me to look guilty to get rid of me."

"How could you?" the woman beside her said. She turned her shocked face to Marge and the shock melted to a glare. "And you'd have let us eat it. You sanctimonious pig!"

Ben nodded at the woman and said to Marge, "There's a flaw in your logic. I don't need a reason or an excuse to get rid of you. I could kick you out anytime I liked."

"I didn't do it!"

Ben held up his hand and the woman yelling at Marge quieted.

"This is my home. I could've thrown your ass out at any time."

Marge stood to face the crowd. "See! I told you he was a bully—"

"Shut the hell up. I'm sick of listening to you. If I were a bully, I'd have kicked you out ages ago." Ben glanced at the ten people who lived in his basement. He didn't know many of their names, but they all looked shocked and scared. "She'd have killed you without a second thought." They stared at Marge now, and Ben turned to the crowd. "She'd have killed the ten kids who live in my house, innocent children, to kill my family." He glared at Marge, silencing her protest before she uttered it. "Except for Jill, right? You had plans for Jill." He turned and kicked Tim's foot. "He told us all about your plan. Well, told might be misleading. He blamed you. Said if you'd gotten us the meal on time, he'd have won. He said the entire thing was your idea, but that he hadn't planned to kill anyone. You were supposed to knock us out. I saw you meet with him with my own eyes. So, tell me, Marge, will it knock us out or kill us?"

"He's lying. Of course I had nothing to do with it! I explained why you saw me with him. You can't possibly believe a word he says. He's just trying to cause trouble."

"Remind me again?"

An angry flush crept up her neck and settled into two bright red patches on her cheeks. Her lips were clamped so tightly they'd whitened. Ben lifted an eyebrow and tapped his foot

"I'd gone looking for you to apologize," she finally bit out.

"So, you walked all the way up to the barn to find me instead of pulling me aside down here, where I was. Where you knew I was. But, do go on. What was so urgent that you had to seek me out to apologize about and while doing that you just happened to run into Tim and his cronies."

"You remember perfectly!"

"But you don't. I believe you said you were sorry for your poor attitude. That the shock had made you a tad over-reactionary." He lifted his eyebrow, and she nodded.

"And yet, here we are with you accusing me of the same things you claimed to be so sorry of accusing me of just yesterday."

He held a hand to his ear and leaned forward. He straightened and smirked when she said nothing. Ben scanned the crowd until he spotted Sharon. "Sharon, did she come apologize to you? She spoke so sincerely of how bad she felt for causing your husband's death. She expounded on how guilty she felt for the affair and assured me she'd come and speak with you to beg your forgiveness."

"I didn't get a chance," Marge said as Sharon said, "No," in a voice laced with contempt.

"Did you force him?" Sharon asked.

"You don't have to force men," Marge snapped, then cleared her throat and smoothed her shirt, taking a deep breath and pasting such a false look of sorrow on her face that Ben laughed.

Marge glared at Ben a moment before turning back to Sharon. But she wasn't really speaking to her, Ben noted. She was eyeing the crowd, gauging their reactions, and he could practically hear her weighing the odds and deciding what to say that would get them on her side.

"I'm sorry he died, but that was hardly my fault. I shouldn't have come to see him, but he begged me. He said it was urgent we speak. And since he was in charge of the storm cleanup, I went. We weren't having an affair—"

Ben slammed his hand onto the table so hard the bowls rattled. "One more lie from your mouth, and I'll shoot you dead right now!"

He pointed over his shoulder at the man tied beside Tim. "Do you know that man?" Without waiting for her to answer he went on— "He knows you, and he knew Sharon's husband. Say nothing or tell the truth but so help me God, if you further tarnish her husband's name to her face, I'll kill you! Sharon isn't a liar! She saw you with her own eyes!"

Marge swallowed hard and opened her mouth. She closed it and opened it twice before saying, "Yes, we were having an affair." Marge glared again at Ben and said, "This is none of your business. It's none of anyone's business!"

"Did you force him!" Sharon yelled.

"Let it go, Mom," a young man seated beside her said and tried to pull her back to her chair.

"Don't you want to know, Josh?" Sharon took the man's hands and rose beseeching eyes to Ben.

Josh said, "I loved Dad, but he wasn't a saint."

Marge crossed her arms and turned back to face Ben.

"I didn't force him, don't be ridiculous, and I'm finished talking about this. You have no right to question me," she said to Ben. She half-turned to say, "Will he threaten you too and make you reveal the things you're not proud of? Haven't you all made mistakes? We had an affair and I was going to apologize privately. What else could I do? The man is dead. What would telling her about our affair accomplish?"

"It proves your character," Ben said. "She begged you for truth, and you repeatedly called her a liar. You'd still call her a liar, and not to save her feelings— she saw you. She knows the truth— but to save your reputation.

"You bitch," Sharon muttered, but she sat back down and looked angry now, not heartbroken, which, Ben supposed, was the best he could hope for.

Ben gestured to the tied and gagged men. "And now they claim poisoning my family was your idea. That you added the poison. And we all know you're a liar!"

Marge said, "But I didn't poison anyone. If he says I did, then he's a liar. Maybe there's not even any poison in it."

"Then eat one bite. I mean, you could be right. Maybe they

were all lying. After all, how would they get the poison? It was locked up beneath the storage room beneath the bakery. Sure, you had access, but they didn't. So, go ahead, have a bite. Prove I'm mistaken in believing them or that it's just a harmless concoction to make us sleep like Tim claims you promised."

"But they're liars, and everyone had access to the storage room at some time or another."

"You begged to be allowed to help for the memorial and I agreed even though you'd already been fired. And you were down there a long time yesterday," Claire said thoughtfully.

"She was," Trish agreed, and her horrified expression changed to disgust. She stood and faced the crowd. "I sent her down for a box of pie tins, and she was down there a good thirty minutes. I'd thought she'd forgotten and went myself after the first batch of pies came out, and she was just coming up the stairs. The tins are stacked right beside the door. So what took you so long?"

"I was down there, but it wasn't that long. That's not proof. There is no proof because I didn't do a thing!" Marge resumed her seat and crossed her arms over her chest.

Ben said, "We aren't here to figure out your guilt. We're here to see who else might've been involved. I'm sorry, I don't know your name," Ben said to the woman sitting beside Marge.

"It's Margret— Maggie Owens," she said nervously.

"Well, Maggie appears innocent of the poison scheme. She was going to eat the stew and those two men were about to. But the rest of you…"

He trailed off as they began to loudly proclaim their innocence. He let them talk and turn to the crowd to beseech them for alibis and character references until the din grew so loud he couldn't make out who was saying what.

He slammed the gavel onto the hunk of wood and the crowd quieted as if he'd fired a gun. "Let's ask Tim, shall we?" Without waiting he yanked the gag from Tim's mouth. "It appears you've told the truth. At least about who was involved. Care to accuse anyone else?"

Tim laughed and spat, the globule of spit landing on the table. He hadn't been spitting at Ben but Marge.

"Nah, none of them others were in on it except Spence and her. It was her plan, and she botched it. We didn't mean to kill anyone just take the guns for ourselves to even it up so to speak. It ain't fair you have all the power."

"Liar!" Annie screamed, muffling Marge's protest of innocence.

Ben shook his head at Annie, and she sat. Meredith began to cry, and she leaned over the baby's head to coo to her.

Tim's gaze narrowed on Annie, and he eyed Ben with dawning realization. Fear replaced the anger in his eyes, and he hunched, staring down at his feet. "I swear, if you just let us go, we'll never trouble you again. We'll go far away and won't bother anyone."

Ben said sadly, "You're a thief and a liar and if we let you go, you'll murder the first person who crosses your path if they have something you want. We'd be fools to let a danger like you roam our hills. "

"We can't just kill them!" Trish burst out, then slapped her hands to her mouth.

"Trish— I hate the necessity, I really do, but no one here will be safe with a murderer on the loose."

She dropped her hands to say, "No one died though."

"It wasn't from lack of trying. Thirty-two people live in my house. Ten of them children. If we'd eaten that food, we'd all be dead. And while I agree, attempted murder isn't the same as murder, it's still a very serious crime. Are you willing to gamble that he goes away? What's to stop him from hiding in the woods and ambushing the next group of men who go out hunting? And then, when he has their weapons, what's to stop him from coming back here and doing whatever he likes? Do you want to be at his mercy, Trish?"

Tim smiled at Trish, the expression ghastly in his sweaty face. "We were just trying to even things up. I swear no one was going to get hurt!"

Ben could see that his hands shook now. *It was sinking in that he would pay for his crimes,* Ben thought with vicious satisfaction.

"Even if I believed the threats we heard you make in the barn were empty boasts to get the men on your side, the chainsaws, the choosing of women— I know you had plans for Jill. What can you say to defend that?"

Tim stared at him mutely.

"It was a dangerous game you played, and you lost.

"What are you talking about?" a man yelled from the back.

Ben ignored the shouted questions and turned back to Marge. "We've given you a chance to confess. Which is more than fair. You say they're liars, and I agree, but there were other witnesses with no reason to lie."

"I told you why I was speaking with him, I was looking for you," Marge said.

Ben turned from Tim. "It doesn't matter. Doug, call Phil."

The crowd gasped as one when Phil limped inside. The bruises on his face were clear testament to a serious fight. He glared from his one good eye and pushed through the crowd to reach his wife.

Annie yelled, "He tried to murder my husband— thought he had, the prick! And then he had the nerve to come and tell me how sorry he was that Phil fell in the water! We should hang him!"

Ben stared at Marge who rose her hands to cover her face. He shifted his gaze and scanned the crowd. "Phil warned us, saved our lives, saved your lives. Tim had some big plans. He'd have been a dictator who'd give Stalin nightmares. I hope that we can live together here and make fair laws but right now, this is still my land, and I'm the sheriff. And I say potential murderers get executed. As hard as that is to hear, I just can't see any other way for us to be safe. This wasn't a crime of passion or an accident. They're too dangerous to have around."

"I didn't hurt anyone," Marge said weakly.

"True. And you aren't that dangerous without help. I don't think you could overpower anyone to steal their gun, but I don't think I want to give you the chance to prove me wrong or talk someone else into helping you."

"I'll go away," she said.

"She wouldn't last a day," Pat muttered.

Ben knew it too. Marge was too soft. Even with supplies she wouldn't make it very far. But she didn't deserve pity, he reminded himself.

He banged the gavel. "So be it then. The ten of them will be hanged, the three who admitted their crimes and gave honest testimony will be released across the river with three days food and a blanket each and she's banished with them. If anyone is caught helping them, they'll be banished as well. If they're caught plotting, I'll hang them all."

"Ben," Trish gasped.

Clair put an arm around her shoulders and whispered something.

"Sentence to be carried out immediately." Ben banged the gavel again.

"Got the trees already picked out," Wayne said.

"Let's go, assholes." Kate prodded Tim with her rifle.

"You can't just let her go!" Helen yelled, sounding as angry as Ben had ever heard her as she pushed through the crowd by the side door. "She was going to murder my entire family and she gets to just walk away?"

"Mom—"Anne rose to hug her mother.

"No, Anne, it isn't right. She should hang with the others!"

The crowd began muttering, most agreeing with Helen, and Marge began to cry, grabbing at Maggie's sleeve. "Don't let them.

I'm sorry, and never meant for anyone to be hurt." She continued to babble; the words mangled by sobs. Maggie shook her off and stepped away, brushing at her arms as if the contact contaminated her.

Ben was actually surprised none of the others sitting at her table tried to help her, but they all glared and nodded along with Helen. Although, he supposed, he shouldn't be surprised they'd quickly abandoned her when she'd brought them down with her. If Phil hadn't warned them, if Tim had accused, they might be going to the gallows too. Or everyone here might be at Tim's mercy...

A sick feeling bloomed in his stomach, burning over the knot of anger that had kept his muscles tight since Phil had snuck into his room. He'd never done a person violence before today and the thought of killing these men in cold blood sickened him. But if he let them go, he knew they'd be back and be even more ruthless. But having no choice didn't make it any easier.

A scuffle broke out as Dave gestured the men forward. The crowd outside began yelling and a shot rang out. Ben reached for his gun, hurrying for the door.

Another shot rang out followed by two more in quick succession, and he couldn't tell who'd shot, the ringing in his ears made it hard to pinpoint sound.

Sound resumed within moments with a shrill overtone that matched the clanging in his head as he pushed through the people trying to run from the doorway. He could hear men cursing and then Kate swear.

"It wasn't me!" Tim yelled.

Kate snarled, "Get up, asshole, or I'll drag your ass!" She shook the man she pulled up, saying, "Try that shit again, I dare you! You okay, Wayne?"

"I'm good!" Wayne called back, "Nice shot, Kate. Thanks!"

Kate lifted the rifle and hit the man before her with the stock, knocking him to his knees. "You face forward. Turn again, and I'll think your trying something. Now get your ass up and walk!"

She reached down to yank him up, but he fell forward.

Wayne said, "Stay back, Kate. We'll get him."

"I could just shoot the fucker right here and save ourselves the hassle of dragging him to the woods."

Wayne laughed and Ben muttered, "You're not helping."

Kate stood back glowering. *She was tougher than him*, Ben mused as he bit back the sour tang of vomit. The air smelled of blood and fresh feces with an underlay of gun smoke that made his stomach roil painfully. Blood had splattered her face and covered the floor.

She didn't look at all upset to be standing over the corpses of the men she'd just killed. She nudged the body by her toe. "Fucker had it coming. He went for Wayne's gun and almost choked him to death before I got a clear shot."

"Quiet down!" Pat yelled and the exclamations behind Ben died down.

He leaned over Ben's shoulder to get a view and shook his head. "I'll get a crew together to clean this up. I guess we should tie them together or something."

Kate grinned at him and again nudged the corpse with her toe. "Think there's instructions on that in one of the encyclopedias?"

"*Har har*," Pat said and turned back to the main room, telling the people there, "Exit through the back door. Ben has this under control!"

Ben said, "Thanks, Kate."

She jerked her chin in acknowledgment, not relaxing her grip on the gun. "*De nada*. I told you I got her back. These fuckers make me sick! I'd shoot them all right here except I don't want to waste the bullets."

"You can't do this," Tim pleaded. "We didn't hurt anyone! Not even Phil. Not really. We roughed him up a bit but—"

Ben glanced away from the spray of blood as Tim shrieked and held a hand to his bleeding nose. Kate gestured with her rifle. "Go or you'll wish you had. I think hanging is too good for you. We should stake you out in the woods or feed you to Mrs. Ming!"

Ben and Wayne exchanged amazed glances and Wayne guffawed, then broke into laughter when Kate glared.

Ben had no idea how fierce Kate was although he should have. She'd always been tough and not one to shy away from violence, but this cold-blooded anger was new and surprising. It was clear to him she meant every word and wouldn't turn a hair at feeding Tim to the tiger. It was clear to Tim too. He closed his mouth but stared at the watching crowd with pleading eyes.

Ben waved Anne back, but she said something to Jill then hurried to catch up, pushing through the crowd gathering by the door to reach them.

"Go home, sweetheart."

Sweat beaded her brow and her face was pale but resolute. "No. I should be there. I don't want to, but I should."

He glanced over her head at the mummering crowd and sighed hard. "It won't be pretty," he warned in a whisper.

"I'm not stupid, Ben." She gave him a guilty wince and took his hand. "Sorry. I didn't mean it like that. I understand you want to protect me from these horrible things, but if I'm in charge, I need to be there. It's cowardly to order a death but not see it through yourself.

"You didn't order it—" Ben jerked as Helen shouted, "Ben Windsor, there is no way you're letting this murderous piece of filth walk away!" Helen pushed through the crowd yanking Marge with her.

He'd forgotten all about her. He wished he'd never met the woman, that he could pretend it hadn't happened. He rubbed his temples, and Helen's glare dimmed a hair, but she shook Marge's arm hard.

Ben said, "No. You're right. She should come with us."

"You can't," Marge said in a quavering voice and fell to her knees.

"Hang her!" a man shouted, and in seconds, the crowd was arguing.

"Enough!" Ben bellowed. "Her guilt is clear, but god help me, I don't have the heart to order a woman hanged. So— we'll banish her."

"I'll die," Marge gasped through her tears. "Please, Please, give me another chance! I can be useful." She folded her hands and gave him a ghastly smile.

"I know things. I could work in the kitchens or something—"

"Shut up!" Helen snapped. "Kate!" she called when Marge continued to plead.

Marge held her hands to her face and cried, and Ben wasn't the only who felt sick. He examined the white strained faces. Most looked shocked. Only a few appeared angry, and he wasn't sure if it was with Tim and his group of thugs, or Marge and her poisoned stew, or he and Anne for surviving the attacks.

"Yes, Ma'am?" Kate asked, nudging Ben aside so she could stick her head through the doorway. He moved so she could see past him. He tended to forget what a small woman she was, she had such a big presence.

Helen said, "Take her far out in the woods and leave her there just like we found her."

Marge clutched her shirt tighter, straining the sleeves across her broad shoulders, and lifted pleading eyes to Ben. Before he could say anything, Helen snapped, "Those are my clothes she's wearing, and she can't have them! If anyone wants to give her the clothes off your back, be my guest, but consider she was willing to leave you all naked."

"No! I never—"

"How did you think we'd get any new cloth without Anne, you

idiot! I heard Phil. I know what you planned!" She whirled and rose a fist at the crowd. "I don't want to hear one more word about my daughter from any of you!"

"She's a witch," Marge said and wiped her face on her sleeve, turning glaring eyes on Anne.

Ben almost felt sorry for her, she was so desperate, but she'd been willing to murder his entire family to take the farm although he thought her a fool for thinking Tim would keep his side of the bargain.

Marge continued pleading to Helen, "You're a good Christian woman and should see she needs to die. I was doing it kindly. She'd never have known. We can't let a witch live!" she yelled louder when the crowd began to mutter.

Ben wanted to kick her, and it must've shown on his face because she scrambled away from him on her hands and knees.

Helen slapped Marge's pleading hands away. "My daughter isn't a witch. You're a greedy whore who'd do or say anything to get what you want. My daughter has a talent, That's all! She was born with it! And don't try to pretend you were doing it for us. You planned to make Jill your slave. You're disgusting!" She slapped Marge, rocking her head back and leaving a red print on her white cheek.

The crowd stare at Helen as it they'd never seen her before but with a new weary respect.

Ben was shocked too and glad his mother had agreed to remain at Angie's. He never wanted to see her so angry and afraid. Her sorrow was hard enough to watch.

Kate grasped Marge's arm and began dragging her to the door while Marge screamed curses at Helen that changed to a shriek of pain as Kate changed her grip, twisting Marge's arm and yanking her up, pushing her now with her arm twisted high behind her back. She'd done it quickly and made it look easy, and Ben made a mental note to ask for some lessons.

"This is murder! Help!" Marge screamed as Kate dragged her through the door. "I didn't do a thing! You're all murders! I—" she let out a sharp oof and sagged, grunting with pain but unable to gasp out a sound.

Kate shook out her hand, flexing her fingers and thrusting Marge forward with a hard shove.

"This is a nightmare," Anne murmured.

"We'll get through it," Ben said and strode after Kate.

In the End is the Beginning

Sunday Evening 1/28

The smell of Ben's own vomit wafted to him on the frigid air, obscuring the smell of death. Ben wiped his face with a trembling hand and straightened to peer around, but no one had followed him into the trees.

He sagged against a tree trunk as he considered what he should do next. His hopes for a normal life had been irretrievable dashed with the hangings. He could never go back to being a simple farmer. The people in his care would expect his protection now. They'd expect him to uphold a fair law, to be judge, jury and executioner.

Another spasm gripped his stomach, and he vomited again.

"Ben?" Anne called softly.

He wiped his mouth and face with snow and stepped away from the tree as she came through the trees. He was struck by her strangeness as if seeing her for the first time.

She wore the cloak Jill had made her. She'd left the fur hood down and the matching mittens dangled from a silver cord along her side. The deep purple cloak flowed to her feet and was cinched with a silver belt lined with small plaques of SECs.

Jill had formed her matching jewelry, a wide bracelet, an ornate necklace, and a headband all formed to hold essence that shimmered behind their diamond-like shells. In her right hand, she carried a bigger ball of essence. Her left trailed along the trunks of the trees and the leafy branches of the shrubs she passed.

He knew she was using the essence contained within the plants and ground to seek him, and it rose the small hairs on his body.

"Here!" he called and went to meet her.

She greeted him with a hug and rested in his arms long enough that he grew chilled.

"I'm sorry," she said when he pulled away.

He smiled ruefully and tucked her arm into the crook of his elbow and began heading slowly back to the farm. They'd buried the men on the rough bank of the river downstream from them. Ben hoped the corpses would rot quickly in the moist ground and obscure all traces of them. He wanted to forget the sights and sounds of their deaths but knew he never would.

He said, "They'd have tried to take the farm from whoever owned it. It had nothing to do with us personally. You did nothing wrong. Your only contribution to this fiasco was making it possible to reach and help so many survivors. You are who you are, and I love you. I've never regretted us, not for one second. I meant and still mean every word of the vow I made you." He kissed her temple and traced the side of her face with his fingertips. "None of that was your fault. Or mine either. They chose their fate."

"And Phil?"

"Earned a second chance. We'll have to watch him. I think he was way more involved then he said, but I also think this was a lesson he won't forget." He slowed as the sounds of men talking reached him. "We've had some hard shocks, and I'm sure they'll keep coming. It's going to be difficult, probably more than I can imagine, but we aren't alone in this, Anne."

She released his arm to hug herself, rubbing her arms as if she were cold as she turned to the sound of voices.

"It gets harder every day. There's more of them and they want more from us. I hadn't realized how thin the veneer of civilization was."

He took her hands and kissed them, then drew her close and embraced her, using his own cloak to wrap them both.

I must appear a strange sight too, he mused.

He still wore the blood-splattered, essence-formed clothing Jill had formed for him. The pants resembled black jeans and the shirt was the same dark purple as the clothing Jill and Anne wore cut in a western style, but the buttons glittered like gems and his belt was formed of thin plaques of essence. He made a mental note to ask Jill to make him a barn coat, but he planned to keep the belt. Having essence on him for his maker wife or daughter to use might be lifesaving someday.

Snow began drifting down, and Anne gazed up at the sky with a troubled expression. "I almost wish we'd run away."

"And left them all to fend for themselves?"

He laughed when she flushed guiltily. "Don't think I haven't considered it, but I truly believe you have a gift from God. And with great gifts comes great responsibilities. We can help shape the future, Anne. Sure, it'll be hard work but when did that ever stop us?"

"I thank God every day for giving me a man like you. I was so blessed."

He frowned and smoothed her hair back, not liking the beaten tone of voice. "We *are* blessed, and this isn't the end, it's a new beginning."

She smiled up at him, her gray eyes clear and full of love. "*In fine est pincipium—*"

He rose an eyebrow.

"In the end is the beginning," she whispered, leaning closer to kiss him.

The End

Coming Soon

STORM WROUGHT
Chronicles of the Makers 2

The world has descended into chaos and it's every man for himself.
Can an unskilled Maker enforce law and order when the rest of the
world is against them?
Will she have enough to time to hone her craft and build a new
empire, or is man destined to go the way of the Dodo bird?

Books By S.M Savoy
Available Wherever Books are Sold

S. M. Savoy